THE COLOURS OF CORRUPTION

by

Jacqueline Jacques

HONNO MODERN FICTION

First published by Honno in 2013

'Ailsa Craig', Heol y Cawl, Dinas Powys, South Glamorgan, Wales, CF64
4AH.

1 2 3 4 5 6 7 8 9 10

A catalogue record for this book is available from the British Library.

Published with the financial support of the Welsh Books Council.

ISBN 978-1-906784-53-9

Cover Image: *Street in Venice*, 1882 by John Singer Sargent
Cover design: Simon Hicks
Text design: Elaine Sharples
Printed by Gomer Press

To Jack, Abigail, Caiden and Teagan

Acknowledgements

This book came about as a result of the Escalator Scheme run by the Writers' Centre in Norwich and an Arts Council (East) grant. I must thank Joan Deitch for encouraging me to 'go dark' in the first place, Michelle Spring for her invaluable mentoring at the outset and Janet Thomas for her cheerful but rigorous editing at the end. Most of all, I thank my family and friends for their stout support as always, through thick and thin.

Chapter 1

June, 1893

Archie touched his tongue to his lips. Market smells. So strong he could almost taste them: the stink of the fish stall, beer fumes belching from the pub across the road, bruised fruit fermenting and horse dung, steaming in the summer heat. And smoke …

That puzzled him. Not tobacco smoke, not chimney smoke, not food frying. More like wood smoke than anything.

He turned from his easel to lean out of the window. Horses were whinnying, pigeon wings beating in panic, street cries and banter dying away as shoppers and sellers alike snuffed the air.

'Fire!' The sky beyond the church spire was shimmering, turning black as thunderclouds. People ran, women picking up their long skirts and shopping bags, dragging small children away. Whistles blew, hand-bells rang. Archie dunked his brushes in thinner and hopped around the room, pulling on his shoes.

'Archie?'

'Go home, Ida,' he told his model. Still tucking in his shirt, he snatched up a bag of pencils, a sketchpad and clattered down the stairs. 'Same time tomorrow!' he managed to yell before his front door slammed.

Out on the street, the greengrocer was putting up his shutters; his queue had disappeared, drawn more towards catastrophe than carrots. 'Catch you up, Arch,' he promised as his lodger began elbowing through the jostling crowd.

By the time Archie reached the burning store on the corner, bucket chains had formed from various pumps and wells and the sign 'Wylie's Second-Hand Furniture' was weeping sooty tears.

Archie joined in, his bucket slopping, slurping, as he dashed towards the roaring flames, forced to duck away from the searing heat as he aimed his slosh of water, hoping it didn't fall short. 'Get out in time, did they?' he said over his shoulder.

'Dunno, mate.' Bert, the tobacconist two doors down from the police station, passed Archie the next clanking pail, happy to let the younger man, with his superior height and longer arms, swill the water past the blistering window frame. '*Closed* was on the door,' he said as Archie turned to him for the next bucketful, 'When there was a door ...'

Archie blinked as sweat and smoke stung his eyes. The air was hard to breathe. Black ash fell like snow. 'What about Daniel?'

'Too 'ot to stop indoors – he'd've took his sandwiches outside, eh?'

But if he had, where was he now? The shopkeeper should have stood out in the crowd, being a head higher than most, with bushy beard and grizzled mane. His booming voice alone usually made him easy to find.

A creaking, a slow splintering and the upstairs came crashing down. Everyone jumped back, gasping and crying out, flinching from the sparks. The smell of burning wood and polish was sickening. No one inside could survive now, surely?

'Dear, oh dear.' The woman from the flower stall used the

2

moment to wipe her face with her apron, but her eyes continued to fill.

'How'd it start?' someone asked.

Did it matter? Archie swallowed. Wylie was gone.

He stayed until the fire was out, more or less, and then, scorched and sorry, his auburn thatch singed, his eyes bloodshot and sore, he walked back up the road. Fires were common enough this long hot summer, forest fires mostly, but Walthamstow was little more than a large village on the outskirts of London and still had clapboard cottages at its heart, and timber-framed buildings like Daniel Wylie's. Tinder-dry, they were always at risk. But why hadn't the man saved himself, let the damned furniture burn and claimed on the insurance? Unless he'd been trapped, hurt in some way, caught under heavy furniture? Archie sighed and shook his head. Poor Daniel, Archie mourned, head bowed, hand to heart, and discovered his bag of drawing-materials still slung across his chest. He'd had neither the time nor the will to use them.

*

It wasn't until the following day that the police were able to pick their way across the floor of the devastated store through to the back room. They found Wylie's charred remains in a pile of wood ash, with only a signet ring to identify him. It lay beside the body where his left hand might have fallen, with a bunch of keys which had presumably been in his trouser pocket. His clothes and extremities had burned clean away. Although what remained of his body was charcoal brittle and black, accidental fire was not the cause of his death. According to the local *Journal*, close examination of the skull had revealed a bullet wound above the right ear, an exit hole below the left. Daniel had not escaped the inferno because he was already dead. Murdered.

Cruelly, he was then hauled on top of a pyre of dining-room

3

chairs, like a Guy Fawkes, and set alight. What was that all about? A respectable shopkeeper on a bonfire in Victorian England? It was barbaric.

The neighbours, deaf and blind, claimed to have seen and heard nothing unusual: no one entering or leaving the shop around the time in question. They were used to furniture being moved around the shop during the dinner hour. They hadn't realised that Will Beswick, who usually helped with the lifting, was out of town at a two-day auction in Chelmsford, his presence verified by a dozen or more members of the public and the landlord of the Blue Lion Inn. Beswick arrived back with a cartload of furniture and no shop to put it in. He sold it off in the market for as much as he could get and then disappeared, cart and all.

Near the front of the shop, in the still smouldering embers of what had been a sales counter, the police discovered an empty cash box, clumsily forced open. If the murderers had been after money they'd have been sadly disappointed. Daniel had banked the week's takings the day before.

Who could have murdered the furniture man and, more to the point, why? As far as Archie was aware, Daniel Wylie had had no enemies. He was a good man, a churchgoer. Where most men would whistle popular songs, Daniel seemed to know only hymn tunes. In the three or four years since taking over the business, he had become known for dealing fairly with buyers and sellers alike. His second-hand furniture was always treated for woodworm and polished to an attractive sheen before being offered for sale at a reasonable price. If, like Archie, you wanted to kit out a largish room with the basics, you couldn't go wrong with Wylie. And say the painter wanted to include a chandelier in a portrait, or a fancy footstool, Daniel would willingly let him bring his sketchpad or easel into the shop. An obliging sort of chap, he had been known to put aside any cheap picture frames he came across and to give Archie first refusal.

The police, too, were at a loss – until Mary Quinn turned up.

*

Fear lent her pallid skin a wraithlike transparency that would have challenged Rembrandt. She crept into the room at the sergeant's bidding and stood trembling, as if about to collapse in a heap of rag and bone. In the silence he heard the rasp of rough dry skin, as she twisted her hands.

'Come in, have a seat.' Archie sprang to his feet.

She shrank away, gnawing her lip.

'We won't keep you, then, Sergeant,' he said, his eyebrows lifting with the smallest of hints. They had it down to a fine art after three years. Frank Tyrell would put the kettle on and stay discreetly out of the room until the drawing was well underway. In Archie's experience witnesses found describing a suspect difficult enough, without the distraction of the law breathing down their necks. But even with Tyrell gone, the girl stood nibbling her fingernails, hardly daring to look at him.

Lord, was he that frightening? He sat down quickly to minimise his height and bulk. Or had she been listening to gossip? He knew what the neighbours thought about the artist in their midst and his loose morals. If he had been a skivvy like this poor little scrap, *he* might have found him a little daunting.

She had been cleaning for the widow, Mrs Chinnery, who had rooms over the chandler's, when she had spotted a man on the other side of the road, pressed against Wylie's window, banging and signalling for the owner to open up and admit him. Half an hour later the missus had made Mary shut the window for the smoke coming in.

According to Tyrell, the girl had only spoken up this morning. Like many, she was in fear of policemen and had spent sleepless nights making up her mind to tell her mistress, who had straightway marched her up to the police station. 'Tell them what you told me!' she'd rapped. 'Tell them you saw this man acting suspiciously.'

That was when they had sent for Archie.

Affecting indifference, he opened his sketchpad at a clean page, chose a pencil, and began drawing, relying on the old trick to break the ice. It worked with children. A sigh of long skirts and a whiff like a balled-up dishcloth told him that she had taken her seat. He looked up, expecting to find her absorbed in his comic sketch of the police sergeant, with walrus moustache and bulbous nose, but instead her baleful blue eyes were fixed on him.

She turned her attention to the wall where a faded etching of the queen headed up a list of dos and don'ts for those who could read. From the intensity of her gaze and the movement of her lips he guessed she only had the rudiments.

Lord, this wouldn't do. Her testimony was all they had to go on.

'There's no rush.' He forced a smile. 'Take your time. Try closing your eyes – that sometimes helps.'

That was asking too much. Almost perversely, she fastened on Archie's box of newly sharpened pencils, watching, he supposed, for them to wriggle and grow teeth. Suppressing a sigh, he raked his fingers through his damp auburn hair and asked her questions about height, build and colouring, trying to get a picture in his mind of a monster who would murder a decent chap like Wylie.

He had to get it right. There were no shortcuts: comic sketches like the one he'd done of Sergeant Tyrell wouldn't do for police records and, contrary to current theories, there really was no

6

criminal 'type'. Wrongdoers were not easily identifiable by the thickness of their skulls or caveman's physiognomy, and the caricatures featured in *Punch* magazine and the like were unhelpful. Perhaps a shifty or threatening manner might give them away but their features, give or take the odd scar or broken nose, were not remarkable – no more so than those of law-abiding citizens. In this case the suspect seemed to have been a fairly well-to-do young man, wearing a light-coloured, three-piece suit. Archie was forced to lean in close to catch the words. Her breath was sour, the lilt Irish.

'Collar and tie?' he asked.

'Yes, sir,' she whispered.

'Hmm,' he said, overcoming his doubts, 'and on such a hot day, too.' Where the hell was that tea?

'Collar and tie, sir,' she insisted.

As he selected his first fine-pointed pencil, the tea arrived, the policeman withdrew and Archie watched blunt finger-ends add a greedy six lumps of sugar to her cup. There were biscuits, too, to be dunked, sucked and swallowed with relish. Lord, the girl was famished. No wonder she looked so washed out. Not a speck of colour in her face apart from those startling ultramarine eyes, all but lost in the dark saucers of her skull. Little by little as the tea went down, her lips grew less pale and with a touch more vigour she began describing a young man in his middle-to-late twenties, shorter than Archie, who stood up for comparison, his hair grazing the low ceiling. 'Not your build at all, sir, not so broad in the shoulders.' Her man had a high forehead beneath a brown bowler hat or derby, a long, narrow jaw, sandy or fair hair, pale eyes and 'rabbity' teeth. At Archie's prompting she remembered cheekbones, 'Sharp, no meat on them at all,' adding, shyly, not without a touch of admiration, 'not like yours, sir.' Feeling her eyes on him, he kept his own on the drawing and changed to a softer pencil for shading under the bone. Oh yes, she recalled a moustache, big and bushy, like Sergeant Tyrell's. Instinctively Archie's fingers strayed to his own upper lip, his gingery stubble – Tyrell had got him out of bed this morning – and, becoming conscious of her appraisal, returned to the task in hand. It wasn't the first time a witness had used him as an *aide mémoire*. 'And *he* hadn't the side whiskers, sir. Nor a dimple in his chin,' she added, almost cheekily.

As they went on she grew bolder, letting him know that the eyes he'd drawn, that she'd approved earlier, were set too close, 'Too piggy altogether,' and the eyebrows were too heavy. He tried again with larger irises, further apart.

'No-o-o,' she dared to groan, 'nothing like!' Setting his mouth in grim compliance he erased this effort also. 'Oh.' Her pout said it all. 'I'm a nuisance, amn't I? Hadn't we just better forget it?'

'Not on your life,' he said. 'You're very good. Most people would have used these much earlier.' He was referring to his collection of 'visual aids' created over the three years he had been working for the police: pages of head shapes, noses, mouths, chins, brows, jaws, hairlines, ears and, of course, eyes. From his folder he selected drawings of deep-set eyes, 'normal' eyes and more protruding eyes. She chose from the third sheet and, without hesitation, a pair with long upper lids. 'There's your man.' While they were at it, could she see the noses, sir? She did believe his was thinner than the one Archie had drawn.

He continued erasing and re-drawing at her dictation until suddenly he knew how it went. This was a face he'd drawn before! Quickly he flipped the page and began afresh, drawing now with swift strokes, shading around the nose and to show the fullness of the lower lip. 'Sure an' you have him, sir,' she said, catching her breath in wonder that he'd seemed to read her mind, 'that's him exactly.' He erased smudges of soft pencil for highlights on the cheekbones, the forehead, just as he had before, and finished him off with a collar and tie and a derby tipped back on his head.

'The very man, so it is,' said the girl, shrinking back in something like horror. 'It's uncanny.'

No. There were no Other World spirits at his shoulder, no angels. It was just a knack he had, getting the witness to relax, letting her talk, listening carefully.

He called in Sergeant Tyrell, told him they were finished and, with his face set against any giveaway show of emotion, slid the sketchbook along the table towards the older man. 'See who it is, Sergeant?'

'By crikey!' He leaned round Mary Quinn and moved his spectacles further down his nose to peer over them. 'That's Mad Tommo Hegarty, that is!' His nostrils flared with distaste. 'Well, 'e *as* come up in the world.'

'You know him?' She sounded more alarmed than surprised.

'Not as well as I'd like,' the officer grumbled. 'Give us the slip last time. Your first case weren' it, Mister Price?'

Archie jerked his head in acknowledgement, remembering the disappointment when, after all his efforts, the villain and his accomplice had got away. He had a sudden thought. 'I'd better let the Kingtons know.'

'If you would, Arch – uh, Mister Price. Let's 'ope we can catch the blighter this time.'

'Bastard,' said Archie. 'Hanging's too good for him.' He glanced at the girl with sudden regret for his rough language, but she was hardly a lady. Indeed, the way she was staring at them both, you'd think she might add some epithet of her own.

'Come on, you,' said the policeman, curtly. 'You're done 'ere.'

9

She turned on her worn-down heel and followed him out of the door.

Archie was still packing up his materials when Tyrell returned. Tearing out the page he said, 'I'll get a poster done, then.'

The policeman grunted assent, his mind clearly elsewhere, on the next steps in the investigation perhaps, consulting the files, alerting the rest of the force, writing up his report.

'First thing in the morning all right?'

'Sorry? Oh yeah, thanks, soon as you like.'

'She was good, wasn't she? The girl, I mean.'

'Mm-hmm.'

'You don't think so?'

The sergeant took a long breath, scratched his forehead. 'In so far as she went, Archie, she was spot-on. I mean, the man she's described is Mad Tommo, no doubt about it. He was there. But there's gotta be at least one other person involved. At least.'

'Oh?'

'Think about it. Hegarty's an evil little worm, wiry but short in the arse. Even s'posing he done the killing, he ain't gonna be strong enough to lift the dead weight of Daniel Wylie up onto that pile of chairs all by himself. I mean Wylie was at least as tall as you, Arch, and a few stone heavier. I doubt you and me between us could have raised him above shoulder height, alive or dead. So I'm wondering, when, where and how did his mates show up? Was they already in the shop when the Quinn girl spotted Hegarty or did they come after?'

'And who were they? Was it Hegarty's idea?' Archie was enjoying the puzzle. 'Why, most of all, *why*?'

'I don't see Hegarty as the brains behind this, Arch. He's more your smash-and-grab bully-boy. Look what he done to that Squire Whatjemacallit …'

'Mowbray.' The old Squire been smashed to a pulp. Archie's friend John Kington, coming across the killers just after the attack, was lucky to escape with his life.

'Mowbray, that's the one.' Tyrell nodded. 'No, Tommo's just a mindless thug. Whoever killed Wylie planned it, done his research. Knew Wylie shut up shop between twelve and one, knew Will Beswick'd be away and he'd have Wylie's undivided attention. But what was they after?' He paused, his heavy brow furrowed in thought. 'Not the cash – he'd already banked the week's takings, the day before, according to his wife. He'd a known that – whoever done it – shopkeepers round here bank on a Friday. Carry a big float on Market day, you're asking for trouble. And then there's the shooting. Hegarty's more at home with a shillelagh, we know that.'

'He's had three years to learn how to use a gun,' Archie pointed out.

'True, very true, Arch, but I don't see our Tommo as a gun man, somehow.' He shook his head, defying argument. 'And piling up the chairs like that, making a bonfire, what's that in aid of? The man's dead. Who they trying to impress?' He tapped his fingernails on the table and pursed his lips. 'No, it's not as simple as it looks, mark my words.'

*

They paid the artist a guinea for his pains. They gave Mary Quinn nothing. Helping the police with their enquiries, albeit reluctantly, was, after all, no more than her civic duty.

Easily sloughing off a sense of injustice on her behalf, Archie bounded down the steps of the police station, looking forward to a plate of eels and mash, when he saw her ahead of him at the crossroads, waiting for a gap in the traffic. Should he slow down, pretend he hadn't seen her? He'd spent a lifetime ignoring such people. Their interests were not his, their God not one he recognised. She stepped out into the road and hastily jumped back, crossing herself, as a horse and carriage rounded the corner in a choking cloud of dust and dried clods of dung. A brewer's dray ground by on the other side, pulled by a pair of massive Shires.

'You look that way and I'll look this,' he said, taking her bony elbow in his palm and dodging a butcher's boy on a bicycle. Skivvy or not, she was still a woman, and manners learned at his mother's knee were ingrained. 'It wasn't so bad, was it?' he asked when they were safely across, wiping his hand, where he'd held her, on his coat. 'I'd say we did a good job between us.' She stared hard at the ground. Any minute now she'd bob a curtsey. 'In the interview room, I mean.' He smiled, but there was no response. The creature was struck dumb by his attention. He really should stop teasing her, tip his hat and walk away. Some wicked impulse prompted him to persevere. 'You seemed decidedly anxious in there.' The frowsy hat dipped lower; blunt fingers came up to scrape loose hair behind the ear. 'But there was really nothing to it, was there?'

She flicked a glance at him. 'No, sir,' she said, twitching her mouth in what might have been a smile. Why did he get the feeling that what she had just done carried tremendous weight for her? Poor wretch – he realised, in a life so close to the gutter, a visit to the police station must either be a glorious highlight that would keep her in gossip with her ragged cronies for weeks, or unendurable torture.

'Not that it wasn't of critical importance,' he hastened to add. 'The police have been after that scum Hegarty for years. Your evidence will nail him, once and for all.'

He caught the flash of her eyes as she muttered, 'Always supposin' they catch him …'

She was right. And if Hegarty found out who had fingered him, he would make it his business, his *primary* business, to silence her. She had been very brave in coming forward, very brave indeed. There was more to her than met the eye.

In fact, he couldn't help thinking, with a few hot meals inside her and something decent to wear she'd be almost passable, with those thick black lashes and that delicate bone structure – 'a face full of bones,' his mother would have said. The way her head was poised on that skinny neck was very pleasing, very pleasing indeed. Just so long as she didn't open her mouth. They had no conversation, these people, no education, just a lot of empty chit-chat. But as one thought struck him so another took its place, a scheme …

'Come along,' he said firmly, and taking her arm again, steered her into the fragrant pie and eel shop. She protested a little, struggled feebly, but it was clear as day that she couldn't believe her luck. She was like a child at the high counter, her eyes misting as she followed each chunk of stewed fish ladled into the dish, each drop of hot parsley liquor puddling the mash: her moist tongue actually licking her lips. He told her to find a table and he'd bring over the food.

Tears filled her eyes as he put her plate before her. 'It's too much altogether,' she whispered. But one greedy mouthful followed another, freeing her tongue at the same time. Hardly pausing for breath, or even to chew her food, she prattled on about the news of the week, the fire at Wylie's.

'Couldn't I feel the heat of it with the window closed, hear the roaring of it?'

Slow down, slow down, finish your mouthful, he wanted to tell her. Her manners were appalling. He could scarcely bear to watch her, blathering away with her mouth full of fish and green

13

parsley. Any minute now she'd abandon her knife and fork and stuff the food in with her bitten finger-ends. Oh God, this was such a mistake. Could he possibly invent an urgent appointment and leave her to it? Now there was an idea.

But even as he slipped his hand into his pocket to consult his watch, she was off on another tack: her daily grind. Apparently Mrs Chinnery wasn't the only lady she 'did' for. As if he gave a tuppenny damn! Mostly she cleaned houses and shops. Up and out by four in the morning, she'd have swept up the sawdust at The Horse and Groom, emptied the spittoon and cleaned the lavvies before Mister Reeves opened up. That done, she'd take herself down the road and mop a shop floor or two before knocking on Mrs Chinnery's door at eleven on the dot.

He was hardly listening. Head aslant, he studied her face, thinking, Lord, Lord, why does she spoil her looks with that dreadful tuft of crimped hair and that cheap fluff of feathers on the brim of her hat? And a regular encounter with soap and water wouldn't come amiss. Quite apart from improving her 'bouquet' she'd be almost pretty with those sky-blue eyes, bright now and animated, those flyaway eyebrows and that delicate skin. A good scrub and he might be able to do something with her. In fact, she'd make a striking picture.

In fact …

His bag of materials sat beside him on the bench. But the white wall tiles were too cold, the high-backed booth too functional and, besides, he'd seen something similar in the Academy by one of the new French artists, with an eminently forgettable name. But he could still see the painting of that derelict couple, the woman drinking absinthe, also at a marble-topped table, looking completely unfocused, un-posed. Funny the impact it had made and it wasn't even well done: the brush-work was crude, the colours dull. And yet it said something a more 'finished' painting somehow could not. Degas – that was the chap. The galleries in town were agog with him and his cronies, with their preference for common subjects, realistic scenes.

If this was the coming thing, perhaps he, too, should …

He closed his eyes to focus on a vision fast-forming in his head, of a raggedy-Annie, a dirty little immigrant, hardly connecting to the real world except to clean it. She would be in the foreground looking out of the window, her washcloth laid aside as she stared at the shocking scene across the street, the burning building, the wild-eyed horses, flames, devastation, death. He could use the sketches he'd made for the *Journal*.

And her. He'd use her.

Oh, this would be very different from his usual style which, he had to admit, had hardly changed in five years and still owed much to the tenets of the Pre-Raphaelites, his idols at college. Like theirs, his paintings were designed to lead the viewer away from reality's imperfections, to a world of make-believe where only the most beautiful and luscious of leaves and fruits grew and the most beautiful and luscious of people lived. Like Ida, all peaches and cream; like Charlotte, another Jane Morris, with her dark hair and pouting lips; Gussie even had the Titian colouring so beloved of Rossetti and company. He aimed so to consume his viewers with beauty that they failed to see that in Victoria's England things were flawed, were smelly and noisy, were in fact downright ugly.

This new work wouldn't pull any punches. On his way home he'd buy some long flat-headed brushes, some tubes of ready-mixed paint. Stand aside Pre-Raphs! Enter true realism.

He would paint this girl exactly as she was: bony wrists, dirty neck and all, and he would show her humanity in every brushstroke. He would be holding a mirror up to poverty.

Photography be damned, this would be ten times more real, more telling.

He gulped down the food now, hardly tasting it. He couldn't wait to get started. Casually, delicately, as though the act of arranging the segments of fishbone around the rim of his dish was oh so absorbing, he explained what he had in mind, if she would deign to sit for him. They could go now, well, when she'd finished eating. His studio was just up the road. 'No need to change. Come as you are.'

She blushed. She scooped up the very last crumb of her mashed potato and slid off the bench. Her dish clattered against the marble top as it caught her sleeve and she pointed the knife at him in a dangerously different grip. 'Oh no,' she said, looking him in the eye as she backed away, 'you've got me wrong there, mister. You'll not buy me with a plate of fish. You'll have to find someone else for that sort of thing, so you will.'

What sort of thing? Surely she didn't imagine he would stoop to … good God! He watched, speechless, as she left the shop, and held out his hands to Bernie, the restaurateur, in complete bewilderment.

Bernie was more concerned about the girl's empty plate. She'd made off with his cutlery.

Chapter 2

Mary ran down the High Street, the knife up one sleeve, the fork up the other, the eel and its lovely juices swilling in her belly. Thinking she would be sick and that'd be a waste of it, she slowed to a walk when she was sure he wasn't following. Jesus, Mary and Joseph, she thought, gulping air and crossing herself, wasn't that a narrow escape?

She had only herself to blame, of course. She'd known what he was like. Nobody spoke to her directly, the girl polishing the brass fittings on the door of the Conservative Club, but the shrill voices of the stallholders floated over to her.

'Fair dos,' said the one they called Charlotte, laying out her knick-knacks, 'he pays all right – shilling an hour, and eighteen pence for specials.'

'*Specials*, what's that?'

'You know – bare-arsed.'

Shrieks and squeaks and '*Lawks!*' had Mary straining her ears to catch their drift.

'Well, I tell ye ...' went Charlotte, lowering her voice even further. Mary couldn't make it out, not over the rattling letterbox. She turned her attention to the doorknob.

'Never!'

'Oh yes! Ain't nothing sacred with painters.'

'And you let him, Charlotte Wiggins. What was that then, *extra* special? Gawd 'elp us, no wonder he always looks like he's just got up, with them bedroom eyes, an' all.'

'Oh he's lovely, Bess, but I tell ye, gel, you sit for him, you wanna watch you don't come out with a sight more'n what you went in with! 'Old up, here's yer old man.' Their laughter ended abruptly. 'So, Bessie, what d'you think of me new line, eh? Little black cat for luck and you can have green eyes or red. Go on, treat yourself.'

The missus at the pub didn't mince her words, either. 'A wolf in sheep's clothing,' she reckoned. 'Melt your heart, he would, with that smile of his and *could* I let him have half a bitter on the slate, just till he gets to the bank? Cheeky beggar! I soon told him what for. Course, we all know where his money goes, at a shilling an hour. Them silly geese – if their mothers only knew …'

And she was one of them, another silly goose. A prize eejit. Oh, she could kick herself. But how could you *not* trust a man who could see into your mind and transfer what he saw to paper? Down to the last button and whisker? What he did was amazing. There was magic in his fingers. He listened hard, to every blessed word, bending his head in close, a flea jump away. And breath like honey.

She should have known it wasn't kindness that had him offering her dinner. Why should he? The likes of her? And him with ladies a-plenty, real ladies in pretty dresses? But she'd been so very faint with hunger she hadn't thought what he might want from her. Doing that shameful thing in the police station had used up all her strength, and the biscuits with the tea no help at all. Sure, and when had she ever sat down to a proper dish of fish and parsley sauce?

Fish *stew*, maybe, if she could beg a few fish heads in the market. 'For the cat?' she'd wheedle. But they knew, the butcher and the fishmonger, and all their customers, too, that the marrowbone 'for her little dog' and the fish heads would end up in the cook pot, alongside any carrots and onions that had rolled off the barrow, or the leaves off cauliflowers, or soft tomatoes. But it wasn't the same as eels and mash you hadn't had to cook yourself. That was special.

Mammy made the best fish stew in the world. 'Feeding the multitude,' she called it, with a herring or two off the boat and the shellfish the children gathered in from the beach: crabs and razor-shells and winkles. Cooked up with some praties and a few pot herbs, you'd think you were a queen at a feast. Even when Da died of drowning Mammy could make do with the scraps from the filleting down on the quayside. But then the fish stopped biting and the boats came back empty more often than not and there was no work for anyone, men or women. Sooner than live off seaweed and nettles, gulls' eggs and what few shellfish were left now that everyone was picking them, the nine children dwindled to six, then five, then four as they all went for a better life in England. After Brian went it was her turn. And here she was, alone and making what she could of it. She supposed she'd never see Mammy again or many of the others, come to that.

She crossed the road to 'Uncle's' and, sucking them clean before she went in, pawned the knife and fork for sixpence. The old man gave her a squinty look, like he knew they were stolen, and so he should, but never mind. Needs must.

Nearing the end of the High Street now, she breathed shallow against the foul smell of the Lea and its marshes. The hot weather had dried the river to a slow, lazy sludge. What boats and barges there were kept to the middle and their crews wore scarves over their noses like thieves.

19

There was that kid again, the one that looked like her brother Michael, his hair so thick with dirt you couldn't tell its colour, eyes sunk with starvation, and skin like sooty candle wax. His feet were bare, his clothes in shreds. She hadn't said anything to the police, but the other day, while she was looking in Underwood's at the hats, he'd been pestering Mister Wylie on the doorstep.

'Clear off, sonny,' the big man had said. 'Nothing for you here.'

She hadn't heard what he'd said, but Mister Wylie had taken it badly. 'May God forgive you, you evil little runt!' he'd shouted, purple with rage. Next thing, the door banged, the *Closed* sign went up and the kid was away down the street, holding his ear and hollering.

It wasn't like the furniture man to clout a child. Generally he was praising the Lord for a glorious day and God-blessing anyone who stopped to look in his shop. If business was slow, he'd maybe sit outside with a bowl of soapy water and a cloth to clean a looking-glass or a pretty lampshade and to pass the time of day with passers-by. But the little fellow had really upset him. As the boy's rusty wheezing faded away, Mary couldn't help but wonder what he'd said that was so bad.

Perhaps *he'd* had a hand in the murder. Perhaps he'd got his Da to pay the man a visit; set fire to his store for spite. She almost laughed. Daft idea, Mary. The police were convinced that Tommo Hegarty was their man, thanks to her. All they had to do now was catch him. And soon, please God. She crossed herself. She couldn't have him wondering who had grassed him up. He'd know soon enough, at the trial, when she pointed her finger at him there in the dock. But they'd have him in irons by then.

What was this boy thinking of, hanging round the pub on the corner, bothering the fellers as they came through the door? He was asking for another thick ear or worse. The Railway Tavern was a den of roaring boys, and charity the last thing on their minds.

'I'd run along, if I were you,' she said to the boy, as she came up, 'anywhere but here. They eat you little ones for dinner.'

''*E* won't.' His dirty face was streaked with fresh tears, she noticed, and the bones of his cheeks were nearly through the skin. '*E*'s a toff.'

'Who's that? Your Da?'

'Ain't got no Da.'

'Oh.'

'No ma, neither.'

'Who looks after you then?'

'Me pals. Least they did.' His mouth turned down and his eyes filled with tears as he gazed longingly at the door of the Tavern. He could only have been five or six, not much more. Limbs like twigs. 'But they went and left us,' he said and a new tear washed a pathway through the dirt on his cheek.

What could she do? He shouldn't hang around here hoping for handouts from mindless drunks. He'd get more than he bargained for. He said his name was Jim. It was what his ma had called him before she 'run off with some geezer over Tottenham'.

She sighed. 'Want a biscuit, Jim?' His eyes lit up like magic and he cuffed his snot with an almighty and unsuccessful sniff. She felt for the biscuits she'd palmed into her pocket up at the police station. She'd been going to give one to Dolly but what the eye didn't see …

It was gone in a flash and he turned his gaze on her pocket expectantly, as a dog would: knowing there were more.

She sighed again. She couldn't take him home. Dolly would have a fit, another mouth to feed. There were places for waifs and strays – orphanages, the Workhouse – where he'd have a roof over his head, at least. 'Look, you come with me, Jim, and I'll give you the other one,' she wheedled. She'd take him to the Sally Army up the road.

He squinted up at her. 'Giss it nah!'

'No, let's just go and see these people I know. They'll take you in.'

'Gimme a bickit, first.'

'No.'

'Gimme, gimme!' He stamped his little bare feet. She couldn't torment the poor little mite and in the end left him, munching greedily, searching frantically for any dropped bits and crumbs – much good would they do him – and refusing to budge from the spot. A faint thought fluttered through her mind that perhaps she should fetch a policeman, but it scurried away in fear. Not even a needy case like Jim warranted more words with them.

With a heavy heart she left him to his fate, looked for carts and bicycles coming round the corner, and picked her way across James Street.

Chapter 3

Archie threw down his brush with a grunt. His painting of Ida Sutton among the pillows was dull, dull, dull! It was a pretty pose, improved, he thought, by the addition of the flowers, scattered symbolically over the sheets, broken-stemmed, with falling petals. It would pay the rent. But it wasn't how he wanted to go on. It wasn't real. It didn't *say* anything except that Ida was the well-fed daughter of a local farmer, who brought Archie butter and eggs and posed for him in exchange for drawing lessons and mutual sexual satisfaction. But only he knew that.

He cleaned his brushes and palette and set out to walk to Woodford, hoping the fresh air would energise him, spark off some new ideas. If only Mary Quinn had agreed to sit for him. The image came to him again, of a skinny neck, limpid eyes, a frizzy tuft of hair …

Soon the cries and bustle of shopping were behind him and he was striding along leafy lanes with his jacket flapping. Breathing deeply, he raised his face to the breeze, let it rinse his hair and scour his ears. Days like this reminded him of his boyhood in South Wales, of skittering over the fields of a Sunday with his brothers and the dog, down to windy Llantwit beach, Mam and Dad following more sedately, by road, with the picnic things in the trap. Even in those days he took his drawing kit in a bag over his shoulder, to sketch the sea-birds, the thrift and thistles, in between clambering over the rocks, looking for fossils, larking about in the sea. He was Mr and Mrs Price's best hope, the gifted son. Not for him the family shop or the mines, or even teaching in the local school. He came to London to pursue his craft, to the Slade School of Art, and thence to Walthamstow to ply his trade. No good going back to Wales, London was where the customers were. Walthamstow was a bit of a backwater but it was up and running, with the railway into town, and lodgings were cheap.

Even the slog up Forest Road was pleasant, past the spacious homes of the rich, where the air tasted of fresh-mown grass and roses, past the pumping station at the top of the road, crossing over finally into shady woodland, where the paths were dappled with sunlight and birds sang.

He struck out along the main track through the forest, made dusty and rutted by cartwheels and hooves. It was almost as busy as the main road, the small carts piled with dirty fleece from a late shearing or empty chicken crates. People passed in both directions, on horseback and on foot, carrying bundles, driving cows, pigs and geese. The minor paths, though quieter, were given a wide berth after what happened three years before. Squire Mowbray had been waylaid and murdered, and poor old John Kington, Archie's college pal, coming along behind in his mule cart, had been attacked and left for dead.

According to John, he'd been taking what he thought was a quiet route home through the forest, enjoying the cool shade of the trees and the end of a successful day at the Epping Fair. He'd sold all Lizzie's jams and cakes and most of his tiles, taken a dozen big orders, and his cash box was full.

He thought little of seeing two shabby-looking coves by the

path, one bare-chested in the summer heat, cooling his dirty feet in a stream, the other further off, pissing into a holly bush. John had his dogs to protect him and these were tinkers, he thought, heading down to the evening events at the fair.

He called a greeting as he went past, raising his hat. The one standing buttoned his fly and, when he turned, gave a surly nod of acknowledgement. The fellow by the stream simply scowled. The sun angled its beams between two tall oaks, lighting up a rope hanging down from one of them. John only remembered that when giving his statement to the police. At the time he simply noted that the dogs were uneasy, setting up a low growling, their black lips creeping back from their teeth. Without warning Duke leapt from the moving cart, snarling and slavering, sensing the chance to sink his teeth into something meaty, while Queenie clattered around in the cart, barking excitedly, her one blue eye looking mad.

John reined in the mule. 'Duke, Queenie! Quiet!' By then the taller of the men was yelling and kicking the collie away. The dog dodged and snapped, determined to get past the man and onto something in the bushes. Rabbits, thought John, and he jumped down to sort it out. Suddenly Queenie was there, too, barking furiously and earning herself a kick in the ribs that made her squeal.

'Hey, you, no need for that! Duke, heel!' he cried, bewildered both by the dogs' behaviour and the men's overly violent reaction. 'Leave! Duke, Queenie, that's enough. Heel, I say.'

But the bare-chested one never gave them a chance. From nowhere he produced a cudgel and, with a savage oath, caught the bitch a cracking blow across the muzzle. She fell at the man's feet and he swung the cudgel again, killing her.

'Queenie!' John moaned, stooping to her. She was warm

25

against his boot, but heavy, lifeless, a gash starting to bleed into the black hair between her ears. 'Queenie! Queenie, girl.'

'You get away now, lessen you want a taste o' this.' The man was hefting the club against his palm. It had to be made of iron to break a dog's skull.

'You bastard!' John's voice broke. 'There was no need …'

'Get away, I say, or I'll do for yer.'

Duke had come over to lick his mother's wounds, whimpering.

'Come on, Duke,' he urged gently, tugging on the dog's collar. 'Let's get her home.' But as he struggled to lift the bitch, Duke turned to face the enemy, his eyes glowing red, rage welling in his throat.

'Clear off and take the animal with you,' yelled the taller man, backing away from the dripping teeth.

John was now in fear for his life. 'Come, Duke!' he managed, 'Heel, boy!' As he dumped the dead dog in the cart, the movement jiggled the cash box.

'Hah!' cried the dog-killer and he raised his cudgel to strike again.

When he came to, John found he had company under the holly bush. Flyblown and almost faceless with beating was the local bigwig, Sir Timothy Mowbray, done to death on his way home from the Epping Fair, and robbed blind, literally. His eye had dropped from its socket onto his cheek. John must have happened on the killers just after they'd done.

He was in bed for weeks recovering from his head injuries, and poor pregnant Lizzie left to run their pottery business single-handed. But he was able to describe his assailants to Archie, who'd drawn their likenesses for the police. They'd put out Wanted posters, though too late to catch the bastards. That track was now patrolled regularly by mounted policemen, and a notice set up by the managers of the forest, the City of London, warning travellers to take care on these paths. The Mowbrays' influence was far-reaching.

Archie's sketches had done some good, besides securing him a job with the police. Local people recognised John's attackers, identifying them as Tommo, Mrs Hegarty's youngest lad, and Brian Rooney, a more recent immigrant.

Maureen Hegarty of Railway Cottages, Chingford, hadn't seen her son in months. He was away with the tinkers, as far as she knew, and for all she cared the devil could take him and his wicked ways. Rooney was a likeable fellow, she said, who first came to the house calling on her daughter, Maggie. He lived by his wits, it seemed, and Maggie, quite rightly, told him to sling his hook. She directed the police to Rooney's lodgings in High Beech.

The landlady had re-let his room when he failed to return after a week. She had kept his few possessions and, when pressed, handed over to the police some worn clothes wrapped up in a bit of oil-cloth, two popular novels, a pile of penny-dreadfuls and, more usefully, a studio photograph of his younger self in the bosom of a large family. On the back was the address of a photographer in the small town of Ennis, and the warning that *Negatives are kept for twelve months only*.

Further enquiries revealed that on the day after the murder Hegarty had travelled on the up-train from Chingford to the end of the line, but there the metropolis had swallowed him up. Fellow passengers described him as a ratty haired, gamey-smelling hooligan dressed in the fine linen shirt, frockcoat and breeches of a man of means. The riding boots drew their attention particularly, footwear out of place on the early morning train to

London. The tinkers had presumably divvyed up the contents of the Squire's purse and John's cashbox and gone their separate ways, one on the Squire's prize chestnut mare, one in a mule cart which was later found abandoned at Chingford station and returned to its owners.

So what on earth had induced Hegarty to return? Family? A woman? And why Daniel Wylie? What had a scoundrel like Hegarty to do with that good man? Was he back to stay? If so, where was he now?

Archie's thoughts were interrupted by a milk cart trundling past, chains chinking against the churns, the horse's hooves thudding on ground made hollow by rabbits, and the driver giving him a cheery 'Evening!' A cloud passed over the sun and Archie shivered, looking from left to right as though he might see a pair of footpads standing in his way. He wasn't at all sorry to leave the track at the fingerpost to Woodford and, cutting through quickly to the High Road, crossed over and turned down Tubbwell Lane, to the Kingtons' pottery.

When he heard the howling child and thrashing water through the window, he almost turned tail. He'd come at a bad time. But the door opened and there was John Kington about to go out. Leaning on a stick, he looked a much older man, twenty-six going on sixty, his eyes red-rimmed, his skin white and clammy as the underside of a flatfish. He looked ill, or drugged.

'Well, look who's here,' said the tile-maker sharply, his mouth twitching with sarcasm. 'Find it hard to keep away, did you?'

He *wasn't* any better. Since his beating he had become cynical and dry, not the wild bohemian of their student days. Now he was one of the few people Archie knew who could take the wind out of your sails with a word. It was the main reason he hadn't visited in weeks. Lizzie, now ... but Lizzie was off limits. He'd

28

come to realise that he'd let her go too easily all those years ago. More fool him.

He tried explaining how busy he'd been, what with painting and police work. Just this afternoon he had been round at the printer's preparing a plate for the press …

The interest was fast draining from Kington's face. So he came to the point and was dismayed to see John crumple over his stick, as though stabbed by the news. He would have fallen if Archie hadn't caught him. The tile-maker pinched the bridge of his nose as if to rouse himself, growled, 'Hell and damnation!' and led the way back indoors.

Before his eyes adjusted to the dim interior Archie could have believed the slender figure kneeling motionless before the tin bath was carved out of stone. Her skin, her clothes, her headscarf were uniformly grey. Then as a brimming jug emerged from the water, he realised that her moving arm was pink and alive, washed clean. His eardrums split as the jug tipped over the child's head.

'Last one, Clara – keep your eyes shut!'

'Lizzie!' her husband hissed through teeth bared in pain. 'Lizzie, we have a visitor!'

Archie's smile was apologetic; he was intruding. John shouldn't have let him in knowing that Lizzie would be embarrassed. 'I'm sorry, I'll …'

'Yes, indeed,' Kington interrupted, waving his arms like a conductor trying to bring an orchestra to order, 'he's come to tell us that my murderer is back amongst us and to bar the windows and bolt the doors. Isn't that so, Archie?'

Archie frowned. *My murderer.* He knew his friend was haunted by the fear that Hegarty would return to finish him off. 'Not at all,' he tried to reassure him, 'it's just that they might need you to testify if they catch him.'

'He knows I can identify him.'

'Oh, John, how many more times? He doesn't know who you are, where you live or even that you're still alive.'

But Lizzie's tight lips and the look that passed between husband and wife, told Archie the truth of the matter. In her opinion he *had* been murdered, the John she knew. And John was perfectly aware of this.

The child stopped crying and blinked up at Archie with long wet lashes. She smiled in delight, recognising her 'Uncle Art!' while the water splashed and swirled around her legs.

'So, how's my best girl?' cried Archie, dropping to his knees and kissing the wet cheek. 'What was all that noise I heard? It surely wasn't Clara, was it?' The child shook her head in barefaced denial. 'Must have been your Ma, then, raising the roof. Lizzie, really! What a fuss to make!'

The child's giggles were irresistible. Lizzie used the small respite to whip off her protective scarf, revealing flaxen hair scragged into a tight bun. It made her face seem even greyer, her grin dingy and her eyes, fringed with grey lashes, gleaming pieces of sea-glass. 'I'm a mess,' she apologised. 'Been sweeping out the pottery ready for glazing tomorrow.'

'You're fine,' he assured her. She really was, one of the best. Different from the bubbly, high-spirited girl he'd known at college, but he supposed marriage did that. 'Now then, see,' he said, giving Clara his full attention, 'I've brought some lovely ripe plums from my friend, Bob, but he said I must only give them to a good girl who doesn't mind having her hair washed. That'd be you, would it?' He winked.

Glancing at Lizzie, he said, 'I just thought you should know that a certain, em, Irish tinker, has shown up again in connection with another, em, incident,' not wanting to use the M word in front of a bright two-and-a-half-year-old. 'So maybe this time they'll catch the – the –'

'*Bastard* is the word you're looking for.' Kington seemed to be overtaken by pain so crushing he staggered, bumping into the table.

Lizzie jumped up. 'John, John, sit down, for goodness' sake. Don't go out,' she pleaded. 'You really don't need a drink.'

She slid a quick glance in Archie's direction, afraid she'd been disloyal, said too much. He met her eyes with sympathy. He'd guessed where John had been headed when they'd met.

John could hardly speak, holding his head with his hands. 'No-o,' he agreed, struggling upright. 'I'll – I'll go up to bed, take a spoonful of jollop.'

'Do you have to?' she sighed, and turning to the visitor standing helpless in the middle of the room, said, 'Archie, I'm sorry, would you be a dear, just keep an eye on Clara for a minute?'

The two climbed the stairs, Lizzie half-pulling, half-carrying her husband. Archie could hear a murmur of voices, footfalls and thumps overhead. He rolled up his sleeves, knelt by the bath and wiped the child's face dry with a towel. Then, producing sweet plums from his pocket, he conjured them from behind her pink ears and stoned them for easy eating with his penknife. When her mother came back they were singing '*Daisy, Daisy . . .*' and blowing soap bubbles.

The woman smiled but her eyes were troubled. 'It's getting worse. Any sort of stress and he's like this.'

'He seems to be in real pain, Lizzie.'

'Mmm,' she murmured, her twisting mouth casting doubt on John's illness.

'What do you mean?'

She shook her head, frowning a warning that the child had ears. 'Let's just say that it's convenient, the pain. It's the medicine that's the problem.' Turning her attention to Clara she asked, 'Have you been playing nicely with Uncle Art?' Then she looked up at her visitor. 'We're so pleased to see him, aren't we?' She picked the dripping flannel out of the tub and swabbed her own face with it, becoming human again, vestiges of her younger self showing through.

'Have a plum,' he offered.

While she was upstairs putting Clara to bed, he took the tin bath into the yard, emptied it onto a clump of thistles and hung it on the wall of the house beside a larger one. The door to the pottery was closed, with dust and cobwebs obscuring the windows, but you could feel the heat from the kiln. It must be unbearable working in there in this weather. Poor Lizzie, from pampered daughter of an art teacher to perspiring skivvy. She'd come a long way.

Archie wiped his feet on the worn backdoor mat and went through into the scullery. A stack of plates and dirty pots was waiting to be washed. He went back to the yard and filled the kettle from the well.

*

The sun was low in the sky when he returned to his studio and his wet canvas gleamed in the light from the window. Pink and soft as a marshmallow, Ida's image simpered at him over its nicely rounded shoulder, the sheets tastefully rumpled. He sighed. Wrong, wrong, wrong! He took the painting off the easel, careful not to smudge it, and propped it against the wall. There were just the finishing touches to do, a few more petals, a candle stump. In the meantime … he took a blank canvas from behind the wardrobe, already primed and prepared.

32

Tomorrow he'd get someone in, someone who could look poor and frail. Who, though? Charlotte? She was altogether too intense for this painting, too spiky and mealy-mouthed, reminding him of a ship in harbour with its sails tightly furled. Gussie was too vibrant, too smug. Maude? Too matronly. And Lizzie was off limits. Damn and blast it, why was Mary Quinn's image so persistent?

A sketchbook was on the table. A soft pencil, a few swift strokes, and there she was, staring through a window at a burning building: a small-boned, thin woman. Goddamn! It even had her face. He tore it off the pad, levered a drawing pin off his notice-board with his penknife and pinned the sketch where he could see it.

Well, someone would come along; they usually did. In the meantime he would improvise. Choosing his larger brushes he used *terre verte* to block in the woman's face, neck and hands. When it was dry, in a day or two, he would paint over that unearthly bilious green, and transform it into pearly translucent skin and hopefully by then he'd have his sitter.

Right now the light was going. He glanced up. The pigments were changing colour as the setting sun brushed the glass jars, and the junk in the oddment box – driftwood, animal bones and pebbles – was turned into miniature golden statuary.

It was time to light the candles and close the shutters.

But the sunset wouldn't be ignored. Quickly he ground more pigments – crimson, orange and yellow-ochre – mixed them with linseed oil and moved his easel to the window. He breathed in the sight, feeling energy coursing through him as he transferred the colours to canvas with swishes of his largest brush. Then he trailed an intense phthalo blue between them and, putting his brushes aside, played and danced among the clouds with his bare fingertips.

'Archie-eee!' There was a gang of them outside: Eddy and Wally from the boxing club, with Abel Stevens, whom he'd sparred with once and come off worst. Stevens taught at the boys' school halfway down the High Street: gymnastics and games.

'Said to knock you up!' Jonah White called up. True, this afternoon at the printer's, he'd felt like an evening out. Now he was too busy enjoying himself.

Gussie and Charlotte were beckoning. 'Come on, big man, come for a jar!'

Holding up his palette and his filthy hands, he gave them a crooked smile of regret and they replied with gestures of understanding. No use trying to drag Price out when he was in full flow. He'd be no fun.

'See you, then, Arch!' With a final wave they piled through the swing doors of The Horse and Groom opposite and immediately left his thoughts. He might have heard back-room singing and rowdy laughter as the hours passed, but apart from a reactive smile he ignored the distraction.

As the pub emptied and the sky turned purple-black, and later when the lights went out up and down the street, he worked on from memory. When it was done he gave a sigh of pleasure. Glorious. A perfect background for his ragged girl. No need for a burning building. Gazing out of the window at that sunset would be enough. His sitter's thoughts would, of course, be drawn to her little grey home in the West. That's what he would paint. A ragged Irish girl dreaming of home, a look of intense longing on her face. Dammit, she *had* to be Irish, with the milky prettiness of Mary Quinn.

It was almost midnight. He paused before the moon's pockmarked face: he really should do a moonscape, the High Street in shadow, the bluish-green light of the gas-lamp on the corner, the darkened pub, each tiny pane of glass picking up the reflections of a girl, another poor wretch, begging, soliciting. There'd be a carriage, a man – no, a man's hand, all you could see of him – beckoning from the window. He took up his sketchbook, quickly drew the scene, tore out the page and pinned that to the notice-board also.

Lord, he was high, he was flying. He closed the shutters and blew out the candles. His head dented the pillow but his mind was still fizzing.

And it was *her* image he saw: Mary Quinn lying on a dirty straw pallet where fleas hopped and bedbugs bit. Were there dirty children lying nearby and a feckless drunk of a husband who beat her?

Poor little scrap. She'd been so scared this morning, trembling like a cobweb in a draught. But she'd managed well, surprisingly so. Usually the *victims* of violence had the best recall, as if trauma somehow heightened their powers of observation, the odious face of their attacker imprinted on their memory. But Mary Quinn was not a victim, not even an involved witness. She had glanced out from an upstairs window across the street and seen a man behaving strangely. That was all. Yet she had described him in detail. Archie frowned. The way she'd told it, the man had had his back to her *and* he was wearing a hat. So when had she seen his face?

He sighed. Of course, Hegarty had turned to speak to Wylie, and he must have removed his hat to go inside the shop. Even so, she'd had only a fleeting glimpse of the murderer, but what an impact it had made.

Almost as lasting as his image of her.

Chapter 4

He jerked awake to the sound of Bob's cart arriving from the farm with the day's vegetables. He stuck his head under the pillow, determined to ignore his landlord's early start, to sleep through the wooden shutters going up, the market coming to life. A cockerel crowed close at hand, answered by another across the road; a pigeon pranced along the gutter and Archie gave up the struggle. Besides, a plan was forming in his mind. He kicked off the covers.

Throwing on some clothes he took the stairs two at a time, colliding with the greengrocer as he burst through his front door onto the street. A sack of something went flying. 'Sorry, Bob, sorry!' he muttered, stopping a rolling cabbage with his foot as though it were a football. He left the man scratching his head, clearly unhappy to think Archie was shooting over to The Horse and Groom at six o'clock in the morning.

But he was too late. Fresh sawdust was already on the floor, counters gleamed, glasses sparkled. A clutch of saucy charwomen invited him to join them in a night-cap before they caught the bus home. Regretfully he had to say that it was a bit early for him. But he *was* looking for someone to clean his studio, one morning a week. Nah, mate, they said, they worked nights down the pickle factory. Mornings was spent akip, afternoons and all if, with a bit of luck, the old man was in work. Mrs Reeves said he had just missed her girl, Quinn, who was always on the lookout for work. A grafter, she was. She'd do a good job. She gave him the address of one of the old millworkers' cottages down past the bottom end of the High Street.

'Cop'mill Lane, next the marshes,' she said with an additional warning to watch his step and to keep his hand on his ha'penny.

'Eh?'

'There's all sorts down there,' she confided, leaning across the bar, 'prozzies, tea leaves – make mincemeat of a nice boy like you.'

His smile assured her he'd be all right. He could handle himself. He set off to walk the mile or more to Mary's house, suddenly conscious of his rolled shirtsleeves and, Lord above, his carpet slippers. But as he side-stepped through the bustle of stall-holders setting up, nobody gave him a second glance. All far too busy: carters unloading, horses stamping, men shouting as they threw sacks and crates and bolts of cloth to each other.

By pure chance, he found her, or rather he tripped over a pair of worn-down heels sticking out from the entry to the boot-and-shoe emporium. Not a good advertisement. Soapy water slopped from her bucket as she turned and soaked the sacking she was kneeling on.

'Sweet Jaisus, mister!' she cried, jumping up and brushing at the wet patch on her skirt. 'Would you look what you made me do!'

'Mary, Mary Quinn!' The feathers in her hat were frowsier and her dress dingier than he remembered, but her eyes were as blue, her lashes as black, her mouth as prettily formed.

'Oh, it's you!' she cried, her brow clouding with bad memories. 'Well, you've caught us on the hop and no mistake!' Ignoring him, she rearranged her skirt and knelt back down on the bare step, squeezing out a dirty cloth to sop up the puddle beside her. When she found him still standing there she said, with a dismissive twitch of her feathers, 'You'll have to excuse me, Mister Price, I'm working. They don't pay us to talk.'

'I wonder if you'd reconsider.'

'Reconsider?'

'Sitting for me.'

'Oh, for the love of …' She swivelled round and glared at him. 'I thought you'd come to tell me they'd caught that monster – that Mad Tommo – and I could sleep easy in my bed again.'

'Not as far as I know, Mary. But they will, I'm sure of it, thanks to your description.'

'So he's still abroad.' She glanced fearfully past his legs as though the murderer might be lurking among the market stalls, hiding behind rolled-up carpets or racks of ladies' dresses.

'Don't worry about him, girl. He's never going to know it was you gave him away.' He crossed his fingers behind his back. Eventually she'd have to point him out in an identity parade and testify in court. She must know that. 'The picture, Mary?' he persevered.

'Picture? Listen, Mister, will ye leave off about the blessed picture! I'm not doing it, so I'm not.' This was new, this boldness. The spark in her eyes would have been at home in a smithy. 'I'm sorry to disappoint you, *sir*, but I'm not some old tart will do it for a bowl of fish soup and shilling or two.'

'I'm very glad to hear it.'

'I'm not, and it's no use you standing there laughing. I've heard all about you, Mister Price, what else you expect for your money, and you can whistle if you think I'm coming near your place at all.'

'All I *expect*,' he countered, 'is that people sit still and quiet while I paint their portrait.' What am I, he thought, blasted

Bluebeard? Who's been spreading tales? Gussie, Maude? Or Charlotte over there, unrolling her tarpaulin, pretending she hasn't seen me. Charlotte had stripped off very happily at their last sitting, and fairly thrown herself at him afterwards. Not that he'd refuse any reasonable offers freely given. Trying to stand on his dignity in his slippered feet, he said, 'They told you wrong, Miss Quinn,' hoping his voice carried. 'I paint pictures, that's all. Sometimes of women, but I paint men too *and* children. I certainly wouldn't get the police asking for my help if ...'

'*They* don't have to take their clothes off.'

Lord, she was sharp. He struggled to keep a straight face. 'My dear girl, nobody *has* to take their clothes off. But if the narrative demands it – the story in the painting I mean – and the sitter agrees, well ... look, I've been painting nudes for years. It's what an artist ...' He took a breath, and the smell of the heavy leather footwear inside the shop caught at his throat. Was she even listening? Dirty water dribbled into her bucket as she wrung out her cloth. Soap bubbles slid into each other, describing her frowning visage in multiples of quivering turquoise and magenta. He tried another tack. 'I – I've made a start on the painting if you want to take a look.'

'Get a whore in, did you? Give *her* a fish dinner?'

A blinkered horse snickered into its feedbag, stamped its foot. Did she have to be so shrill? The man with the jockey scales had frankly stopped setting up and was regarding them with interest, his gleaming brass weights in his hands. Across the way, Charlotte's shawl was quivering across her narrow shoulders.

'It's an idea,' he said, with a sudden rush of temper. 'I don't usually. But perhaps I will. One of them might be glad of some decent money for a change. A shilling an hour, tea and biscuits thrown in.'

As he turned on his heel and started back up the High Street, through the market coming to life, he could hear behind him the rhythmic chirr of the scrubbing brush accompanied by a defiant *too-ra-loo-ra* humming. A sweet voice. Well, she was thinking about it. She was definitely thinking. He picked his way across the road, between carts and horses, apple-crates and steaming mounds of dung. He stuck his hands in his trouser pockets like an errand boy and began to whistle.

*

Her conditions were harsh. There would be no nakedness, no more than one button undone, no lying down at-all-at-all, no hanky-panky and he was to leave the window open so she could shout for help if it came to it. She would take off her hat and let down her hair, remove her shoes if he insisted, but she would want sixpence an hour extra. Take it or leave it.

He couldn't believe he hadn't painted her before. It was like coming home, as if his painting muscles remembered her somehow. Her fey looks, slightly feral, slightly ethereal, seemed to cast a spell over the entire painting, shedding light in unexpected places, shadows in others, dictating colours and brushwork, almost as though she and not the sun were the source of light in the picture. As she leaned forward, raising her head, so his brush made the right, the perfect, connection with the canvas, tracing the glorious line her neck made against the painted sunset. Her chin was so sweet a curve as he sculpted it with his thumb that tears salted his eyes. A shadow here just under the fullness of the trembling lower lip and oh God, he was happy, having captured an in-breath, a gasp of long-throated ecstasy that rich buyers could not help but find titillating.

She was, in fact, *Mrs* Quinn, she told him, lifting her face to the now leaden sky, while big drops sputtered on the cover of the cats' meat stall. She could do dreaming so well, a real actress. 'Sure and I'm a widow-woman, Mister Price, and have been these last three years or more.'

Perfect. Perfect. No thug of a husband to object to her sitting for him, no squalling brats with demands on her time. And no prim virgin, either. He might yet persuade her to pose nude. While half his mind was nodding with possibilities, the other buzzed with colours, selected brushes, worried about this nostril – *more magenta in the mix* – the fringe that the curling tongs had burned and split – *a dry brush, unmixed iron oxide, and the merest smudge with a fingertip* – and that tidemark formed by infrequent washing. Should he put it in? Should he not?

Pauly was a darling man, she declared, but he'd died building the new houses in Highams Park, the houses along the railway line. And no, thanks for Archie's concern, she wasn't entitled to compensation as it turned out. The men should have checked the scaffolding before putting it up, to be sure that the planks weren't soft with rot. Their fault, not the owner's. So. And now she scrubbed floors for a living and lodged with an older woman, Dolly Brett, a seamstress who kept her awake from dusk 'til dawn with her snoring and snorting, and from dawn 'til dusk with a racket of machining.

So, was she born in Ireland? Not that he cared one way or another but she seemed happier talking than not. He added more blue to the mix on his palette. And still it wasn't quite drab enough for the open collar of her dress, where it defined the cylinder of her neck. He wanted it drab and drear and dull as ditchwater in contrast to the translucent skin. More raw umber perhaps. And just a touch on her teeth. They weren't pure white, after all – far from it.

Yes, in beautiful County Kerry. She could remember the green hills, the sea flooding for miles at low tide. You could see two skies, so you could, one reflected on the wet sands and the little shells left behind by the waves, pink thrift blowing in the salty air. Her eyes were almost black with nostalgia, her nostrils flaring to catch the salty air. 'Hold that look, Mary, there's a girl.'

He told her that he also had salt in his veins. Mam came to Llantwit Major in South Wales from England, as governess to a rich maltster's children, and married Bryn Price, the local butcher. So Archie, despite his first name, was part Celt. He could speak Welsh, if pushed. But when Mary spoke in Irish he didn't understand a word.

As he painted he learned that her brothers and sisters had come to England one at a time, each paying the next one's passage. She'd paid for her younger brother, Michael. Conceptua was still at home with Mammy as Michael had died of the cholera. Da was dead, too, of drowning.

'What did you do? I mean, how did you scrape enough money together for your brother's passage?'

'What else would I do but what I do now? I had fine ideas about going into service, but no one would employ an untried bog-trotter straight off the boat.'

'That's hard.' He stroked in a pink highlight on a button. 'So where did you live?'

'My big brother, Brian, found me lodgings in Chingford, down the road.'

Her husband, Pauly, was from Waterford, over here as a boy. Too old for school by then, he'd never learned to read and write. But he could lift and haul with the best of them. London was like a hungry spider crouching in its web, sending out railways to fetch in the workers at the start of the day. Office workers needed houses to live in, cheap and cheerful for them at the bottom of the ladder, bigger and better for the climbers. And didn't houses need labourers to build them? So that was what he did until it killed him. She blinked and sniffed, and the artist stilled his brush a moment, out of respect. They'd met at a ceilidh, she went on, recovering: an Irish gathering, with music and dancing and Pauly playing the tin whistle, plaintive and sweet, to bring tears to your eyes. Then it came to her turn and she sang *Marble Halls*, with her friend Kitty Flanagan doing the harmony, and he came over afterwards and asked her to dance. That was the start of it. They'd had a year together, was all, six months of that as a married couple.

'I've heard you sing. Cleaning that shop front,' he reminded her. 'You've a lovely voice.'

'When there's something to sing about.'

He looked up, hearing her voice dull and flat now, without colour, without hope, and the rain, in a sudden squall, spattered her face and hands and the front of her dress. She stepped back, breaking the pose, wiped her cheeks dry with her fingers and pulled down the bottom half of the window.

It was time to stop anyhow. He let out his breath. What a session! He'd been on fire for three hours. Now he was exhausted. What he needed was a drink and a woman, though not this one.

He watched her winding up her black hair, slipping her bare toes into her shoes, treading down the backs and scuffing across the floor to the easel, eager to see what he'd made of her. 'Well there y'are,' he said, standing back to give her room. 'What do you think?' This close, the smell of her made his nostrils flare, stale beds and stewed tea, with a salty tang reminding him, inexplicably, of home.

Tears sparkled on her lashes as she gazed at her portrait, just the head and neck complete. 'You've done it grand, so you have … made me look like a lady.'

Lord, he hoped not. That would defeat the object.

But it was true. Painted against the sunset's glow, she could have been one of John Waterhouse's heroines, the very Pre-Raphaelite romantic guff he was trying to get away from. What could he do?

He glanced at Mary in her ugly old 'passion-killer' hat. 'Sorry?' he said. She had been speaking. Where had his thoughts taken him?

'I don't suppose,' she repeated with an anxious cock of the head, setting the feathers quivering, 'have you heard at all – did they catch your man that did for Mister Wylie? That Tom somesuch?'

No, of course, she didn't read the newspapers. 'Tommo Hegarty. No, I don't believe they have even a smell of the man.' Seeing her crestfallen look, he added, 'But it's early days, yet.'

'He's got away with it then, like before.' Her mouth pouted disappointment.

'I wouldn't say that.' He explained that the felon had probably hopped on the train to London, hoping to lose himself in the bustle of the city, lying low until all the fuss died down. But the Met – the London police – were good and they'd be keeping a watchful eye out. 'Don't you worry – they'll get him. Sooner or later.'

'He won't come here,' she wanted to know, 'looking to find the one who informed on him? To – to silence them?'

Poor thing, she was terrified. 'Lord, no,' he reassured her. 'He won't want to be seen round here, not with his picture on every tree and lamp-post.'

'But when they catch him he'll want to know who told you what to draw.'

'He can ask away, I won't tell him and the police certainly won't. No one else knew, did they?'

'Mrs Chinnery.'

'Ah,' he said, 'the woman you clean for. Well, I'm sure the police

44

warned her about keeping quiet, for her own safety if nothing else. In any case, he'll find out eventually, Mary, when you point to him in court and tell the jury what you saw him do. You know that, don't you?'

She nodded mutely, her eyes showing the whites.

'But they'll have him handcuffed and under police escort. He won't be able to come anywhere near you. And then they'll take him out and hang him. You've nothing to be frightened of.'

'Oh,' she said. Then she held out her hand, palm uppermost. 'Three hours,' she said, 'that's four and six.'

Yes, let's not forget her wages, he thought. Well-deserved. He felt in his pocket for two florins and a sixpence. It was more than she earned in a week cleaning and she pocketed the coins quickly, barely hiding a gurgle of delight at money so easily made.

When she was gone, he turned back to the painting. Of course the ragged dress would make it clear she was no lady. But there must be no doubt. Others made their narrative clear with clues: broken eggshells, a bird escaping a cat's claws, a discarded glove. He thought for a moment. What did he have?

By suppertime he had collected half-a-dozen 'art photographs' – the kind he used for life-drawing to save the model's blushes. Vague and foreshortened they would litter the table beside his model as a Hogarthian prophecy of moral decline. Likewise, the shadowy bolster propped drunkenly against the studio wall would be an explicit artistic device for those with eyes to see. And the shawl, fallen to the floor in languid confusion, could only symbolise wantonness and corruption.

Next session he would paint the dress, then the hands and feet, and tell her that the rest was background for which he didn't need her. She must have no notion of the narrative, the liberties he would take. Good Lord, she would never sit for him again.

Chapter 5

With what he made from his posters and a couple of landscapes that Charlotte sold for him on her bric-a-brac stall, Archie was able to pay for a photographer and to place an advertisement in *The Art Magazine*. Within a week of its publication he had received a number of written enquiries, more than one comparing his work favourably with Holman Hunt's *The Awakening Conscience* and asking for a viewing.

He sent replies arranging appointments. When they came, one hadn't realised how big the painting was; he'd never be able to fit it in the chaise. Another, a silver-haired old codger, with a pince-nez and trembling hands, claimed to be an art collector and said that he'd understood the price included framing. Oh really? Archie was polite but showed the old cheapskate the door. A third was concerned that the sunset would clash with his red-flocked wallpaper. The advertisement had given no clues as to colour, only to composition.

When Archie opened the front door to a large, loudly dressed gent, the strident clamour of the market drowned out what he said. Archie thought he was asking directions.

'No, my friend!' The man slapped his side in amusement, but his laughter degenerated into a coughing fit and Archie had to wait until he recovered to learn that this was Norbert Streeter, an entrepreneur, who had come to look at the painting. 'My agent drew my attention to your advertisement and since I had business over this way …' He gestured vaguely down the road.

On the wooden stairs he stopped to get his breath and to tell Archie that he had just bought a house on Hampstead Heath and was looking for works of art to add to his collection.

He stopped again in the open doorway to catch a wheezy breath and to take in the disarray that was Archie's studio. His face only brightened when he saw 'The Immigrant' on the easel and he bore down on it, creaking floorboards and breathing heavily. The advert had hardly done it justice, he declared. The girl, so pale, so wide-eyed, you could almost touch her, feel her trembling, and so cleverly painted. The skin was almost transparent. That throbbing vein in her temple, the hint of dryness on her lip, her hair, thick and black: she was a delight. Look at the wear in her dress, the loss of nap, the hanging button, the fraying hem and cuffs; contrast them with the richness of the sky behind her. And the poor, chapped hands, the bitten nails. Oh – he snatched off his bowler and clutched it to his chequered waistcoat as though declaring his love – it did your heart good to see passionately painted work like this.

Passionate? thought Archie. Well, yes, the man might just have put his finger on it.

'Why didn't we see it at the Academy?'

Archie explained that the Summer Exhibition had been and gone before he'd even started the picture.

'Well, I can't say I'm sorry,' said Streeter. 'You would have sold this for sure and I want it.' He wagged his head in wonder. 'It's what I *call* a painting.' He creaked across to the window and scanned the street, hoping, perhaps, to catch a glimpse of a certain dirty bundle of rags. He turned back. 'You know Sickert?'

'Not personally,' Archie had to admit. 'He was a couple of years ahead of me.'

'He, too, draws doxies and drabs in situ. Gloomy rooms. Drab drabs ...'

Archie had to wait for another fit of laughter followed by coughing to subside, for the man to dose himself from a hip-flask, before he could explain that Mary was not a prostitute but a cleaner, a skivvy.

'But I thought ... well, you certainly had me fooled. It's in the detail, you see – what the butler saw through the keyhole.' As he bent to do likewise – to squint at the out-of-focus litter of photos – the late afternoon light was a greasy smear on his scalp. When he rolled back on his heels to assess the composition as a whole, thrusting out his belly, tucking his chin into a soft cushion of fat, his eyes gleamed and his lower lip was wet.

'What you're suggesting, young man, is that this is a girl who doesn't mind getting down and dirty.' He winked as if they shared a smutty secret. Using finger and thumb, he wiped the drool from the corners of his mouth. 'This is what she is, a tasty little drab, put on earth to save us men from torment and our wives from harm.' He was already reaching into an inside pocket for a thick roll of bank notes. 'How much?'

Archie blinked as the man licked his thumb and peeled off the price, there and then. It happened so quickly, almost without his realising. But he felt none of the thrill that a successful sale usually brought. On the contrary, he felt unclean and wanted to protest that it had all been a mistake. The painting wasn't finished, wasn't for sale, certainly not to a lardy lech for ogling and lascivious fantasy!

But too late, it was done. Now, of course, he couldn't help but see the painting through Norbert Streeter's eyes. Was that how he'd secretly wanted Mary Quinn to appear, a tempting morsel from the gutter? Suddenly he hated it, couldn't wait to be rid of it. He chewed his inner cheek until he tasted blood and made out the receipt.

'So if you would crate up the painting, Mister Price, my man will be over this way on Wednesday afternoon. You will be in?'

Archie wrote out the receipt and the provenance, detailing the title of the painting, the name of the sitter, the materials used, his own name and address and to whom he had sold it, for how much and on what date. Streeter read it over, pocketed it and reached for Archie's hand. 'Pleasure doing business with you.'

Business, was that all it was?

He could never explain the wrench he felt when he loaded the crate onto Streeter's cart a few days later and secured it. All the – yes – *passion* that had gone into its execution and it was goodbye to 'The Immigrant', as if she had never been.

But what was this? The driver was handing him an invitation, all bevelled edges and *Norbert Streeter Esq. requests the pleasure* in cursive script. Archie's buyer would be holding a housewarming party in a few weeks' time and, inexplicably in Archie's view, requested the artist to be there. On the back of the card he explained that Archie might like to see 'The Immigrant' framed and hung and Streeter would like to introduce him to a few of his friends and business associates who might be interested in commissioning paintings. A postscript, penned in contrived haste, gave away the true reason for the summons: *'Bring the sitter along. I'd be charmed to meet her in the flesh.'*

Before Archie could extend his sincere regrets, Streeter's man had whipped up the horse and rattled off down the street.

*

The long terraces of derelict cottages had once housed mill workers but the copper industry had died years ago and, by the looks of things, the cottages too. The roofs were caving in and mossy and, at Mary's house, the number '35' dangled precariously on a piece of wormy wood by a single tack. The gate scraped open onto a small front yard.

He rapped on the door, there being no knocker, and waited. She should be home by now. He tried peering in through the window but the small panes of glass were bleary and flawed, and hung with heavy wooden blinds. A faint curl of smoke wound from the chimney, stale smells of stewed tea, cabbage and cat pee seeped through gaps in the woodwork. After a second knock, the door cracked open. A sliver of a suspicious face showed: an eye first, then a nose and mouth.

'What?'

'I, em …' It was difficult talking to pieces of a face, difficult to find a focus. He tipped his hat. 'Would it, I wonder, be possible to speak to Mrs Quinn?'

The door opened wider and there stood an attitude. She may have been in her thirties or forties, her brow puckered, her wire spectacles drawing attention to strained, puffy eyes. Her hennaed hair hung in ringlets in the old style; her narrow bodice was stuck with pins and threaded needles; a tape measure embraced her shoulders. So this was the seamstress, the one who snored.

'No gentlemen callers,' she recited in the flat tones of the marshes, and made to shut the door. The crack wavered but stayed, wedged by his boot. Her parting, straight as a ruler and showing grey roots, tipped up to reveal eyes sparking anger or panic.

'I just need to deliver a message.'

The woman got her breath, and exhaled defeat. 'Who shall I say it is?'

'Price. Archie Price.'

'Mary!' she cried over her shoulder. 'Your painter wants a word!' Turning back to the door-stepper, she treated him to a crooked smile that softened her eyes, sweetening her face. 'Won't be a jiffy, sir.' She turned to shout again, but Mary was peering round the door, her expression venomous.

'I've sold the painting, Mary,' he said.

'Haven't I told you not to come down here?' Her voice was shrill as she tried to shut the door.

'But ...'

'You could have told me next week, so. Tuesday, ten o'clock, we said.' She kicked the toe of his boot to dislodge it and went on kicking.

'I thought you'd want to know about the painting,' he persisted.

'It's you has sold it, you that's getting paid.'

She had a point, of course. Little by little his foot yielded to her determined efforts, and the door slammed shut as he was bawling, 'The buyer wants to meet you!'

There was the snick of a lifting latch and, with a tentative creak, the door reopened. She was ready for bed, with her wrapper barely fastened, her long black hair unpinned.

He was entranced. 'S-sorry – I've disturbed you.' Of course, she had an early start and went early to bed as a consequence. 'I won't come in.'

It was as if he hadn't spoken. 'Why? Why does he want to see me?'

'He's invited us to a party to show off the painting. You're to be there as a guest of honour. I thought you'd probably need time to fix up a dress, something to wear. Maybe your friend can ...'

'Who is it?'

'The buyer? A man called Norbert Streeter.'

Her mouth fell open, her eyes widened with shock. 'Are you

serious, Archie Price? Nobby Streeter, by all that's holy! Did you *say* I didn't go with the painting?'

His heart flipped with foreboding. 'You know him?'

'*Of* him.' She shifted her gaze, jerked her head down the street. 'He's, em, "friendly" with some of the girls in the lane.'

'You mean …' Archie frowned.

'Oh yes, a regular visitor.'

'But he's rich – he could have his pick of any …'

'Sure and hasn't he a taste for the raggle-taggle sort. The nearer the bone the sweeter the meat.'

'Mary.' It was a rebuke. He hated hearing her talk this way.

'That's what he does, and that's who you've sold my picture to, you fecking eejit!'

'Oh, Mary.'

As he slowly pulled the gate to behind him, shrill voices permeated the rickety walls as Mary relayed the gist of their conversation to her friend. He was sure he heard the words 'pimp' and 'slaver'. Oh Lord, his head was splitting. What had he done?

Chapter 6

Streeter's new home was an imposing redbrick mansion with a Palladian entrance, white Corinthian columns and portico, and a gravel turning-circle; in the centre a fountain played into a small lily pond. Archie's cab crunched to a standstill at a flight of stone steps. The import-export business, whatever it involved, certainly paid well, but it wasn't slavery, Mary. How could it be? Slavery was abolished long ago. How could Streeter possibly carry on that sort of trade under the noses of the police? He paid the driver and went in.

The grandeur of the interior took his breath away: vaulted ceilings, lots of wood panelling, and chandeliers reflected in enormous mirrors over great stone fireplaces at opposite ends of the room. And there good taste ended. Streeter's agent may have told him what to collect but not how to display it, how to give each piece enough room to breathe. Big-bottomed settees rubbed cheeks with dainty lacquered cabinets; heavy velvet curtains, swathed, fringed and tasselled, provided a backdrop to life-sized statuary. Archie wasn't flattered at having 'The Immigrant' set among Nobby's trophy stuffed bears, stags' heads and waterfowl in glass cases. His poor girl was framed, imprisoned, in heavy ornate gilt that doubled the size of the work and diminished her. Flanked by Aubrey Beardsley eroticism and Toulouse-Lautrec can-

can dancers, she looked lost and helpless, completely out of place. Perhaps that was the idea.

Archie pressed his lips together, breathed a heavy sigh of resignation and, snatching a glass from a waitress gliding by, sank the contents.

'Archie Price, the man himself!' Here was his host bearing down on him, puffing like a steam train in a shot-silk frockcoat with, fast on his heels, a bewigged and portly gentleman, shiny with sweat. 'So glad you could come!' Streeter brayed, insincerely. 'And where is the lovely young widow? Everyone is quite taken with her.'

Were they, indeed? There were a few guests gathered around his picture, talking knowledgeably, gesticulating with cigars and gem-encrusted fingers, as if she were a Gainsborough or a Reynolds. He wondered if they would find her so interesting in the flesh: small, dark and menial, half the size of her portrait, with broken shoes, a tattered hem and a horrifying hat. Surely they would tell her to run along, be about her chores? *He* had made her into a work of art. Only he had been able to see her potential, or so he liked to think.

'Mary sends her apologies, Mister Streeter, her regrets. She couldn't come, I'm afraid. She's a working girl, as you know, and has to be up and out by four in the morning to scrub floors.'

Lord, who was he shaming here, Mary, Nobby or himself? But he couldn't repeat what Mary had said as she left his studio that afternoon: that she knew Streeter's game, that he was a raving pervert and he wasn't getting his hands on her!

Streeter leered greasily. 'Silly me, I should have thought of that. Never mind, there are more ways of killing a cat.' His self-congratulatory laughter turned into a roiling cough he couldn't control. He wheezed, rattled and hawked; doubled over a silk handkerchief, his face puce, his eyes bulging. Archie turned his head, politely, as if to admire a large ivory elephant with gold tusks and trappings. Well-crafted and, no doubt, very costly but too ornate for Archie's taste. On the other hand he'd have given the world to have possessed the lovingly made chair beside it, a Morris and Company original. He ran his hand over the smooth wood, following the line of the exquisitely curved arm.

When he turned back, Streeter had regained his breath and some of his dignity. He tapped his great nose, purple with thread-veins, and sneered, 'You'll see, Mister Price,' before resuming his progress around the hall, in search of someone with more to offer. The portly gentleman trundled after him like a coal truck, chuntering sadly.

Well, that brush-off was plain enough. Pretty damned conclusive. Mary was the one he wanted. Archie could leave now for all Nobby cared, though that would be a shame when he could be working the room, drumming up business, as Streeter had more or less suggested. Since his host had abandoned him, he would have to introduce himself to the other guests. He refilled his glass and sallied forth.

Some showed an interest; one or two were keen to see his next painting of Mary by moonlight. Others were really only interested in having their own portraits painted, or their children's. Archie made a note of their names and their requirements.

The word *entrepreneur* appeared on a number of calling cards, but no one seemed willing to describe the exact nature of their business. 'Import-export' was a favourite, typically vague, response, which expanded to 'buying goods in from abroad, to sell here' when pressed.

'Yes, of course, and export is from us to them. I understand that, but what exactly is it you deal in?'

'Whatever people need we endeavour to supply,' a well-upholstered gent offered, as he appraised Archie through his pince-nez.

'Manufactured goods, do you mean?'

'More often natural resources.' He raised an eyebrow at someone tittering. What was the joke? Archie couldn't see it.

'At a profit,' a taller thickset man added. He had dark, penetrating eyes: one of a number of Streeter's guests who seemed to be sizing Archie up, unsure whether to trust this stranger in their midst, this inquisitive painter chappie.

Archie noticed that when he approached certain huddles of men, voices that were raised – apparently settling some sort of a deal – were either lowered or ceased abruptly. He was treated to polite pleasantries. Even oaths were smothered when he came close.

What was going on? Was 'import-export' a euphemism for something shadier: drugs or smuggled or stolen goods? He felt his shirt sticking to him. Why was he being treated like a visiting cleric? Did they perhaps know of his police connections? Had Streeter or one of his business associates in Walthamstow seen Archie ducking in and out of the police station in the High Street, or had he been seen chatting to a bobby on the beat? Might he be on dangerous ground here? Perhaps the sensible thing would be to withdraw before they set on him. Honestly, Arch, he asked himself, is it so important for you to preserve these loud-mouthed crooks in paint, or their brassy wives or their dim-witted progeny? Well, yes. He needed the money.

He paused to down another glass of champagne. The trouble was, his curiosity was aroused. What sort of house was this? Would his painting be safe here? Perhaps he would take a look upstairs. Traffic between the two floors seemed pretty brisk. Was there a card game? A casino? Now that would be one way of whiling away an hour or two.

In front of him, an elderly stick-insect of a man was making his stiff and stately way up the long staircase, arm-in-arm with a much younger woman. A local dignitary of some sort; Archie had had a halfway intelligent conversation with him earlier about the Arts and Crafts Movement. He thought the girl must be his granddaughter from the way she was resting her head on his shoulder. Husbands and wives would never display affection like that in public. Unless they were newly-weds, of course; there was always that.

At the top of the stairs, Archie discovered several of Streeter's guests heading in the same direction, towards a pair of closed double doors at the end of a wide corridor. Old Spindle–shanks rapped for entry and, as the couple was admitted, Archie had an impression of noise, light and laughter before the door closed again. It looked like the party was continuing up here with entertainment of some sort.

He knocked in turn.

'Do you have an invitation, sir?' a frock-coated attendant enquired.

Archie patted his pockets. Now, where had he put it? Damn, it was in his overcoat. A flunkey had taken it from him when he arrived, he explained.

'The auction is by *special* invitation only.'

Auction? Streeter hadn't mentioned an auction. But it would be interesting to see how much some of Streeter's art collection fetched. It occurred to him that this might be the fate of his own painting: to be auctioned off to the highest bidder. Perhaps this was how Streeter made his money. He assured the doorkeeper that Mister Streeter would want him to see this, that he was the artist who had painted Streeter's latest acquisition – the picture he'd called 'The Immigrant', on the wall downstairs. 'Archibald Price is my name.'

'I'll have to check, sir, if you wouldn't mind waiting here a moment.' Leaving Archie stranded, he presumably scurried off inside to seek advice. Archie gave the door a gentle push and it opened enough for him to see the backs of the latecomers, Spindle-shanks and his lady, among many who were craning their necks to see over the heads in front, and standing on tiptoe or some, even, on benches. From the doorway Archie could only guess at the merchandise on display. The hubbub ceased as though at a conductor's baton and one lone voice prevailed: that of the auctioneer, whom Archie could see on a raised dais. 'We come now to lot number nine ... dark meat from Africa, fresh off the boat, if you get my meaning. Now then, what am I bid, gentlemen, for this lovely young creature?' A harsh male voice cracked an order in a language Archie did not understand. 'What a little treasure, eh, gentlemen? And so biddable. So – who'll start me at twenty guineas? Do I hear twenty? Fifteen then? Fifteen guineas, one for every year of her age. I have fifteen ...'

'Sir, sir!' Oh, Lord, the attendant was suddenly back, insinuating himself between Archie and the crowd, ushering him inexorably out of the door. 'Excuse me, sir, Mister Price, Mister Streeter requests that you join him downstairs.'

'What are they selling?' Archie wanted to know, though now he had a fair idea.

'I couldn't say, sir – would you mind going back downstairs now, sir – the entertainment is about to start and Mister Streeter requests ...'

Archie stood outside the closed door, utterly at a loss. People were bidding on young girls, in order to own them. But slavery was illegal.

What a fool! How could he have been so blind, so naive? Flesh. Flesh was what they imported and exported. Mary was right. Streeter was a slaver, and what a narrow escape she had had.

Queasy, and hardly thinking straight, he opened the nearest door, hoping to find a bathroom. But it wasn't. There, on a four-poster bed, frolicked a bare-arsed man and two, no, three naked women. 'Oh Lord. Oh, sorry, sorry,' he murmured, backing out and shutting the door. Luckily, they were all too engrossed to care. As he stumbled away down the corridor, he saw another door open and a scantily dressed woman appeared, beckoning.

'Coming in, dear?' she said. 'On the house tonight. Old Nobby's in a generous mood.'

Dear God, he thought, as he made his excuses, this magnificent house, with its beautiful trappings, was no more than a knocking shop.

Downstairs again, somehow, Archie stood by the piano, feeling naive and foolish, not knowing what to do. This was a den of big business crooks, pimps and procurers. A word out of place and he could find himself in serious trouble, *dead* trouble. Perhaps he should leave now while he was still in one piece.

But he didn't *want* to leave. He was curious. He hadn't yet given up on the idea that here were men desirous of having their pictures painted.

He made his way round the edge of the room, sat down in an armchair by the fireplace and, taking his sketchbook from his pocket, began drawing. The pencil shook for a while, as he waited for someone either to challenge him or to crack open his skull with a handy silver candlestick. But as he drew Streeter's portly coal-truck, then the entrepreneur in the blue waistcoat, he grew calmer. Drawing was to him like deep breathing and no one seemed to mind. What else would an artist do?

Over by the piano a young woman was about to sing. She had a few words with the pianist and gave him some sheet music to arrange on his stand. Underneath the heavy rouge she was pretty enough, thought Archie, but the curling ostrich feathers in her hair cheapened her and her dress, swathed scantily over her full white bosom, left nothing to the imagination. The pianist gave a trill on the white keys, a signal, apparently, for Streeter to speak.

He cleared his throat noisily. 'Ladies and gentlemen – I believe we have one or two.' He waited for the laughter to die down. 'Allow me to introduce my protégée, currently appearing at the Hackney Empire, my own little Irish songbird, Kitty O'Grady. I think you'll like her. Kitty …' He nodded, extended an arm and the pianist bent to the opening bars.

Her voice was unexpectedly sweet and pure, belying her appearance: the song one that Archie had never heard before, something haunting and lilting from the wild western world. You could hear the sea and the rushy sedge and a lone piper sitting on a treeless hillside, his hair blowing in the wind. The braying voices stilled, the clatter and clink were silenced; the room was spellbound. And when the song ended the applause was genuine if somewhat perplexed, the company perhaps a little uncomfortable to find themselves so moved.

Her next song, *I'll Take You Home Again, Kathleen,* was rather too sentimental. Embarrassment found release in sniggering, and some jokers pretended to dash tears from their eyes. But her last song, *Ta-ra-ra-Boom-de-ay,* hit their mood exactly. The bawdy lyrics, sung with winks and bumps and grinds, got them all joining in the 'Boom-de-ays' and fisting the air. When she took her final bow the applause was ecstatic. She smiled and, it seemed to Archie, singled him out for a heavy lascivious wink.

Oh Lord, he didn't want to be noticed, he was simply waiting for the right moment to disappear, but he put down his sketchbook and clapped along with the rest. As she left the podium, he saw her stroke Streeter's cheek in passing, turn and blow him a kiss. The fat man leered after her for a long moment before resuming his conversation with a couple of plumed and painted drabs. The singer, meanwhile, flushed and excited, made her way directly to a tall, distinguished-looking gent and hooked her arm through his to discuss, with an odd sort of fervour, Streeter's latest acquisition – Archie's painting of Mary Quinn. As her friend turned to her with what seemed to be a sour remark, Archie's pencil froze. That profile! He felt a single bead of sweat trickle down his neck; the pencil slipped from numb fingers and rolled about the floor.

That face! Archie knew every plane, every crag, having drawn it once before.

Brian Rooney was hardly recognisable as Tommo Hegarty's sidekick. Tastefully dressed, well-groomed and softly spoken, he seemed every inch the gentleman. But his wealth and bearing, Archie knew, had been dearly bought with one man's life and another's health and happiness. Picking up his pencil, he was fuming to think how such villainy could be rewarded. He began drawing again. The police would be interested in this. In fact, he remembered, there was a price on Rooney's head: twenty guineas put up by the Mowbray family. He could do a lot with twenty guineas.

Rooney was frowning at the painting, stroking his jaw. The girl spoke to him, but the Irishman ignored her, continuing to stare at the painted face, as if transfixed. The woman leaned in and drew his attention to the artist, sitting across the room, sketching. When their eyes met, the singer gave Archie a thumbs-up of approval. But Rooney's face contorted with loathing. Turning his back to Archie, plainly drunk, he staggered over towards a tray of drinks that was doing the rounds.

Archie wasn't altogether surprised when the girl from the Hackney Empire slid into his lap a few minutes later. 'Kitty O'Grady – I do nude if you're interested,' she announced, 'erotic poses, two guineas an hour.' Through her ostrich feathers he saw Rooney among Streeter's entourage, heatedly arguing with their host.

Distracted by the girl's warm fingers loosening his cravat, her soft lips nuzzling his neck, he lost sight of the Irishman. Next moment, it seemed, a tall figure was blocking his light and hauling a protesting Kitty O'Grady off his lap. Rooney reached in and, breathing whiskey fumes, grabbed Archie by his shirt-front, snarling, 'Leave her be, you bastard,' his fist raised to demolish Archie's good looks. He jerked a glance around, a confrontational dare to those nearby and, in that small instant, Archie was able to gather his senses, bring up his left elbow in defence and hit out with his right, making contact with hard bone. His opponent fell into the arms of a surprised bystander and was immediately heaved back towards Archie, who was out of his seat and on his toes in time to miss Rooney's next punch which hit the back of the chair. It rolled away on its castors and into a side table, landing Rooney on his knees and a valuable piece of pottery in pieces on the floor. Cries of 'Fight! Fight!' had already broken out and a rhythmic stamping. Archie jigged about waiting for the wild–eyed man to struggle to his feet and relocate him. As he did, Archie swung a right, knocking the man's head sideways into his left, again catching the jaw. The drunk staggered back and an almost certain fall was blocked by the crowd, who righted him and sent him back for more. There was a cut on Rooney's eyebrow, and he frowned to focus. Now they were toe-to-toe, both deflecting punches, ducking. Streeter's voice bellowed, 'Oi! Oi! What's all this about?' For a fleeting moment, Archie couldn't think of an answer. Something to do with a woman? He lunged forward with a right and felt Rooney's knuckles connecting with his cheekbone. Shaking the pain away, Archie now went for the exposed solar plexus. Unfair, but, hey, he had to end this. Rooney doubled over, winded, and as he was straightening up, Archie hit him square on the jaw and laid him out flat.

Streeter was thumping him on the back. 'Mister Price, you surprise me!'

'Surprised me, too,' he managed to say, tentatively prodding his sore face. 'Didn't realise I'd upset him. He only had to say …'

Somehow he found himself sitting down, in the same chair, with a drink in his hand and Kitty O'Grady, her hand on his knee, smiling up at him. 'Sorry, Nobby – spoiling your party.'

'Not at all, not at all. Nothing's spoiled, apart from your man's good looks.' Jerking his chin at the unconscious Rooney, he gestured to a couple of footman to deal with the mess. 'He's for home, methinks. Pop him into his carriage. I'll bill him for the vase in the morning.'

There would be no round two. Archie was a hero and suddenly everyone wanted to be his friend, buy him drinks, give him orders for portraits.

Leave Kitty O'Grady be? That would be easier said than done.

*

Some time later, he found himself draped over Streeter's staircase with his shoes in his hand, his shirt unbuttoned and hanging out of his trousers and his cravat loose about his neck. The smell of sex, and Kitty O'Grady's heavy perfume, was all over him, though she was nowhere to be seen. Oh Lord. Sound and vision seemed to arrive in surges of clarity. On the crest of one such, he seemed to be speaking to Norbert 'call me Nobby' Streeter. Sense receded. Next he knew, a flunkey was helping him to his feet, advising him that his cab was still waiting, clocking up the fare.

'You'll have to get a move on, sir, if you want to catch the last train. Where are you going, sir? Yes, yes, I'll tell the driver. Perhaps you'd better put your shoes on, sir. Did you have a coat?'

Archie drained a glass that had magically appeared beside him and allowed Streeter's servant to help him down the rest of the stairs. Weaving his way around the remaining guests, he eventually found his host. 'Thank you for a perfectly lovely evening,' he lisped. His mother would have been proud.

'On the contrary,' said Streeter, with a nod and a wink, 'thank *you*. Perhaps I can return the favour some day.'

Return what favour? What had he done?

Before he could ask, someone thrust his hat into his hands and hustled him through the front door to the waiting hansom. Somehow he must have paid the cab fare and boarded a train at Liverpool Street with his return ticket. His next conscious thought was being shaken rudely awake by a guard, who put his mouth close to Archie's ear and cried, 'Chingford Station, end of the line! Sir? This is as far as we go.' When Archie growled a protest that he didn't want to go to Chingford, the man simply repeated the information.

'Lea' me alone!' he begged, curling into a ball. But the guard showed no mercy. 'Chingford Station,' he insisted for a third time. 'End of the line. Out you get, mate.' He opened the carriage door, hauled Archie upright, gave him a shove and a boot in the pants for luck.

Lying there on the platform, the unhappy drunk seemed to dream or remember someone, at some point during the evening, asking him for Mary Quinn's address, but for the life of him he couldn't remember who, or what had happened. He wouldn't have betrayed Mary, surely? Had he, hadn't he, written it down, or was that Kitty O'Grady's? He could almost see himself writing *35 Coppermill Lane,* and the ragged edge of a torn page.

Judas!

In a panic, he sat up and slapped his pockets. There were his keys, his diary, his wallet full of calling cards, a little folding money left from his transaction with Kitty. But not the … no, no, it wasn't there. He remembered sketching the singer. Oh God, he must have left the book by the bed, beside her fan and reticule. Or had he handed over the entire sketchbook, the way an organ grinder's monkey hands over the takings? To whom? To Streeter ? All those drawings! Lord – and Mary's address! Oh God, the fat man would be round there in his carriage, scooping her up, rags and all.

He found a seat in the unheated waiting room and huddled into his coat. His knuckles and his face were sore, but not as sore as his heart as he shivered the night long, not so much with cold as with the enormity of what he had done, the trouble he was in, the enemies he'd made. One thing was certain: he had to get to Mary before Nobby did.

Chapter 7

Her duster froze against the mirror. 'What do you mean, you don't remember?'

'It's all very hazy. I might have fallen asleep and dreamt it. But I'm missing my sketchbook.'

'And you might or might not have this memory ...'

'Or dream ...'

She gestured impatiently. 'This picture in your head – of writing down my address, tearing out the page ...'

'Part of the page – the bottom half.'

'And giving it to that pimp?'

He scratched his nose in shame. 'I believe I may have done.'

'You believe! You believe!' She kept her voice low while managing somehow to shriek, refusing to look at him directly but speaking to his reflection, that frightful-looking cove on the other side of the bar, bruised, pasty and hung over, in need of a wash, a shave and a comb. 'So what would you have me do now, *sir?*' she demanded, with heavy sarcasm. 'Now that I daresn't go home?'

She seemed to know how it worked. He supposed she saw it every day down at her end of town.

Rubbing at a mark low down on the huge glass, looking through it, beyond it, into nothingness, she searched for a solution.

He spoke carefully. 'I had a long time to think about it last night before the milk train started out.'

'*Think?* In that state you could still *think?*'

'I sobered up quickly. The cold night air …'

'So what'll I do then? Should I run away with a gipsy out there on the marshes? Or do away with meself altogether?'

'Mary!'

'Don't you Mary me, you – you auld soak!' She whirled on him with a glint in her eye that made him glad the bar was between them. 'I should have known. You're no better than the rest of them. You're feckin' useless, Archie Price, so y'are!'

That hurt. 'Hear me out, Mary, please. It may be for the best.'

'How can it be?' She fought against the tears of fury and fear that filled her eyes, and pressed her lips into a grim white line to hear what he had to say.

He took a deep breath. 'I have some friends out at Woodford who might take you in. The man was set upon and badly beaten three years ago, as a matter of fact, by your friend Hegarty … What?'

It was one of the things that entranced him, the eloquence of her features. She was so easy to paint: every nuance of feeling found expression in her eyes – darkening now with pain – in the shadows brushing her brow, in the teeth biting her lip. She was gripping the sill of the counter to keep from falling.

'Sorry, of course he's not your … are you all right?'

She nodded, but was unable to speak, and he went on, stealing anxious glances at her from time to time. 'The wife, Mrs Kington, is doing her best to keep everything going – their tile-making business and looking after their little girl – but she needs help. You'd be doing them a big favour.' He took a breath. 'Whatever you do, don't go home. I'll go and see Dolly for you, tell her you'll be away indefinitely, and fetch any bits and pieces you may need.'

'She'll want paying, so she will. The rent.'

'Leave it to me.'

A familiar rasping voice broke in on their conversation. 'I'll do you a character, ducks, shall I? A reference? Give us a minute to empty these ashtrays.'

They both looked round, startled. They hadn't noticed her coming in from the saloon bar, her heavy footfalls muffled by sawdust. Her florid face beamed and Archie's heart sank.

'Mrs Reeves …' His anxiety must have shown in his face.

'Oh don't you worry, son, it won't go no further. Your secret's safe with me, safe as houses.'

*

Mary assured the Kingtons that she would work hard for her keep; cleaning, laundering, cooking and minding Clara, freeing Lizzie and John to carry on their business. John looked troubled. He had Lizzie take Mary into the garden while he spoke to Archie alone.

'You haven't thought this through, Archie.'

'What do you mean?'

'I mean you're putting us in danger, Clara and Lizzie, me. Don't you see? Don't the police have their own safe houses?'

'I haven't told them yet.'

'Well, perhaps you should. If she's a witness in the Wylie case they'll need to know where she is. And that's another thing – suppose Hegarty comes out here looking for her? He might well recognise me and bump us both off. Find somewhere else for her. The police won't want all their eggs in one basket.'

'I'll tell them, I will, just as soon as I get back. But Hegarty is not going to come out here, John. Why should he? He doesn't know witnesses even exist. He thought he'd killed you.'

'The posters – someone had to describe him.'

'Doubt he ever saw them. He was away on the train before they were drawn. And the latest posters are nothing to do with your run-in with him. All he knows is – if he's seen them, that is – someone must have spotted him in the High Street around about the time of the murder. Could have been anyone. Certainly not you or her! You're all perfectly safe here.'

John drew on his pipe, discovered that it had gone out, relit it with a taper from the kitchen range and sucked as though it were a life-saver. 'I don't like it, Archie,' he said, blowing out a tremulous stream of smoke. 'I really don't. And where are we going to put her, anyway? I'm not having Clara sharing a room with a skivvy. I suppose we could make her up a bed in the woodshed, but even then you must know I can't pay her. Since the Kentwell Hall contract fell through we're down to bread and point. We had to let the apprentice go …' His voice tailed away and he stared, not at Archie massaging his aching temples, but at his own plight, his bleak future.

'She's my responsibility, John. I got her into this, selling her portrait to that – that animal. I'll pay for her bed and board, if that's all right.'

John's eyes narrowed to slits. 'Don't tell me you're …?' A scowl of distaste creased his face. 'My God, you are! You're sweet on her!'

'Absolutely not!'

'You ridiculous man! She's – God, she's scum!'

'You've got it wrong,' he blustered, 'you don't understand.'

'What's to understand? It's obvious. This Streeter chap isn't the only one who fancies a bit of Irish, even if she does stink like a wet dog.'

'John, that's not … I feel responsible, that's all. Give her a chance, man. She's a good little skivvy, she really is.'

John was silent for a moment. He could hardly turn away

domestic help freely given, thought Archie. 'How long for?' said his friend, at last.

'Until they put the buggers behind bars, I suppose, until it's safe for her to go home. Could be weeks, could be months, I don't know.' Taking John's prolonged pipe-puffing as an encouraging sign he went on, 'I know it's an intrusion, a stranger under your roof when you're used to being on your own, just the three of you.'

John snorted. 'The more the merrier,' he said, with grumpiness giving the lie to his words. He took his pipe from his mouth. 'And what about the wherewithal for this project? I take it you're flush, for once.'

'I sold a painting, didn't I? That's what got us into this mess. And you never know, with Mary helping out here you might just manage to meet your targets. If it doesn't work out, I'll …' He sighed hopelessly. 'I'll think again. And John, I don't want her to know I'm subbing her. I don't want that interfering with – with anything.'

'Oho,' said John, with a knowing look, 'so you haven't actually got around to bedding this one. What's come over you, Archie? Lost your touch? Or are you frightened of catching something?'

Yes that was probably it, thought Archie, though not nits or fleas or lice. Nor disease, unless you could call poverty a disease.

*

Lizzie wouldn't hear of Mary sleeping in the woodshed, but set her to work straight away on the attic. She could clear a space, Lizzie insisted, put up the old iron bedstead. Anything the girl couldn't use she was to pile up under the eaves: chairs, chests, boxes, lamps, pictures. She would find the bed stacked in pieces against the far wall, the horsehair mattress with it; the flock mattress was rolled up in one of the trunks, together with a quilt, pillows and blankets. Bedlinen was in the downstairs cupboard beside the range.

John went to the forest to collect firewood. He had a headache, he said. The fresh air might clear it. Lizzie watched him go with a frown.

'He finds it difficult, Archie,' she sighed.

'What?'

'Coping.'

'What do you mean?'

'He … he lives in constant fear.' She pressed her lips together. 'That he'll die and leave Clara and me stranded, that we'll starve, that I'll leave him, that the hens won't lay, that the roof will fall in, that those tinkers will find out he's still alive and come round here and do the job properly, so that he can't testify.'

'They're not tinkers any more.' He told her about Rooney being at Streeter's party, leaving out the fisticuffs. 'They're rich now. They've far bigger fish to fry.'

'It wouldn't make any difference if they were dead and in the ground,' she said, 'he'd find something else to worry about. His nerves are stretched to snapping. The slightest little thing goes wrong and he's off out, like now, or off to bed, hoping that whatever it is will have gone away by the time he gets back. If you ask me, that crack over the head did more damage than we realised.'

'The headaches getting worse, are they?'

'It's not headaches, Archie, it's him, who he is becoming – not the man I married.'

'What do you mean?'

'Not now, Arch,' she said. 'You go and help the girl. I need to see to the kiln.' She looked at him and smiled wanly. 'Thank you,' she said, 'for thinking of us. I'll be glad of the help – and John – he'll get used to it. Give him time.'

71

Between them he and Mary assembled the little bed, slotting the iron pegs of the uprights into the frame of springs and, leaving her to wrestle with the mattresses, he bundled down the stairs with a couple of rolled-up carpets.

Even on a good day they would have been heavy and awkward to hang across the clotheslines. With a hangover and lack of sleep he was already fagged but, as he picked up the willow beater and began to attack the first one, he saw, instead of carpet, the limp body of Norbert Streeter. Clouds of choking dust became his victim's cries and screams. He smacked his smug face, whipped his lardy hide until the blood ran and, running backwards for more impetus, did away with him altogether. Lizzie came out of the pottery, holding Clara by the hand, to laugh as he gave a repeat performance with the second carpet. She didn't realise he saw this one as himself, the fool who had got the poor girl into this predicament.

When he remounted the narrow stairs, tugging on the rope rail for leverage, ducking to mind the low ceiling, with his guilt limp on his shoulder, the bed was made up and Mary's cheeks were flushed, her eyes bright with excitement. She had never lived in such a room, she declared, her hands clasped to her breast, with carpets on the floor, two mattresses on the bed, and the sun coming in the skylight. She had even found jugs for hot water and cold, which she put at either end of a shelf, for want of a washstand, with a spotty old mirror between. In front of this she put a wooden crate on which she placed a chipped enamel bowl for washing, and stood back to admire the effect. Gazing at the graceful arch of her spine, her head inclined so perfectly in quizzical assessment, Archie was suddenly aroused. Lord, he was rock hard, almost groaning, visualising himself flinging her down on the white coverlet and flattening the flock.

What a monster he was, with Lizzie just downstairs, and Kitty O'Grady's smell still on his skin!

Saying he must take Clara off Lizzie's hands for a while, he turned and left the room, covering his shame with his hat.

When the master of the house shambled home with his pathetic barrow-load of firewood, Mary was in the kitchen, rattling pans, and Archie and Clara were feeding the chickens.

'She can cook?' John seemed surprised.

'Apparently. It may only be cheese and potato pie but it's marginally better than bread and point.'

Chapter 8

To Archie's profound relief his sketchpad was delivered to his door, owing three ha'pence postage, payable to the postman. It was the way the railway returned lost property where a forwarding address was written inside the cover. It must have fallen from his pocket when he'd curled up on the seat of the train. How incredibly obliging of whoever had found it; though, he supposed, it wasn't much use to anyone else since you couldn't eat it or spend it or wear it. The stub of pencil was missing from its loop on the spine of the book but that was the least of his woes.

Feverishly he riffled from the back cover through a few empty pages to the last entry, and stared at the explicit nude on the rumpled bed – the singer, Kitty O'Grady. If he'd had any doubt there was her name, her address, written in his own hand. God, after all that booze he was surprised he'd been able to function, let alone draw, least of all write. He flipped a page and there was the pianist, a hearty-looking chap with a handlebar moustache. Didn't remember drawing him either. The heart-stopping thing was that the keyboard was torn across. He could just make out the indentation the pencil point had made, forming words across the feet of some ugly mobster on the following page. And yes, when he scribbled across it with a soft pencil those indentations formed the name, Mary Quinn, the number of the house and the name of the road where she lived.

At the police station, Sergeant Tyrell sighed and scratched his bald spot. 'Well, we've all done silly things in our time,' he said, with a touch of condescension, which meant he had never done anything that came within a million miles of getting drunk and incapable in a criminal stronghold. 'But some good came of it, I suppose – spotting Brian Rooney for one. He scrubs up well, I must say.' He leaned back for the full glory of the brocade frockcoat, the side whiskers. 'Pity you never thought to see him safely home ...'

He leafed through the sketchbook Archie had pushed across the counter. Bent closer. 'You know, some of these faces are not unfamiliar. This one, now ...' He tapped a sketch with a tobacco-stained finger. 'You wouldn't want to meet him on a dark night – not without good back-up. That's 'Bully' Watkins, that is. Lovely chap, lovely family – all of 'em bastards, in fact and in deed.'

'He said he was in import-export, like the rest of them.'

'Import-export, my eye! In clink most of the time. And lookee here, who's this? Give us a minute and I'll put a name to him.' He squinted sideways at the page and puffed on his pipe, rocking slightly with the effort. 'By crikey!' he cried. 'Charlie Philpot, a dirty little embezzler! So he's in with the big boys now, is he? Very interesting!' Tyrell rubbed his hands together and continued turning the pages. 'Don't know this one. Looks like a vicar.'

'They don't all look like scum, Frank. Cedric Carrington is a bank manager and I guess, with that cherubic face, you'd trust him with your life savings. But he has to be as bent as a tin guinea, fingers in all sorts of dodgy pies.'

The next page showed a long-legged stick-insect of a man, the one Archie had followed up the stairs to the auction. 'That one, that kindly old greybeard, turns out to be Lionel Partridge. He runs an orphanage in Stoke Newington: a real humanitarian, you'd think. I had a long conversation with him and he has the very best credentials – an Oxford degree, qualifications coming out of his ears. I couldn't help wondering what a man like that was doing at Streeter's party. They couldn't have much in common. And then I saw him going into an auction Streeter had laid on.' His blood chilled as it had that night. His face set hard.

'Auction? What – paintings and that? Funny thing to have at a party.'

'Except these were people they were auctioning, Frank. That's the sort of party it was. They were selling slaves from Africa.'

'What! But – but that's ille …' He stopped mid-word, realising that the law meant nothing to Streeter and co. 'You sure about this?' he asked more quietly.

'Sure as I can be. In fact, I had it from Partridge himself. When he realised I was sketching him, he came over and had a look, asked me if I would come over to the orphanage and paint him properly. He also asked me if I liked little children and, like a fool, I thought he wanted to interest me in adoption. Not as a breed, I told him, though there were one or two exceptions – my brother's boys and little Clara Kington. But, of course, that wasn't what he meant at all …' He glanced over at the policeman who was grimly taking notes. 'He obviously supplies some specialist need.'

The sergeant frowned as he tried to take in Archie's meaning and then his face twisted in horror and anger. 'Oh, bloody hell!'

'Hard to believe such men exist.'

'An orphanage, you say?'

'In Stoke Newington,' he repeated. 'I believe I have his calling card, if you're interested.' He shuffled through his wad of cards, selected one. 'Here it is – Saint Anne's. Lord knows what goes on over there. I suppose if I did his portrait I could find out.' He took out another card. 'This is Carrington's place, over in Chiswick. I'm off over there next week to paint his daughters.' After a moment's thought, he tapped the whole pack into shape and handed them over.

The officer leafed through them in silence. What an impossible job policing was, thought Archie, trying to ferret out these vermin.

'So,' the sergeant said at last, 'Charlie Philpot wants his picture painted, does he? Whatever next? And oh, dearie, dearie me, look at this – vanity thy name is Chalky White.' He rolled his eyes and tutted over the names on the cards. 'So the family can remember what Pa looked liked before he went inside.' Archie hadn't thought of that. 'Brian Rooney didn't want your business then?' the sergeant observed.

'We didn't get a chance to talk,' was all he said. Instead he drew a rough sketch of the Irishman, snarling, with his fist raised, ready to strike.

'Ha! No shillelagh then. But according to your John Kington it was Hegarty did all the damage.'

'Rooney was there, Sarge. He could have stopped him.'

Tyrell shrugged. 'I doubt it. They don't call him Mad Tommo for nothing.' As he spoke he tapped the cards into an uneven pack. 'Mind if I hang onto these, Archie, just to update the records – latest known address sort of thing? I'll let you have them back. And I need to start a few new files,' he said, staring hard at the sketch of Lionel Partridge, 'if you wouldn't mind leaving the drawings for a while. They could prove useful.'

'Well, I …'

'I'm sure the petty cash will stretch to a guinea. Will that do?'

'Keep them and welcome. I can see them all in here.' He tapped his temple.

He also had them in his diary: places to go, appointments to keep. In just two days' time he was required to call at Cedric Carrington's Chiswick home to begin sketching the banker's two older daughters, Maud and Lilian, aged ten and twelve, for a painting that Carrington insisted was to be on the lines of Gainsborough's 'Linley Sisters'.

Afterwards he called in at the police station, as had been arranged, although he had nothing out of the ordinary to report – he had had his work cut out trying to keep two high-spirited young girls quiet and unmoving for more than two minutes at a time.

He found Tyrell fizzing with impatience.

'They're clever, these bastards. See them waltzing round town you'd think they was walking on water. Church on Sunday. Good works. Soup kitchens, almshouses, you name it. Talk about covering their tracks. Bleeding royalty couldn't manage it better. The Port of London boys have upped the checks on all incoming ships and there's not a sign of human cargo. They must stop off to unload on the way in. Checked their books with a fine-toothed comb and there's nothing. Nothing that doesn't add up, I mean. Whiter than white the lot of them. You *must* be able to get something on one of the buggers. You're our only hope, Archie. Our inside man, if you like.'

Archie didn't like. If he were found rooting around in Carrington's big house, he pointed out, he'd be asking for trouble. In any case, he was relegated to the library at the back of the house. No chance of spying on anyone there. In fact, while he was painting the girls he had to put up with their governess, a Miss Nugent, sitting in the corner, on chaperone duty.

Tyrell fumed about wasted opportunities. 'Can't you put something in the old girl's tea? Cosy up to one of the parlour maids? Get her to tell you what's going on?'

What Archie did was complain about the light, blaming the cold January skies, the nights drawing in. 'It's really far too dark in the library to see the girls at their best. Their skin looks almost grey ... no, Cedric, I'm sorry. Oil lamps would be worse. They shed an unnatural yellow light. No, we need full daylight to bring out the bloom of their cheeks, the sparkle in their eyes. I could leave the portrait until the summer,' he offered, hopefully. But Carrington didn't want to wait.

The banker moved Archie and his sitters upstairs to the nursery, the younger children, both boys, being away at school. It was at the front of the house over the entrance hall and had long windows. Apart from the bars to prevent little children falling out, Archie had a perfect view of all the comings and goings.

His Chiswick days were Wednesdays and Fridays to avoid Mrs Carrington's tea parties and the girls' dancing and singing lessons. He would begin at around nine, mixing paints and working on the background. Carrington insisted on a completely unrealistic summer woodland setting to match Gainsborough's, and left Archie books and prints of foliage and flowers to copy. At ten-thirty prompt, the sisters came in from their studies in the school-room, accompanied by dough-faced Miss Nugent and her knitting, and Archie might spend the next hour or so painting Maud's hair and bodice or Lilian's chubby hands. When the sun – what there was of it – moved around the side of the house, the girls and their governess went also, to stretch their legs before lunch. For the rest of the day Archie worked from his sketches and, on Fridays, when Carrington was home early, leapt to the window to see whose carriage had just drawn up in the street outside.

Some he recognised, some he didn't, but a sketch was usually enough for Tyrell to identify them. Archie became acquainted with George 'Pretty boy' Clancy, Billy 'The Dip' Meadows, who must have struck lucky, and Josiah Fox, a thickset builder from Walthamstow.

One Wednesday evening they all arrived together on the stroke of six as Archie was leaving. Streeter greeted him like a long-lost friend. 'Any more paintings for me, lad?'

Lionel Partridge said he would see him at the orphanage in a week or two. 'Drop me a line when you're free.'

If only he could have listened outside Carrington's study and taken notes, but his employer held the front door open for his leaving, and he missed his chance.

About the same time the following Friday he was on the landing, ready to depart, when he heard voices below in the hall. Carrington was ushering someone out of his study. Archie backed into the nursery and, leaving the door ajar, hid in the shadows, listening hard.

'I'm glad you're coming in with the rest of us. You've made the right decision, I can assure you. You can't go wrong with Nobby.'

'So how soon will I get my money back?' The voice had an Irish lilt and a familiar ring to it.

'Within the month, I'd say. *The Eastern Star* leaves Tilbury first thing Wednesday. They're rounding up the cargo as we speak. I'll let Nobby know tonight that you're putting in two hundred. Then I'll pop round and see Partridge. He'll need an advance. He has the job of drenching the little bastards, de-lousing them, feeding them up. You don't get much for dead meat crawling with vermin.'

'These aren't anybody's children, are they? They won't be missed at all?'

'Look, the way I see it, we're doing the city a favour, cleaning up the streets.'

'And I'll double my money, you say?'

'Guaranteed, my friend, more than double. We're all winners – the orphanage, the ship owners and the buyers.'

'They'll give them a home, won't they, a roof over their heads?'

'They'll give them *work*, my friend, and plenty of it. But don't you worry, it'll be the making of them.'

'Well then, Cedric, thanks for the tip. It's grand doing business with you, so it is. You must come over to Shoreditch, one day soon. Bring Mrs Carrington and the children.'

As the butler saw the visitor off the premises Archie hurried to the darkened nursery window, breathing fast, his heart hammering. He hooked back the curtain in time to see Brian Rooney stepping up into a cab and waited until it was clattering off down the road before coming out, closing the nursery door loudly and bundling down the stairs. Well, now we know, he thought: Wednesday on *The Eastern Star*. Tyrell would be able to shoot the entire enterprise out of the water. He knocked lightly on Carrington's door and popped his head round.

'Just off, Cedric. See you next week.'

'Oh Archie … How'd it go today?'

'Getting there, slowly.'

A freezing mid-winter squall whipped his scarf across his face as the door closed behind him. The cold was making his cheeks ache but, as Archie gave directions to the cab driver he was in a fever of excitement. This was a chance to nail the lot of them. With that crew behind bars Mary could come out of hiding.

Tyrell heard Archie out, smoothing his moustache with thumb and forefinger. 'Excellent, excellent,' he said, at last. He went over to the telegraph machine and sent a long message, stopping only once to check, '*The Eastern Star,* you say, Tilbury Docks?'

*

The Port of London Authority police boarded *The Eastern Star* on Wednesday the fifteenth, arresting captain and crew as they were about to set sail with their human cargo. At the same time, back in Chiswick, Archie was setting up his easel in the Carringtons' nursery, hopefully for the last time. To return, week after week, to the house of a man who made money out of children's pain and suffering had been hard to do. Were these the *natural resources* Streeter's 'entrepreneurs' had referred to? Goodness knows what sort of life Carrington and his pals were committing them to. There was no doubt in Archie's mind that these little slaves would be sent underground to build railways, or exploited in factories, or made to work inhumanely long hours on settlers' farms. *Or sold to child molesters and fetishists.* Every bone in Archie's body urged him to put his fist through the painting, denounce his employer as a vicious beast, an evil bastard, and leave honestly. But he had to see the day out. If Carrington suspected for one moment that Archie had a hand in what was to come he would have him killed.

The governess took her usual chair in the corner of the nursery while Maud and Lilian continued some petty squabble they had begun at breakfast.

Archie was painting the fading heat of argument into their cheeks when he heard a commotion in the hallway: Carrington's angry voice and the stern warnings of arresting officers.

The girls ran downstairs immediately, leaving Archie and Miss Nugent watching from the window, as Cedric Carrington was forcibly marched down the front steps into the waiting wagon. His cherubic face had lost its bloom to fear. His wife was screaming at the police constable and pummelling his shoulders with her bare fists, hampered by Maud and Lilian who were dragging on her sleeves demanding to know what was going on.

Carrington's secretary, a bespectacled young man, was also in handcuffs. He had only done his job, he kept repeating.

It was Archie's turn next. A policeman saw him at the window and bounded up the stairs to twist his arm painfully behind his back and steer him down into the jolly-wagon, with Archie protesting all the way that he had done nothing wrong; he was just a visiting artist. He supposed they had to include him, to make it look real, though the cold clasp of the handcuffs, the rough-handling, the sweat and fear were real enough. Suppose they'd got it wrong?

Plain-clothes policemen brought up the rear bearing box-files and ledgers.

They let him go later, as had been agreed, the Port of London Authority being happy to take full credit for the raid.

*

When Archie woke with a jolt from nightmares that made his heart beat and bounce like a smithy's hammer on an anvil – dreams where he was being hunted by masked men, tortured in damp cellars and killed in dark alleyways – he prayed that they would all be locked up for a very long time or shipped off in the hulks to the ends of the earth, never to return. The worst of it was that no one by the name of Brian Rooney had been taken.

'Changed his name, I betcha,' Sergeant Tyrell assured him. 'Couple of Irish taken – could a been one of them. At least they're all behind bars: Streeter and Partridge, your lovely bank manager, a dozen or more. Refused bail, of course. You did well, Archie. Good job.'

Kitty O'Grady didn't know any Brian Rooney, she maintained. The man she'd been talking to at Streeter's house was Kelly, she was sure of it. Rory Kelly. She didn't know him very well. He was a stage-door johnnie, was all. And no, she'd never been home with him. Didn't know where he lived.

Archie Archie pulled on his socks. 'He objected pretty strongly to your sitting on my lap.'

He was drunk, she said. She'd given him no encouragement at all.

Archie sighed. He didn't believe her for a minute. And what about Nobby Streeter? How well did she know him?

Ah now, she and Nobby had an understanding, strictly business, so it was. He was her agent and took a slice of whatever she made on the stage. But that was it. No how's your father, nothing like that.

Unlikely, he thought.

But otherwise he was pleased with Kitty, and she with him. She said she'd sat for that other painter, Walter Sickert, but he'd given her a wishy-washy face that could have been anybody. At least Archie made her look like herself, every last inch of her.

He sold that painting for eighty guineas and no regrets at all. Still he hankered after a skinnier body, with suffering in her blue eyes and work-sore hands. He told himself that now that Norbert Streeter was behind bars it was safe for Mary Quinn to come home.

Chapter 9

The Kingtons agreed to a week's leave. It was all she needed, Mary said: grateful just to pop home and see Dolly was all right, make a few visits. The first, it was agreed, would be to Archie's studio. He had a particular painting in mind and he would need her to wear the wrapper she had left behind in her dash to Woodford. It was dirty, she fussed. Life at the Kingtons meant that she was now used to taking a weekly bath and washing her hair from time to time. She smelled sweeter and her clothes were clean. Even her teeth were whiter. She couldn't or wouldn't understand that for Archie her grubby wrapper was exactly right. If she dared to wash it, he warned her, the deal – one and six an hour – was off. A florin, she haggled. He raised his eyes to heaven but agreed.

Wearing the wrapper meant changing out of her coat and work dress on arrival. As the garments flopped over the top of the screen, he imagined her naked and within reach, and he thanked God for his all-concealing smock. With her black hair hanging loose around her shoulders and over the arm of the chaise longue, he could scarcely keep his hands off her. Could she hold her chin at this angle, with this shoulder slightly lower? Up a little more. Yes, just like that. Leaning a bit to one side? Not too far. He put out a hand to make the adjustment. But his fingers trembled, suddenly clumsy. She flinched.

'You're all painty, Archie.'

He leapt back behind the easel. That was perfect, if he could just catch that look. 'No, don't talk, you'll spoil it.'

Outside, the sounds of the market hung like a mist of busy, gossipy breath on the frosty air. Inside the room was silence, broken only by the shift of coal in the grate, Archie's dabbling as he bound the pigment with oil, mixed the colours on his palette, and the whisper of brush against canvas. With tenderness he outlined her poor hands, the fingers all calloused and blunt. The one at her throat, so exquisitely poised as though holding to herself precious memories, quite took his breath away. He thought he knew who she was thinking of, could almost see her husband's image in her pupils. She wasn't free, would never be free while Pauly lived in her head.

When she demanded, without breaking pose, 'Why are you friends with Mister Kington?' his brush skittered as at some loud and unexpected noise. So much for mind-reading! He'd been completely off track.

'I ...' He wiped an unwanted dab of flesh pink from the painted lap, perplexed by the question and her impertinence. 'Why do you ask?'

'You're not alike, not at all.'

He resisted the temptation to fish for compliments, understanding that the question had sprung from real concern. 'He hasn't been unkind to you, has he?'

Mary merely waggled her head, signifying secrets.

Now he really was worried. 'He hasn't done anything improper?'

'No!' she protested. 'What are you thinking? No, nothing like that.'

She stared into the middle distance as the pose demanded, her lips perhaps a little tighter than before. He waited, brush poised, but she would give him no more.

He said, at last, painting again, and thinking he knew what she meant, 'He wasn't always like this.'

'That's what *she* says, poor lady.'

'What's going on, Mary? Is there something I should know?'

She gave her head a shake. 'It's not ...' Her stubby finger-end had found its way to her mouth. 'No,' she declared, pausing to nibble the remaining corner of a fingernail. 'I – I've said more than I should, so I have.' She turned her head away and he heard her sniff. She seemed very affected.

He sighed, wanting to slap her hand down. She'd moved completely out of position.

'Sure,' she mumbled, 'and amn't I the old blabbermouth? It's between the two of them. I shouldn't be telling tales.'

'Mary.' He needed her to be still, not agitated. He clicked his fingers, to remind her where she should be looking. But her mind was somewhere else entirely.

'Let's take a break,' he sighed, defeated. 'I'll make some tea.' The kettle was red-hot as he took it off the fire with a cloth and poured boiling water into the teapot. He was glad of the activity, the chance to ease his neck, his shoulders. No other sitter made him as tense.

Her voice startled him, sharp and cutting. 'Sure an' you don't need me here at all, Archie Price – couldn't you paint me from memory?' He turned from pouring the tea and found her leafing through his drawings. Boiling liquid spattered the floor. He yelped. There were some things he really didn't want her to see ...

'I – I need to try out different expressions, different positions,' he reasoned, covering a particularly explicit nude with her cup and saucer.

'In the altogether?' she objected. 'It's taking liberties, so it is. Who's to know I don't take off my clothes for you?'

He knew. 'I have to exercise my imagination, Mary.' It was a little lie. 'Didn't your Pauly have to practise on his whistle every day to be able to play a tune beautifully?' Her mouth was screwed tight, her eyes looking sideways but she was listening. 'And I have to practise drawing you so I can get the painting right. Practice makes perfect, don't they say?'

'A good memory, ye have,' she observed. 'Anyone'd think you had a photo to copy.'

'You, too,' he said, hoping to turn the conversation. 'I don't know how you were able to remember Tommo Hegarty so precisely. I mean you could only have seen him clearly for a moment or two. He was looking into a dark window with his hands shading his face …'

Her cup jiggled against her saucer. He must have touched a nerve. She pushed the china safely onto the table. Her fists dropped into her lap and her knuckles whitened as she forced herself to remember. 'When he asked Mister Wylie to let him in, he turned into the sun …'

He pictured the scene. 'Briefly,' he nodded partial agreement. 'That's what's so remarkable. In my experience only the *victim* of a crime can recall their attacker so vividly, after so short an encounter. Fear somehow imprints the face on their memory.' Or arousal, he might have said, lust at first sight. 'But you weren't a victim, just a casual spectator.'

Her eyes became hard blue stones. 'Are you calling me a liar?'

'No.' He frowned, perplexed. He'd meant it as a compliment. 'No, not at all. I'm saying that you have a special gift to be able to remember so – so accurately …'

She pushed away from the table, her eyes blinking tears.

'I have to go.'

'Mary, Mary, I'm sorry. Oh don't take on – I didn't mean to upset you. That's the last thing, the very last …'

'I can't stay here,' she said. 'Not with you thinking bad things about me.'

Bad things? Did she mean the erotic sketches? Oh Lord. Oh damn. He'd never meant her to see them.

She went behind the screen to dress, came out to twist up her hair before the mirror, fastened it with pins and pulled the awful hat down over it. Her face was white, her eyes glacial. When he proffered the money they'd agreed for the sitting she didn't attempt to take it, regarding it instead with disgust. 'Keep it,' she said. 'Buy yourself a proper whore.'

He heard her step on the stairs, the front door slamming, the wolf-whistles fading as the barrow boys spotted a likely target and then hurriedly changed their minds. Her look, he knew, could damage a man.

He ran to the window, threw it up. 'Mary!' he yelled after the small scurrying figure. 'I'm sorry!' But he was competing with the 'Apples-a-pound, pears!' of the street traders, the 'One yard, two yards, three for a shilling!' Either she didn't hear or she didn't care to.

Chapter 10

'Didn't I tell you?' Mary yelled at the woman, throwing down her crust in fury. 'If anyone ever comes to the door asking for me, you were to tell them I'd gone away and you didn't know where …'

'Which was true enough *last* week – you left me right in the dark.'

'Because I know you cannot keep your trap shut. Jesus, Dolly, you don't tell that smarmy devil he's just missed me! Where's your brains, woman?'

'But he said he had summat for you, work or summat,' Dolly wailed, pulling at a ringlet until it was stretched as far as it could go. She stroked the tuft across her top lip, like a baby with its bit of blanket. Her pale eyes reddened.

'Sure and we know the sort of work he has in mind, do we not? On me back with me legs in the air!'

'Now you don't know that for sure,' Dolly countered, letting go the curl, which, trained by nightly rags, sprang back into place beside her ear.

'What I do know is that you and Archie Price are the biggest blabbermouths in England and between the pair o' yous, I'll be turning tricks for Uncle Nobby this time next week.' She took a despairing breath and stared at the ceiling for inspiration.

Nothing, just spider webs and floorboards. Sighing, she sat down, picked at her crust of bread and condensed milk and thoughtfully sucked her sugary finger. 'It was definitely him, Nobby Streeter?'

'Said so, didn't I? See him often enough, up *The Railway*, chatting up the prozzies. Big fat baldie-locks, nice line in waistcoats and cravats.'

'But he's supposed to be in clink …'

'Well, he might have been once but he ain't now. He was round here, knocking on the door and asking for you.'

'Oh Dolly!'

'I mean you shoulda said summat when you come 'ome yesterday. Or today, even. 'Stead a boring the socks off me about Peter the Painter and where he puts his brushes, you coulda told us who to look out for.'

'So what did you tell Streeter exactly?'

The woman stared into her tea.

'Dolly!' Mary slammed her fist onto the rickety table making the crust bounce on the plate, the candle sputter and the seamstress sit up straight, curls bouncing anxiously. 'What did you *say*?'

'I – I said you was visiting your pal over Chingford and I was expecting you back tonight,' she said in a rush, clamping her lips on words it was too late to check.

'Tonight!' roared Mary, gripping the table edge. 'Sweet Jesus!' Pushing away to stand up, she knocked the chair flying. 'Mother of God!' She shoved her hands into the nest of her hair and scrunched it hard, trying to focus. 'And what did *he* say?'

'He said he'd come back later.'

'Later *tonight*?' Mary spat. She could cheerfully have slapped that silly face, knocked the specs off and stamped on them.

'Sorry, Mary.'

'*Sorry?* That's going to save me from a fate worse than death, is it? *Sorry!*' She packed a fistful of venom into the word and Dolly quailed.

Mary turned away, rubbing the back of her other hand. What was she going to do? If she didn't look sharp he'd be at the door and she'd be slung into a cart with a bump on the head. She righted the chair, crossed to her cubby-hole and flung the door back so hard that its momentum swung it closed again. She kicked it open again and again, growling with irritation.

'Mind, Mary, you'll have it off its hinges!'

Mary summoned all her strength and kicked it again, relishing a thrill of perverse pleasure when it bounced.

'Mary!' The taller woman came from behind and grabbed the door. 'Don't take it out on the door!'

'I'll take it out on you, then!' she retaliated, transferring her kicks to the woman's legs, losing her impetus in a tangle of skirts. 'You'll be the death of me, Dolly Brett!' She went on kicking until Dolly caught her wrist and bent her arm back. Freeing her wrist at last and grabbing Dolly's ringlets with both hands, Mary shook her stupid head like a colander of greens.

'Ow, ow, let go, let go-o-o!'

Mary twisted around, found her feet on the floor and threw the woman away from her in disgust. Dolly lay whimpering on the bed. 'Damn you, Dolly,' muttered Mary, sniffing tears, 'you've really landed me in it.'

'Serves you right. Look what you done, pulled half me hair out, you bitch.'

'Dozy cow.'

'You're the dozy one, getting yourself mixed up with bloody sex maniacs.'

'All I did was let Archie paint my picture. It's not my fault there are evil men about, using it to pleasure themselves. Oh Dolly,' she wailed, 'he's going to come round here tonight and pack me off to some brothel for God-knows-who to have their way with me.' She gulped. 'God help me, what am I going to do?'

'You best get going then, ain't ya? Run away.' There was scorn in her voice.

Mary reached under the bed for her bag, pushing aside a gazunder and a sack of potatoes. 'Get up. I need to pack.'

Silently, Dolly rolled off the bed and held back the door.

'Get on out of it, then.'

But Dolly hung about, clearly anxious about something.

'These are yours,' said Mary, thrusting the curling tongs at Dolly. 'I'll do without.' That's what she was waiting for. The older woman snatched them up and went to put them back on the mantelpiece. Mary seized the moment to whisk her hand under the pallet.

Where was it? Her fingers played over bits and buttons, silky ribbon, polished ivory, a stub of … Archie's pencil rolled away and a glittering trinket dropped to the floor. One of a pair. Worth something, but Jesus, Mary and Joseph, she didn't want to be reminded of *that one*, so she didn't! She should have slung them in the dustbin with his letters and flowers but you can't, not gold. She kicked it under the bed where the broom never reached. '*M* for Mary,' he'd told her – the lying toad – but she could neither wear them nor pawn them, useless bloody things. That *M* was for Murder, she knew for sure. If she tried to sell them they'd string her up, an' all.

At last her scrabbling found Pauly's tin whistle, scratched and worn, touched by his lips, his breath, his fingers – all she had left of him. Into the shopping bag with it. He'd been buried in his one good suit of clothes and his work boots, and everything else had been hocked to pay for the funeral. Cleaned her out.

Dolly was back, a beaky jackdaw eyeing the battered old bag and wondering what had gone into it. There wasn't much: just a change of clothes, an apron, hairpins, comb, a mashed bit of stick she used for her teeth, a face cloth …

The rest of her stuff was back at the Kingtons'. Well, it could stop there. She wouldn't go back. Not with your man the way he was. He despised her. When he could bear to look at her, it was like she was shit on his shoe. And he never remembered her name. She was 'that slut' or 'the skivvy', at best 'the girl' or 'Archie's bit of fluff'. Never mind that she could hear every word he said. He couldn't bring himself to address her directly. It was always through his wife. 'There's a crease in this shirt, she can do it again. Can't she make a decent brew? Tell her to keep the noise down,' when she was singing to Clara. He wasn't much nicer to the little girl or the missus. 'Get this child out of my hair. What do you look like, woman? Don't answer me back.' With a slap for good measure that'd make your teeth rattle, miserable git.

Not to mention the other thing and the man full grown. She was sorry for the missus but she wasn't beholden to her, nor to Archie for that matter. She didn't owe him a brass farthing. She'd call in on her brother. He'd know of a fine big house to take her on, where there were a dozen servants or more. She'd make friends, girls her own age who could share a joke. She'd forgotten how to laugh.

'Don't go, Mary,' said the now contrite Dolly. 'You can hide downstairs until the geezer goes away. I'll tell him you're not back.'

'You don't tell him anything. Not a single word. You don't even answer the door.'

'I'll send him up the painter's.'

'You'll do no such thing, Dolly Brett, promise me!'

'What do you care? He's a dirty-minded letch, doing pictures of you in the nuddy. Didn't I say he was only after the one thing?'

'Well, he can whistle for that, to be sure. But, Doll, he's never laid a finger on me and only draws what other men are thinking. He doesn't deserve a visit from Nobby's crew.' He'd taken liberties, sure, but he'd never meant her to see those silly pictures. No, it was the other thing. He was getting too close, too close. She bit her nail, spat it out. 'Look, Dolly, if Nobby comes back, don't go to the door, will ye now? Go down the cellar and stay there.'

'I ain't going down there. Never know what you're gonna find – spiders, all sorts. I hate it down there.'

'Well, go to bed then. Make out there's no one home. Don't do any more work tonight, put the light out, lock the door and get an early night.'

'What about you, gel?'

'I'm off.' She fastened the buckle on the bag. Shrugged on her shawl, jammed on her hat and skewered it with two pins. She'd pick up the rest of her stuff some other time.

'Where you going?'

'You think I'm telling you, you great gab?' She wished she hadn't been so quick to throw Archie's money back in his face. Her stupid pride'd be the death of her. If she went anywhere tonight it'd have to be on Shank's pony.

'But you'll be back?'

'Don't count on it.'

'I tell you, Mary, I ain't minding your place for you no more.'

'Sure an' I wouldn't expect you to,' said Mary briskly, knowing the woman would never turn her away. Picking up the cat, she tickled its ears 'til its eyes closed in ecstasy. 'I'll just have to sleep about the room how I can, like you do, Puss.'

'Take a lantern, duck.' Dolly's voice softened. 'It's black as Newgate's knocker where you're going. Put some matches in your bag and a candle end. This one won't last the night. 'Ere, come on, gel, give us an 'ug.'

There was a knock on the door.

They sprang apart, making the sign for silence, fingers on lips, eyes wide with fright. Had he heard them? There was a scuff of feet that came to the window, silence as he tried to peer in past the blinds.

Something moaned but it wasn't him, just wind in the cracks, curling the fog that leeched from the damp walls.

Dolly shooed with her hands, meaning that Mary should make herself scarce. 'Go, go,' she mouthed, 'down the cellar. No, wait!' Stuffing the bread into the empty mug, she pushed it and the plate into Mary's baffled arms and shunted her to the cellar door.

Yes, yes, she cottoned on. Dolly wasn't such a dumb cluck. If he saw the table set for two he would know Dolly wasn't alone. With one hand clutching her tea things to her chest, the other the lantern, Mary began a shaky descent as the cellar door closed quietly behind her. She had hardly reached the bottom of the steps when the door re-opened and her bag came tumbling after, followed by some tinkling coins – a shilling piece, a tanner and a few coppers. Thanks, Dolly. This time when the cellar door closed the bolt slid across, making sure.

Mary put the tea things on the copper, pocketed the scattered coins and then returned to the top step to spy, her eyes level with the jagged bottom of the door. 'Just a minute!' she heard.

Don't do it, she urged her friend silently. But a blast of cold air whisked across the floor, catching up dust and cotton strands and cat hair, making her eyes water. The front door was open. Mary blew out the lamp. If Streeter saw light straining up from the cellar he'd know immediately where she was. There were voices: a lilting Irish and Dolly's flat twang. Not Streeter, then. His man perhaps. It was a faint hope. She knew who it was.

'No, sorry, mate, not yet.'

Another query and then Dolly again.

'Dunno. She said tonight for definite.'

There was a sharp sound of movement, feet scuffing and Dolly yelping, 'Oi, no, you can't come in!' The front door slammed closed.

Mary crossed herself. 'Thanks be to God,' she whispered and gathered her bag to her, ready for Dolly to let her out.

But instead came the sound of a whimpered, 'Leave go, you!' followed by a thud and a scuffle and someone falling against the cellar door, with a rattle of bolts and latches. Mary gasped and crossed herself again. He was inside the house, and he was pushing Dolly around. Those were squeals of fear and pain. Oh Dolly. The door shuddered again as the seamstress fell against it and slithered to the floor. A fold of her dress skimmed the gap at the bottom of the door. Mary ignored the dust and the rust from the big iron hinges showering her hat and her face; she blinked it from her eyes as she strained to hear Dolly's voice. But there were just moans, muffled moans that could have been the wind.

Don't hit her again, you bastard. Leave her alone. But he ignored her silent pleas, ignored his own conscience if he had one and, into the bargain, kicked the cat, which yowled as it skittered across the bare floor and thumped against the wall. Then a heavy quiet fell.

She didn't dare push against the bolted door. In any case, she was probably safer down here than anywhere else. Tears scalded her cold cheeks. 'Oh Dolly,' she hardly breathed. Her trembling fingers reached up to touch the wood where she thought the woman's head might be, as if she might transmit healing through the door. 'Dolly, be all right, will ye, darlin', please be all right.'

There were his boots crossing the cellar's ceiling. She shrank

97

down into the dark steps, squeezing her eyes shut against discovery. She heard the back door open and felt that draught. She dared to breathe. He was going outside to relieve himself.

'Dolly,' she whispered through the crack, 'Doll, are you all right?'

'Mary! Clear off!' came a hoarse breath. 'He says he's stopping till you get here.'

'Who is it?'

'Dunno. Some Irish.'

'Are you hurt?'

'A bit.'

'Dolly!' Tears stung her eyes. 'Oh sweet Jesus, Doll, get out.'

'I c-can't, mate. I'm done for.'

'I'll fetch a policeman.'

'Just go, I'll be all right. I've got me scissors in me pocket.' The silly cow would get herself killed. Now he was coming back with a clump, clump, clump, not even wiping his feet. Poor old Doll must be gnashing her teeth, those she had left. It was one thing she was hot on, keeping the floor clean for the dress material.

There was a scrape of chair legs, a creak of dry old wood as he sat down. She could just make out long shiny boots, and her heart beat faster. Sure and she knew those boots. *She knew those bloody boots.* One left the floor as he crossed his legs.

Dolly's hand dropped down where Mary could see the needle pricks in the finger.

Oh Jesus, will ye go away, puss! Here was the cat now, stretched against the cellar door, scratching to be let in, away from those boots. She just had to put her finger under the door to stroke his bony paw. But she wouldn't.

The chair scraped backwards along the floor, the boots

squeaked the short distance towards where she lay sprawled along the cellar steps.

'Move yourself!'

'No, I ...' Dolly's voice.

Another thump and his fingernails clipped the door. No protest from Dolly, just the sound of the breath leaving her lungs and the swish of her dress sweeping the floor, as he dragged her limp body out of the way.

The bolt rattled back but Mary was gone, sliding down the steps, her dress riding up round her neck, scraping her knees but landing with both feet on the mud floor.

The door squealed open on a column of light. The cat padded down the steps. A lantern probed the shadows up and down and round the cellar, missing her by a heartbeat.

The cat, as if primed to distract, jumped up onto the tub and with another leap disappeared through the mossy vent near the ceiling. Good cat. Satisfied, the man went back up the steps, locking the door behind him and Mary, listening behind the sacking in next door's cellar, breathed again.

*

They had been here, according to Dolly, since the cottages were built: connecting cellars, forming a long passageway under this part of Walthamstow.

Sometimes there were doors to push aside, sometimes a ragged bit of dirty curtain or sacking, sometimes just an opening where the door had been used by desperately cold people for firewood, but there was always a way through. No one dared be the one to say no and brick up their entry or block it off. There'd be hell to pay if you did, from the thieves who used the 'rat-run' as a quick getaway. On she went, cellar after cellar, under the cottages, never minding feral eyes that were lit by the lantern light, sleeping bundles of rags, puddles and piles of ashes, orange boxes and broken chairs, dirt and smells. Where the houses ended, the tunnel became a huge wormhole running alongside any cellars rather than through them. This was the High Street. She travelled faster, trying not to think about Dolly and what was happening back at number 35. Words on boards would have told her the nature of the premises above, had she her letters and could read them. She knew the tobacconists by the sweetness of the air, so hereabouts would be the police station, though they had no cellar and no knowledge of what went on down below. Here was Taylor's the cheesemonger and Bishop's the tripe-dresser. Sweet Jesus, you didn't need a board to tell you that. Soon she would come to Archie's greengrocer, with an earthy smell of boiling beetroots, and then round the corner into Hoe Street, where the cellars began once more and the going would be slower. Eventually she would be at the railway station and boarding the first train out of Walthamstow. Hopefully the one-and-ninepence Dolly had given her would take her to Liverpool Street. From there it was but a short step to Shoreditch and big brother Brian. He'd give her money.

As the night wore on she saw no light but her own and her hand holding the lantern grew colder and colder. She put down her bag to pull her shawl tighter, the shawl that Mammy had knitted all those years ago. It had worn thin, so it had, no defence against the cold wind in the passage that never died away. In the early hours, she found a brick copper already alight for Monday's wash and the water beginning to seethe and boil. Unable to resist the warmth she sat down on the dirt floor and rested her back against the heated walls of the tub. Her eyelids began to droop.

'You stop there, little love,' said a voice when Mary stirred, 'you look done in.' Just a woman about her work, a refuge.

So she slumbered on. Even though her fingers dreamily twitched to scrub and slap clothes on a washboard; even though her nostrils flared with the familiar smell of hot suds and she heard the bubble of sheets on the boil, the stream of water as they were lifted out for rinsing, she didn't stir. Steam filled the cellar and her nostrils with soapy warmth, turned back to water on the cold walls and ceiling, and dripped onto her hair, her skin. But she didn't really come to until she heard the clank of the mangle, the heavy old rollers turning, squeezing out a splash of cold clear water into the bucket underneath. She opened her eyes and found the woman had brought her hot bread and milk to break her fast.

'On the run, are you, dear?'

It was prune-faced Mrs Ives, who ran the haberdasher's. Well into her seventies, with dyed black hair and hooded eyes, she told the girl that she always put the whites on early, to get them pegged out in the yard before she opened up the shop at nine. A woman on her own, she had to organise. She'd add cold water for the coloureds, leave them to soak and rinse them through at dinnertime.

Mary shivered. The method she understood, the kindness she didn't.

'You cold, little love? Here, have my shawl – I'm roasting.' It was a patchwork of crocheted squares, same as her own, made from scraps of wool. 'No, keep it,' she said when Mary protested, 'I'm glad to give them away. Knitting and crochet, it's what I do while the customers 'as a look round. I sits in me corner, behind the cash box, listening to the gossip and keeping busy, like an old spider in its web.'

Mary snuggled into the warmth with a sigh and the tears came by themselves. Mrs Ives patted her shoulder and said, 'There, there, dear,' but she made it clear she didn't wish to know about the intruder at number 35, insisting that she preferred not to know why people used the passageway. She held her pink and soggy palms to her ears when Mary begged her to call a policeman for Dolly. 'Please, Mrs Ives, he's vicious.'

'And how did I get to hear about this, little love? I'd have to explain how a wandering girl found her way into me cellar. The boys in blue'll investigate and it'll be, "Oho, a secret passage, eh? Who'da bloody thought it?" Old Mister Big –' She jerked her head to indicate another interested party. 'He wouldn't take kindly to it. You know what happened along the road. Paper patterns and cotton reels make a pretty blaze, but burning wool don't smell near as sweet as burning wood. Now I'm fond of me little shop and me customers are fond of me. So I watch and listen but me lips is sealed.'

To pay her back for her kindness, and to put off thinking about her next move, Mary took over the mangling while Mrs Ives starched collars and cuffs in a china bowl. If the devil were to come down here looking for her, she could always sling a dipper of boiling water at him, if the worst came to the worst.

They shut the damper on the fire and took the washed whites up to Mrs Ives' backyard to hang in the freezing cold, the wool-woman insisted that she'd sooner see it blowing about in the coming snowstorm than trailing in the mud of the cellar floor. Because Mary had helped, it was all done and they were back indoors, putting on the kettle, with some minutes to spare before opening time. Mrs Ives tipped some of the steaming tea from the cup into the saucer and blew on it. Then she slurped it up, never taking her eyes from Mary's face. 'Aaaahh!' she went, smacking her lips, and replaced the cup in the empty saucer.

'Well, dear, I've had a think and I might be able to help you. What if I gave you my widowed sister's address in Bow? Mrs Ferris will be glad to put you up for a day or two, give you time to gather your wits, take stock. She might even take you on, teach you the trade.'

'Oh,' asked Mary, 'what does she do?'

'She makes a fair living, dear, that's all you need to know.'

In between saucers of tea she wrote a letter of introduction to her sister. At one point, as she was melting the brown wax to drip and seal it, she bent her head towards the floor, listening, drew in her breath and let it out, relieved. 'No. It's all right, dear. I thought it was *him* going through but they're going the other way. Just got off the train, I expect.' She pressed her signet ring on the wet seal and blew on it. 'There now, that's two birds killed with the one stone – you and my sister, both sorted.'

Mary winced. The saying made killing sound easy. Was it? She thought of fish bashed until they stopped twitching, of chickens, their necks twisted until their heads came off, a pig stuck with a knife and strung up while the blood flowed into a pail. It had to be done and she'd done it. But it hadn't come easy. Poor Dolly must have stabbed him with her scissors to stop him coming after her. Good old Doll, loyal old Doll. Please God.

Mary's face twisted as she recollected the pain of being punched to the ground, beaten almost to death. You'd say or do anything to make it stop. Anything.

Mrs Ives flipped the *Closed* sign to read *Open* from the outside, fiddled with a tiny tin of violet cachous, popped one into her mouth, picked up her knitting. Mary put her new shawl over her head against the chill of the morning, and set out, with a ping of the doorbell and a generous silver three-penny bit in her pocket for the omnibus. She hadn't refused it, though she was still in two minds.

As she waited at the stop across the road, she stamped her feet in their thin shoes. She couldn't feel her toes. She'd have more purple chilblains to tend tonight, wherever she was going.

Her glance fell to where steam leaked out at ground level, making it look like the pavement was cooking. Women up and down the street, all over the land, were busy doing the Monday wash, in their cellars, in their sculleries, boiling shirts and sheets and drawers in a soapy broth. Up went the steam, puffing and billowing into the cold air, into a sky that threatened snow.

She thought of the studio round the corner and of the artist trying to finish his painting without a model. Poor Archie – too clever by half, he'd almost figured it out. She'd had to run, so she had, never mind that she'd wanted to stay. He was in with the police. And *they* would have her guts for garters. She'd asked Mrs Ives to pop round to the greengrocer's lodger, tell him she was all right. And Mrs Ives had pursed her lips and said she would when she got round to it.

Here was the bus coming. Mrs Ives stood in her window, among the sewing silks and cross-stitch canvas, nodding encouragement, her thin lips whispering, 'Slip one, knit one, knit two together, pass slipped stitch over,' like a spell under her violet breath.

With a nod of her head Mary made her decision. The bus went all the way to Shoreditch and it was cheaper than the train. She'd call in on him first. Tell him her troubles. He had connections among the criminal fraternity and influence. Her brother, Brian Rooney, could stop this, if anyone could.

Chapter 11

He scooped her off the doorstep and swung her up in the porch, so high she could have touched the cobwebs.

She yelped, 'Put me down, put me down, you eejit!' with agitation, not delight.

'In the name of God, Mary, what's the matter? You look ill, girl. Come in, come in, and tell me all about it.'

He showed her into his front parlour where it was so warm her nose began to run and her feet and fingers to ache. A manservant came to take her hat and shawls and bring them tea. Brian sat her down in a cosy armchair, so high in the seat her feet came off the floor. He looked so tall and fine, with his hair trim and the side whiskers, a real gentleman in shirt and trousers and braces – carpet slippers, too. She hardly knew him after all this time. In fact, she felt quite shy as she explained why she'd come.

'Streeter's after you?' he roared. 'By God, I'll swing for him. He's gone too far, so he has.' He went about the room, stabbing the poker at the fire and moving ornaments back and forth, running his fingers through his black hair. 'I knew no good would come of it.'

When she leaned back in the chair, trying to read his face, he explained, 'I saw your picture hanging on his wall.'

She gasped, 'You were there, Brian? Hobnobbing with those crooks?'

'It's what I am and I must have been or I wouldn't be telling you, would I?'

'Wouldn't be telling me what exactly?'

He scowled, and his blue eyes pierced her to the quick. 'That I saw me own sister, me own flesh and blood, had had herself painted like a Jezebel for all to see!'

'How can you think that?' she reproached him. 'I sat for the painting for a bit of cash, was all, and I made sure I was decent. I had nothing to do with the selling of it, or where it was hung, or who saw it. An' I wish to God anyone had bought it but Streeter. For isn't he after putting me on the game?' She bit her lip. 'I had to go down the cellar to hide and leave Dolly to face him.'

'Face Streeter? He's out?'

'His man.' At least she hoped it was Streeter's man, better him than the other.

'You weren't followed?' He went to the window and twitched the blinds.

'No, no, there's ways out o' the place he would never have known.'

'I see.' With his back to her he was nodding grimly; turning he said, 'And the seamstress?'

'He beat her up, the devil. Pray God she's still alive.'

'How did he know where to find you?'

'Archie – the man who painted the picture, Archie Price – he was at that party, too. He wouldn't have told them in the normal way, but he got very drunk.'

He frowned and pressed his lips tight on some grudge or other. 'I saw him, strutting around, lording it: look at me, aren't I the clever one? I – I –' He hesitated. 'I didn't like him.'

She sprang to Archie's defence but her brother clung to his opinion.

'He's the one gave Streeter ideas,' he insisted, 'painting you to look like a whore.'

'He did not! He made me look grand, so he did. He even …'

'What?'

She gave her head a shake. 'Nothing.' She'd been about to mention the Wanted poster Archie had drawn at her dictation, but it wasn't a good idea. 'Brian, if you know Streeter you can put him right. Tell him I'm your sister and he's to leave me alone.'

'I could and I will. By God I will.'

'Brian, you – you weren't involved in that affair down at the docks, were you, with the shipload of little children …?'

'What? How could you even think it?'

She didn't know whether to believe him or not. He couldn't lie straight in bed, that one. When he'd sent the money for her passage, he'd written to Mammy that he'd earned it on the railway. When she came over she found he was a thief, light-fingering around to make ends meet. He caught her shaking her head in sorrow.

'I may be a wrong 'un, Mary, but I'm no slaver. Sure an' isn't all my money tied up in bricks and mortar?'

She gazed around at the room, at the high ceilings, the huge windows. It was a grand house, to be sure. Three storeys up and one below. With live-in help to wash and clean and fetch and carry, he was doing well.

'I've two more of these,' he explained, 'let to tenants, and I'm selling this for twice what I paid. Property is the key, Mary – buying and selling. You speculate to accumulate, don't ye know? People are flocking to London and they need homes. Your Pauly knew that. I make more money now than I ever did thieving.'

'Pity you didn't learn that sooner.'

Brother and sister exchanged looks containing words that if

107

uttered would have reduced them both to tears. Brian nodded and his mouth twisted in a sour look. And so he might, she thought.

Over tea and cakes, he showed her the plans for his new house: spread them out on the table and pointed out the bathroom and the bedrooms, the reception rooms, the servants' quarters and the kitchen with running water and gaslight.

'You decide, Mary, which room will be yours?'

'Mine?'

'I'll not have you showing yourself off to painters in order to put bread on the table. Who knows where it'll lead. You're coming to live with me, like the queen in her palace, and Lord Nobby can pick the bones out of that, so he can. You'll have your own sitting room, your own bedroom. It'll be your home. And if it works out, we'll have Mammy over and Conceptua, too.'

A warm glow spread up from her itching chilblains, prickling her legs, her shoulders, the backs of her eyes. She hugged herself, smiling happily. She didn't need to go for that job with Mrs Ives' sister after all. Wasn't it fate that had urged her to stay on the bus to the end of the line? Her brother would look after her. 'Oh Brian, I ...' Her eyes blurred with tears, and she dashed them away as she leaned over the table to see the plans, to decide whether a room at the front overlooking the street would be preferable to one at the back. And look at the big garden to walk in and to plant with trees and flowers.

'But suppose you marry?'

'You know it's unlikely. My little sister has spoiled me for all other women.' His wide grin was charming and she could almost have believed him. 'No,' he went on more seriously, 'any wife of mine will bring money to the match, I'll make sure of that, and I'll buy another house, and you can keep a room for us staying over.'

It sounded too good to be true.

Her eye wandered down and down. Written at the bottom of the blueprint was a signature she couldn't decipher but below it were typewritten words that she had seen before. They'd been painted on the side of the cart that had brought her dead husband home. She put her teeth together, made the sound of '*f*' and then '*o*' and then '*s*', built it up: '*Jos-iah*'. The next word was easy: '*Fox.*' It was the same man. Her heart sank. Her dreams dissolved.

'Brian!' she cried. 'This man, the builder – he's the one Pauly worked for!'

'Is that the truth?' He looked astonished, but looks, especially Brian's, could deceive.

She told him how her poor husband, rest his soul, after wrestling with his conscience night after night, had gone to the boss about the dangers of cutting corners when building the cheaper houses along the railway. Instead of using traditional mortar, the brickies found themselves trying to bind ash-adulterated bricks with an inferior lime-based product.

'It never dries out, Brian. You can pick it out with your fingernail. In bad weather the rain comes in. A strong wind will blow the walls down. They're death traps, those places.'

Pauly had pointed out to the builder how cheap timber and badly pitched roofs were adding to the dampness of the dwellings. If they weren't crushed by collapsing walls and ceilings, the tenants became ill with coughs and colds and rheumatics; some died. Fox said that he would look into the matter but he never did.

As clearly as if she'd seen it with her own eyes, the scene played out in her mind like a magic lantern show. There he was, her sweet boy, stepping along the scaffolding on a bright new morning, with a heavy hod on his shoulder full of bricks. She'd made a pad for him, a cushion to strap on under his shirt because the loaded hod chafed his skin and made it bleed. He was whistling, cheerful because Fox had promised to change his ways, and because of the baby coming, and was looking up at the height of the walls when he stepped onto a rotten plank. His foot went through and down he came, bricks and all, twenty feet or more, landing on his back, his arms thrown out like Christ on the cross. The plank came down, too, the men on the site told her afterwards, splintered in half, wet with mould and rot and smelling like death. How on earth he hadn't seen it …

'You told me it was an accident.'

Her eyes focused. She looked at Brian's plans for his new house, at Josiah Fox's signature. 'A *convenient* accident, Brian. Pauly was a troublemaker and he was got rid of. No one dared complain about shoddy materials again. They all knew what would happen if they did.'

'You think the rotten plank was put there on purpose?'

'Of course it was.'

'But Josiah wouldn't have gone climbing scaffolding with planks of rotten wood.'

'He wouldn't have dirtied his hands, no.'

'Who was it then? I'll kill the bastard.'

She shook her head: she'd said too much. 'I don't know,' she lied, and dropped another lump of sugar into her tea, stirring it thoughtfully while he continued to frown.

'Yes, you do. Tell me who it is.'

'It's done now, Brian. It's all taken care of.'

'You're not caught up in anything bad, are you, Mary?'

'Not that I can't handle.'

'And you reckon Josiah Fox paid this bastard to do it?'

She nodded. Her brother rubbed his chin and stared at her without speaking. She shivered. What was going on in Brian's mind? Was he thinking who he knew in Fox's employ that would kill a man? He'd know if he put his mind to it. Or was he wondering how he could get out of the contract with Fox?

'You see, Mary,' he said, at last. 'I've sunk a lot of money in J. Fox and Son, a *lot* of money. What I paid out for the new house is nothing, a drop in the ocean. The man thinks of me as a friend; the firm is one of my ventures. It is in my interest that they build houses cheaper than they can sell them for, the bigger the profit the better.'

He took her breath away. She put her cup on the table before she dropped it or threw its contents at him. 'No matter who has to die?'

'I'm sorry about Pauly, so I am.'

'Sorry,' she echoed faintly.

'If I'd known …'

'If you'd known.' Her mouth hung open as she forced herself to face her brother's admission. 'What would you have done, eh, Brian? Had a word with your precious Mister Fox and got him to mend his ways? I don't think so – your profits might have suffered. You make it your business not to know.' She could hardly breathe for anger. Brian tried to calm her by saying that his new house, that she would live in, was built from the finest materials. He'd been over there yesterday and it was just grand. Not a sign of damp.

'So that's all right, is it?' she cried. 'So long as you're home and dry? Eh?' She jumped up, heedless of the tea spilling over his precious plans, screaming, 'You're a killer, you *are!*' beating at her brother's chest. 'You stand by and let it happen, as you've always done!'

He caught her fists and held her until she was quiet. 'Mary, you don't get it.'

111

'Oh, I do,' she said, her breath shuddering as she pushed away from him. 'I cannot live in your fine house, an' all those people dying – Pauly, too. It isn't right.'

He shook his head, clearly baffled. He had never given a tinker's curse for anyone but his own, not for the sufferings of those he robbed and let die, not for the hardships they had to face because of him. Never gave them another thought and not about to start now.

Years ago, she remembered, on a stormy night, they'd stood together on the high ground above Lahinch and watched a cargo ship being lashed and battered by the Atlantic ocean, going down before their eyes and the men drowning. She'd wanted to take the boat, go out to them and he had held her back. The boat was their livelihood and she his sister. Those men, who were nothing to him, had grasped at anything that might stop them going under, beam or barrel or rope or sailor. They would push any man down, their best friend even, to steal a last mouthful of air. She'd watched it happen and done nothing at all to help. Just like him, now.

She wished she'd never come to London, a terrible place; she wished she'd never come to see her brother in his true light. Life was hard enough in the old country, with smoky old peat for a fire and a useless bit of land so waterlogged it would only grow rushes and heartache. The praties and the cabbages in the backyard and the fish from the sea were all that stood between you and the grave. But it was better by far than a life of greed, where good people turned to thieving and murderers got off scot-free because people like her brother let them. She longed for home where the last trees in the land turned sideways, grown bent by the everlasting breeze off the sea, where the houses were made of stone, and limed inside and out, pure against corruption, where the women were warm and kind, and always ready with a cup of tea and craic. The men though, the men were something else altogether.

Chapter 12

By Monday Archie was at his wits' end. He'd finished a bottle of whiskey the night before, and woken this morning with sticky eyes and the headache from hell stamping about in pit boots. It was another murky day, the sky bruised and menacing, the light all wrong for painting. What he should have done, of course, was start something new, something that demanded the softness of candlelight, a still life, perhaps. But he was no Cezanne. He couldn't get excited about apples in a bowl, or twinkling bottles and glasses. He needed to be inspired by a living, breathing, blood-in-her-veins woman, and where was she? Where the hell was she?

Monday was washday and Archie generally took his laundry to the washhouse, where, for a few pence, some woman would have it clean and ready for him to collect by Friday. But today he hadn't the heart. It was skewered by guilt. He sat in his dirty clothes and wrote Mary a letter, begging forgiveness. He read the last line again and remembered, with an exasperated butt of the head, that she couldn't bloody well read, so he threw it on the fire. It turned black, soft and fragile, and blew up the chimney on a draught.

He took up a lantern, wound a scarf about his neck and tucked it into his coat. He'd go and talk to her.

As he trudged down the High Street the first snowflakes began to fall, and the squeak of pulleys accompanied his steps, as the women reclaimed their clothes from lines strung from one side of the street to the other. By the time he reached the crossroads at the bottom the snow was swirling madly, and he was walking in his own cocoon.

Mary's cottage in Coppermill Lane looked deserted: the windows blind, the chimney cold, the hollows in the roof filling with snow. He gave the door a desultory knock, waited a minute or two, and walked back to join the shivering queue for the public omnibus. It was fair to assume that she had gone back to the Kingtons, despite her misgivings. By the time it arrived at the Waterworks, the bus was creaking through snowdrifts and the horses were steaming. The driver said he was turning back. If anyone wanted to go to Woodford that night they'd have to walk. So Archie got off and lit his lamp. He would take a short cut through the forest rather than risk getting stuck in drifts.

Instead he got caught up in brambles hidden by the snow, snagging at his laces, wrapping round his boots. Once he tripped on a root and fell, sprawling, though his lantern landed safely. He rolled onto his back, and stared up into a cathedral roofed in white, with pillars and supporting beams and an absolute silence that felt like prayer. If you painted a scene like this, no one would believe you.

It was late when he arrived at the pottery.

*

Lizzie had just got Clara off to sleep. Poor girl, she'd never looked as exhausted. No, she said, wearily, Mary hadn't come back to them. She pulled the heavy blanket back across the door and it ballooned in the draught until she trapped it with a bolster. Woodsmoke from the fire in the range stung the eyes.

'You've tried her home?' She frowned at his anxiety. 'I shouldn't worry, Archie. She's probably off visiting her friend in Chingford or her brother. She said she might pop across while she had the chance.'

'Her brother?'

'The older one, Brian? He's not far away. Shoreditch, I think.'

He'd forgotten she had family in London. Of course, that was where she'd be. With renewed hope he blew out his lantern, kicked off his boots and hung his cloak across two coat-pegs to dry, explaining that they'd had a falling-out, that he hadn't seen the girl since Saturday.

'A falling-out? You mean she slapped your face and told you to put it away.'

'Not quite. She, um, she found some nude sketches I'd done of her.'

'Oh, Archie!' she cried, more in anger, he thought, than dismay, 'just as things were looking up!'

He guessed she was more worried about her own loss than his. She must have found the last few days a trial without Mary's helping hands. John, too. Since Mary's arrival the tile-maker had been able to leave Lizzie in charge of the pottery while he went out with the mule cart to see customers and drum up business. He'd even hit on the idea of selling kits – boxes of tiles, with spacers, cement and grout – and had visited local markets demonstrating how customers could transform a tired old fireplace with a new design. The day he came to Walthamstow's High Street he had sold box after box of his Japanese cherry-blossom, his cormorant and fishes, and his dragonflies and water-lilies. Mrs Reeves had asked, only the other day, when he was coming again. Mary had been good for business.

'She'll be back,' he said with more assurance than he felt. Now he was doubly penitent. It hadn't occurred to him that, because of him, the Kingtons would suffer. He sighed. His 'faux pas' with Mary had far-reaching effects.

'John not about?'

'Upstairs,' she said. But when Archie set foot on the stair, she put a hand on his arm. 'Best not.'

'Bad day?'

'You could say that.'

'I thought he was getting better.'

'No.' Looking glum, she touched her hand to her cheek and across her mouth in what seemed like a gesture of despair. Then, looking her guest square in the eyes she changed the subject. 'Let me get you a cup of tea,' she said, rushing her words as though steam-driven. 'Sit down. Have you eaten? You must be starved after walking all that way. And don't even think of trying to get back tonight. You can have Mary's bed or scrunch up on the sofa. Take your pick.'

'What's his problem?'

'You'll see.' She picked up the kettle with one hand, the water jug with the other.

Before long he was settled before the range with a hot mug of tea thawing his hands, wearing two pairs of John's socks, and she still hadn't answered him. Again that gesture, that turning away, cradling her jaw. At last she said, 'I ... oh, Archie, I feel awful burdening you with this. But I have to tell someone.'

'Lizzie, for goodness sake, this is me. If there's anything I can do ...'

'He's an addict, Archie. To laudanum. That's where he is now, sleeping the sleep.'

He made a sound of disgust and stared at the ceiling, shocked to the core. John Kington? His clear-eyed, cool-headed friend? The genial genius, who had designed some of the most beautiful tiles the world had ever seen? He could see now why Mary had been so upset. 'I thought it was insomnia and – and headaches.'

'It is, but the way he copes is to have another nip from his little brown bottle and then the pain is of hypothetical interest only.'

'Oh, Lizzie, you shouldn't have to …' He didn't finish his sentence. It was understood and beside the point, anyway. She had married John, not him, and she had to make the best of it. They both did. 'I knew he was relying on it pretty heavily when he was first injured but I assumed he'd knocked it on the head.' She winced, and he realised he'd made a dreadful pun. 'Oh, damn – sorry, sorry!'

'He does try,' she said, blinking tears at the clock on the wall. 'Sometimes he can go for days without a sniff of the stuff but the strain starts to show, bursts of temper, violence …'

'Violence?'

She turned to face him and now he saw the marks on her face. Livid red fingermarks. She'd been trying to hide them.

'He did that?'

She grimaced. 'It wasn't him. Not the real John. This is the addiction.'

'I – I … Lord, Lizzie, I had no idea, you poor girl.'

'No, it's not something we brag about,' she said with a touch of sarcasm. 'You wouldn't have known at all if you hadn't caught us on the hop.'

'Lizzie, I'm so sorry.'

'I know.' She swallowed, using her fingers to smear away the tears. 'And no, there's nothing anyone can do.' She filled her lungs with the smoky air and turned to face him with a brave smile. 'Well, Mister Price,' she said brightly, 'I must get on. Have you read the newspaper? You don't mind amusing yourself while I do the ironing?'

Newspapers were heaped on a nearby chair. As he leafed through them, he came across a sheaf of tile designs.

'These are lovely! At least the laudanum's good for something.'

'What? Oh, I'm afraid not. They're mine.'

'You're designing now?'

'Someone has to.'

'I thought opium was supposed to enhance the creative powers.'

'It does, but the market for erotic fireplace tiles is sadly limited.'

*

Mary's smell was in the pillows, in the sheets, in the towel hanging by the wash bowl. She'd rigged up a makeshift wardrobe with a broom handle wedged between the chimney breast and the outer wall, and there he found two of the dresses he'd bought her from the second-hand stall, a coat and a pair of boots. She hadn't reckoned on snow, then. But, presumably she was warm in the bosom of her family. They'd look after her.

He thought of his friend on the floor below, deeply asleep. He wondered what was going on in his head right now. From all accounts, his dreams would be vivid. Both Coleridge and Mary Shelley had written works of genius with opium swirling in their brains. The Pre-Raphaelites swore by it. So many writers and artists had lived by the drug. Died of it, too.

He thought of Lizzie, of her tile designs. Drawn with the aid of compasses and ruler, they were a pleasing mixture of mathematical and natural shapes, reminiscent of work he'd seen in the National. Art nouveau, they called it, exotic rather than erotic, strange and affecting. He could see them taking off …

He was woken by a sound, a scuffle, a cry. He lay there straining to identify the voice. Had Mary come back? Had Clara woken up? Had something happened downstairs? It was still dark, though it was hard to tell. The attic skylight was covered in snow.

'You *pig*!' Lizzie's words carried clearly on the white silence. The next sound was a porcine grunt followed a broken, 'You can stew in it by yourself.'

What had upset her?

One door closed, another opened. There was a murmur of female voices; one, a childish treble, was querulous, the other, a whisper. 'Go to sleep, baby.' Nothing more.

In the dim grey morning, more sensed than seen, the sound of the shovel against the well-cover woke him and the cockerel, both. Like him, the creature sounded confused. Lizzie couldn't need more water already?

'Help yourself to bread and cheese,' she flung at him as he arrived in the scullery. 'Tea's in the pot.' She looked sleep-starved and raddled. Hair loose, dressing gown hardly knotted, boots wet with snow. The place was full of steam as large kettles of water brewed on the kitchen range. The copper was alight. Was it washday again?

'What's up?'

She held up her hands: don't ask.

'Lizzie?'

A heavy sigh. 'Your friend, the pig upstairs – so out of it he can't control himself. Sweet dreams, wet dreams, it's all one to him. Another mess on the sheets for me to scrape off and boil. God knows what's in his head to give him loose bowels. But one thing's for sure – he's not going to clean up after himself in that state, is he?'

'Let me help.'

'Fine. You'll need a peg for your nose.'

*

The room stank like a midden and Lizzie hugged her stomach and dry-retched. 'No,' she said, recovering with a rueful smile, but looking pasty. 'It wouldn't help, on top of everything.'

119

Archie went to open the window straight away, but the practical wife insisted on lighting a fire first. John was to be stripped naked and washed. He'd freeze to death in the raw air. Though maybe that wouldn't be such a bad thing, she added caustically.

Between them they got John out of bed and onto a chair with newspaper beneath him. Then Lizzie tenderly cleaned and washed him by candlelight, while Archie stripped the bed.

'See, I have two babies, Archie,' she declared, 'though one's out of baby clothes now.'

This was what Mary had to put up with, Archie realised. This was what she hated about John Kington. And of course, this was why the Kingtons would never visit him and stay overnight, however many invitations he sent. So many things explained. He made a vow to himself, as he wiped and dried the rubber sheet, never to touch the drug. His dreams were pretty enough.

Back in bed, clean and tidy and smelling sweet, John was still comatose. Lizzie picked up the pile of soiled bedding, dumped it out on the landing, picked up the empty enamel wash-bowl and began loading it with the scrubbing brush, face flannel, carbolic soap.

Archie struggled with a window frame swollen with ice. When at last he succeeded in opening it, he stood for a moment or two, breathing in great gulps of fresh air, even though it seared his lungs and stung his nostrils. Snow was piled deep on the sill and clinging like moss to the brickwork. Looked like he was here for the day.

He turned to her. 'You can't go on like this, Lizzie.'

'What can I do? I can't abandon him to his little brown mistress.' She nodded at the bottle on the night table. 'Much as I'd like to. I keep hoping it will get better, that he'll come back to me. But I don't know that he ever will …' Tears ran unchecked down her cheeks, her nose, her chin, and Archie, unable to gather both her and her cleaning materials into his arms, took out his handkerchief and wiped her face.

'Oh, Archie,' she mumbled, leaning her forehead on his shoulder, 'what am I going to do?' With an effort she pulled away to stare at the shifting and sparking fire as if there were hope there.

'Mama, Mama …' Clara padded barefoot across the cold floor.

'All right, darling. I'm coming. Take that bucket of dirty water downstairs, Archie, there's a dear.'

Someone once said, probably his mother in a sentimental mood, that no matter how much a woman loves her husband, she loves her children more. So Clara must have been loved more than words could say.

Chapter 13

'Oh no, dear, I can't see you today. I don't see no one without an appointment.'

As Mary started back down the steps, heavy-hearted, her feet dragging, the woman addressed her again. 'How far gone are you, dear?'

She didn't know how to answer her. It might have been fear or grief or lack of sleep that made it seem as though the woman was talking gibberish. Frowning, she gestured across the chilly street to where the bus had dropped her. 'I – I started out from Walthamstow this morning and then to Shoreditch. Now here. A fair few miles, I shouldn't wonder.'

'Eh? Walthamstow, you say?'

Mary explained that she had been sent by a Mrs Ives of Hoe Street, who gave her thruppence for the fare.

'Winnie sent you?'

Mary returned to the woman in the doorway a little more hopefully, and presented the letter.

'Why didn't you say so, you silly girl? Getting me all mixed up. I *thought* I didn't have another appointment 'til three o'clock.' She opened the door wide onto a dark hallway. 'Come in, come in, it's too cold to stand about. Only best be quiet, eh? I've a lady akip up there. Her gen'leman'll be back for her at eleven. Come through and we'll sort you something out. I might be able to fit you in next week.'

Untimely darkness promised snow and the woman picked up an oil lamp to light their way through the house. Mary felt the walls of the hallway swallowing her up, pushing her inexorably towards a small dim room at its end, so uncomfortably full of things it reminded her of an overstuffed stomach. Two huge wing chairs before the fire took up most of the space but Mrs Ferris had also managed to squeeze in an upright piano and a music-stool and, in the window, a desk and chair. In all the houses she'd cleaned, Mary had never seen so many knick-knacks and folderols, aspidistras and birdcages. Every shelf and tallboy had its own lace trim. Even the gloomy paintings were fringed with tassels and it not even Christmas.

Mrs Ferris put the oil lamp on the mantelpiece and motioned her visitor to a chair, sinking heavily into the other with a grunt of fatigue. After checking the seal, she prised open the letter and moved her glasses down her nose. As she read, her frown deepened; she raised her eyes to Mary's and sank her head into her shoulders in a show of embarrassment.

'What must you think of me, dear? At cross-purposes, wasn't we? There was I thinking you was one of my ladies and all the while you was, well, come to lend an 'and ...' She skewered her large behind further down into the chair. 'Winnie knows how I'm fixed, dear, what with my last assistant leaving me so sudden. Thought she could start up on her own, and good luck to her.'

Mary noted the word 'assistant' and swallowed. She'd imagined she'd be doing plain and simple skivvying for an elderly woman on her own, be a maid-of-all-work, but 'assistant' might mean something more.

'See, I can't do it all, dear, not run a business and the house, as well. Not at my age, with screws in all me joints.'

Screws? More like nuts and bolts. As she held out her hands for Mary to inspect the girl winced, seeing the knobby joints of acute arthritis. Mrs Ferris prised off a mishapen shoe to display a throbbing bunion, corns and hammer-toes. Mary took a slow breath as an idea occurred to her. She needed this refuge.

'Why don't I fix those toenails while I'm here? Would you have some scissors or a nail file?'

'Oh,' said the woman, startled. 'Oh,' and then, 'bottom shelf.' She indicated a low cupboard wedged into the space on the other side of the chimney breast. Mary found the tools she needed, pushed her chair in closer, then sat forward so that Mrs Ferris could rest her foot on her lap. The old woman kept further comments about this fortuitous turn of events strictly to herself.

After the third or fourth thick yellow toenail had been successfully filed down and trimmed, she piped up, as though nothing out of the ordinary were happening, 'You said, "while I'm here …"'

'Sure an' I might not suit.'

'I see.' As Mary snipped away, the woman said, 'You're a good girl, Irish or no. You spots what needs doing and you gets on with it. I see what my sister likes about you. What will you do if I don't take you on, eh?'

'I don't know, missus,' she whispered, flicking a nail paring into the fire.

'Speak up, dear, everything's going – hearing, eyes, wits.' Her little joke.

Mary cleared her throat. 'It'd have to be the workhouse, again.'

'They've taken you in before, dear?'

'Once,' she admitted, hanging her head. 'After my husband died.'

'A bad time.'

124

'The worst.'

'But you rallied, you see. That's what I like. A bit of pluck. You pulled yourself up by your bootstraps.'

Bootstraps? If she had any, mebbes. If Mrs Ferris wouldn't take her on she'd be poorly off, so she would.

The operation complete and no snags, no complaints, Mary sat back in her chair and, while she waited for her hostess to re-read the letter, surreptitiously dug her hands down the sides of the cushion to wipe off the old woman's smell. Suddenly Mrs Ferris's glasses appeared again over the top of the note, with curious eyes behind them.

'Winnie tells me the police might be wanting a chat with you.'

Mary's hand flew to her throat, reminded of the horrors she'd witnessed. If Dolly were dead, the police could be out looking for her right now. The neighbours would be sure to say they'd seen her. Fear slipped in sideways and set her pulses racing. Best be honest. Forming her words as clearly as she could, so the woman would be in no doubt, she told her the same as she'd told Mrs Ives, about having to leave Dolly to her fate. 'But he might have left her alive, missus,' she said, without much hope, 'since it was me he was after.'

'What's he want *you* for?' the woman demanded.

'He was sent by a terrible man, Mrs Ferris, a man in prison who made his money selling women and children into slavery.'

'So you ran off. And who can blame you, dear?' A thought struck her. 'Here, 'e don't know you come 'ere to me? No, course not,' she re-assured them both, reaching across and patting Mary's hand. 'Oh, you're shaking like a leaf, dear. Just a minute …' She levered herself out of the chair and limped to the piano. Mary watched her in confusion. Surely she wasn't going to play them a tune to perk up their spirits? The woman was a puzzle, sure enough. But instead of sitting on the piano stool Mrs Ferris opened its lid and removed from its depths a bottle of liquor and two glasses. 'I don't usually, not so early in the day. But my next lady ain't till three, and you looks like you could do with something to settle your nerves.'

She poured two small glasses of the dark liquid and gave one to Mary. 'Madeira,' she said, as Mary sniffed at it suspiciously. 'Sip it slow and wrap it round your tongue. It's strong stuff. But don't you go getting a taste for it, dear. I keeps it for emergencies and I don't want to find the level gone down after you've been in here doing the grate or feeding the canary.'

Mary gazed at her benefactress over the rim of the glass. 'So you'll take me on, will you, missus?' she hardly dared to ask.

'If Winnie reckons you'll do, you'll do. Irish never done *me* no harm. And we widder women must stick together. But I do have to know a bit more about you, dear.'

Mary nodded, sipped the sweet, fruity liquid and coughed so violently her new employer had to slap her on the back. She tried again. This time she didn't cough and the glow flooded her veins very pleasantly indeed.

'Now, dear,' said Mrs Ferris, resuming her seat, and downing her own drink without any trouble at all, 'you'd best tell me what you can do. I need someone who can turn their 'and to most things.'

So the snow drifted past the window and Mary, warm and safe by the fire, told the older woman how she'd more or less run the Kingtons' household while the master and mistress tended their pottery.

In a room over their heads a bell tinkled.

'That's her. Awake and ready for tea and biscuits. I'll show you where.'

It seemed that Mary was to start work immediately. The kitchen adjoined the room they were in, down three steps. Mrs Ferris lit the gas lamp on the wall, revealing a floor tiled in black and white stone, easy to keep clean. There were plenty of saucepans hung on the walls, copper jelly moulds and colanders, a dresser stacked with crockery, a scrubbed table and a chair to sit on while you sliced your cabbage or scraped your carrots.

In the immediate left-hand corner was a coal cupboard.

'When the coalman comes be sure and count the bags when he brings them through, dear. He'll "do" you else. You can count, can you?' She nodded happily as Mary reassured her.

The kettle was bubbling on the range, steaming up the windows and a plain oval mirror close by.

'Black-leading of a Tuesday – tin and brushes under the sink.' She indicated the copper built into a corner of the room. 'And laundry, as and when needed. We does things a bit different here. You'll see, dear.'

In the opposite corner was the pantry, stocked with bins and jars and packets of food, eggs in a bucket of isinglass, a meat safe and a covered cheese dish on a marble slab. The mice would have a hard time of it. Under the window was a large butler's sink with whites in soak and a smell of bleach. And, joy of joys, a hand pump for water and a pipe to an outside drain. No trips out to the yard, no lugging heavy buckets through, no cellars. Oh, this was easy living altogether.

Mary took off her shawls and her hat and hung them up behind the door, then donned the long white apron and the frilly cap she found there, picking a long brown hair from the cap before putting it on. She rubbed a patch of mirror to bob a look at herself. And didn't she look the part, a proper housemaid? She let out a sigh of happiness. As part of this household, for two

127

shillings a week and bed and board, no one would find her, not Streeter or anyone else. She might even grow to like it, and never more yearn for the old places, the sea and the mighty cliffs of Moher and the Burren carpeted with flowers in the springtime.

Pushing up her sleeves, Mary set to work and in a few moments had her hands washed, the tea made and was following Mrs Ferris up the stairs with a tray. They came to a door on which her mistress knocked.

'Are you presentable, dear?'

On the narrow bed, as pale as the sheet she sat on, a young woman in a nightdress slowly raised her head. 'Is it done?' she murmured. Her cheeks were wet.

'It is, dear. All bar the shouting, as they say. I've told you what to expect, haven't I? Plenty of newspaper. Bundle it up and burn it, dear. Think of it as fish heads or butcher's lights, a shame and a waste but better luck next time. Now you drink up your tea the girl has made and by the time you're dressed your young man will be here, ready to take you home.'

Mary's eyes were open wide. What had happened here? Was it, could it be that Mrs F ... that this young woman had ...? She tried to breathe normally, tried to still the jiggling of the spoon in the saucer as she handed the hot drink to the girl, whose own hand shook. Mary stared at that hand, white and plump and no wedding ring.

Sure enough the doorbell sounded and Mary went downstairs to answer it. A gentleman was stamping the snow off his boots. He banged his hat against his coat and gave it to her with his gloves. 'Who shall I say?' she enquired, lowering her eyes.

'That's all right, Quinn,' Mrs Ferris interrupted from the landing. 'You can come up, sir. She'll need an 'and down the stairs.'

From the hall, Mary could hear the murmur of crisp, businesslike voices. Five minutes later Mrs Ferris's lady crept gingerly down, one stair at a time, gripping the banister with one hand and holding on tight to the man in front with the other. Her face was drained, her eyes dead. Behind them Mrs Ferris was tucking a wad of notes into her reticule. Mary was in no doubt now. What was going on here was a sin, so it was.

As Mrs Ferris closed the door behind them, she said shortly, 'No names, no pack drill, Quinn. Best not.'

*

The bed-springs were clean of bugs. She let the mattresses drop back into place and spread her hands over the flowery eiderdown. She had never had an eiderdown before, plump with feathers. Her room was perfect. No cobwebs, no cracks in the ceiling. No fleas. There was a fire laid all ready to light, a coal scuttle, a proper wardrobe to hang up her dresses when she fetched them from Woodford, and a rack for shoes! There was a washstand, a chamber pot, and curtains at the window. Everything she could ever have wanted. After all her troubles she had landed on her feet.

Mrs Ferris wasn't so bad. Kind, like her sister, Mrs Ives. In fact, they were alike in many ways, besides their florid looks and dyed black hair. They were both widows, both ran businesses to keep the wolf from the door and both liked the womb-like comfort of small, stuffy rooms. But there the similarity ended for, whereas Mrs Ives was a knitter of warm comfort, Mrs Ferris was an unraveller, an unmaker, her trade one that every good Catholic should abhor as the Devil's own work. But what choice did a poor girl have who was hounded from pillar to post by lustful men?

Mrs Ferris had explained to her that she would be required, at first, merely to be on hand in case of complications, to watch and

129

learn. There were perhaps two or three cases a week, sometimes more, sometimes less. In between appointments Mary would cook and clean and generally do what was needed on a daily basis. The house was larger than the Kingtons' with more furniture to dust and polish, but she considered she was fortunate.

After a bit of bread and cheese and a quick cat's lick with a feather duster, at three o'clock she was ready to show the next client into the 'operating' room where hot water and towels were ready and Mrs Ferris's instruments spread out neatly on a side table. The bedlinen was clean on and a fresh nightgown hanging up behind the screen. Everything was spotless.

The lady put on the nightie and lay down on the bed and Mrs Ferris showed Mary how to drip a tincture onto a pad she'd put over the lady's nose and mouth. Five minutes to allow her to go 'under' and then they pulled the nightie up 'out of harm's way', slipped a rubber mat under her backside, and screwed a wooden board across the bed, with straps to hold her dainty white feet in place. Then they put on rubber aprons and the old woman went to work.

Drip, drip.

When Mary saw the things being inserted into the lady's insides, things that reminded her of shoe-horns and button-hooks, and heard Mrs Ferris explaining what she was doing with each, she had to shut her ears and look away. This was a mistake. This of all jobs was not for her.

'No, my girl,' instructed Mrs Ferris firmly, 'you gotta watch, you gotta take it all in, 'cause there'll come a day when I won't be able to do this no more. You'll be down my end and I'll be up there doing the dripping.'

Never in a million years!

Drip, drip.

When Mary saw Mrs Ferris' face rising over the swollen belly like a full moon, concentration in every wrinkle, when she saw her knobby old fingers pressing on the lady's soft skin that still bore the marks of her stays, palpating, almost listening, she had to hold on tight to the bedpost and try not to think.

Drip, drip.

When the nozzle of the suction pump went in and strings of blood and slime came out, when the lady groaned, 'No-o-o,' even though she was fast asleep, Mary felt the tears running down her own face. Felt her own knees soften, her insides drag in sympathy.

'That's enough now, Quinn. Don't do that no more. The drip, dear, that's enough. Don't wanna overdo it, do we?'

'No,' she heard herself agree faintly. No, they didn't want to overdo it.

And then it was Mary's job to swab the lady down, pad her privates and tie the tapes, tidy the bed and pull the nightie decent. Then she put the rubber mat and aprons in a bucket to scrub, took the soiled towels and the coversheet down to the scullery and put them in the sink with those from the morning and added a spot of bleach. In an hour there would be no trace of blood. In a day or two the sheets would be sparkling, boiled, starched and ironed, and on the bed ready for the next customer.

But she wouldn't be here. Holy Mother, her knees were still weak, wanting to fold up under her to beg God's forgiveness. Or she would go to hell, she surely would.

After her tea, the lady left on the arm of her young man, disappearing into the blizzard as if they had never been. As Mary closed the door her employer came creaking down the stairs. Now was her chance.

'Mrs Ferris, I don't think I can …'

'Course you can, dear.' Her voice had a steely edge to it.

'But it's a mortal sin, so it is.'

'It's an act of kindness to a poor woman who never asked for all this. It's the man God won't forgive for taking advantage of her in the first place.'

'It's killing an unborn child.'

Her employer's eyes were hard black coals. 'What unborn child? I never see an unborn child. Did *you*?'

'But when she gets home ...'

'That's her business – a miscarriage. Common enough.'

'Oh Mrs Ferris, I'm sorry but ...'

Mrs Ferris opened her hands, as if freeing a bird. 'You must do as you think fit, dear. It's a shame 'cause I thought you would suit. Just light the copper before you go, dear, and rinse the whites for boiling. I can probably manage after that. If you wouldn't mind washing up the tea things and hanging up your cap and apron.'

Mary did as she was bid – tidied her room, packed her bag and put on her hat, Mammy's shawl and then the one Mrs Ives had given her. Felt in her pocket for money and calculated that she had just about enough for the fare back to the Kingtons. Better the devil you know, she thought, coming downstairs and opening the front door.

There was snow past her ankles! The street was deserted. No buses, no nothing, and what would she do but wander the dark streets in her thin shoes, getting wetter and colder and more and more lost? They'd find her in the morning dead as a doornail.

'God works in mysterious ways,' said Mrs Ferris, coming up behind her and closing the door to the icy world, 'His wonders to perform.'

Chapter 14

It had stopped snowing and a pale sun was out. While Lizzie boiled the sheets, Archie, with Clara at his heels, saw to the mule and chickens, chopped wood, cleared the yard, spread ashes to avoid slipping, built a snowman and threw snowballs at his paper hat.

John lurched downstairs as they were sitting down to a midday meal, looking more sheepish than the mutton stew they were eating. 'It snowed! And Archie, old fellow – how long've you been here?'

'He comed in the night when we was asleep,' Clara volunteered.

'Why? The floozy's gone and not before time. Oh, of course ...' He tapped his nose sickeningly. 'Being Irish she couldn't help herself but blather about my night-time frolics, and you came to see for yourself.'

'She didn't say a word, John. She just ran off. I came to see if she was here.'

'Sounds t'me like you're tied to her little finger, Archie, old chap. Good riddance to her, I say.' He fell into his chair, picked up his knife and fork and sat, fists on the table, waiting for his food. 'So now you know the worst,' he drawled. He seemed almost euphoric. 'A regular sideshow, aren't I, Lizzie?'

Lizzie quietly served him a dish of the steaming soup and passed him the cruet. 'Powdered glass?' she said, with a bitter smile. 'Arsenic?'

His hand shook as he took the salt. 'No more'n I deserve,' he confided in Archie, his eyes glistening with maudlin tears. 'Lizzie shoul'n't have to purrup with this,' he slurred.

'Oh God,' sighed Lizzie. 'Go back to bed.'

'You should get help,' said Archie. 'Get yourself admitted to a sanatorium or something. They have places where they'll look after you while you break the habit.'

'Pay a fortune for a – a strai' jacket an' – an' a padded cell? You're joking.'

'I'll do it for nothing,' said his wife. 'Lock you in the woodshed when you start getting the shakes and shove your food under the door. You can rant and rave as much as you like in there. I'll let you out when you're nice.'

He waved away her threats. 'It won' happen again.'

'Pie-crusts and promises,' she said.

'No, I mean it, Lizzie.'

Her smile was grim as she turned back to the little girl in the high chair. 'Come on, sweetheart, one more mouthful and you're done.'

'No, Mama, no put Pa in the woodshed.'

'Not even for a little while?' she wheedled.

The child shook her head firmly.

'Oh, all right, then. Now,' as if it were some sort of pact they'd made, 'one more mouthful. Good girl.'

When Clara had finished her meal to Lizzie's satisfaction, they went upstairs for a story and a nap and a heavy silence fell between the two men. John loaded and lit his pipe. Archie leaned his elbows on the table and stared glumly at the drawing he'd made the night before with Clara's crayons. It was a profile, obscuring the bruising on her right cheek. Lizzie had pinned it on the wall beside the range. Her voice rose and fell in the room over their heads.

John regarded Archie quizzically through the fragrant smoke, before removing the stem from his lips. 'Come on then, let's have it.'

'What?'

'You're going to give me a lecture, aren't you?'

'I wouldn't waste my breath.' He shrugged. 'You know what you have to do, and you can, I know you can. Just as three years ago you decided you weren't going to bloody die under a holly bush. You beat those murderers and you can beat this.'

John turned away. 'I didn't beat them,' he muttered. 'This'll kill me, finish the job for them.'

'Well, don't let it. For Christ's sake, do you want them to win?' Archie felt like shaking his friend, forcing him to show a bit of fight, but he had to keep his voice down. 'What about Lizzie? She doesn't want you dead.'

John heaved a deep and sorry sigh, self-pity wrapping him round like a cloak in water, getting heavier, dragging him down. 'She'd be glad to see the back of me. I'm draining her dry.'

Archie couldn't deny it. 'She wants you well, John, alive and well. She's giving all she's got to keeping your marriage afloat.'

'Waste of time. It's finished, sunk without trace. She should take Clara and leave. Go home to her people. Unless – unless *you* want her …'

'*What!*'

The man was crazy. His brain was addled, his expression sly and crafty. 'You've always fancied her, Archie. With me dead you can have her. I bequeath her to you.'

'Don't talk such utter rot, John. You aren't going to die. Why should you? And Lizzie loves *you*, she always has.'

'She thought I was the better bet, Arch. You were a dreamer, going nowhere. At least I had my father's pottery behind me. I just had to carry on in his footsteps and she'd be made. But I can't do it any more. The business is going to the dogs. I've lost the will. I can't even design – and *she* surely can't. Just look at these monstrosities!' With a sneer of disgust he shook the sheaf of Lizzie's designs at Archie.

'What's wrong with them? I can see them working well. Bright colours, highly glossed, the tiles could be just what the business needs …'

'Dross.' Ignoring Archie's shocked protests, he ripped the drawings across and across again, levered off the lid of the stove and dropped them into the flames.

Archie fumed, thinking of the care Lizzie had taken over the designs. That her own husband should … She was right – he had changed beyond recall. How could she bear to live with this boor?

Sick or not, John read his mind. 'It's the way I am now,' he said smugly. 'They've done for me, those Irish bastards!' He sat down at the table and propped his head on his hands. 'Don't stare at me like that – I'm not a freak show!'

Archie was ready to leave now, snow or no snow. John was beyond saving. When Lizzie came down he'd make some excuse and go. He pulled a newspaper off the chair and sat down. It was Saturday's *Clarion*. He scanned the headlines but hardly saw them for the thoughts whirling in his head. What about having John committed? What about forcibly depriving him of the drug? Locking him in a room to dry out? Persuading Lizzie to leave her husband, let him fend for himself? He shook the paper, tried to concentrate on the news. Something about Gladstone and his second bid to settle the Irish question. Would Gladstone resign again? Would John ever recover?

And then something caught his eye that drove every other thought from his mind. He stared at the small paragraph near the bottom of the page. The heading: *Release for East End Traders*.

The journalist described how experts had scoured Cedric Carrington's accounts, how they had gone through his files and those of everyone else implicated in the child slavery case, including the ship's master, but had found nothing, not one scrap of evidence on which they could hold the merchants.

The money paid into Streeter's account by his backers was just that, perfectly legitimate funding for the voyage of the steamship *The Eastern Star* to Sydney, Australia and back again. It bought fuel, crew, food and drink, livestock, all the supplies needed for a long voyage to the colonies. As for the goods to be traded, there were the usual bolts of linen, tea, coffee, salt, medicines, artefacts, soap, but nothing remotely connected with child prostitution or slavery. Those children in *The Eastern Star's* hold were a dozen or so of Wapping's homeless urchins having a game, playing at stowaways. Thankfully they'd been discovered before the ship had set sail. Little scallywags! It was all a terrible misunderstanding.

The accusation that Partridge had supplied children from the orphanage was completely scotched. The orphans at Saint Anne's were well and accounted for. And when questioned, every child said that they missed their own parents but were grateful, indeed happy, to be raised by dear Mister Partridge and his helpers. At least they had a chance of making a decent life.

So the charges were dropped and Norbert Streeter, Cedric Carrington, Lionel Partridge and the rest were released back into society without a stain on their characters.

Archie's palms were sticky. Mary wouldn't have read the papers.

She couldn't. And this was Saturday's, the day Mary had fled from his studio. Streeter had been released on Friday, the day before. He'd have had plenty of time to think about his creature comforts, about satisfying his lusts. He might even have her by now. Maybe that was where she was. Oh God.

'I have to go, John,' he said, throwing down the paper and getting to his feet.

'Not on my account …'

'Nothing to do with you. Nobby Streeter's on the loose again.'

He glanced at what his friend had been drawing and froze. No tile design this, unless the man had gone completely off his head. He had drawn a room with damp peeling paper, a cold, bare floor, with knots and uneven grain, the boards disappearing to a vanishing point somewhere beneath a rumpled bed. Barely covered by a ragged quilt, a naked sleeper tossed and turned, her slender arm thrown across her face. A man in a frockcoat was leaning over the bed, a man whose arm was raised and whose hand held an open cut-throat razor.

'Branching out, are we, John?' enquired Lizzie, coming up behind Archie, resting her chin on his shoulder. He could smell her warmth, the soap on her. Could almost have turned his head and kissed her poor cheek. 'But look, you've forgotten the price.'

'What?'

She took his pencil and wrote *1d* in the corner. 'It's the cover for a penny-blood, isn't it? In rather poor taste, if I might say so.'

'How d'you mean?'

'I mean Archie's worried witless about Mary, and here you've drawn her having her throat cut.'

'Why should it be her?' His eyes were round with assumed innocence. When he turned to catch Archie's horrified reaction, his puerile grin was sickening.

Chapter 15

He found Tyrell alone and tetchy. Yes, he'd heard the news about the freeing of the East End scum at the weekend. Yes, it was a travesty, but these things happened. Unless they could catch the buggers red-handed and find witnesses willing to testify, there really wasn't much hope of putting them behind bars for good and all.

'What about – I mean, do you think they'll work it out – that I was the informer?'

'Why should they suspect you more than any other? There must be a few who were in the know, at the bank ...' He counted them off on his fingers. 'The workers at the orphanage, servants, drivers, other gang members with a grudge, the ship owner, the captain, the crew. Any one of them might have objected to the trade. No, you should just carry on as normal, keeping your head down, painting your pictures, worming your way into their confidence.' He gave his moustache a downward stroke and Archie a sideways look before adding, 'And keeping your ear to the ground.'

'I can't.'

But Tyrell wasn't listening. 'We could put you on the payroll, do you see? You could be our inside man, our undercover agent, reporting any new developments.'

'You're joking!' said Archie with a mirthless laugh. 'Think about it – another operation is foiled, the police turning up out of the blue, arresting everyone in sight. Don't you think I'd be top of their list of suspects, especially after this last fiasco – the artist who happened to be painting in the next room? They're corrupt, not stupid, Frank.'

Tyrell's mouth twisted in disappointment. 'I had to ask. We need all the help we can get.'

Archie stared at his wet boots, chewing his lip. He was a jobbing artist, taking work where he could. He wasn't a policeman. He wasn't even an upright citizen, couldn't remember the last time he was in church. Granted, he hated the rotten business some of his customers were involved in, but it put a roof over his head, money in his pocket. Dirty money, he reminded himself, but what Tyrell was asking him to do was bloody dangerous. He could wind up dead.

As if answering his thoughts, the telegraph machine started chattering in the corner. Tyrell left his post to take down its message, his dejected spine straightening to martial attention as he translated the Morse 'dits' and 'dahs' into English words.

Archie took a breath. He needed to report Mary missing. In the light of Streeter's release, it was important that she be found as soon as possible. He would put it to the sergeant as soon as he'd finished.

Tyrell looked up, his irritation magically transformed into beaming bonhomie. 'Don't stand there shivering, man, warm yourself at the fire. Good God, your trouser bottoms are soaked.'

There was a pause in transmission. Tyrell took the opportunity to explain that he had been waiting for this particular message for a long time. But Inspector O'Connell over in Ireland had been busy on another case, Irish nationalists or something.

But now it was here.

'See, you saying Brian Rooney's well off now, dressing the part and that, give us a bit of an idea. Do you suppose his poor old mum over in the old country is getting the benefit?'

Archie remembered how they'd traced the mother through an address on the back of a family photograph they'd found at his lodgings. She'd maintained that after the Epping murder her son had stopped sending money home, that he was probably dead. But Archie had proved otherwise.

Tyrell turned to the machine, and wrote down a few more words before the chattering abruptly stopped. 'By crikey!' he cried. 'Come and look at this, man!'

Having just started to thaw out, Archie was reluctant to leave the fire. Nevertheless, he found himself looking over Tyrell's shoulder and reading:

BRIDGET ROONEY SITTING PRETTY STOP RECEIVES REGULAR ANON MONEY ORDERS FROM VARIOUS ENGLISH POST OFFICES STOP ALL HER CHILDREN HELPING OUT STOP

'We could have her for receiving,' the sergeant remarked, back to stroking his moustache, his eyes slitting at the prospect of arresting some poor old Irish biddy.

Lord, thought Archie, the law's take on things was certainly different from his. He carried on reading:

BRIAN AND MARY IN LONDON AREA STOP IRENE AND GERALD IN MANCHESTER STOP KATHLEEN IN HOLY ORDERS LIVERPOOL STOP CONCEPTUA HOME WITH MAM STOP MICHAEL DECEASED STOP HOPE THIS HELPS STOP P OCONNELL

'So he's a good son to his old Mum,' Tyrell sneered. 'She'll be well pleased when she finds out how he paid for her new sofa.'

Archie shrugged. 'She certainly has a brood: one in Holy Orders, one a white slaver. Where do the others fit in, I wonder?'

The machine started up again, and Archie went back to the fire. Over in the corner the sergeant became more and more excited. 'By crikey,' he muttered again and, 'would you Adam and Eve it?' He tore off the postscript and, with a prodigious smirk across his face said, 'Just cast your eyes over this, Archie.' His eyes were gleaming. 'This'll put the cat among the pigeons.'

Archie read it, gasped and read it again:

IRENE ROONEY MARRIED ALBERT FRICKERS STOP MARY ROONEY MARRIED PAUL QUINN DECEASED STOP

It was worse every time he read it. He couldn't speak.

'Which makes little Mary Quinn,' Frank Tyrell crowed, '*Mrs* Mary Quinn, our star witness in the Wylie case, Brian Rooney's blasted sister!'

Cogs and spindles clicked and spun in his brain, as the mainspring unwound. His sister! *'Leave her be!'* rang in his ears. The fight. Not over Kitty O'Grady at all, but Rooney's very own sister that Archie had painted surrounded by smutty photographs, drunken bolsters, discarded shawls. Was the pretty immigrant dreaming of home or waiting for her next client? Presumably she was now safe under Brian's roof in Shoreditch. She'd probably told him all about Streeter's perverted interest in her and got him to have a quiet word in his leader's ear.

So, in one way, Archie could stop worrying. In another, what was she telling her beloved Brian about the drawings of a certain randy young artist? Could he expect a visit from the brother? He rubbed his nose protectively.

'That family photo, Frank, the one Rooney left behind at his lodgings …'

The file was already out and the photo easily found. Head to head, policeman and artist pored over it.

'Which one do you think is her?' Tyrell wondered.

'Third youngest, she said. So not the baby or the toddler. That'd be her brother, Michael. This little girl, then,' he said, stabbing a finger at an elfin child who scowled at the camera as if casting an evil spell. Good Lord, he knew that look. That was Mary, no doubt about it. The family resemblance was striking. They all had that same set to the eyes, the same nose, the same jaw line.

Were they similar in other ways, too? Rooney had the devil in him certainly, opting for a life of crime and even now he was rich, investing money in the child-slavery project. And Mary was a damned liar.

No wonder she had been able to describe Tommo Hegarty so accurately. He was her brother's pal, his sidekick. Mary must have shaken Tommo's hand, poured him tea, handed him his hat and coat, not to say his cudgel. She might even have kissed the bastard goodnight.

Yet, his thoughts ran slower, she didn't hesitate to inform on him, implicate him in Daniel Wylie's murder.

'What's she up to?' he said aloud.

'Eh?' said Tyrell.

'She *knows* Tommo Hegarty, must do. She knew damn fine it was him outside Wylie's but, even so, even though he's her brother's friend, she's willing to testify against him.'

Tyrell smacked his fist into his palm. 'More than that,' he said, 'she wants him dead, hanged for murder.' A smile like a snake's spread across his face. 'We'll have you in for questioning, Mrs Quinn …'

'Ah, no, you won't, I'm afraid.'

'Eh?'

'It's what I came to tell you.' He cleared his throat with an effort. 'Mary's gone missing. I've been looking for her. She wasn't at home when I called yesterday and she's not at the safe house. My fault,' he confessed, 'I – I'm afraid I upset her and she ran off.'

The change in the policeman was immediate. The joy and the self-congratulation fell away. His shoulders sagged then, with blazing eyes, he exploded. 'Unbelievable!' He held up hands to heaven. It was the first time Archie had seen him lose his temper. 'I trusted you to keep an eye on her, you moron!'

Archie's regret was deep-felt. He knew he'd let everyone down, himself included. 'The people I sent her to believe she's gone to visit her brother in Shoreditch.' The sergeant's eyes were still blazing. 'It has to be the same brother, doesn't it? Brian, I mean.' He nodded at the contraption in the corner. 'Seeing that Michael is dead and Gerald is in Manchester.'

'Shoreditch? It's like a blasted rabbit warren over there. And organised. They got hidden passages, lookouts, secret signals. Someone sees the police and they knock three times on their wall, the neighbours hear it, do the same. It goes all along the street and your villain's out the back, over the garden wall, and away. We'll never find 'em in Shoreditch!'

'Or she might be home by now. Perhaps one of your men could take a little stroll down the road and check.'

'Damn and blast you, Archie Price! You have the gall to—' Tyrell spun his book around for Archie to see. 'Take a look at that, boy – that's today's "to do" list, that is. Nearly five o' bloody clock and still no end in sight. I've got a man off sick. I've got two officers in the back room writing up a sheep-stealing at Chapel End. I've got young Beckett trying to make sense of a snarl-up at Bell Corner – brewers' dray overturned in the snow, beer all over the shop and traffic at a standstill. I've got a drunk in the cells with a broken head. I've got a petty theft, a stabbing and the two sheep stealers, all needing to have statements taken. I've got thieves and murderers vanishing into thin air, dogs missing, children missing, jewellery missing, I've got my bloody work cut out. If you want to check on Mary flaming Quinn, Archie Price, I suggest you do it yourself!'

Chapter 16

All this way down the slush-puddled High Street for nothing! She hadn't come back. Still at her rich brother's, if she'd any sense. But suppose she had, suppose she was lying in there with her throat cut? The windows were dark, but when Archie tried the door it was bolted on the inside, so someone must be about. Archie rapped harder, threw snowballs up at the bedroom window. Get up, and let me know you're alive!

Damn John for putting morbid ideas in his head.

The pane of glass broke with a single blow from the half brick he found. Carefully he pulled out the jagged slivers, reached through to unfasten the catch, and pushed up the lower sash.

Hooking one leg up to the sill, he found his way blocked by a piece of furniture jammed up against the window and loaded with all sorts.

It took a moment to identify a sewing machine and a garment in the making. He set the lantern down in the snow and, after a tussle with the blind, managed to push the table away from the wall, setting off a tinkling avalanche of bobbins and thimbles. He straddled the window sill, ducked in his head and trunk and then brought his other leg through. There wasn't room to stand upright, the ceiling was meant for a smaller breed of man, but he recovered his lantern, pulled the window shut and crossed his fingers.

Nothing. No challenges from curious neighbours, no police whistles. Just the slats of the blind rat-tatting in the draught and muffled sounds coming through the thin walls: a baby's wailing on one side, a man aptly singing, *'Oh dear, what can the matter be?'* on the other.

Apart from the sewing-machine there was nothing whole in the entire room. Every stick of furniture sagged or leaned or was dented or sprouting stuffing. Tucked away behind a ragged door Archie found a small bed with a straw pallet, a greasy blanket and a dirty ticking pillow. A child's: no, Mary's, he realised with a start. That was the smell on her wrapper – burnt potato skins and woodsmoke, and tea brewing on the hob. Right now the fire was out and the tea stone cold, but the smell lingered.

His breath came quicker and the back of his neck prickled. There was someone behind him. He turned. She was there, over in the corner, very pale, very still, watching him!

'Mary, thank God, you're …' As he brought the lantern up, he gasped. She had no head. It was a dressmaker's dummy, with a wooden screw for a leg. What a joke! 'Oh Lord!' he breathed and misted the air.

He backed into a chair and sat down hard. It creaked on legs as unsteady as his, as he set the lantern down on an equally rickety table. In its pool of light, mouse droppings speckled a cloth and mingled with stale breadcrumbs on a plate. Dried tea leaves lined a chipped enamel mug. This meal had been eaten days before. A tin of condensed milk had been left with a spoon in it. A couple of dead flies lay embalmed in the sticky syrup. Flies. At this time of year and in this freezing temperature. Lord, what a place!

Rat-tat-tat went the blind and an icy draught blew down his neck.

Poking out from behind a jar of spills on the mantelpiece was a rent-book in the name of Dolly Brett, a pawnbroker's ticket for *'pr. white sheets, 1/6d,'* and a fading photograph of a young man clutching a tin whistle to his chest: dear departed Pauly, he presumed. There was a letter, as well, addressed to Mary, with *'c/o Leytonstone Workhouse'* scored out. Someone there had re-addressed it, sent it on here but it was still folded and tucked, with the seal intact. The workhouse! Poor Mary, there was so much he didn't know about her. The writing was clumsy, almost illegible, but he could make out another address on the back, the sender's presumably: *13A Mount Street, Bethnal Green.* He wondered if Mary was waiting for someone to read it to her. Perhaps Dolly was also illiterate.

He tucked the letter into his back pocket.

There were two more doors on the other side of the fireplace, one bolted, that opened onto a smelly back yard. Steps led down to a cellar from the other one. A cat streaked past him, meowing piteously and making straight for the tin of condensed milk. It must have been trapped down there.

So the two women spent their drab little lives in this one dilapidated room with something similar, presumably, upstairs and if the front and back doors were both bolted on the inside then that was where the person who bolted the doors must be.

As he mounted the stairs, treading quietly so as not to wake the sleeper, his lantern shook and he climbed in the company of long leaping shadows that flung themselves before him.

Archie could see a single bed pushed into the alcove created by the chimney breast. The other alcove was draped with a blanket to form a cupboard of sorts. Half-made skirts and dresses hung from hooks in the roof timbers, obscuring his view, but he could just make out a simple washstand against the far wall, with ewer and bowl. The wooden floor was bare as were the walls, there being no wallpaper, just a thin and patchy whitewash between the timbers. He stopped, listening hard through the loud banging of his heart. Had he heard a sound overhead? There it was again, a slithering and then … a flummock in the yard below. Snow sliding off the roof.

He paused to let his fright subside and then climbed the last few stairs and stood as straight as he could. It smelled up here. Really bad. And more flies. He batted them away and lifted the lantern high. Took a step into the room. Damn, he shouldn't be here. For there she was in bed, tucked up tight against the freezing cold, snuggled into a lovingly stitched patchwork quilt. But something wasn't right. He brought the lamp closer and felt his skin prickle, his stomach lurch.

Oh shit!

Her pillow was dark with blood, as were the chimney breast and the two walls. Her orange corkscrew curls lay in it.

Not Mary. Thank God, not Mary. He rocked back on his heels.

But at the same time, here was her friend, her daily companion, lying with her white and waxy face to the wall. Her throat hadn't been cut but something had been stuffed in her mouth and a large pair of dressmaking scissors protruded from her jugular. Dead as dead – days dead – with maggots feeding and bluebottles laying their eggs and butting into his lantern. Where had they come from, those flies, with snow on the ground? Down the chimney? Through cracks in the walls? His eyes swam, his ears pounded. He felt for the bedside chair and sat down; he crouched over, his head between his knees, and closed his eyes. He never wanted to open them again.

But he couldn't stay here: the smell was making him heave. He dared, at last, to look from the dusty floor back towards the bed, where the quilt spilled onto the floor and a dark hem protruded.

Better not touch anything, he told himself. Let the police … But he just had to check.

He lifted the quilt.

Under the covers Dolly Brett was fully dressed apart from her shoes, but the dress was stained. He lifted its hem to reveal a torn shift and the sheets soaked with blood. What had he done, her attacker? Would rape make so much blood?

And then he gasped. Those scissors. Oh God.

This had to be Streeter's work or one of his thugs. Dolly must have let him in, and he had dragged her upstairs, beating her into submission. She couldn't scream for the drawers stuffed into her mouth. No, her murderer must have knocked her unconscious otherwise the neighbours would have heard her cries as he'd ripped off her drawers. They'd have raised the alarm, wouldn't they?

And at the end of her torment, he had stuck the scissors in her neck to finish her off. Archie focused on those scissors. Where would they have been? On the sewing machine downstairs? The mantelpiece? Or in her apron pocket when she came upstairs? Had she threatened him with them? He had to've been the last one to use them, the bastard. And blood had spurted everywhere – walls, bed, floor. It appeared to have dried now. But not before the murderer had trodden in it. Footprints led to the stairs, clear as paint. Archie stumbled down after them, his hands numb, his legs without strength. There they were again, fainter now, leading to the cellar door. The *cellar* door? He hadn't seen anybody down there when he'd let in the cat. But it was the only unbolted door …

He brought the lantern up slowly, hardly breathing, so that he could see all the steps down, and the entirely bleak, entirely empty cellar.

No one.

His mother's basement had been an Aladdin's cave for a child growing up in Wales, lined with twinkling jars of preserves, and smelling of lamp oil and grated soap. This was as cold as the grave and smelled as bad. Creatures had died down here. He swung the lantern to reveal crumbling walls and a dirt floor, huge cobwebs hanging like the sails of ghostly ships, tree roots, and the dirt and debris of half a century packed into the angles and crevices of a room.

It was so bare. Where his mother's cellar was a storehouse bursting with supplies, here was just a scrape of small coal, a tree stump chopping-block and a few sticks of firewood chopped from boxes and crates from the market. Dominating the space was a brick copper, with a dipper and a copper stick. No soap, no grater. Not even a bucket or a mangle. Not a sign of life.

He shivered, his mind full of the scene upstairs. Better go back up and fetch the police. The murderer must have escaped some other way, out of a window or across the roof. Then he noticed a length of sacking beside the copper, flapping in the draught from upstairs, and revealing, when he lifted it, a dark opening. He went through and found himself in next door's cellar.

The twin of Dolly and Mary's – number thirty-seven, presumably – was just as dirty, almost as barren. The only difference was light straining through the knot-holes and cracks in the ceiling boards, and creaking feet walking back and forth accompanied by a woman's voice: 'Hush, baby, hush!' Here, a smell of soap lingered with warmth from the copper and ragged baby clothes were strung on lines across the room.

Connecting cellars, eh? Perhaps these were Dolly's special friends or relatives. They would have to be close, people who would trust her not to make off with their laundry. He felt he was trespassing and turned back to Dolly's place.

On the wall facing him was a rickety looking latched door that he hadn't noticed before. This had a number *33* painted on it. Another connecting cellar? It was. This time the number *31* was chalked on the facing wall and no attempt made at covering the gap through.

Were all the cottages connected? Tyrell had said there was an underground passage in Shoreditch. Was this the same? If so, the police clearly didn't know about it.

The floor was puddled and muddy, strewn with coal dust and splinters of wood and, like any well-used footpath, bore the traces of through traffic. There were the prints of shoes and bare feet, big ones, smaller ones, human and four-legged, and the continuous single track of a wheelbarrow. And there were *his* footprints again, the murderer's, no longer bloody, but clearly patterned, smaller than Archie's size tens, heading towards the single numbers at the top of the road.

Archie followed, his handkerchief pressed to his nose against the stench of urine and faeces, of rodents, of damp. He passed places where fires had been made, where lines of laundry hung; he saw buckets and bowls, and a tin bath containing a quantity of water and fish swimming; he passed a hutch, a writhing nest of ferrets, their eyes shining red in his lantern light – a light that was growing increasingly dim, he realised with a stab of horror. The wick was burning low, was already guttering into the melted wax. Damn, he breathed, as it went out. No help for it, he had to turn back or be lost forever in the dark. Fumbling his way to the previous opening he began counting. Twenty-three, twenty-five … Damn and blast! Water slurped. He'd nearly had the tin bath over. He'd forgotten about the damned fish. He stood, rubbing his bruised shin, listening to the tinny clunk as a tail smacked the side.

A spark of light appeared in the loose weave of the sacking at the next opening. He froze. Told himself to wait quietly – didn't want to give them a fright, whoever it was. The opening gradually filled with light, the drape lifted and a small figure scuttled through, a hurricane lamp disfiguring the face above it.

It was a boy, a scrawny bundle of rags. He yelped to see a man towering before him in the dark, and would have darted away if Archie hadn't caught him. He squirmed like a wild animal, trying to bite the hand holding his skinny shoulder.

'Hey, hey, hey,' cried Archie, 'calm down! I'm not going to hurt you.' The boy still tried to wriggle free. 'Here, you've dropped your sack.' He snatched it. 'Look,' said Archie, 'my lamp's gone out. I need a favour. I'll *pay* you.'

The word worked its spell and the boy stopped struggling. Eyes big with fear narrowed in speculation. ''Ow much?' he demanded in a voice rusty with weeping.

Archie reached in his pocket, found a coin.

'A copper?' jeered the boy, treating his benefactor to a display of decayed teeth. Archie wondered how old he was. Seven? Seventy? So small and spindly and yet his face looked old, pinched, with the look of a scavenging fox.

'Do you know this passage well?' he asked.

''Oo wants to know?'

Archie introduced himself and explained that he'd come down here looking for someone. But his lantern had gone out. 'I'll give you thruppence if you can find me a decent candle.'

The boy spat on his hand and held it out for Archie to shake. 'Done,' he said solemnly. 'Come on.'

With a show of confidence he led the way to a cellar further back where he climbed up onto the copper and, holding his lamp high, began examining the bare wall behind it, next to the flue, tapping and feeling carefully. 'Gotcha!' he cheered, and dragged out a loose brick. He plunged his hand into the cavity. When he turned back he had in his grasp a rusty tobacco tin which he shook hard.

'Nah!' he determined. 'Tacks!' He prised it open for Archie to see how right he was. Archie firmed the lid back on while his companion stuffed his hand back in the hole. The next tin seemed more promising and he forced the lid with strong little fingers. A paper of matches lay there. He extracted one and struck it against the brick wall. 'There'yah!' he said triumphantly. For a moment he was just a child fascinated with fire.

Archie explained that a match alone wouldn't do. He needed another candle. Undaunted, the boy ferreted around in the brickwork once more, up to his armpit this time. The cavity had to be wider and deeper than Archie had first thought: a regular safe dug out of the clay behind the wall. He heard heavier objects being moved around. This must be where the householder kept his tools, an axe for chopping his firewood, a hammer perhaps, soap. Eventually the boy fished out a two-inch candle-stub, which Archie took.

He thought of putting a penny in the hole to pay for it but suspected the boy would be back, as soon as he was alone, to steal it. It occurred to him that unless he hurried back to Dolly's and locked her cellar door the boy would be rifling through the house and finding all sorts of horrible things. He mended his lantern and lit it, while the boy sealed the hidey-hole.

'You knew it was here?'

'Or next door,' he said. 'They all got their secret places. 'Ave to 'ide stuff else it gets nicked.'

'But *you* know and, presumably, there are more like you living down here?'

He shrugged. 'Yeah, ain't nuffin' safe.'

Dear God, thought Archie, life at this level was hopeless. Dog eat dog. He sighed and changed the subject. 'How far does it go, this passage?'

'Cost yer,' the child bargained.

For another sixpence he found out that if he continued in this direction he would soon reach the High Street and could continue on to St Mary Road. He'd come out in a well in one of the gardens backing onto the railway line. From there to the station and away.

In the other direction lay the marshes and the river.

'Don't you go pinching to the traps,' the kid cautioned.

'The traps?'

'The filth, the rozzers – or you'll cetch it, you will.' Making an ugly face he drew an unequivocal line across his throat.

'Who'd do that?' Archie was amused. 'You?'

'Ain't funny, Mister. He does you for pinching.'

'Pinching?'

'Snitching, grassing ...'

'Who's "he"?'

'Oh Gawd!' The kid jerked his head and tutted at Archie's ignorance as he held a dingy length of material aside for the boy to pass through.

'What's his name?'

The boy made a face. 'Dunno. See him, mind. See him do people and all. He's got a shooter.'

Archie knew what a shooter was. This wasn't funny at all. 'And this man lives down here, does he?'

'Nah! He's a toff, inne?' He bit his lips realising he'd said more he'd meant to. He looked furtively over his shoulder. 'Best be off.'

Archie understood. The deep black shadows had dirty ears and eyes. He swung his lantern high. The curtain twitched and the boy was gone.

*

He unbolted Dolly's front door and let himself out, fastening the latch behind him. The street was still slippery and he couldn't help thinking, as he fell into a privet hedge, earning himself a shower of snow down his neck and up his sleeve, that if he'd gone via the underground route he might have fared better. But he was damned if he was going back to that foul place in a hurry. He slipped again.

Damn and blast it, the police station was more than a mile away up the High Street. He must report the murder. Dolly wasn't going anywhere, poor soul, but whoever killed her was and he already had a few days' start, it looked like. Archie put on a spurt and half-walked, half-ran, in the middle of the road where traffic had thinned the snow to slush.

Halfway up, he passed the ruins of Daniel Wylie's shop, covered in snow, still boarded up, still the subject of ongoing police investigations. Black and white. Except it wasn't, was it? Nowhere near open and shut. He stopped stock-still in the middle of the road. If the underground tunnel went up the High Street on the left-hand side, it must go under Wylie's. And that was how the murderers had got in! Through the cellar. Though if it went as far as the station it must cross over the road at some point. Before or after Wylie's, though? That was the question. Dammit, he should have followed it to its end.

Too late now, he was nearly home and fit to drop. He'd leave it till tomorrow.

The Horse and Groom, opposite his lodgings, with its licence for 'dramatic entertainment', was doing a roaring trade. Vehicles were lined up nose-bag to tailboard on both sides of the road, the horses wearing blankets, and the queue of eager theatre-goers stretched down past the Congregational church. Stamping their feet in the melting snow and blowing their nails, creating their

156

own fog of excitement, were several he recognised: shopkeepers, stall-holders, friends. But he didn't stop. *'The Demon Barber of Fleet Street'* in the pub's saloon bar was the last thing he wanted to talk about.

Once he might have been keen to see the actor Herbert Pickering as a maddened Sweeney Todd, but tonight he couldn't even look at the poster. A man wielding a cut-throat razor? He could scarcely believe that he had been bent over that very copper plate a few months before, etching a suitably manic gleam into Pickering's eye.

In fact – it occurred to him now – John Kington would have seen that very poster when he came to the market selling his tiles a month back. He would have studied it critically, knowing Archie had created it. And that, of course, was what had fuelled the idea for *his* drawing of a woman being murdered in her bed. He, Archie Price, had sown the seed. Was it only this afternoon? In all likelihood – give him the benefit of the doubt – John had simply been lampooning his poster. Well, be that as it may, now it was real. A seamstress had been stabbed twice with her own dressmaking shears, and from now on Archie would see everything through a blood-red haze.

As he was passing the pub, someone held the door open to let the first few patrons go inside. Archie caught an inviting waft of tobacco smoke and beer fumes, saw people squeezing past each other to get to or from the bar, holding brimming mugs of mulled wine and ale high over the heads of the crowd. Not tonight, Archie, he cautioned himself. Keep walking, boyo. Police station first stop. Dolly was dead, Mary was missing and a vicious murderer was on the loose. Tyrell had to know.

But there was the chestnut seller, his brazier glowing in fiery contrast to the black night sky. Archie's blood still ran cold, seeded with ice, and the smell of roasting nuts was almost painful. 'Buy, buy, buy, buy!' cried the man. 'A penny a twist to keep out the cold!'

He stopped, remembering that he hadn't eaten since that meal at the Kingtons. He crossed the road and joined the little crowd round the brazier.

Sucking in air to cool the hot mush in his mouth, he poked his head round the door of the pub, thinking that a hot toddy might not come entirely amiss. Just to steady his nerves.

Percy Reeves manned the ticket desk by the saloon bar door, posting sixpences into a cashbox and issuing tickets, which the customers solemnly handed over to Mrs Reeves before they went in. Already the 'auditorium' was filling up with excited punters.

'Archie!' Percy cried, through the fumes from a stubby cigar. 'Coming to see the show? Only a tanner, mate.' Ash spilled down his waistcoat, unnoticed. The customer he was serving peered at the newcomer, as though he might know him. The man, better-dressed than most, with flaring nostrils and a superior air, did strike Archie as vaguely familiar and he tipped his hat, to be polite. But he couldn't put a name to him. Probably just someone he'd seen shopping in the market.

'Another time, Perce. I'm a bit pushed tonight.' His spiced wine was too hot to drink fast and Lord, it hit the spot. He'd just have the one and then, hopefully, still be in time to catch Tyrell before he knocked off. He really didn't want to unburden himself to the night shift.

'Come on, mate, you deserve a break,' cajoled the booth operator.

Archie must have looked baffled.

'Been at it all day, ain't ya?'

Lord, he thought, nothing got past Percy Reeves. He supposed

158

he must be looking pretty done in after finding that body.

'See you up there, beavering away.' Reeves jerked his chin towards Archie's studio across the road.

Startled, the artist followed his gaze. Downstairs – what he could see between a horse and the next carriage – the greengrocer's shutters were closed tight, the potatoes and onions sealed in for the night.

Upstairs, a light was on.

Chapter 17

He crossed the road quickly, dodging puddles of melt water and steaming piles of dung.

He hadn't been home since Monday and any light he might inadvertently have left burning would have guttered and gone out long since. The only other person with a key was his landlord. Perhaps Bob was up there, having a look around before he went home, assessing the damage after the dinner party last week. It was all right – they'd scraped the candle wax off the floor and got the wine stains out of the rug. Or perhaps Bob had let Ida in, or Kitty, in Archie's absence, before heading off home. Perhaps he'd left a note …

Archie opened his front door and closed it quietly behind him, climbing the stairs with tired legs and a shiver of apprehension. No sound. He turned the handle, not knowing what to expect. The breath left his body.

The light came from an oil lamp on the mantelpiece. Its beam, reflected in the mirror, shone out over a wreck of a room. Cupboards were flung open, paintings and rolls of bare canvas strewn about, sketches and posters were torn off the wall, screens and chests overturned, bedclothes were ripped from the bed, and a wad of paper was burning in the grate, floating page by page up the chimney. His drawings of Mary!

'What the hell!'

The door to the back stairs was open and a gale was blasting through, creating a small snowstorm of pillow feathers. As he went across to shut it, he thought of Streeter. Had the gangster rumbled the cause of his arrest? Was this wreckage to pay Archie back?

A crunch of glass made him whip round. The intruder moved into the light and Archie realised he knew this swaggering bully boy in his brown buttoned suit.

'Where is she?'

Archie couldn't think, couldn't breathe. 'What? Who?'

'You know who.'

Oblivious whether he was treading on tubes of paint, packets of flour or butter, the man smacked a thick iron cudgel into his left palm as he advanced. He meant business.

'If – if you're talking about Mary Quinn, I don't know where she is.' Archie backed away, his heart pumping wildly as he cast about for a weapon of his own. 'I'd like to help you but I – I've been looking for her myself.' He slapped his pockets. *Where was his damned penknife?* 'I was in the middle of painting ...'

The iron bar smashed down on the table, making Archie jump. 'I'm not come to play games, Mister. You know right enough or what's *this* doing here?' He snatched from his shoulder what Archie realised, to his horror, was not a scarf but Mary's dirty old wrapper. It had been on the bed. Archie's blood boiled. The bugger recognised Mary's wrapper. He *knew* it, knew it was hers. Christ Almighty! A hundred implications milled through his mind. He could almost see the thug's cloddish fingers on Mary's bare flesh.

'Put that down, you bastard!'

But the bully made an insolent face and twirled the wrapper round his head. Archie lunged to grab it, swiped with his other fist. The man danced back, evading the blow and sniggering. While Archie was unbalanced, the Irishman used the moment to rip the cloth in two, his smile a twisted gash of glee.

'You moron!' yelled Archie, shedding any last vestige of reason. He aimed another ineffectual punch, knocking off the man's bowler. 'It was a prop! She wore it for the painting!' He gestured towards the easel and the man turned to look. Archie knew full well that he would only see what he wanted to see, believe what he wanted, but the distraction gave him a chance to back towards the dresser. 'I painted her in it,' he insisted, choking on fury, 'that's all.'

The short ugly laugh was one of crude disbelief, and, curling his lip, the wrecker swiped along a shelf with his iron bar …

'No!' Archie screeched.

… sending jars of linseed oil and pigment crashing to the floor.

'You swine! That stuff costs!'

'Where is she?'

'I don't damn well *know*!' he cried. 'She's not at home.'

'No,' he agreed. So he'd been to the cottage. With a gasp, Archie realised *this* was Dolly's killer. He'd wielded those scissors. Those were his bloody footprints on the bedroom floor. But he hadn't got his murdering hands on Mary. Nor would he, if Archie could help it.

He breathed hard for control, tried to remember what they'd taught him at the boxing hall. Keep moving, dance, duck and dodge. But his feet seemed to be nailed to the floor with fear. His brain was numb. 'I haven't seen her since Saturday and she left in a hurry – didn't tell me where she was going.' Keep talking, he told himself, and maybe, just maybe, the devil would take his search elsewhere. 'Perhaps Nobby has her already?' With his hand behind him, he felt for the drawer handle, praying it didn't stick.

'Nobby?'

'Nobby Streeter?' The man's jaw dropped with puzzlement. But surely? A fleeting doubt popped into Archie's head: perhaps he wasn't in the pimp's pay, after all. 'Big gangland boss?' he prompted. 'He's been after her for a while.'

'Why's that then?'

Dear God, he was thick. 'He wants to put her on the game.'

'You're lying.'

'Please yourself.'

'The woman at the house said she was in service to a tiler and you'd know where.'

Oh, Dolly, you didn't? You stupid cow.

'Not any more. She left there – couldn't stick it.' He mustn't go looking there, laying about the pottery with his damn cudgel. Lizzie – oh God keep Lizzie safe! 'She could be anywhere – I dunno. Looking for another job, or – or she could have gone to her – to her brother over in Shoreditch!' God that was inspired! His hand slipped into the drawer. 'Yes, yes, that's where she'll be.' From the murky depths of his desperation an address bubbled up. 'Or have you tried Bethnal Green? Mount Street? She has a friend there, I …'

'What do you know about Mount Street?' The bullyboy thrust himself up close, his eyes pink slits, the muscles in his neck bulging. 'Eh? Eh?' He poked Archie's chest with the cudgel. His brown incisors were bared to bite and he spattered Archie with flecks of saliva.

'Get away!' snarled Archie, whipping out the carving knife. 'Get out of my house or I'll kill you, you dirty little shite.'

But the cosh simply whacked the knife from his grip. Archie yelped. 'Oh will you now?' jeered the thug. 'Tell me, where is this tiler's?' He swung the bar again, too fast to dodge. It connected

163

with Archie's chin, almost lifting him off the floor before he fell. He spat blood and a tooth. Before he could give full attention to the throbbing in his mouth, the kicking began. He saw the brown boot coming a split second before red-hot pain smashed into his eye, smelled polish as it connected with his nose and cheek. He heard a crack in his ribs and, before he could lift up his knees and bring his arms across to protect his stomach and groin, one boot and then the other found these soft spots. Somewhere, someone was screaming. He vomited chestnut pulp and spiced wine, gasping and begging no more. No more, please. The kicking stopped. But as he thanked God or his persecutor, he became conscious of a blur, a shape bending down, picking something off the floor, considering it and moving across towards the easel.

'Don't!' he cried. He could hardly see, but he knew what the bastard was about.

'Where's the place? The tiler's?'

'She's not there.'

Moaning, crippled with pain, he was forced to watch as the man stuck the carving knife in the painting and began cutting out Mary's face. 'No-o-o,' he groaned. He had to stop him. Somehow he had to roll over and crawl across the floor, grab the brown-booted foot. He rolled, put out a hand and then felt the worst pain of his life as the man stamped on it. Ground in his heel. Archie may have screamed before passing out …

His head thudded. He dearly wanted to stay in the dark, out of it. But pain made one eyelid spring open, while the other stuck tight. He blinked. He had to see what was causing this agony. He shuddered. His 'D-o-on't …' was disbelief.

The man had one knee on the crushed hand, and his face was quite still and concentrated as he sliced the knife across Archie's exposed wrist. There was a momentary glimpse of white bone and then blood everywhere.

Speechless with fear and the desperate need not to pass out again Archie summoned all that was left of his energy. He twisted away and made a wild grab at the knife with his left hand, but the thug was quicker and held it to Archie's throat.

'Don't think I won't, pal,' he menaced. 'One more makes no difference.'

'So what's stopping you?'

In the split second his aggressor took to ponder the question, Archie managed somehow to buck, wriggle and kick, and the knife went skittering away across the floor. But the man raised his fist, and Archie knew that this time there'd be no getting up.

Chapter 18

It was late when Tyrell turned into the High Street, arriving as the last of the theatre-goers climbed into their trap, noisy with drink and the horrors of the play. As the driver whipped up the pony, the wheels churned up a filthy mixture of fresh horse dung and muddy slush and the police officer had to flatten himself against the greengrocer's shutters to avoid being spattered.

There were no lights in Archie's room. Percy Reeves and PC Stanley Beckett were already waiting at his street door with lanterns, pink with cold, their eyes watering.

'Took your time, didn't you?' said Reeves. 'We was just thinking about breaking the door down.'

'Came as fast as I could,' puffed the sergeant, as he took off his gloves. 'Cheshire was out. His wife gave me the keys.'

'It might be nothing, but better safe than sorry, I always say.'

'Quite right, Perce. The lady seemed quite agitated, though I couldn't make out if that was because of your play or Archie Price's shenanigans.'

As he fitted the key into the lock, the publican started in again about the old girl who came over queer in the play and had to go out for a breath of air. Served her right, in Tyrell's opinion. You watch sensational twaddle about throat-slashing barbers, you must expect to come over queer. He'd already heard from the lady

166

herself how thumps and breaking glass had alerted her and the roast-chestnut man to a different drama across the road. Blood-curdling screams had sent them scuttling up to the police station. By sheer luck he and Beckett were still there, waiting for the night shift to take over.

'Save it for later, Perce. I'll take your statement in the morning. You cut along now. It's been a long day and I expect Bertha will need you to help finish up.'

He didn't take kindly to being dismissed, it was plain to see, but this was a police matter and if there was any trouble Percy Reeves would just be in the way. It was probably just a storm in a teacup anyway, the artist larking about with his mates.

At the top of the stairs they found the door to the studio unlocked but with something heavy jammed up against the other side. Beckett, a decent scrum-half for his old school team, put his shoulder to the door, heaved, strained and gradually inched it open. In the lantern light the exposed floor was streaked with blood.

'Oh my God!' cried Tyrell. 'Archie.'

Beckett squeezed through the gap he had made. His hand beckoned. 'Lantern, Sarge!' The door shut again. 'Jesus Christ!' Tyrell heard his muffled voice.

'What is it?'

'Eh? Oh, hold on.'

Tyrell heard grunting and groaning, bumping against the door, light and shadows playing under it, a murmur of apology, more puffing, and a dragging sound. The door opened. 'Had to move the poor blighter. Quick, get in here, Sarge. I'll fetch the doctor.'

Archie Price was laid out on the floor where Beckett had left him. He was barely conscious, his eyelids fluttering, his face drained but livid with bruising. The blood, pooling on the floor and staining his clothes was from his right forearm where a deep cut oozed across the wrist-bone. It looked as though some mad sod had tried to cut his hand off. There was the knife, a domestic carving knife. It lay on the floor, stained red and sticky.

While Beckett hurtled off into the night, the sergeant found an oil lamp, lit it and, removing Price's boot, bound the injured arm with its lace, to act as a ligature above the wound. Then, hissing and cursing with vicarious pain, he tried to make Archie as comfortable as he could with pillows and blankets. The slightest movement made him groan and Tyrell realised there were hidden injuries. The hand was a real mess. It was washed with blood from the wrist wound, and the fingers were swollen and bruised with the tread of a heel printed on the skin in paint and what looked like flour. The fingernails were split and torn. Someone had really had it in for poor old Archie.

Beckett had dragged old Doctor Anthony from his surgery, abandoning the last of his sick and elderly patients. 'It's no trouble, no trouble at all,' insisted the wizened little medic. 'If they're really ill, they'll come back tomorrow.'

'Shouldn't we try and get him to hospital?' Tyrell asked.

'And just how do you propose getting him there? In your handcart?'

'Snow's nearly gone. We can take a cab.'

'No cabs out there. Street's empty. Let me have a look at him.' He pushed his glasses to his forehead. 'Hmm, you did right with the tourniquet but it looks like he's lost a lot of blood already. I'll know better when I've examined him.' With a grunt of discomfort he got down on his knees to examine the patient, gently murmuring encouragement but at the same time prodding and pushing at the poor man's anatomy, attempting to gauge the vigour of the groans. He gazed up at the ceiling for internal vision.

In between he told them about Holmcroft, the new hospital up the road. They might take him in. Originally a small children's hospital they'd only recently moved to Orford Road, to extended premises, and now they took in adults, too.

'We'll put him in my buggy,' he said, 'and hope they have room.' Only then did he ask Beckett to hold a pad of lint over Price's nose and mouth, and drip some tincture onto it. The artist slumped into deep unconsciousness, allowing the doctor to clean and stitch up the arm.

'This will heal. It's just a flesh wound,' he decided. 'You'd need a hacksaw to get through bone or a butcher's cleaver. Now I have seen ...' He clearly thought better of telling them the worst horrors of his practice. 'Suffice to say,' he went on, 'if the attacker had cut as deeply on the underside he'd be dead by now.'

After stitching and dressing the wound he turned his attention to the hand, feeling carefully along each bone, around each joint, bending the fingers if they would bend, flexing them.

'Wait,' said Tyrell, when he saw that the doctor was about to clean off the oil-paint with some of Archie's turps. He found a piece of paper and took the heel print from the damaged hand. 'Could be useful,' he said grimly.

The doctor then set the crushed fingers between wooden spatulas and bound them with bandages. 'A temporary measure,' he explained. 'I'll see him in the morning and he can tell me himself what hurts and what doesn't.' It was pretty clear that the attacker had stamped on the hand and ground the bones. They might have broken or splintered. He turned to Tyrell with a look of complicit dismay. They were both wondering what the hell Archie Price would do if he couldn't paint.

The young man had also taken a hefty clout on the jaw. In Doctor Anthony's opinion a heavy object had been used which had probably knocked him out. He had lost a molar and swallowed a lot of blood but his jaw was intact, which was something of a miracle. He was strongly made. At some time during his ordeal he had been severely kicked. At least one rib was cracked, maybe two, and would be uncomfortable for a while, but thankfully his breathing was not impaired. It remained to be seen whether the other internal organs were functioning normally. As he bound the ribcage tightly, Doctor Anthony expressed an expectation that the patient would make a good recovery. Apart from the hand.

'Bed-rest and quiet should do the trick.'

The doctor bathed and anointed Archie's facial injuries, and then, and only then, agreed that that the policemen might lift the patient. 'Put him on a blanket and we'll get him downstairs. Careful, he's heavier than he looks,' he warned.

Tyrell couldn't help thinking that they were doing more harm than good as he and Beckett heaved and struggled to stop the comatose patient bumping on the stairs or into the narrow walls. But it was the only way. Archie needed round-the-clock care and who would provide it, in that midden of a studio? As carefully as they could, they loaded him into the buggy. 'Fetch a bowl, Sergeant. He's likely to spew up and all the better for it, but I don't want it all over my upholstery.'

Tyrell collected the bowl, Archie's toothbrush and shaving kit, another blanket against the cold, and for the first time really saw the damage to the room. The painting on the easel was cut to ribbons, the head and neck of the portrait removed; jars had been smashed and spilled, powders and lumps of coloured pigment trodden into the floorboards making perfect footprints for the records. There was the carving knife which the perpetrator must have handled in his attempt to cut off the hand. He shivered at the savagery of such a notion. Brushes were strewn around like a child's game of pick-up-sticks, some snapped underfoot. The screen lay in pieces on the floor, the couch had been slashed down to the springs and half-burnt papers had spilled into the hearth, the top one with a perfect thumb-print where someone, either Archie or his intruder, with blue paint on his hands, had held it before shoving it on the fire.

There was a book in circulation, it was rumoured, a book called *Fingerprints*, which made the claim that everyone's were unique. Apparently the Met were very interested. If correct, you could probably identify criminals from the fingerprints they left at the scene of the crime, which would make his job a lot simpler. If only …

He took the wad of charred papers for safekeeping and found they were from a sketchbook; the drawings were of Mary Quinn. 'By crikey!' he murmured. He couldn't send that one to Scotland Yard. 'Oh dear, Archie Price – been letting our imagination run away with us, have we?' After a bit of a hunt, he eventually found a decent one to pop in the post in the morning. It'd help in their search for her. As he turned out the lamp, locked the door behind him and pocketed the key, he reminded himself to hang onto it for a while. It was a crime scene and would have to be thoroughly gone over. In any case you couldn't have Archie going back to the room in that state. He was one of their own. A valued member of the team. Gifted.

Though whether he'd be much use to them when he recovered was another matter.

*

When he visited the patient next morning, he learned that they'd all had a rough night of it. Mister Price couldn't seem to understand that he had to stay in bed. Very agitated he was.

They'd found him on the floor once, writhing in pain. Kept saying he had to talk to the police, he had a murder to report, and his other concern was for someone called Mary. Was that his wife? He was worried that she was going to die. Couldn't she come in to see him, put his mind at rest?

Tyrell explained that Mary was a witness in a murder case, and one of the artist's models. Her portrait was damaged in the affray. It was probably the picture he was worried about. He had no wife, no family really. Tyrell believed the man's parents lived in some god-forsaken village in south Wales. There were friends closer at hand whom he would inform about the incident.

'Well,' said the nurse, 'he was thrashing around like a fish on a hook. He wouldn't stay put. Had to sedate him in the end. And that was a battle in itself. You'd have thought we were trying to poison the man. Got it down him in the end. But of course he'd swallowed a lot of blood and that all had to come up. After that, he seemed to settle down for a while. He's asleep now.'

Chapter 19

He was dreaming. Mary's portrait was on his easel but, instead of dewy freshness, he could only paint her skin in the curdled textures of age. Though he loaded the brush with luscious young flesh tints, somehow the effect was old parchment. Blotches as on a rice pudding. Her clear blue eyes became cloudy, absorbing any sparks or highlights he put in, and bruised pouches appeared beneath them. The lashes and eyebrows became sparse and the definition of those lovely swallows' wings was lost. The skull shone through the fading hair, flesh hung from the bones as bags and jowls, and shadows gathered in the hollows: a foretaste of death. No good, no good.

He wiped off the paint, cleaned his brush, mixed the colours afresh. As before, each time he touched brush to painting she aged. What was happening?

Fever invaded his dream, hot then cold with the chills of guilt. He'd done this to her. His stomach clenched with remorse. He worked harder, wiping off the paint with a rag, scrubbing it, scouring it down to the bare canvas, trying again. His hand hurt with the effort. It ached unbearably.

He uttered a cry of pain and she heard him. She turned towards him out of the pose, and it wasn't Mary Quinn at all, but some stranger in white, starched and official. A nurse? Was this a hospital? Was Mary here – hurt, in pain?

'Where is she?' he cried, looking around in desperation.

The woman's head wagged from side to side. 'Don't you fret, Mister Price. Whatever it is can wait.' She smiled.

'No, no!' he cried. 'I need to see her.'

'He won't be told,' she complained.

Another voice, this time, a man's. 'Easy, Archie, easy, old chap.'

Through a blur he saw Sergeant Tyrell, wind-chafed and pink, removing his helmet. A young uniformed officer sat beside him.

He tried to sit up. He had something to tell them. God, what was the matter with his hand? It was on fire, so he leaned on the other elbow to raise himself up but his ribs screamed and his face and his groin. Goddamn it, he couldn't move.

'Frank ...'

'You're doing yourself no good, you know, getting all excited.'

He remembered what it was he needed to tell the sergeant.

'She's dead,' he managed to lisp over the hectic beating of his heart. His lip was swollen, his jaw would hardly move. He swallowed and tasted blood. His head was full of blood.

'Now you don't know that, Archie.'

He shook his head, swallowed again.

'It's all right, son,' said Tyrell, reacting to his panic, 'we're onto it. We'll find her, don't worry.'

He didn't think they'd quite got it, but it was too much effort to argue. He fell back on the pillow with a grunt of pain. 'He's looking for Mary,' he told them. 'He'll kill her, too.'

'He won't kill her, mate, don't you worry. She ain't no good to him dead. Get some sleep.'

Maybe he did. The sun was painting the inside of his eyelids red and purple, black and green. He opened one, put a hand over the pain of the other, and saw the two policemen. Why were they still here? They'd said they were going to find her.

'Mary,' he reminded them.

'They're out there now, door-stepping. Someone will have seen her.'

'No-o,' he wailed. 'I was coming to tell you. Dolly's dead. Not Mary. Dolly Brett, the dressmaker!'

Slowly, painfully, he made them listen.

'Dolly Brett?'

'Mary lodged with her.'

'Was Mary there?'

'No, no. That's why he came to me, looking for her.'

'In the cottage you say.'

'Yes, in bed.'

'Get down there, Beckett. Take a doctor. Oh and get a photographer.'

'Right, Sarge.'

'Now then, Archie, in your own time ...'

With difficulty, pausing every now and then to lick his split lip, to explore a soft new gap between his teeth with his tongue, to spit out blood, or to cough a rib-racking cough, he described coming upon the man trashing his studio.

'He thought I was hiding her, I suppose. When I wouldn't tell him where she was, he tried various ways to persuade me, mutilating my painting, even attempting to cut my hand off. But I couldn't. I couldn't.' He dashed at his swollen eyes with his wrist. 'Even if I'd wanted to,' he sniffed.

'You lost a lot of blood.'

'A lot more besides,' he murmured, in shame.

He'd made a poor show of it altogether. He could never show his face in the boxing ring again. Apart from one glancing thump

175

on the chest, he'd not hurt the man at all. His famous 'knockout' punch that had floored bullies at school, floored Brian Rooney, had grazed his assailant's ear and knocked his hat off.

On the other hand, one blow of the villain's cudgel had decked him. He should have seen it coming, parried it. Being taller and heavier, he should have been more than a match for the slighter man. He should have been able to overcome him, march him down to the police station and seen him slung into a cell, but the man was too quick and light on his toes while Archie had lurched about like a drunken bear.

'You were exhausted,' offered the policeman. 'The shock of finding Dolly, the walk home in the snow. *And* he had the element of surprise.'

No excuses. Since he'd met Mary he'd failed her in every way. He'd talked her into sitting for him and painted her in such a way that degenerates were even now lusting over her, wanting her for their own foul ends. His own lurid sketches of the girl, which she had found, had turned her into a fugitive. And now he'd let a murderer slip through his fingers who would find her and kill her if he had half a chance.

'Hey, now,' said the sergeant, disturbed more by the man's tears than his injuries, 'don't take on. You did all you could. Take it easy now. We can do this later.'

Archie shook his head. They needed to get after him now. Stop him.

'He mustn't get his hands on her.'

'You really think he means to hurt her?'

'Of course – he'll kill her. She's betrayed him.' Then he realised what was missing. 'I haven't told you, have I?'

'You recognised your attacker?'

'Yes.'

176

'One of the Hampstead crew?'

'No.'

'Who, then?'

'Tommo Hegarty.'

*

'They found her.' It was Tyrell, removing his cycle clips, breaking into the monkey chatter of Archie's thoughts. His heart jumped up like an eager puppy. Mary! Was she safe? From the look on Tyrell's face he guessed not. 'She's dead all right, your Dolly Brett.' Archie sucked his teeth in disappointment. 'A right mess he made of her, an' all. Animal!' Carefully, avoiding water jugs and kidney bowls, he placed his bulging saddlebag on the night table beside Archie.

She wasn't *his* Dolly Brett. Dolly wasn't his concern any more. Mary was the one. If that mad bugger had beaten *him* senseless, tried to cut off his hand and tortured and killed Dolly, heaven alone knew what he would do to Mary when he found her. If he had a grain of humanity he would shoot her. Get it over with quickly. That was how they'd killed Daniel Wylie. He turned to share his theory on the Wylie killing with the sergeant, but the image of a ragged child came to him, his gleaming eyes reflecting a match flame, his decayed teeth forming the word, *'Don't!'*

Don't give away the secret of the 'rat-run', he'd advised. When was that? *'Or yore be for it, you will.'*

Yes, if no one – over the many years the 'rat-run' had been in existence – if not one single soul had had the courage to *'pinch to the traps'* the threat of reprisal must be very real. So perhaps he'd save his knowledge till he was not so vulnerable. Right now, he couldn't even get out of bed.

In any event the police officer's eyes had glazed over, fixing, no doubt, on a crime scene not two miles distant. He shouldn't be here, nursemaiding Archie, they both knew that. He should be down at Dolly's, finding clues that would lead them to her murderer.

'Look,' he said, 'you don't have to keep coming back here. I'll be fine – if you want to get off ...'

'I've not finished with you yet,' said the policeman. 'I need to take some prints.' He produced a strange kit from his saddlebag: Archie's boots minus a lace, several sheets of foolscap, a tube of watercolour paint and a large paint brush.

'What's all this about?'

'Bear with me, Arch.' The policeman explained that he wanted to take prints of Archie's boots, in order to distinguish them from Hegarty's. In the studio the smaller tread had indented blood and paint, charcoal, flour and butter; in Dolly's, there were two sets of prints, one smaller than the other, and bloody.

'Oh.' One-handed, he drew back the bedclothes, made to get up.

'What are you doing?' Tyrell cried.

'I thought you wanted me to put my boots on.'

'Ridiculous man!' Tyrell gently pushed him back against the pillow. 'You stay put. I just need your permission to do this.' So saying, he painted the soles and heels of the boots in undiluted blue paint and pressed them onto the paper. 'Beautiful!' He was clearly proud of the results. 'We'll just wait for it to dry.' Then he had another bright idea: taking Archie's left hand, he daubed the pads of his fingers and thumbs with paint and took prints from them. He explained to Archie fingerprints were said to be unique to the owner. If this was true, he should be able to tell Archie's prints from Hegarty's at both scenes of crime.

'I'm impressed!' quipped the artist, albeit feebly. Tyrell didn't get it.

178

He cleaned his hands with a wet flannel and lay back in bed, exhausted. 'Oh God, I feel so useless, lying here, doing nothing, when she's out there somewhere and he's gaining on her.'

'You don't know that.'

'I do.'

'And just what do you think you can do in your condition?'

'Something. Anything!' He had a plan but when he threw back the blankets and put one foot on the floor to take a step towards his boots, red-hot pain scythed through his groin and into his belly. 'Aaa-gh!' He crumpled, his head swimming, and would have collapsed if Tyrell hadn't caught him. Lord above, he hadn't realised how deep the kicking had gone.

'Back into bed this instant, young man!' A wizened creature appeared at the door. When Archie continued to slump on the edge of the bed, the policeman and the visitor, by tacit agreement, each grabbed a dangling leg and forced it back under the blankets.

When he'd finished gasping and groaning he was introduced to Doctor Anthony, who had patched him up last night.

'You probably won't remember me,' said the old man as he attached his stethoscope to his ears. 'Breathe in!' he commanded with martial abruptness.

Archie breathed in half a lungful of air. Full inflation hurt. He didn't remember the man but understood that he had probably saved his life. Exhaling, he thanked him.

The doctor examined the injured hand again and found that bones in the first and third fingers were indeed broken. They would be out of use, splinted for six weeks. Archie would probably lose three fingernails but they would grow back. The good news was that the tendons were sound. The knuckle joint on the middle finger was badly dislocated but with a little manipulation – *'Bite on this, young man!'* – it was soon realigned.

'Well done, well done, sir!'

The ordeal left Archie white and sweating.

'A few sips of water, Mister Price, if you please.' He held the glass to his lips. 'That's the worst over,' he promised him, 'provided nobody stamps on your hand again. Now I have to warn you that there is likely to be a weakness in the joint for a while, so we'll splint the three fingers. Don't make that face,' he said sternly, catching Archie's look of horror. 'You're lucky you're young and fit. You should heal quickly. Of course, cracked ribs are no picnic, but they're better than broken any day. Yes, with strong strapping and a sling, you can probably go home in a day or two. And, provided you don't do anything silly you should be able to renew your painting activities in six weeks or so.'

'But I have to …'

He raised his hand. 'No arguments, young man. You must simply make up your mind to it. The time will pass soon enough. You'll do permanent damage if you rush things.'

'No, you don't understand. I have to go home. I can't afford to stay in hospital. I can't pay their fees – or yours, come to that. Particularly if I can't paint.'

'Don't you have parents who can help you out? Or one of your clients? Hmm? Oh, we'll find a way, my boy, never fear.'

*

No sooner had word got out that Archie was laid up in Holmcroft than his neighbours started arriving, puffed from the walk up the hill, windswept and wet, to load the night table with flowers and sweets, homemade biscuits, apple pies and lemon and honey cordial. Mrs Reeves from the pub brought him a pot of stew, still hot from the stove. 'You could starve on hospital food, boy.'

Bob Cheshire, Archie's landlord, brought oranges from his stall and a box of dates, 'Fresh off the boat, Arch!' Oh, he remembered, when he was serving the woman from the wool shop with spuds and greens, she said she had a message for the artist upstairs. 'Tell him Mary's all right. She asked me to say.' And no, she wouldn't say no more. She knew where Mrs Quinn had gone, knew she was safe, and that was all.

When Archie slumped back on his pillow in relief, hardly breathing, Bob was worried. 'Archie, mate, you look like you've gone ten rounds with Tom Cribb!'

'Feel like it, Bob, and that's the truth. Lord, she's led me a merry dance.'

'That's women for you.'

'I suppose so.'

''E's give you a right shiner there, Arch, if you don't mind me saying so. Bastard burglar!' He mouthed the abuse, to save the nurses' blushes, and comforted himself with a date from the box he'd brought Archie. 'Be a month a Sundays cleaning that lot up.'

'Be few scars, they reckon. Oh, you mean the studio! I'm so sorry about that, Bob.'

'Not your fault, Arch. Get that Greek whatname, cleaned the stables …'

'Heracles,' Archie supplied.

'That's the chap. Get him and my missus on the job – have it done in no time, flat.'

It hadn't occurred to the police or to Archie to ask how Hegarty had gained entry. Seeing Bob made him think about it. Not through the front door. How would he, without a key? After killing Dolly on the Sunday night he must have made his way along the 'rat-run' with the blood still wet on his shoes, and holed up somewhere until Tuesday night, after Bob shut the shop. He'd then walked under the shops until he came to the cellar where Cheshire boiled his beetroots and kept his barrels of vinegar. He'd broken down the cellar door, forced his way into the shop and sneaked up Archie's back stairs.

'What do I owe you for the damage, Bob?' Archie asked quietly.

'That's all right, mate. Like I said, it only needs a good scrub out.'

Archie looked about. The patients in the other beds were asleep or out of the room. He kept his voice low. 'No, I meant for the cellar door.'

'The cellar?' Honest Bob looked decidedly shifty.

'It's how he got in, isn't it, via the passageway?'

'What – what passage is that, then?'

'Oh come on, Bob. The one through the cellars, from the marshes to the station. It must cross over to our side somewhere.'

His friend frowned and lowered his voice. 'Two doors down, Williams' Dairy. But you ain't meant a know about that, mate, you wiv your "connections", like. Coppers best left in the dark, see?'

Two doors down. So the tunnel *did* go under Wylie's. He was right. He assured the greengrocer that he wouldn't pass on that piece of information. He knew what was good for him.

His friend looked doubtful, and blew out his breath. 'Well, yeah, the door's fixable. The bolt's still on. It's the jamb that's a mess where the 'asp was screwed on. Old wood, see. Just as well, perhaps or I'd be looking at a new door.'

'How much to have the jamb replaced?'

'Five bob should cover it.'

'Get it done then, would you, Bob? I'll foot the bill.'

'Thanks, Arch, you're a toff. And listen, we don't mention the passage, ever. Got it?'

Archie made a sign to show his lips were buttoned. The police wouldn't hear about the passage from him. Though they'd be bound to find out about the connecting cellars for themselves at Dolly's. 'There's something you can do for me, Bob, if you wouldn't mind. On top of my wardrobe …'

The hospital authorities were glad to accept his painting of the parish church, St Mary's, in lieu of payment. And Doctor Anthony was equally happy with the promise of a portrait when Archie recovered the use of his hand.

*

'Oh, what has he done to you?' cried Lizzie in shock.

And what has *he* done to you? thought Archie with a pang of anxiety as he kissed her cold cheek. Something – worry or lack of sleep – had deepened the saucers of her eyes.

She'd come as soon as she could, she said. 'Had a fright when the policeman came by on his bicycle, face as long as a kite. "About your friend, Archie Price," he says in this deep dark voice. Dear God, I thought we'd lost you!'

Archie shivered.

The child didn't smile at all, but stared at him in horror from behind her mother's skirts, as though, in all her baby years, she had never seen anything so freakish and repellent.

They were both pink-nosed and frozen, from the mule-cart, and relieved to be indoors in the warm. 'Sit down, sit down,' he said waving his sling at the single upright chair beside the bed. As Clara let herself be gathered onto her mother's lap, she didn't take her desperate gaze from the half-closed eye, the swellings and bruises and healing scabs, and her lip began to quiver.

'It's all right, darling. Uncle Archie had a nasty fall and hurt himself, but he'll be better soon.' The little girl seemed unconvinced. Her mouth turned down, her eyes brimmed and Lizzie hastily tried another tack. 'You know how you fell in the yard and scraped your knee and I kissed it better and put a bandage on? Well, it's good as new now, isn't it? And so will Archie's face be – good as new, in no time at all.'

'Waaah!' went Clara, causing the other patients to slide down in their beds and pull the covers over their heads.

'Clara, Clara! Hush, sweetheart, it's all right, I'll be fine, I promise. Look, have a ju-jube. Everything is better for a ju-jube.'

'Kiss better, Mama,' she pleaded through a pink dribble of jelly.

The two sick men emerged, peering over the blanket-stitching to catch the couple's confusion.

'Kiss him eye.'

Lizzie did as she was told and, as Archie felt her lips brush the bruise, he closed the other also, relishing her closeness and resisting an almighty urge to kiss her back.

'Kiss him poor hand.'

That was easier, though his heart galloped and he had to suppress a smile of delight.

'Mouf ...'

Luckily a kindly nurse happened by, who enticed Clara away to the children's ward where there were toys and other children to distract her.

'Sorry about that,' said Lizzie. 'I had to bring her. John's childcare leaves a lot to be desired.'

That said it all, he supposed. 'It's lovely to see her, Lizzie. And the kissing better,' he grinned, 'you should patent it.'

'Every mother knows it,' she said, blushing.

'Well, it's preferable to the cure for dislocated fingers.'

She bared her teeth as he described Doctor Anthony's rough treatment, cringing in vicarious pain. 'Archie! You poor thing! As if you hadn't been through enough.' Gently, she took his broken hand in hers. 'I expect he thought he'd killed you, didn't he?'

'Doctor Anthony?'

'Idiot! No, Hegarty. He's getting careless. He left John for dead, too. Gosh, I'll bet he and Rooney couldn't believe their luck when that heavy purse of Squire Mowbray's fell into their laps, and our cashbox into the bargain. Who'd have thought two prize fools would fall into their trap on the same afternoon!'

With a wan smile he told her about the police discovering that Mary was, in fact, Brian Rooney's sister.

'No! I don't believe it! And she came to work for us? She kept that well hidden.'

'She wanted to keep her job.'

'You could be right. She certainly worked hard and Clara loved her. We all did … perhaps not John so much.'

'That figures.'

'Mmm, well, at least we know she's safe.'

'How so?'

'Well, that's where she is, I expect. At her brother's. If you hear from her, Archie, please tell her that we'd love to have her back. We could afford to pay her properly if we were both free to work in the pottery.' Her brows knitted. 'No need to tell John that she's related to Rooney.'

'Hah!' He thought better, too, of filling his friend in on the details of his search, how he'd come across Dolly's body and an underground passage to boot. He sighed, 'I'm sorry, Lizzie. You're back at square one. Why couldn't I leave well alone? I spoiled everything.'

Her hand covered her mouth and her frown deepened. 'Suppose Hegarty gets wind of her living with us? He'll … Oh God, Archie. He might want to finish what he started.'

'Lizzie, love, Hegarty thinks Mary went to work for a tiler. A *tiler*, not a tile-*maker*. Somehow he got it wrong. Perhaps we can thank Dolly Brett for that. So he won't be looking for a pottery.

He has no idea where you live or that you have anything to do with Mary. In any case, I told him she'd left your employ, which was true. Oh, don't look so worried, Lizzie.' He rubbed at his splint. 'Sorry, I'm not being much help.'

'No, you are.' They lapsed into a silence, busy with their own thoughts. At length, she took a deep breath. 'I'd better go and collect Clara.' They could hear her squeals of excitement from the next room. 'Can't have her enjoying herself too much.' She gave him a half-smile.

'Before you do, Lizzie, would you do something for me?'

'If I can.' Poor girl, her voice betrayed her weariness.

'I need to send a letter, and it's difficult to write left-handed. Drawing's not too bad, but my writing's illegible.'

'Who's it to?'

'A man called Cedric Carrington. I was in the middle of painting his daughters when this happened.'

'One of the *Eastern Star* people? The banker? I saw his name in the paper. You're working for *him?* Oh, Archie, you're not mixed up in any …'

'Of course not, silly. I'm just painting the picture. The police know all about it.'

Enlightenment suddenly dawned. 'It was *you*, wasn't it?' Luckily, any would-be eavesdroppers now had visitors of their own. '*You* told the police. Oh, Archie, I hate your involvement with that crew. Cedric Carrington, Norbert Streeter, they're awful men. Oh Lord, I'm so afraid you'll be, you'll be …'

He covered her hand with his own.

'If not killed,' she went on, 'then corrupted, somehow, tainted with evil.'

Did she think him so morally weak? 'There's no chance of that.'

She gave him a quizzical look, such as his mother might have given him. She knew him so well, his appetites, his whims and fancies.

'Look, I know the dangers. I'll be very careful.'

'You'd better,' she said darkly. 'So, what do you want to say to this horrible man?'

'I need to tell him that I won't be able to finish the painting.'

Lizzie frowned. 'No, what you need to tell him, Archie, is that you *will* finish it, as soon as you're able. Explain what happened, that you're in hospital because Tommo Hegarty beat you up.'

'How am I supposed to know it was Hegarty?'

'Well, you've seen the Wanted poster, like everyone else. Tell him Hegarty tried to coerce you into giving away Mary Quinn's whereabouts. Ten to one the bank manager will spread the word. Thick as thieves, don't they say? It'll go down well at a dinner party or over a single malt. A talking point.' She regarded him with a kind of pity. 'You don't get it, do you?'

'Not really.'

'Word will get back to Brian Rooney,' she explained with infinite patience. 'You say he's one of them.'

'Oh, he is!'

'Then *he'll* warn Hegarty off. He's her brother, get *him* on the case!'

God, I love you, Lizzie! What he said was, 'Bright girl. Now all we need is something to write on.'

A nurse obliged with a sheet of paper and a pencil and Lizzie wrote at Archie's dictation, folded the letter into a packet, addressed it, sealed it in the post office across the road and stuck it with a postage stamp. Clara proudly dropped it in the pillar box before Lizzie lifted her up onto her seat behind the mule, made her secure and set off for home.

When night came, Archie found it impossible to sleep. Pain

found him whichever way he turned, and his thoughts darted feverishly from Lizzie and John, to Rooney and Mary, from Cedric Carrington, Nobby Streeter, Dolly Brett and Hegarty, back to Lizzie and those healing kisses ...

There was something Lizzie had said, that was gnawing at his memory with brown rodent teeth. What was it, for heaven's sake?

The night nurse took pity on his restlessness and offered him a sleeping draught. Not laudanum, she assured him, as he gratefully took the glass from her. The howls and whimpers of sick children in the adjoining room, the groans and snores of his neighbours ceased to trouble him, and three hours before the nurses roused them all for breakfast, he slept.

Chapter 20

Two days later, towards evening, Nurse Ogilvie showed a windswept visitor into the ward. As the tall man removed his hat, Archie froze, recognising the long planes of his ruddy cheeks, the bright blue eyes, so like his sister's. 'Someone to see you, Archie – a Mister Kelly,' she said, inclining her head towards the man's broad, well-tailored back. 'All right?' she mouthed, eyeing the riding whip the man was slapping against his boot. What would she do if he said no, he wondered, smother his visitor with her apron?

Archie was sitting on the bed, ready to go home, with clean dressings and shirt and the sponged and pressed trousers Mrs Reeves had sent up the day before. They smelled strongly of the turps she'd used to get out the stains. A nurse had helped him on with his socks and boots, and his outdoor clothes were laid out, waiting for Bob Cheshire to collect him as soon as he finished up at the shop.

He was a sitting duck.

'That's fine, thank you, nurse,' he said, mentally crossing his fingers. Putting on a brave face, he said to his visitor, 'So we meet again, Mister Kelly.'

'Is there somewhere we can talk?'

'The day-room?' Lord knows he didn't relish a tète a tète with

Tommo Hegarty's partner. He struggled upright and, leaning on his stick, limped to the door, gesturing for 'Kelly' to go ahead.

When Holmcroft had been a private house, the day-room had been the family's library and there were still shelves of books lining the walls, newspapers on the small tables, and comfortable armchairs for the walking wounded and their visitors. An old gentleman in a dressing gown had dozed off before the fire.

'Take a seat,' invited Archie, indicating an empty chair by the window and lowering himself gingerly into one opposite. Though they said his ribs were mending, he was still unable to bend without pain and under his clean woollen combinations his body was black and blue.

'I will,' said the man, polishing a dew-drop from his nose with a silk handkerchief and wiping the wind from his eye. 'Sure and 'twas a grand ride over the marshes there.'

Following his gaze out of the window, Archie saw a mare tethered to the rail, burnished to conker brightness, tail swishing, head tossing against the bit. A spirited mount, groomed and blanketed, it made the other nags in the drive seem like a different breed. Was this the horse he'd stolen from Squire Mowbray?

'I wondered if you might come that way,' said Archie.

'You were expecting me?'

'I thought Mister Carrington would acquaint you with my situation, knowing that you would be concerned for your sister's safety.'

The man arched an eyebrow but said nothing. He would be difficult to hoodwink.

'She is your sister, isn't she? Mary Quinn.'

'You think so?'

'Wasn't it her honour you were defending that night at Streeter's?'

'Ah yes, the fisticuffs …'

Trusting that the man had been too drunk to have a clear memory of events, Archie persevered with the lie. 'Yes, I wasn't sober but I do remember your warning: "Leave my sister alone!" I understood you to mean that you didn't want me painting her again.'

The man rubbed his forehead. He clearly remembered something of the sort.

'Regrettably, you were too late. I'd already started another.' Ignoring Rooney's scowl, Archie went on, 'It's one of my best. A moonlit scene.' He gestured helplessly. 'She needed my money and I needed Nobby Streeter's. He seems to like her looks. There was another painting but it was only half finished when she ran off.'

The scowl deepened, the fists bunched. 'Ran from *you?*'

'Nothing I did. It was when I told her I'd met you and told her that you'd taken against my painting her that she …'

'Ran off,' he put in, with an understanding nod, pursing his lips. 'She would, so.'

He was an intelligent chap. How did he get caught up with the likes of Mad Tommo? Archie shuddered, recalling the wild gleam in Hegarty's eye as he raised the carving knife to cut off his hand. He could quite see him killing old Squire Mowbray in a fit of temper, mashing the man's face with his shillelagh. He couldn't imagine Rooney being as violent. Rooney was more controlled, more circumspect; even now he was weighing him up, trying to work out the truth.

'I could have finished it without her,' Archie went on. 'She has a – em – a memorable face. But, unfortunately, the man who did this –' he indicated his ruined hand and face '– destroyed my painting as well.' He couldn't resist adding, 'Perhaps you've heard of him? Tommo Hegarty?'

191

'You mentioned him in your letter to Cedric,' Rooney said, matching Archie for assumed innocence. 'He's wanted for murder, I understand.'

As are you, Brian Rooney, Archie might have said. By association. By not lifting a finger to stop it. But now was not the time to confront the man. Once a ruthless footpad, Hegarty's partner-in-crime had come a long way in three years. His brogue was not as thick as Hegarty's and he had all the trappings of one of Streeter's 'entrepreneurs'. You couldn't trust a man like that.

In as level a voice as he could muster, he informed his visitor that the police thought that Hegarty had murdered Mary's landlady, presumably to ensure her silence.

Rooney's eyes widened in shock. 'He *killed* the woman! Dear God, he's beyond—' He took a moment to gather his wits, and from his expression Archie inferred that, whatever else, Brian Rooney was no friend of Tommo Hegarty. 'Mary was after telling me about a bullyboy come to the house. She thought it was one of Streeter's rowdies, and so she ran out the back – came straightway to me.'

'*Streeter* was behind it?'

'No, no. It's what she thought but she was wrong. Nobby denies it and I believe him. You say it's Tommo and that makes more sense. By the saints, though, I'll not forgive myself if she falls into *his* hands again.'

'He's mistreated her before?'

The brother bit his lip, realising he'd said too much. 'You have no idea where she can be?'

Archie swallowed. 'I hoped she was with you. Otherwise I don't. I believe she has a friend over in Chingford …'

'Maggie Hegarty, Tommo's sister,' the visitor replied. 'No, she'd not long come from there when I saw her last.'

'Is she the singer?'

'Singer? No.' He managed a smile. 'Maggie doesn't sing. Kitty Flanagan's the singer. You heard her at Nobby Streeter's do, so you did.'

'I thought … no, that was Kitty O'Grady?'

'Kitty *Flanagan*,' he insisted. 'O'Grady's her stage name. He made her change it.'

'I see.'

'I doubt you do. She's under Nobby's protection, as Mary might have been if she hadn't taken against him.' Strangely, he sounded peeved.

Archie shuddered. 'But Kitty,' he began. The Kitty he knew was the one who'd sung *Marble Halls* at the ceilidhs with Mary? Jesus! Kitty with her loose ways, her sugar-daddies. Mary was friends with her? Perhaps he had Mary all wrong. Making her out to be some sort of saint when in fact, she was … well, he really didn't know. But that was how Rooney was acquainted with Kitty, of course. No stage-door johnnie – he'd known her in Ireland, his sister's friend. They'd simply been renewing old acquaintance when he'd seen them at Streeter's. They'd both recognised Mary from the painting.

'I don't think Mary has any idea that Kitty has become a, em, is a – a singer on the stage,' he told his visitor.

'The least of it,' muttered the Irishman, and abruptly changed the subject. 'Well, she has me jiggered – my sister, I mean. I haven't a notion where she might be. But I'll put it about that I'm looking for her, that I'll pay for her safe return. I'll find her, don't you worry.' His expression was grim. 'Leave Hegarty to me. I'll see he doesn't harm the girl.'

'You know where he is, Mister … Kelly?'

The blue eyes frosted over; the mouth became a thin line of muscle. 'If I don't, I'll find out.'

As he walked Rooney outside and watched him ride off across the cobbled yard to the road, Archie felt his load lighten. He could see Rooney calling on Hegarty and putting the frighteners on the little rat, so that he'd scuttle back to Ireland dragging his tail behind him. He felt he could almost stop worrying about Mary. Rooney would take care of it.

Bob Cheshire's arrival roused him from a reverie of relief. 'Aye, aye, Arch!' he shouted, over the horse's hooves, the rattle of the cart. 'Ready to go home?'

Archie went in to get his hat and coat and his few toiletries, to take leave of the other patients and the nurses. When he came out again into the foyer, Bob remarked, 'See they've put your picture in pride of place, Arch.'

Indeed they had: *Saint Mary's Parish Church* was already framed and hanging in the entrance hall, opposite the great front door, the first thing visitors saw as they came in. The only other decoration was a large photograph, showing the official opening of *Holmcroft,* the expanded *Leyton, Walthamstow and Wanstead Hospital,* that had taken place the year before. A bunch of local dignitaries, including the founders of the original *Cottage for Sick Children,* a Mr and Mrs Tudor, stood on the steps against a backdrop of uniformed nurses. Doctors and surgeons filled in the gaps, and the whole group stared fixedly at the camera until the flash of phosphorous told them to stop.

Archie's eyes narrowed. There was old Doctor Anthony who'd set his bones, Matron – that formidable lady who'd reprimanded Nurse Ogilvie for paying more attention to one Archibald Price than was absolutely necessary – and Ogilvie herself in the back row. But who was this? A face he'd recorded in his notebook: obsequious eyebrows and flaring nostrils. Archie remembered seeing him sprawled on one of Streeter's sofas, shirt unbuttoned, enjoying the favours of certain feathered and gartered demoiselles.

'Excuse me, Nurse,' he asked as Ogilvie sailed past in billowing white and blue, 'who is this?' He tapped the glass. 'This person standing next to Matron?'

The nurse frowned as her eyes adjusted to the dim light of the hallway. 'Oh, that's Sebastian Mowbray, Archie, owns a lot of property hereabouts.'

'*Mowbray?* Any relation to Sir Timothy?'

'His son. Sebastian is the younger son. The old man was one of our patrons – generous, you know – donated seventeen thousand pounds towards the alterations here.' Her eyes slid sideways. 'But, of course, he was killed, you may have heard, so Sebastian stepped up to represent him at the opening.' She pointed to the man beside Mowbray, heavily moustached and plumply important, the only one to have blinked too soon. 'This is Josiah Fox.'

'The builder,' Archie supplied, having a sour recollection of said Mister Fox, a local man responsible for the spider's web of cheap housing radiating from railway stations in the area. He had tried to beat Archie down on the price of a family portrait. His was one of the few commissions Archie had ever refused.

'And this is …'

'*Lionel Partridge!*' Archie gazed open-mouthed at the skeletal greybeard. A shiver went through him. What was that pederast doing in a children's hospital?

'You know him?'

'We've met,' was all he would say but, as she went on to explain that Partridge was a well-known do-gooder, Archie took in a breath deep enough to crack all his ribs at once.

*

195

The studio was a picture. The floor had been scrubbed to the bone, the shelves were spotless, furniture was polished, the range blacked and shining. The bed was shaken, its pillows repaired and plumped. Clean sheets, fresh-painted shutters, even the windows were clean. Some brave soul had sat on that bird-limed windowsill and washed them, inside and out. Any paintings that had escaped Hegarty's attentions leaned against the walls looking exhausted.

Within minutes of his arrival, Mrs Reeves was knocking at the door with a heavy parcel.

'No, no,' she cried when he tried to take it from her, 'you'll drop it.' Once upstairs in the studio, she placed her burden on the table. 'Three guesses?' she demanded.

'No idea. Was it you?'

'Eh?'

'The cleaning?'

'Not the room, you silly arse! That was Aggie Cheshire and the scrubbers from the pickle factory. I mean this, the parcel, guess what it is?'

'No idea. Groceries?' he asked hopefully.

'Open it,' she urged, clearly excited. But the knots in the string were impossible with his stupid right hand still in splints. 'Oh cut it, cut it.' She couldn't wait. 'Here let me, you don't wanna spill nothing.' When the string was off, she let Archie peel back the brown paper, just as if he were a two year old. 'We had a whip-round.' She couldn't contain her impatience. 'Charlotte said you was coming home and everyone put in.'

'You mean …'

'All the stalls, them at the school, all the shopkeepers, even the Sally Army. Come on, hurry up.'

There were pencils, brushes of all sizes and dozens of tubes of paint, bottles of turps and linseed oil, beeswax, charcoal. Most

196

amazing were the small boxes of pigment: iron oxide, ultramarine, chromium, titanium, zinc, cobalt – replacements, in fact, for the contents of all the jars that had been broken. 'Just to get you started again,' said Mrs Reeves, looking flushed and happy. 'We give the money to your mate, 'Arry, in the printer's. Said he knew where to get stuff. He went up town Tuesday. Done all right, didn't he?' She fingered a long hogshair brush, unscrewed the top of a fat tube of yellow ochre, and put it back again, occupying herself with the parcel's contents so that she didn't have to see a grown man cry.

*

By nightfall, though grateful, he was worn out with people dropping by to wish him well and after he'd seen Bernie Diamond off the premises, having shared a plate of jellied eels with him – better than anything the hospital provided – he locked up and slid home the new bolt that Bob had put on the front door. Then he crawled upstairs and into bed.

It was still dark when an echo of Brian Rooney's voice prodded him conscious. *'You were expecting me?'* Why was he remembering that part of their conversation?

It was something that Rooney's victim, Squire Mowbray, might have said had his attackers given him half a chance. They were lying in wait for him. *For him, and him alone.* John Kington's cashbox was a bonus.

Lizzie believed the brigands had struck it lucky – been in the right place at the right time. But they were well prepared. John had mentioned seeing a dangling rope, one end knotted about the branch of an oak tree, some seven or eight feet off the ground. The robbers had climbed trees on either side of the narrow track to stretch a rope between them, high enough to catch a cantering horseman across the chest and unseat him. If the horse Rooney had been riding was indeed Sir Timothy Mowbray's chestnut mare then it was about eighteen hands, putting her rider high enough. It wasn't luck that had netted the robbers such a big fish. They'd been expecting him.

How had two lowly footpads learnt that a man with a nice fat purse would come along that particular path at around that time in the evening? They couldn't have known he'd win the point-to-point and be ten guineas the richer. But they did know his route home.

The most direct way from Epping Town to Penbury Hall, the Mowbrays' ancestral pile, was along the open road, past Bell Common and across Warren Plantation. Instead, he'd chosen a by-way on the other side of the Epping New Road, behind Ambresbury Banks. He must have told someone that this was the path he'd take, or how had his attackers known where to wait? They couldn't have followed him from Epping; they'd never have kept up with the horse. They wouldn't have had time to get ahead and prepare the trap.

Somebody knew his plans and somebody told Hegarty and Rooney, somebody who wanted the old man dead. His wife? One of his sons, in a hurry to take up his inheritance? A mistress? A rival landowner? A servant with a grudge?

The more Archie thought about it, the more likely it seemed that if somebody at Penbury Hall was trying to hush up their connection to the Squire's death, they might want to silence Mary Quinn and thus keep Tommo Hegarty out of the witness box. Who knows what stories he could tell?

Yes, he was sure he would find the answer at Penbury Hall. But how was he going to weasel his way in there and root around without arousing suspicion?

Chapter 21

When Streeter appeared unexpectedly on his doorstep, towards the end of the week, Archie's heart flew into his throat and lay there ticking. Oh Lord. Was he in for another kicking? Had Nobby rumbled who it was who'd cost him a cargo of sweet young flesh and a spell in prison? Would he shoot him and be done with it?

Nobby had business over this way, he said, and having heard from Cedric Carrington about Archie's misadventure, thought he'd call in on the invalid. Meanwhile ... He clicked his fingers for his man to bring a large hamper to the door from Cedric, who sent his best. The driver led the way with Archie trying to cover his revulsion with fulsome words of gratitude. All the calves' foot jelly in the world would not exonerate a man who would dream of selling little kids. As soon as Streeter was gone he would send the *foie gras*, chocolate, fruit cake, sugared almonds, oranges and whiskey round to the Salvation Army. Well, maybe not the whiskey.

'How very kind of Cedric,' he said, through gritted teeth.

When they were alone, settled before the fire, Streeter insisted on taking Archie's mending hand in both of his and examining its lumps and scars as though checking that they were real. He was very sorry to learn that Archie had been so inconvenienced, he said eventually. Broken fingers were the devil and that dreadful cut ...

Archie studied him. How could you tell a dissembler from an honest man? Did he sweat, as this man was sweating? Did he lock eyes with you to convince you of his innocence? Did he quiz you as to the doctor's prognosis? Whether you would be able to paint again? And why this madman, Tommo Hegarty, was so set against you?

Streeter was either a good actor or was genuinely concerned for Archie's welfare. He swore he'd keep his ear to the ground, see if he couldn't track the bastard down. But – and he leaned in closer to catch the slightest change in Archie's colour or expression – what sort of hold did Mary Quinn have over the fellow, that he wanted to find her so urgently?

'I really couldn't say, Nobby.'

'Could she pick him out in a line-up, perhaps?'

The unexpectedness of the suggestion caught him off-guard. 'I – I don't know how well she knows him, if at all. They're both Irish,' he suggested. 'I recognised him from the poster outside the police station. He's a wanted man.'

'Why did he come to you, I wonder?'

'Well, from the little he told me, I gather he'd called at Mary's home and, not finding her there, questioned the woman she lodged with, a seamstress named Dolly Brett.'

Streeter nodded as though he knew the woman. Of course, Mary had told him that Streeter's was a familiar face in Coppermill Lane. Perhaps he'd even called at the cottage, looking for Mary. He had the address, after all.

'Dolly Brett must have told him that Mary sat for me,' he continued, 'and I suppose he thought I might be privy to Mary's plans. I'm sure the poor creature only said it out of desperation to be rid of him. But he killed her anyway.'

'Killed her!' The man's jaw dropped. 'This is why the police want to question him?'

'It is.'

'So he came to you next. And were you able to help him?'

'No, no! I have no idea where she is.' He explained how his model had taken off in the middle of a painting and that he hadn't heard from her since.

'Something you said perhaps?' Streeter asked, with the quirk of an eyebrow.

Archie sighed, 'I wish I knew.'

Streeter asked if he could see the painting. Archie pointed out the vandalised work leaning against the wall, the canvas drooping grossly from its wooden stresses. The art collector gazed in horror.

'He's taken her face,' he cried, 'her soul! That's diabolical. Good God, the man really is insane!'

'He was trying to get me to talk. But even if I'd wanted I couldn't have told him what I didn't know.'

'Can you save her?'

'I don't …' He realised Streeter was referring to the ravaged painting. 'Oh, I see. No, I'd have to start again, using a new canvas.'

'You have photographs?'

'Don't need them.' To demonstrate, he took a scrap of paper and, pinning it down with his splint, drew Mary's face, left-handed.

Streeter watched, spellbound. 'But you have her! What a gift! And you're ambidextrous!'

'Not at all. It's like pushing treacle, as you see. Writing is impossible.'

'I'd make it worth your while.' He mentioned a figure that had Archie reeling almost in pain. The man was clearly addicted to Mary Quinn. In which case, striking while the iron was still white-hot …

'I wonder, might you be interested in something else?' He limped over to the wardrobe and pulled out from behind it, like a rabbit from a hat, a canvas Hegarty had missed.

The effect was startling. In between wheezing and coughing, he managed to splutter, 'Oh my God!' but not until the attack subsided, a minute or two later, was he able to take in fully the composition of street, moon and milling theatre crowds. When he could breathe freely, his eyes filled with the ragged little busker singing for coppers, and his brow cleared in wonder. 'Is this the one you were peddling at my house?' he asked. 'I didn't realise. The little thing is even more fetching in this than she was in "*The Immigrant*".'

Archie nodded agreement, albeit reluctantly. Much as he hated letting his work go to this awful man, if it bought his safety, he could have it. If Streeter had the slightest notion that someone in his circle had scuppered the *Eastern Star* project, he would be less likely to suspect a man who benefited from his patronage.

'Can she really sing?' Nobby demanded.

'I believe so,' he said, remembering sweet nursery rhyme sessions with Clara.

'Mmm,' her buyer murmured. 'Perfect.'

What did that mean? Was this scheming bull-frog intending to put Mary on the stage with Kitty? Or did musicality add to a slave's market value? With mixed feelings he tucked the thick roll of Streeter's money into his inside pocket.

'So, Archie.' He gathered his hat and gloves. 'You're going to be busy, what with Carrington's girls to finish off and my portrait of Mary Quinn.'

'I am. But after that I'd like to try something different.' He outlined his plan to Streeter, who listened intently.

'You know the people?'

'Hardly. I believe I may have exchanged a few words with the younger brother at your house-warming, but I'd need an introduction …'

'Leave it to me, Archie. I'll have a word with Mowbray for you. Least I can do.'

*

Penbury Hall was old, sixteenth century from all accounts, set in eighteen acres of parkland, off the Epping New Road, some nine miles from Walthamstow. To save himself a long daily commute, Archie took a room at the Forest Gate Inn on Bell Common. After a substantial breakfast, he'd set out along well-trodden footpaths to arrive at the old manor house some forty minutes later, better for the brisk exercise and the sight of greening fields and snowy blackthorn blossom in the hedgerows.

Arriving the back way through an old iron gate, he would skirt the vast vegetable plot and cut across the lawns to where his makeshift 'studio' was sited, some fifty yards from the corner of the house. From here, the stark marble frontage was offset by the warm red brick of the side of the house, and the hard angles of the architecture were softened by the dark green of ancient yew trees. His 'studio', built with William Mowbray's permission and his head-gardener's help, was a perfectly dark, box-like shed, where the only light source was a small aperture in the door fitted with a magnifying glass, not for peering out but to let the outside in. Rigging up his oversized canvas against the opposite wall he had given a satisfied grunt as the image of the mansion appeared on it, in crystal clarity, albeit upside down. Another lens, on a borrowed tallboy, turned the image the right way up and enlarged it to fill the canvas. Safe from the weather and curious eyes, he then traced the outline of turrets, chimneys, windows and doors, in perfect perspective. It wasn't cheating. It was how Vermeer had captured Delft, and Caravaggio his fruity boy.

He painted hard and long inside his *camera obscura*, changing to his left hand when the right began to ache, mounting a stepladder to attack the lowering sky. On his breaks he'd wander the estate, passing the time of day with the outdoor workers and sketching or, if the weather was unkind, he'd head for the kitchen, where a cup of tea and biscuits would be forthcoming, but useful gossip less so. He heard about the cook's son-in-law and his philandering ways. He heard about the boot-boy's encounter with a gypsy woman on Bell Common who'd told him that he would be killed in battle before he was forty. Utter tosh. But as soon as he mentioned the Mowbray murder, they closed ranks and clammed up, casting conspiratorial looks at each other. No wonder the police had had no leads at all until John Kington was able to describe the men who attacked him. Presumably the Penbury staff were protecting one of their own or they were in fear of reprisals. How was he going to get them to drop their guard?

One pretty afternoon in March he took a bottle of sherry along to the kitchen to celebrate his 'birthday' with the cook and her assistant. Never mind that he'd been born in February. Artistic licence, he told himself.

'Here's to you, then, Mister Price – what is it, twenty-one today?'

'Add six to that, Cook.'

'Same age as Mister Sebastian.'

Now there was an opening. 'The Squire's younger brother?' he enquired casually. 'I believe I saw his photograph in the drawing room. Blond chap? You'd never think they were brothers.'

The cook, a motherly soul, with five sons and a daughter at

home, put down her glass to sift flour into her bowl. 'He takes after his mother.' She nodded. 'William is more like his Papa. Always the old man's favourite.'

Archie sipped his drink slowly and re-filled the woman's glass, trying not to appear too interested in her story. She explained that she'd had a lot to do with the boys in her early days at the Hall when she'd been taken on as a nursery maid, cleaning up after them and making them milky junkets and gingerbread biscuits when the then cook was busy. As the boys had grown up so she had worked her way up from kitchen maid to her present position, with Maisie her underling and more trouble than she was worth. Maisie, a robust woman in her thirties, merely grinned and shrugged.

As she cut small knobs of butter into her mix, Cook said, 'Good looks was the root of Master Sebastian's trouble, you ask me.' Her expression was bleak as she proceeded to rub the butter into the mixture. 'My little angel, I called him, with his gold hair and blue eyes. Sweet boy, back then.' Her mouth twisted. Presumably the sweetness was long gone. Archie took out his sketchbook and a pencil and caught her mouth tightening on a grudge.

'Squire said he was a runt, a milksop and needed toughening up. Any excuse and he'd whack him, the slightest thing – dirtying his shoes, messing up his room, not knowing twice times eight.' Spooning sugar into the mix the woman breathed deep and helpless disapproval. 'Then he was … *one,*' she counted each spoonful on an in-breath '… sent away to that school … *two* … and that never helped. *Three*. Gawd knows what went on there but he toughened up in the wrong way, somehow. *Four*. Come over all surly, you know? *Five*. And he'd cheek his old man something terrible. Out'd come the old cane and … *six* … the poor lad'd shut hisself in his room for days on end.'

205

'How about that time he run off from school, Mrs Fowler?' prompted Maisie, beating eggs as though her life depended on it.

'Oh aye. Oh, that were a terrible shame.'

'He come 'ome, she said – I mean, so Mrs Fowler told us – he come 'ome from that wicked place and, you know what?'

Cook gave her a look to shut her up. This was her story. 'Those eggs ready, girl?' She made them wait while she stirred a slop of eggs into her mixture. When she was strong enough, she muttered, 'The Squire flogged him for it.' She swallowed and her floury hands dropped onto the table, wooden spoon and all, as her head and shoulders sagged. Archie topped up the sherry.

The young boy had been horse-whipped before the entire staff assembled on the back lawn to witness his punishment.

'Dear God!' Archie laid down his pencil.

Maisie gave him a satisfied nod that said, *See, I told you.*

According to Cook it had quite broken Sebastian's spirit. She tipped her dough out of the bowl and rolled it evenly with the rolling pin. He had gone back to school when his wounds healed, to whatever punishment awaited him there, returning to Penbury Hall the next holiday, tight-lipped and taciturn. He'd go off on his own, some said to the woods to play with the gypsies. Skilfully lifting the smoothed dough she turned it around and rolled it flat again. Didn't come home till well past supper time, refusing to say where he'd been. When his schooling came to an end, he idled around in gambling dens and – she faltered – and places of ill repute, making all sorts of unsavoury friends.

'And when the old man was killed, rest his soul, Sebastian took his inheritance and went into business with that Nobby Streeter as comes round here. They run a couple a pubs together – one over your way, Mister Price – The Railway Tavern?'

'Sebastian's in with Streeter?'

'Oh aye. Thick as thieves, them two. Up to all sorts.'

Archie finished his drawing of the two women, signed it with a flourish and handed it over.

Maisie cried, 'Ooh, Mrs Fowler! Look at that!"

'Gawd 'elp us, what a fright! Still, I s'pose you better stick it up on the mantel, Mais. Give everybody a good laugh.'

*

It wasn't until a really wet day at the end of March that Archie learned how Hegarty fitted into the story.

Archie and the head-gardener were old friends, having worked on Archie's shed together. Since then they'd exchanged words daily about the weather or a particularly beautiful crop of daffodils that Archie had chosen to sketch, and Archie always threatened to draw Horace Hodge's portrait despite his protestations.

Shaking raindrops from his hair he ducked into the potting shed. 'Phew, what a day! You busy, Horace?' He pulled out his sketchbook and waved his pencil to show his intentions.

'Long as you don't mind us gettin' on with a bit of sowin',' the gardener drawled in the old Essex way.

'Perfect. I don't want you posing. Just be yourself. Look, I'll show you.' He flicked through his book of faces. 'See there's Mrs Fowler cooking.'

'Oh that's her to a T. She allus makes that face.'

'And this is the butler.'

'Oh ah, and that's our Jonah, ennit?' The gamekeeper. 'You been busy, Mister Price.'

'I like to improve the shining hour,' he said, leafing casually through pages of Walthamstow town folk, re-drawn into a new sketchbook for just such an occasion as this. There was Percy Reeves pulling pints, Charlotte on her stall, Nurse Ogilvie dispensing medicine, Bob Cheshire tipping potatoes into a shopping bag, Mary Quinn, of course, scrubbing steps. He swallowed. And came at last to the first drawing in the book: Hegarty's likeness, copied from the one Mary had dictated to him, all those months ago. As he hoped, there was a glimmer of recognition in Hodge's eyes. Mrs Fowler and the rest of the household staff hadn't even blinked at him.

'Hold up, that's young whatsisname? Tom? Tommy Something?'

'Know him, do you?'

'Indeed I do.'

Hardly believing his luck, Archie perched on a large upturned flowerpot while the gardener stood at his workbench, sowing seeds and recalling how, years ago, a certain young barefoot tinker would come to the mansion seeking seasonal work. He'd come up in the world if Archie's drawing was anything to go by.

'Might turn an 'and to 'edging and mowing, picking fruit and that, but you couldn't rely on him. Pull him up for carelessness or bein' late and he'd flare up and walk off the job. Wicked temper on him.'

He gently tamped the tray on his worktop to level the soil and cover the seeds, and stuck in an identity flag before sweeping a pile of papery husks into a bin at his feet. As he sowed another tray with lupin seeds, tipped from a flowerpot of black twisted pods, he went on with his story.

'Any old how, it all come to an 'ead one morning when old Jonah catches him creepin' off down the lane wi' a brace o' pheasants up his wes'kit – whisks him off to the Master at rifle point. Well, Squire don't take kindly to being disturbed in the middle of his breakfast and gives Jonah the key to the dungeon. "Let him cool his heels in there for a while," he goes, and carries on eating.'

'Dungeon! There's a *dungeon*?'

'Oh aye.' He nodded. 'Lookit 'ere.' He pointed through the window. 'See the old door in the wall – just see the top of it from 'ere?' The artist had painted it into his landscape without a clue about its purpose. 'They used it in th'old days for holding wrong-uns 'til the sheriff come by. Empty now. Tried storin' deckchairs in there once but they got the mildew and me mower went rusty.'

Archie returned to his flowerpot, the gardener to his story. 'Door was all growed over with briars so Jonah got us to take the shears to 'er. Shame, a decent *Rosa Villosa,* that were – but we done the job, untied the boy and slung him in. What a place! Damp enough for mushrooms, I'd say. Nowhere to park your sit-upon.'

'You left him there?'

'Had to. Hollering and cursing he were when we locked him up. But what choice we got? What Squire wanted Squire got.'

'A bit harsh, though.'

''Arsh en't the word. He were an old devil, the Squire, ask anyone round here. You heard how he won the point-to-point, year in, year out. Only 'cause no one fancied getting on his wrong side.'

'They let him win?'

'Wouldn't you? There's a few others come away with the prize, but they lived to regret it – their haystack burned down of a sudden or their horse died mysterious-like. Soon as he'd done with his kippers and eggs, he goes down the dungeon and lays into ol' Tommo. Ay, that were his name, Tommo. The Master put the boot in real 'ard. "I'll give you poaching my birds!" he goes.'

The plantsman poked in the last black pill of seed and sprinkled the top with soil, before turning to Archie, whose pencil had come to a halt. 'Kep' him down there all that day and the next,' he said. 'No food, no drink. I ask ye. Starved and freezing 'alf to death, kicked to a bloody pulp – 'tweren't no wonder young Tommo done the old man in, like, when he had the chance.'

'You're guessing, right?'

'It were a guess then. Seeing your picture, him all dolled up to the nines, makes me sure. He done the old man in and made off with his purse, take my word for it.'

'Right,' said Archie, carefully. 'So why didn't any of this come out at the time?'

'No one asked us. Police 'ad their witness – that poor young potter got done over? No need for us to go risking our necks, informing like.'

Archie stared at the floor, littered with seed pods and sprinkled with earth. A long-legged spider scurried through it. So Tommo had a motive, a strong one. But had he the nous to plan his revenge? He *must* have had inside information.

He said to the gardener, 'I suppose he couldn't have been tipped off about the Squire's route through the forest from the Epping Fair? The time he'd be making his way home? That kind of thing?'

'You mean by someone at the house?'

'Could he have had an accomplice? Someone who knew the old man's schedule? I don't know – a stablehand with a grudge, somebody like that.'

'I'm not saying you're wrong, Mister, but where's the point? Anyone coming after Squire would be as bad. They're like as peas, them Mowbrays, in nature if not in looks. Better the old devil you know, be honest.'

'So you can't think of anyone who might have colluded with Hegarty?'

The gardener scratched his head. 'Set him up to kill th'old bugger?' He stuck out his fleshy lower lip and frowned, as though deliberating over the failure of a seed to germinate. He breathed hard through his nose. 'Someone jemmied that dungeon door, helped Tommo escape that time.'

'What?'

'There were talk about Tommo's pals setting him free, they tinkers up the road. Some said it were one of the scullery maids or some other soft-hearted wench. Some said Master Sebastian 'ad 'and in it.'

'*Sebastian?*'

'Back in th'old days, when he were a lad, Master Sebastian went a bit wild like, took up wi' they tinkers up on the Eppin' Road. Some said he and Tommo were close. But I never see 'em together. An' if I did, I en't saying.'

As Archie left the potting shed, the gardener called after him, 'You a grower, are ye, Mister Price? Could ye use some flower seeds? Lupins, *Lavatera*, love-in-a-mist?'

Chapter 22

Rain dripped from the trees and ran in streams down his cape and from the wide brim of his hat, but the horse seemed not to mind, keeping up a steady canter along the path. Rooney hadn't been along this way in years, but remembered Satan's stone from his days in the forest. Everyone else avoided the place except the devil worshippers, who were unlikely to be brewing their poisons and sacrificing their virgins on a wet and miserable Wednesday afternoon. As Tommo had said in his note: *'Best not meet wer peple seeing Hegarty and Rooney togedder will call to mind a sertan Wanted poster and 20 gns reward, dead or alive.'*

It was what they'd agreed when they'd parted, each to go his own way, shake off the dust of Walthamstow and take on a new identity. But Tommo was still Tommo according to the grapevine and still active in Walthamstow, getting involved in all sorts of nasty business. Neither had set eyes on the other since nor tried to make contact, although the builder, Josiah Fox, still used the boy for his dirty business from time to time and kept Rooney informed. Fox had been the go-between in a swift exchange of letters to set up this meeting. Rooney had said that he wanted to see Tommo on a matter concerning his sister, Mary Quinn, and left him to set the time and place. Hearing that the little shit was sniffing around after Mary again, killing and marauding and drawing unnecessary attention to himself, was not good news. He must be stopped, at once and for all.

The wretch was obsessed with the girl, always had been. But Mary had made it plain from the start that she wouldn't have him on a silver platter.

'He scares me to half to death,' she'd confided the very first time she and Brian were left alone in Mrs Hegarty's parlour. 'The other boys are decent enough, and Maggie's a lovely girl but,' she lowered her voice to a whisper and glanced about as if he would climb out from a crack in the wall, 'that one, with his runty looks and rough ways, he makes my skin crawl. He only comes here to get money off his mother, d'ye know, and when she has nothing for him, he hits her, Brian, blacks her eye. He's not right in the head.'

'His brothers get after him, I hope.'

'They do, but it makes no difference.'

'He doesn't touch *you*?' Rooney had to be sure. It had been his fear when she came from Ireland and he'd put her to lodge with the family in Chingford.

'No, but it's only a matter of time. Isn't he forever winking and leering at me? He makes no secret of what he wants.' Her expression hardened. 'I cannot stay here, Brian.' She shook her head firmly. 'I'll find a place in service, go and live in a big house and lock the door against him.'

She never did find that place in a big house, but she did find Pauly Quinn at the ceilidh and went to live in Walthamstow as a married woman. Six months later her husband was dead, and Mary expecting their child. Tommo must have jumped at the chance of killing Pauly Quinn when Fox told him what his problem was. He must have thought that, with the competition out of the way, he was home and dry. Fecking eejit. Life was hard but Mary was fierce, refusing even Rooney's offers of help. She said his money was tainted and she would have none of it.

So she scrubbed floors to keep the wolf from the door and the wolf came sliming around anyways in the form of Tommo, back to his old tricks, she complained, forever hanging about on the corner for her coming home from work. 'See him off, Brian or he'll be the death of me. And you too, if you don't give him up.'

He would have, but along came Tommo one bright morning with the news that would change their lives, by God. Hopping from one foot to the other and smacking the bludgeon into his palm as he spoke. The Mowbrays were going to the fair on Saturday, the sons and their ladies in the open carriage and the Squire on horseback. The old devil was determined to win the horse race: twice round the bounds and back up the Epping High Street.

Rooney hadn't got it at first. Like everyone else, he was looking forward to the fair. It was the highlight of the year and he thought he might enter a few races himself, the sprint or the trial of strength, to impress the girls.

'Don't ye see, Rooney, we're made! *They'll* take the road home and in their own time, too. They won't want to miss the singing and dancing. But the old fella will stay for the prize-giving only. He'll leave before the crowds and take the horse and the prize-money straight home. He'll be all alone on the drovers' track behind the Banks.'

He'd done his homework: he knew the time, near enough to the minute, when the Squire would be riding back around Ambresbury Banks to the big house. He knew, to the inch, how high the rope should be tied. It certainly paid, having friends at Penbury. When he saw the possibilities, Rooney became as excited as Tommo. It was no more than their due, he told himself.

214

Mowbray had come by his house and lands, even his position, by foul means, you could count on it, either him or his old fella or some granddaddy in his distant past laying claim to forest land and forcing the commoners out. What the two of them were about was only 'redistribution', after all. 'We'll just have to hope he wins a fat purse at the race.' He would, of course, as he did every year. Nothing could go wrong.

Had he known Tommo's plans for his sister when they came out of that forest with the deed behind them, he would have killed him then and there. He'd been half inclined to do so anyways, for the murders he'd done, but killing didn't come easy to Rooney, and taking the coward's way out he'd merely divvied up the takings into equal piles. Let the devil take the clothes and the mule cart, while he, being the better horseman, took the chestnut mare. With the gold links in his pocket – the shirt was too bloody to wear – and the wallet warm against his heart, Tommo had boarded the train to London. Never to be seen again.

But Tommo had stopped on the way to try and persuade the young widow to go with him to America. When she would not, he'd left her half dead. But that part of the story had taken its time filtering through to Rooney.

The money they'd taken that day was wasted on Tommo. It was like the story of the talents. While Rooney's investments had borne fruit, hadn't Tommo frittered away his share on gambling, whores and booze, and spiralled him down from a fine house in Bayswater to a flat in Moorgate to a squalid room in Bethnal Green? Now he hired himself out to one gang leader or another. He'd abandoned the mule cart, finding it too slow. He still held on to the boots, though, the fine brown leather riding boots that fitted him like a second skin and kept out the cold.

Rooney had sent Mary a card, eventually, bearing his new

address. No use writing anything else as she couldn't read beyond his name. Only the boys in the Rooney family had received an education.

They wrote to him from the workhouse that she had been brought to their hospital because of the blood she lost, along with the baby. When he came out to Leytonstone meaning to fetch her home, she was pale as a ghost and working in the laundry. No, thanks all the same, she said, she wouldn't go with him. These people had saved her life and she would stay awhile. The child had been stillborn, she told him, and all chance of having more babies destroyed. He'd assumed poverty and hard work had brought this on and she didn't deny it at first. On another visit they told him how she'd been getting distressing letters from a man called Tommo. He'd asked after her health and the baby's and wondered whether perhaps she had changed her mind about going with him to America. If she had he would like to come and see her about it. Recognising his painstaking scrawl after the first one, she had thrown the other letters into the fire, unopened.

'What has he done?' Rooney asked her straight.

But she'd closed her face tight and turned her head away. It was too bad to tell him.

'I'll kill him!' he'd cried.

'And then I'd have that on my conscience, on top of everything else,' she said. 'I'll not have you murdering on my account, Brian, and going to hell. You're still in the clear on that score.'

Rooney blamed himself. If he'd acted sooner, Mary would still have her baby and he'd have prevented murders. Now was too late, but it would be justice, so it would, and maybe a spell in purgatory would see him right.

Today, he'd do it. The still-bare trees hung across the path like a withy basket and the mare was steaming through them, her muzzle flecked with drool. He could see the dark clearing up ahead, the huge stone altar at its centre, evil in the clustering branches, and Tommo's demonic face. He took the gun from his belt, his finger on the trigger and kicked the mare for speed. It would be over in seconds and the world would be rid of this stinking vermin.

Next he knew he was on the ground, the breath knocked out of him, unhorsed by a rope across the path. There's justice. Something vital was broken – he couldn't move and his gun had been thrown wide. And here came Tommo, his rabbity teeth gleaming in a mad yellow grin, rain streaming through his sandy hair, as he smacked his cudgel into his palm.

'It's taken care of,' Mary had said, the last time he'd seen her.

'Well, darlin',' was Rooney's final thought, 'I hope it is, 'cause it's up to you now.'

Chapter 23

A rchie squinted up at the sign swinging in the wind: a Great Eastern Locomotive chuffing through the countryside, smoke billowing from its funnel. He had often passed the Railway Tavern on the corner of St James Street and High Street, but had never been tempted inside. It had a sleazy look, as though pints were pulled and spirits downed but it was another thirst entirely that the customers had come to assuage. Archie was sure he recognised two of the drabs hanging about outside as Mary's neighbours. This one, with the bad skin and scraggy hair, lived over the road: this one, with the missing front tooth, two doors away. Poor creatures, he thought. What a life! Nevertheless, he doffed his hat as he went in. 'Not tonight, ladies.'

A log fire burned in the grate, oil lamps were alight on windowsills and sconces, but a chill crept up through the stone floor. The barman seemed to resent serving him and the few people in the room gave him a cold stare before turning away. He sat down at the end of a bench and, pulling up his collar against the unfriendly draught, recalled the dark tunnel that probably ran directly under his feet, and the blood with which it was tainted. Hot and spicy red wine slurped against the glass as his hand shook and he set it down on the nearest table.

A thought struck him. The cellar passage running under this

place might make those with something to hide more furtive than usual, knowing that in investigating Dolly Brett's murder the police couldn't fail to discover their secret. They might even be wondering how long it would take those investigating the Wylie case to put two and two together. Archie was sure this was how the murdering rats had got into the furniture store.

And that was where Hegarty had come into it: he'd entered the shop in the normal way, bludgeoned Wylie to the floor and then unbolted the trap door behind the counter to let up his accomplices who were waiting below. At whose instigation, though? Archie took another hefty swig of alcohol. If Hegarty was in Sebastian Mowbray's employ …

Stop now, Arch, if you know what's good for you.

He recalled that urchin in the tunnel drawing a finger across his dirty throat like a razor blade. That was what snitching got you, or what did he call it? Grassing? No, pinching. 'Pinching' to the 'traps'. Somehow the 'traps' would have to work out the rest for themselves: the unguessable motive, and the proof, of course.

But he was halfway there.

And Mary Quinn was at the bottom of this mess, he was sure. The closer he got to solving the murders – Wylie's, Squire Mowbray's and Dolly's – the closer he would get to her. He just hoped he wasn't too late.

As he waited to be summoned into Sebastian Mowbray's presence he glanced again at the calling card that had been slipped through his letterbox this morning. Not that he needed to check the time pencilled there, he knew he was five minutes early. He wondered at the reason for the invitation. *'Would you kindly call in?'* It had to be a commission, didn't it? Perhaps Sebastian wanted a painting like his brother's, to go over the bar. Or a portrait. He might want to have his good looks recorded for posterity. On the other hand, if Sebastian Mowbray were the brains behind Hegarty's actions, he might want to finish what his hitman had started, and Archie was a fool to come to this end of the High Street, alone and unarmed, but for his trusty walking stick.

Across the room a huddle of old men doggedly played out their dominoes, sullenly tap-tapping their missed turns and wiping a froth of ale from their moustaches. Watching them, and feeling a little light-headed, Archie had the weirdest sensation that they were putting on an act for his benefit, that secrets were being whispered, about dark subways, about murder.

At last the barman caught his eye and gestured with an unsmiling jerk of his head that Mowbray was now willing to see him. Archie took his toddy with him to the back room. Dutch courage.

It was an office of sorts, with a large desk taking up most of the room, a couple of leather-backed chairs, a wooden roll-down filing cabinet, with signed photographs and posters of actors and music hall artistes scattered around the walls, such as you might expect to see in a theatre agent's office. Some of the faces he recognised from billboards, some acts he'd actually seen at Wilton's or the Hackney Empire or more recently at The Horse and Groom: Marie Lloyd, Hetty King, Abe Cox. And there was his engraving of Herbert Pickering. Another face he knew personally was Kitty O'Grady, though it was some time since she'd sat for him, come to think of it, their friendship having withered away like leaves in winter. He'd assumed she'd found bigger fish to fry.

The owner of The Railway Tavern leaned back in his chair to take in Archie's height in the low room, steepling his perfectly manicured fingers and bidding him take a seat. His features were more regular than those of his brother, William, with the blond looks of their mother. But life had soured him. He was the same age as Archie but already his brow was grooved, his eyes were hooded and his mouth had a natural downturn. Even his smile was grim.

When Sebastian started telling him that the finished *View from a Ha-ha* was now hanging in the dining room at Penbury Hall, Archie's fears subsided. He was not about to be beaten up, it seemed. Sebastian was impressed by the painting of his old home and claimed to remember meeting Archie at one of Nobby Streeter's parties. The old rogue had shown him a couple of half-decent pictures Archie had painted of some little scrubber Nobby had taken a fancy to – very fetching – and Cedric Carrington's little girls looked mischievous and delightful. Looking through his collection of posters he'd come across Archie's name again. He indicated the *Sweeney Todd* poster and another, unsigned, of Florence Leslie as Nell Gwynne. 'These are yours, are they not?'

Archie's nod of assent was tentative. In truth, he was beginning to feel like a naughty schoolboy found out in some wrongdoing he had long since forgotten.

'A distinctive style,' Mowbray observed with an arched eyebrow and a cold eye. 'Memorable, one might say.'

Smooth as butter, slippery as an eel. Archie couldn't get a handle on the man. Sweat trickled down his back. Where was this heading?

'You also record local news events, I believe, for *The Journal*. One image stays in my mind, of that fire up the road. Particularly realistic, I might say: the horror on the faces of the bystanders, the roof coming down – all very moving. Oh, yes,' he said, seeing that Archie was frowning, 'your work does not go unnoticed. It's very good.' A small ingratiating smile. 'Landscapes, portraits, illustrations, posters.' He counted them off on his fingers. 'Quite

221

the all-rounder, aren't you, Mister Price?'

The plummy accent made his words sound even more condescending.

What could he say? 'I take work where I can, as a jobbing artist will. Sometimes a large painting will net me a decent sum to put in the bank, but it's the posters and the illustrations that keep the wolf from the door.'

'Yes.' The fleshy fingers beat a brief rallentando on the blotter before intertwining across the flowery waistcoat. Sebastian gazed squarely into Archie's face. 'If I am not mistaken you also take work from the police, do you not?'

He knew, by God! So this was it, the dénouement, the killer blow. Was he going to call in his henchmen and order them to do away with this two-faced informer or would he do the job himself? He probably had a gun in his drawer.

'I do,' said Archie, brazening it out. 'As I say, I take work where I can. I can't afford to be fussy.'

'You draw Wanted posters.' It wasn't a question.

'Needs must. Anything they want, really, a guinea a time – crime scenes, prisoners in the cells, courtroom proceedings. I also make advertisements for soap and false teeth. What's this about, Mister Mowbray?' Intuition told him to play the injured innocent.

'Is this why Tommo Hegarty tried to kill you?'

'Uh? I don't ...'

'Word has it he tried to cut off your hand. I wondered why at the time, but of course it was for plastering his face over every wall and telegraph pole in Walthamstow.'

'Now that never occurred to me,' Archie said truthfully. 'But yes, he may well have borne me that sort of malice – if he'd seen the posters, if he'd known I'd drawn them. What he *said* was that he was looking for Mrs Quinn whose portraits you saw at Streeter's. He too has a fancy for the girl.'

'I see,' though clearly he was as puzzled as Archie about Hegarty's interest in Mary Quinn. What was the 'history' Rooney had mentioned? It had to be sexual, didn't it?

Mowbray seemed unsettled by Archie's revelation. Again he beat his flat hands on the table and this time reached into a cupboard under the desk and brought out a bottle of whiskey and a tumbler, and then, with a speculative glance at Archie, a second glass.

'Will you join me, Mister Price?' It looked as though his doubts about his visitor had been dispelled and he proceeded to pour two fingers of the golden liquor into each glass. 'I have to say I've heard nothing but good about you, Mister Price. You take every kind of trouble over your work, even, in my brother's case, I hear, building some sort of outsized camera in order to get everything exactly right. No doubt you came here expecting that I would offer you a commission and I won't disappoint you, but mine comes with conditions. Not a word of what I am about to ask you to do must go beyond these four walls. Will you promise me that?'

What he had in mind was a dream of a commission, a fantasy: a huge painting of the great and good of the theatre world, brought together at some sort of gathering or grand ball. Actors and actresses would hobnob with playwrights and directors, music-hall artistes would rub shoulders with opera singers and magicians. Anybody who was anybody in the British theatre would be included. He envisioned a monument to celebrity.

'A cast of hundreds.' Archie marvelled. He took another sip of whiskey, a small one, and rolled the strong liquor around his tongue, counselling himself to be careful: strong drink was his downfall. He had to keep his wits about him. This man had had his own father killed, and how many others? He swallowed, trying to keep his excitement under control. It would be an enormous project. 'Where will it be hung? I mean, I'll need to know the size.'

'Bigger than anything you've done before, I can assure you.' Mowbray inhaled the vision. 'Imagine you're going out for an evening's entertainment at the music hall. Up the steps you go, the grand marble steps, through the swing doors and into the foyer. What an atmosphere: high ceilings, chandeliers, red plush carpets, sweeping staircases to left and right, with gold-painted newel posts and banisters. What luxury! And when you reach the landing what meets your eyes? Why – a wonderful mural, a full thirty feet by fifteen, full of interest, full of glamour. That's my vision, Mister Price, between the twin doors to the Dress Circle.'

A mural! Archie drained his glass. Not quite the Sistine Chapel but not far off. It would have to be painted in situ, working from sketches and photographs, and would have to be measured and planned down to the nearest inch. Those famous faces in the background would be smaller, of course, but at least as visible, as recognisable as those in the front. The work would be seen by thousands of theatregoers.

'So where is this theatre? I'd like to have a look at it before I give you a yes or no.'

'Well,' said Mowbray, refilling their glasses, 'it isn't actually built yet. But I can show you the plans if you're interested.'

Oh yes.

The front elevation showed twin towers at least four storeys high and a grand entrance with steps. Further in, you could see a huge stage with an orchestra pit and seating for many hundreds, in stalls, boxes, dress circle, upper circle and gallery – the 'gods'.

There would be a bar, a cloakroom, fully plumbed lavatories, a kiosk for cigarettes and chocolates.

'We are going to put Walthamstow on the map,' said Sebastian Mowbray.

It was to be a joint venture with Nobby Streeter, their biggest joint undertaking to date. The entrepreneur ran a couple of barges on the River Lea which Mowbray used for transporting merchandise: wine, barrels of ale, coal and lamp oil from the docks. Much the best way – the roads were becoming intolerable. They ran a shooting gallery in Tottenham and a gymnasium in Leytonstone, helping to keep youngsters off the streets. Socially they hadn't much in common. In Mowbray's opinion the Eastender was basically a lout. Although he had been a guest at Nobby's housewarming in October, he hadn't stayed – just stopped long enough to catch the singer. He nodded at Kitty's photograph.

He paused to set down his glass, to pat his blotter into careful alignment with the edge of his desk and straighten a line of pens. Archie, following his movements, recognised this week's copy of *The Era* lying in his intray. It was a journal that Archie also took, containing up-to-the-minute news about the theatre and music halls, the stars, who was playing where, which places were opening, which closing.

'It's an ideal spot you have here,' said Archie, 'close to the station, with gas and water pipes coming through soon.'

'Not here, not on the corner. The crossroads' traffic would present a huge problem. No, it would need to be somewhere rather quieter. Further up the High Street, we thought.' As though regretting a slip, he slid a worried glance at Archie, who smiled encouragingly.

'How long before you start building?'

'Not long, once we have clearance.'

'Clearance?'

'Oh, em, just a few formalities, you know, nothing to worry about. We should be up and running by the summer. I won't ask you to work in dust and rubble, Mister Price. As soon as it settles …'

'Summer? Good heavens I'd better start sketching.'

'But discreetly, I must insist. Not a word of this to your friends at the police station.'

'No friends of mine, I assure you.'

'I hope not. In fact, with this commission under your belt you can safely sever all connection with that establishment.'

In other words, thought Archie, as he wended his way home, stay away from the police or else. Again, in his mind's eye, he saw the waif in the passageway and his dangerous cut-throat finger. What was he to do? Sebastian Mowbray and Norbert Streeter, the scum of the earth, were setting themselves up to be Walthamstow's impresarios. He could, he supposed, refuse their commission and nail his colours firmly to the mast of law and order. Or he could accept their handsome offer.

That wonderful painting! He could see it now, echoing Raphael's *School of Athens*, a symphony of perspective built around the icons of the age, firmly signed by one *A. Price*. He could do it, oh God, he could. It would make his name. And the money, well invested, would ensure he lived well for the rest of his life, free to paint what he wanted, in whatever style he pleased. But that money was tainted with the blood of slaves.

And he knew exactly where the new Palace of Varieties would be sited; knew which friends he would be betraying if he undertook this commission. Percy Reeves was one, Daniel Wylie another and all the people who had contributed to restocking his art shelves, the rest.

Lit by the nearby street lamp, an unpainted hoarding, littered with ragged bills and stickers for musical soirees, circuses, boxing matches, screened the blackened hulk of the furniture shop from curious eyes. It would remain in place while the police investigation went on. That fence accounted for the delay, the so-called 'formalities' to be got over. Presumably Nellie Wylie, Daniel's widow, had been persuaded to sell to Mowbray as soon as she had clearance. No doubt Nellie couldn't wait to be rid of the place that had killed her husband. Mowbray would have got it for a song. *Hah,* he thought wryly, *a song and a dance!*

A music hall halfway down the High Street would kill the Horse and Groom's trade at the top end. If anyone should open a proper theatre, Percy Reeves should. He had the experience, the know-how, the love. He would never forgive Archie for going over to the enemy.

If he went over …

Chapter 24

'In the land of the living, are we?' Frank Tyrell stood on the doorstep, his eyes twinkling with cheer, his moustache bristling.

'Quick – come in!' Ushering Tyrell up the stairs, Archie stopped behind to check the shadows for movement before closing the front door.

'Watching you, are they?'

'Possibly. I'm not supposed to have any further dealings with you lot.'

'Bit of news,' said the policeman, ignoring this last remark. Immediately on entering the artist's flat, he announced, 'Brian Rooney's dead.'

'What!' This wasn't what he'd hoped to hear. 'Where? How?'

'In the forest, where the coven meets, you know?'

He did. It was a ghastly place. They used a natural outcrop of mossy rock as an altar for their demonic ceremonies. Dreadful things hung in the trees around there, animal skulls and dead birds, and an air of evil. 'You mean the devils got hold of him.'

'Too early to say. He was unhorsed with a trip rope – the usual thing.'

'Oh my God, that's Hegarty's doing!' There was no help for it but to describe how he had lured Rooney to the hospital to warn him that Hegarty was looking for Mary. 'I thought Rooney would see him off! But, damn and blast it, I only made matters worse.'

Tyrell nodded terse agreement. 'You should a left it to us, Arch. We was nearly there.' All the same he had to own that no progress had been made in tracing either Quinn or Hegarty, although the police had now established a connection between them.

'Really?'

Under Mary's straw pallet in Coppermill Lane, they had found a stash of keepsakes. A hoard of buttons and ribbons, pretty stones, and an ivory penknife inscribed with the initials *AP*. 'So that's where it went! I had to buy another one.' And a pair of gold monogrammed cufflinks, listed as missing three years ago by the Squire's family. The police had found one of the pair *under* the bed, among the mouse dirt and spiders. 'How she come by them's neither 'ere nor there, the fact remains – the widow Quinn can now be charged with receiving stolen goods.'

How she come by them? Archie's imagination went zigzagging off, chasing a flapping white shirt with twinkling gold in the cuffs. Had she stolen, found or received them as a gift? Somehow he didn't think that Rooney, so clever at covering his tracks, would have given traceable monogrammed gold to his sister. He wouldn't have wanted her implicated in murder. No, it was Hegarty, of course, who hadn't the brains he was born with. *M* for Mary was all he could see. He'd probably given them to her, hoping to curry favour. When, though? It could only have been before he'd taken the train to London, the day after the murder. No two ways about it, Hegarty had spent the night with her.

'They was lovers,' said Tyrell, with conviction. 'He wanted the little widow to go away with him. The shirt come off in the passion of the moment and when he put it back on he forgot the cufflinks, not being used to them.'

'But she *didn't* go with him, did she? She hates him, wants him dead,' Archie reminded his visitor, thinking that this night might be the 'bad history' that Rooney had spoken of. 'No,' he said firmly, 'he took out the cufflinks and rolled up his sleeves the better to batter her.'

'Then the shirt would've 'ad blood on it. I've checked the file and no one who see him on the train that day mentioned blood. A shirt, yes, but no blood.'

His words triggered a thought. 'That shirt would've had blood on it anyway. If it was the Squire's he was wearing it when they bashed his face in.'

Tyrell was keeping up well. 'You're saying that Hegarty took it to Mary Quinn's to wash?'

'Yes, yes, yes!' cried Archie. 'And that's why he stayed the night, waiting for the shirt to dry!'

Tyrell gave a hollow laugh. '*I'm sure.*' And after a long pause, 'She should a come to us with them cufflinks.'

'Perhaps she couldn't.' Glumly picturing the poor girl's state after Hegarty had finished with her, especially if she refused to go with him, he almost missed what Tyrell was saying next: something about bad pennies turning up.

'She must've had a fit when she saw him outside Wylie's last summer – her worst nightmare.'

Archie nodded. He'd pictured the same scene a few times now. 'Wonder if she knows he's on her trail?' he murmured.

'If she's heard about Dolly Brett's murder she does. It was in the paper, along with that piece about you being beaten up.'

'She can't read,' he reminded the policeman. 'And how will she know he was the murderer? The paper didn't print his name.'

'No, I s'pose not.'

'But *you* know.'

'*We* know,' he affirmed. The Irishman's tracks in Archie's room were a match for those in Dolly Brett's bedroom and all through the house. 'Oh, and, this'll make you sit up – both sets a prints led down to the cellars, there and here! That's how he got away, Arch, both times. There's a passage down there, length of the High Street and beyond. Been there for years, looks like.'

Archie spluttered into his tea and Tyrell pounded his back, then apologised as he remembered the artist's tender ribs. 'Hard to credit, innit? All these years and we never knew. An underground passage in Walthamstow! Well-trod and all. Seems like everyone knows about it but us.' He pulled on his moustache, thinking dire thoughts, no doubt, about the ungrateful public whom the police force was devised to protect. 'And there was his prints, distinctive tread, foreign make, size eight. Though they wasn't made for him, the shoes. He was a barefoot tinker, right? Now his feet are too wide for shoes, know what I mean? The upper's spread over the sole, leaving its own mark in the mud. Course you know who *did* have them made – to measure? Old Squire Mowbray. Young William tells me he uses the same Italian shoemaker as his dad. So that's a nice bit of evidence to tie Tommo in with that murder. We got witnesses to swear he was wearing them on the train three year ago. Bit worn now – the tread's quite gone in places, and somehow he's picked up a thumb-tack. My guess is it was that, wedged in his heel, broke your finger, son.'

'A *thumb*-tack?'

'Yeah, like you got up there,' he indicated the notice board. 'In fact,' he said, getting up to examine the drawing pins holding up various sketches and photographs, 'the very same. He must a trod on it when he was thrashing around that night like a rooster on heat. We just gotta get an 'old of them boots and that's all the proof we need.'

He crossed the room and opened the door to the back stairs. 'Course they cleaned 'em up now.' He closed the door and resumed his seat. 'But there was a nice set of prints leading down to that passage.'

Archie cleared his throat. 'You – you don't think,' he ventured, 'that's how they did Wylie's, do you? Came up through the cellar?'

His visitor frowned as he touched a lighted taper to his pipe, sucked and puffed, stuck out his lower lip. 'No cellar there, mate. It's solid stone, that floor.'

'No, it's not!' Archie insisted. 'There's a trapdoor behind the counter. Shift the rubble that's piled there and you'll find it. It's where Daniel used to keep small stuff like footstools and mirrors, easily portable things that might have got stolen from the main showroom.' He described how Wylie had allowed him to rummage through the picture frames down there. 'But then he moved everything up into the shop. He didn't say why. Maybe things went missing.'

Tyrell sagged under the weight of this information, releasing a weary puff of bluish smoke. 'Right, then, first thing tomorrow, I'm getting that shop properly cleared. If you're right that trap door could answer a lot of questions.'

'And then what? You'll release the site for Mrs Wylie to sell?'

He nodded heavily. 'Don't suppose she'll get many offers. Needs a lot spent on it.' Noticing Archie's arching eyebrow at last he demanded, 'What?'

Archie brought him up to date on *his* news.

'By crikey, young Arch, you sure you won't let me put you on the payroll? You're good at this undercover lark. All right, all right.' He fended off Archie's remonstrations. 'All the same I'm gonna ask you to come down the station in the morning and make a statement.'

'He wants me to sever all connection with the police.'

'Well, he would,' said the policeman, tapping his pipe on the fender. 'Perhaps we'd better conduct our business by letter in future.'

'In future?' said Archie. 'Is there going to be much future? I mean for Mowbray? If you can link him in with Wylie's murder he'll be behind bars, won't he?'

'Swinging, with a bit of luck. But it's all gonna take time. All we got so far is hearsay and conjecture. We need solid proof, and for that you're going to have to dance to his tune.'

*

Mrs Reeves ducked over, protected by an umbrella against the steady February downpour. Mary's old wrapper was under her arm, mended and, to Archie's dismay, washed, starched and ironed into the bargain.

''Ere, Archie, that mate o' yourn, the tiler, come down here that time selling them tiling kits – you couldn't give us his address, could you? Got a bit o' business to put his way. That's nice,' she said, over his shoulder, regarding his drawing of Kitty O'Grady. 'Tried to get her for the Christmas panto, didn't we, but she ain't taking on no more work for the time being, they said.'

'Why do you want John's address, Bertha?'

'Toff come in the pub last night, wanted some special tiles for a job he's got on, so I thought of your John. He knocks 'em out hisself, don't he? Bit pricey but the bloke said price was no object. So I took him up to see our fireplace what he done last year.'

'What was his name, the toff?'

'Him down The Railway Tavern. Mowbray, innit? "Yeah," he says, "very nice. Any idea where I can get hold of him?" Well, I knew he lived out Woodford way but I didn't know the road.' She frowned, as she saw the horror on Archie's face. 'What?'

233

'How many tile-makers are there in Woodford. He's bound to find them!'

'So?'

'So he's a horrible man, Bertha. Vicious. Hegarty, the thug that beat me up?' She nodded, her mouth trembling. 'He's Mowbray's hit man, and Mary Quinn can put them both behind bars. It's her they're looking for, to shut her up. And the last they heard she was working for a tiler.'

'Oh my Gawd.' She tried to suck her mistake back through her big yellow teeth. 'You best get on over there, quick. Tell 'em to keep an eye out. Be all right on your own, will you? Got your brolly? 'Ere, 'ave a lend o' mine.'

Chapter 25

Clara was rolling out 'pies' at one end of the workbench, with her family of stuffed toys gathered round, some lying, some propped back-to-back, not to miss what she was doing. She had a thick pancake of grey clay in front of her, a selection of pastry cutters, forks, spoons, wires and meshes, and was totally absorbed, cutting shapes and sloshing water over crumbs of clay, pressing them in with her chubby fingers. 'And not too much water,' she instructed her toys, 'or it'll be a mucky mess like last time.'

Lizzie smiled to hear her own warning repeated. She looked up and caught her daughter's eye, peeping from a dark frond of baby hair. As she pushed it back, another streak was added to an already grubby face.

'But it won't stick on if I don't make it slippy,' the little girl appealed to her mother, her grey eyes wide and earnest.

'Quite right,' said her mother, thinking, poor child, what am I doing to her? She's day after day in here with me, gathering dust, like her toys, like her books, like her thoughts, her ideas. We sing, we tell each other stories, but she should be out and about, seeing and doing, exploring, playing with other children. Oh come back, Mary, we need you.

It was warm and dry in the pottery with the kiln going full pelt, a cosy refuge from the rain. Her own end of the bench was filled with square slabs of stoneware clay. Sheets had been put through the wringer to make them flat and even, and she had cut them to size. Now she was piping on the designs which would be filled with glaze after the biscuit firing. This was one of hers, circles within circles and triangles that would become a central fan-shaped flower, rigidly symmetrical, apart from a spiral stem. She wouldn't show John until it was fired and glazed. If he saw the finished article in all its glowing colours, he might be less hostile to her designs. She would have to choose her moment. She sighed. Good moments were few and far between these days. There was no waking him again this morning. One day, she was sure he wouldn't wake up at all.

She shivered as if someone walked over her grave, as the window darkened and the wet gravel in the yard scrunched. When she looked up a brown horse was ambling past. She wiped her hands on her apron, opened the door, letting in a cold wet blast. The horse was being led towards the cottage by a man of medium height, in a dark cape against the rain and a wide-brimmed hat pulled down over his eyes.

'Hello?' she called out. 'Can I help you?' Her pulse beat a little faster. He might simply have lost his way or he might be a customer, a wealthy one from the looks of him in those fine polished boots, and his horse creaking with good leather. He might be rich enough to want a shopfront tiled or a porch or an entire hospital.

He turned and swept a glance over her. 'Is Mary here, at all? Mary Quinn?'

Lizzie's heart jumped. His face was unshaven, his tow-coloured hair long and greasy, his clothes stained and dirty. He wasn't a wealthy man at all. And there was something about him, an aggression that dared you to defy him. A chill went through her and she fought to appear unafraid, to act normally. This must be the thug sent by that Streeter person to take poor Mary away. Lizzie knew that there'd be no reasoning with such a one. He wouldn't know what pity was. She pulled her shawl over her head and closed the pottery door behind her, pulled it tight until she heard the latch fall into the snick. She prayed for Clara to stay put.

'Mary? I'm afraid she's not here just now.'

'She'll be back, though?'

'I wish I knew. I haven't seen her in weeks.'

'Where did she go?'

'She didn't say, more's the pity.'

'Just up and left, did she?'

'No,' she said carefully. 'She said she was taking a short holiday, seeing friends and family. She should have been back by now.'

His face creased into a suspicious snarl, and her heart bumped against her ribs. 'What is this?' he muttered.

'Sorry?'

'You're after hiding the girl, so you are.'

'Hiding her? Why would I?' But he was already pushing past her to the door. As he yanked it open, there was Clara, teetering on a chair with her grubby little hand extended for the latch. 'Clara!' cried Lizzie, grabbing the child before she fell. 'You silly, silly girl! How many times have I told you …?'

The man was looking around, under tables, under sinks, in clay bins. 'What is this place?'

'It's a pottery. We make tiles. I'm the tile-maker's wife, Mrs Kington. Clara, be still!' The little girl was squirming to get down, whimpering. Lizzie was squeezing her close, too close.

'She works here?'

'Mary? She worked in the house, mostly.'

'I'll be after seeing around then, just to be sure.'

'She isn't here. I told you.'

'Just to be sure,' he repeated doggedly. He clearly didn't believe her. He took her elbow, with Clara still kicking and struggling, and marched them over to the cottage. Opened the door and thrust her inside.

'Mary!' he shouted. 'Come here, when I tell ye. It's Tommo.'

Tommo? Tommo *Hegarty*? Of course, of course. She knew she'd seen that weaselly face before, on the Wanted posters that Archie had drawn. This was the monster that had attacked John and blighted their lives. What did he want with Mary?

'Mary, come down here now,' he bawled up the stairs. No fear he'd wake John, more's the pity. 'Mary, darlin', it's me!'

'You *know* her?'

'Why wouldn't I know her? We're sweethearts, so we are.'

Mary Quinn and this foul creature?

'Rubbish!' It just slipped out, a sneer of incredulity.

The blow came from nowhere and forced her to her knees. Her ears rang and her eyes swam red as Clara was ripped from her arms, howling with fear.

'No!' screamed Lizzie, pain throbbing between her eyes. She could hardly see. 'Not the child! Give her to me, please. Please! Clara!'

'Mama–Mama–Mama!' shrieked Clara.

Lizzie staggered to her feet and tried to prise the man's fingers from the toddler's little legs. He was hurting her baby, bruising the soft flesh.

He chopped her hands away. 'When I get Mary …'

'No-o-o! Look, I don't know where she is, I really don't! Give me my baby, please! I don't even know how to get hold of you if I find her.'

'She'll know.'

And he was out of the door, with Clara screaming over his shoulder, her fingers stretched out straight, reaching for Lizzie to save her. He threw the child across the horse, like an old sack, and mounted up behind her. The horse skittered, reared up.

'Don't you go telling the police, now, missus,' he said. 'Or the babby gets it.' He wrinkled his nose. 'And be quick. I can't be doing with babbies at all.' He galloped down the lane, '*Mamm—aaah*,' trailing after him.

'Please, oh God, please!' sobbed Lizzie, running to the gate, tripping over her skirts. She fell to her knees, beat the ground with her fists, gouged her nails into the wet earth and stones as if they were flesh and blood. 'Oh God, God, God …'

She raced upstairs to John. 'Wake up, bastard, pig! He's got Clara! Wake up!' But for all her curses and cries and pleas and slaps he remained out of it, lost, useless, faintly moaning, smiling, farting.

She harnessed the mule to the cart and drove off after Hegarty and Clara, hoping that some invisible umbilical cord would lead her to the right place. Twenty minutes later she was back, blind with tears, her temple still smarting from Hegarty's blow. She had followed his horse's hoof prints to the crossroads, but there they'd become lost among dozens of others. The mule had pulled the cart straight on for half a mile, through mud and puddles, past field and forest, but her frantic driver had felt no guiding maternal tug. She had returned to the crossroads, and this time taken the left turning, towards London, came back, taken the right towards Epping. Then she'd returned home, having to own that she'd no idea where they had gone. There weren't many people about in the rain and none had seen a horseman with a little girl. No one had seen anything.

She was slumped on the cart in the yard in the rain when, miraculously, Archie arrived on an empty cattle wagon. He must have begged a lift from the market. He jumped down. 'Thanks, mate,' he called to the driver as he drove off. 'I owe you.' Then he saw Lizzie's face. 'Don't say I'm too late?'

Unable to speak, she nodded.

'What's he done? Is John all right?'

'Oh Archie,' she blurted out, 'that Hegarty – he's taken Clara!'

'Oh my God! Where's John?' But he didn't really need to ask.

Alternately wringing her hands and flapping them desperately, she followed him up the stairs, watched him tumble her husband, still sound asleep, out of bed and onto the bare floor, take the ewer from the washstand and empty half its freezing contents in his face. John reared up like a jack-in-the-box, gasping and spluttering. His eyes were staring, the pupils dilated.

Archie shouted into his ear, 'John, can you hear me?' He sloshed the rest of the water down his back. John bucked and drew in his breath with a long rasping sound. 'John! Wake up! You have to hear me. Fight it. Come out of it. Damn you, John, you must!' He put down the jug and slapped the dopey face as hard as he could with his left hand, slapped him again. The eyes began to close. 'John, Hegarty's got your little girl. He's got Clara! Wake up, man!'

'No,' John groaned, his teeth chattering with cold. 'Lea' me alone.'

'Archie, Archie,' said Lizzie, 'let him be. Help me put him back to bed.'

'He'll never forgive himself. When he wakes up …'

'*If* he wakes up,' she said, finding suddenly that she didn't care if he never did. In fact, a pillow, strategically placed and held down, might be a better solution.

'I think he's coming round. Any more water?'

She sighed. He was right. They had to keep trying. 'I'll get some.'

'Cold.'

'Right.'

It took another several minutes of dousing and slapping to rouse him. They marched him up and down the stairs a few times, round the yard barefoot in the rain. Then while Lizzie towelled her husband dry in front of the range and dressed him and tried to feed him tea and biscuits, Archie explained what had happened. The tile-maker was bewildered at first, thinking he was still dreaming.

'What? Clara?' he asked mildly. 'Don't be bloody silly. Why would anyone take her? We have no money for a ransom – it's ridiculous!' And when they told him again, he shook his head, trying to make sense of it. 'Hegarty ... the same, the same one as ... after the drudge? Whatever for?'

When the truth finally penetrated, it was hard to hold him down as he railed against the bastard Irishman who was going to sell his child to white slavers, against the slattern Mary Quinn, against Archie who had brought her to them, swinging punches at them both.

'Call yourself a mother? I expect you to protect our girl, you stupid bitch, you want locking up!'

Archie managed to parry the blows, resisting with difficulty, Lizzie thought, the urge to knock his friend senseless. She merely ducked, being used to these flailing fists, these groggy fits of temper. John wept. He ranted against a God who could let an innocent child be taken by a madman, a murderer. Mostly he scolded himself. He slapped his forehead, called himself vile names, tore his hair and, after a lot of heaving and sighing, eventually lumbered to his feet.

'Well, come on, then, let's go get the bastard,' he said, rocking slightly on his heels, 'that's what all this is about, isn't it? Getting a real man on the case? We can't leave it all to laughing boy here. Good God, Archie, you look as if you've been in the wars. What happened? Fall off your pedestal? Or was it one of your girlfriends getting her own back? Hear that, Lizzie, your darling's got his come-uppance at last.'

'It was Hegarty, John,' said Archie, quietly. 'He paid me a visit, too.'

'*Did* he now? Well I never!' His face soured. 'Jesus, don't we have a police force to do this sort of thing?'

'She's *your* daughter,' said Lizzie in disgust, '*you* do something!'

'Me and my army, eh? Going to slap Hegarty around a bit, too, are you, Archie? God, Clara could do a better job on her own.'

'Stop it, John,' said Lizzie, through bared teeth. 'Just stop it.'

'It's all right, Lizzie, he's not himself.'

'Oh he is,' she said. 'This is normal.'

John glared at her and, in defiance, reached for the brown bottle on the mantel-shelf. But she got there first, knocking it out of his hands so that it shattered on the stone floor. He gave a mighty roar of outrage and fell to his knees as the tea-coloured puddle spread.

'Go on, lap it up, why don't you!' she mocked. 'Lap it up while your daughter is bludgeoned to death!'

Archie grabbed a kettle of water, crying, 'Out of the way!' and swilled the steaming contents over the mess. John scrambled to his feet, ranting and stamping his feet like a thwarted toddler. Then, as if receiving a blow of common sense, he fell into a chair and buried his head in his hands.

'Shall we go?' said Lizzie, when he was quiet. 'We're wasting valuable time.'

'The floor ...'

'Can wait,' she said shortly, looking around for last-minute inspiration. 'Here, you'd better take this.' As she handed him the umbrella, his whole manner changed. Suddenly he was sober, with a sense of purpose, she felt.

'Best thing you can do, Lizzie,' he said, 'is get down on your knees and pray.'

'Later,' said Archie. 'Right now we need her to drive the mule cart.'

Even the mule seemed to sense their urgency as Lizzie flicked the reins. Archie leaned forward in the seat beside her, willing them on. John, sitting on the floor of the cart with his back to them, was at least alert.

She bit her lip. 'Which way? Where is she, Archie?'

'I thought you knew!'

'Mary, I mean. I told you he'll give us Clara if we give him Mary.'

'We can't do that.'

'We must – it's the only way we'll get Clara back.'

'No, I mean I haven't any idea where she is,' said Archie, helplessly. 'She's not in Shoreditch.'

'But ...' She couldn't believe she was hearing this. In all the kerfuffle with John she'd simply assumed that Archie knew where to find Mary. She burst into tears.

'Oh, Lizzie, don't, don't.'

She glanced down. His fingers with their cruel scars hovered uncertainly over her lap as if he wanted to touch her, comfort her, and he couldn't. It wasn't his place to.

'Look,' he said, and his hand dropped away. 'Forget Mary, let's go straight to Hegarty. We'll offer him money. I've plenty in the bank. I've just sold a couple of big pictures. He won't refuse that. Where is he, Liz?'

She couldn't prevent her face crumpling again as she shook her head. 'He – he said Mary would tell us.'

*

Although Sergeant Tyrell immediately tapped out an all-stations alert for the monster, he had no idea where to start looking either. He thought it more than likely that Hegarty had taken the London road. A horse like that – a beautiful chestnut mare, Lizzie told him – would indicate a well-heeled sort of life. Then again, he might be living a life of Riley out in the sticks, away from the smoke and bustle.

'Only his clothes looked good,' she put in. 'Underneath he looked rough – unwashed and pimply with long dirty hair.'

'Then he's probably stolen the horse,' said a policeman called Beckett, 'the clothes as well.'

'Rooney's horse,' said Archie. 'Rooney came to the hospital riding a chestnut mare. Hegarty killed him and took the horse.' With a sudden thought he began slapping his pockets. He found in a back pocket of his trousers a letter he said he'd taken from the house where Dolly Brett was murdered.

It was addressed to Mary Quinn and still sealed. Archie murmured something about Hegarty's violent reaction to his mentioning this address. 'It must mean something,' he said and read, '13A Mount Street, Bethnal Green.'

'You're guessing this is from him.'

'Well, yes. God, I'd completely forgotten. I haven't worn these trousers in a month or more.'

'Open it, Archie,' said John. 'Quickly.'

Archie dithered. 'It's addressed to Mary …'

'We need to know for sure. I'm not gadding over to Bethnal Green to find us knocking up some old Irish auntie.'

Archie broke the seal and opened the letter. 'Tommo,' he confirmed.

'Let's go then,' said the policeman.

Lizzie drew in her breath. '*You* can't go, Mister Tyrell! Hegarty said he would kill Clara if I got the police involved.'

Archie's sideways glance was pinched and unreadable. Then, glancing at his watch, he made for the door. 'John?'

'Hold up,' said Tyrell, 'You'll need help. There are detectives …'

'Can't wait,' said Archie. 'There's a train at twenty past.'

'Quickly, then!' Lizzie fastened her shawl.

'*You* can't go, Mrs Kington!' cried Tyrell. 'It's a filthy place, that part of Bethnal Green, a dump, a slum, populated by derelicts and scoundrels. They've just let it go, the landlords, the authorities. It's got worse and worse.'

'All the more reason, Mister Tyrell. Clara needs her mother in a place like that.'

'But you don't stand a chance against Hegarty. He'll kill you and what will Clara do then? Think, woman.'

'I *am* thinking.'

'No, Lizzie.' John was adamant. 'You'll slow us down.'

'Stay here, Lizzie,' counselled Archie. 'We'll be wanting a lift home when we get back, us and Clara.'

She saw the sense of it, she supposed. 'Be careful, then,' she whispered. 'Take care!' she shouted, as they hurried away.

Chapter 26

If it wasn't one thing it was another. Rain, torrents of it, gurgling along the gutters, down the drainpipes, marching along the pavement like troops of soldiers off to the wars.

She had hoped to have been gone by now. But first it was the snow, then Mrs Ferris had been poorly with a cold and Mary had felt that she couldn't leave her in the lurch. And the time had gone on and now there was another carriage drawing up outside, another 'operation' to be undergone.

The lady was getting out of the carriage, putting up her umbrella. Mary watched through the streaming windows as she headed towards the house and the carriage rolled on down the street. She had come alone, poor girl. But everything was ready. The clean sheets were on the bed, the nightdress on its hanger behind the screen, crisp and white. The instruments were lined up on the tray.

The doorbell jangled. She smoothed her apron, reached for the handle and braced herself. This was definitely the last time. After this she would be on her way.

She took the lady's umbrella and stood it to drain in the hallstand.

'Mary? Mary Rooney?'

'By all the saints!' She would never have known the girl behind all the powder and paint, and the cut of her coat so fine, the lace at her throat and the hat with the spotted veil covering her face. 'Is it ever Kitty?'

'No names, Mary,' Mrs Ferris reminded her, as she sailed up the passage from the sitting room.

'But this is an old friend, Mrs F,' she said. 'We were girls together in Lahinch. Came over to England on the same boat.'

'Fancy,' said Mrs Ferris, in flat tones, and Mary wasn't sure what the lifted eyebrow was for, their shared history or disapproval of the perfume and lace, or something else. 'I'll let you show the young lady up, then, Quinn. You must have a lot to talk about. I'll be there presently.' As she went off to the parlour to prepare herself, she clasped her hands to her mouth almost as if she were praying.

Show the lady up? But, of course, Kitty was here for the same reason as all the others. Even so, it didn't stop Mary throwing her arms around her old friend. 'Kitty Flanagan, by all that's holy. Would you take a look at yourself?' She held her away. 'So grand, y'are.'

'So grand I got meself knocked up, again, like a fool.'

'Again?'

'Oh, this isn't the first time I've visited Mother Ferris. She and I are old friends. I don't know what I'd do without her.'

'Kitty!'

'Sure and isn't it one of the hazards of the profession?'

'Profession?' Was Kitty on the game?

'Oh, not that sort of profession, silly girl, though not far off perhaps. I'm a singer, Mary, like I always said I'd be.'

A singer? So it hadn't been just a dream for Kitty? A dream of singing duets, of being the toast of the town, not just of the ceilidh; Mary holding the tune with her stronger voice and Kitty the harmony? Her friend had gone ahead with it while she had married the good-looking piper. No regrets for that but somehow she felt disappointed for chances missed.

Kitty broke into mimicry. '*Ladies and gentlemen, it gives me great pleasure,*' and she winked lasciviously, '*to present for your delectation sweet and winsome little Kitty O'Grady, all the way from beautiful Galway Bay. Give her a big hand!*'

'O'Grady?'

'It has a better ring to it than Kitty Flanagan, apparently.'

'Who says?'

'The auld fella, my sugar daddy.' She shook her head and swallowed. Then she smiled brightly. 'He put a lot of money behind me and "you have to show your gratitude, Mary". I "tread the boards" at the Hackney Empire for six guineas a week and the occasional shag with a lardy pig. Ta-ra-ra-boom-de-ay!' she sang, fiercely. There was a tremor in her voice.

'Oh dear, Kitty, that's bad.'

Not such a grand life, then, if you had to put up with 'lardy pigs' giving you babies you weren't allowed to keep and love.

They had reached the 'operating room'. Mary took the beautiful coat and hat, hung them up and helped her friend undress.

'Not at all,' said the singer, 'at least I'm doing what I want.' She regarded the tray of instruments with a wry face. 'More or less.' As she lay down in her virginal nightdress she caught Mary's hand and frowned as she traced the rough skin, the burns and blisters. 'Which is more than I can say for you. Whatever are you doing in this line of work?'

'Shaking hands with the devil.'

Kitty winced. 'And there I was thinking you were made, sitting for your portrait, and all. Weren't you Hampstead's sweetheart?'

'My p-portrait?' Her mind raced. 'You were never at Streeter's party, Kitty?'

Her smile was too bright. 'I was the cabaret, doing my party-piece.'

'Brian was there, one of the guests, but he didn't mention seeing you.'

'No?' Kitty frowned. 'Well, I'm not surprised,' she said, a mite too quickly. 'I was so got up with feathers and frills I doubt he'd have known me.'

'He's changed, too. He's quite the gentleman now,' said Mary with a sorry sigh. She could hardly believe what he'd become. Wasn't he the scholar back in Lahinch, with his clever talk, and hadn't Mammy set her heart on him being a priest? But he used his cleverness in other ways. 'Sure and I should have been there, too, but …' She made a face of regret. 'Archie said it wasn't for me – he was the painter.'

'I doubt you'd have made it home again. You'd have been sold off to the highest bidder. Oh Mary, you don't know the half of it.' She paused, flashed her friend another smile. 'I'll tell you what, darlin' – I'll send you tickets for the show. You can bring your man, Archie.'

She felt her colour rising. 'He's not …'

'Well if he isn't, he should be. He's a dish, so he is, with that twinkle in his eye. And he adores you.'

'How can you say that?'

'He's … you can see it in the painting. He has tender feelings for you.'

'No, Kitty.'

'It's true, girl. It's a wonder Pauly lets you sit for him.'

'Pauly died, Kitty.'

'Oh, Mary, that's an awful shame. He was a decent man, with those gorgeous blue eyes.'

Mary sighed. She'd shed enough tears over those blue eyes.

*

It was over. The bloody sheets were in soak, the tea made. Mary took a tray up to her friend to find Mrs Ferris still there, anxiously checking the girl's pulse and mopping her brow. Mary put down the tray quickly. It seemed there were 'complications' – what her employer feared the most.

The rain gusted against the window and Mary stared uneasily at the perspiring white face on the bed. 'How are you getting home, Kitty?'

'The carriage will be back at four o'clock. We've got this down to a fine art, haven't we, Mrs F?' She gave the abortionist a wan smile, raising her pencilled eyebrows.

Mrs Ferris's look was sour. 'Time you gave him his marching orders, my girl. You've paid him back a dozen times over for the start he gave you.'

Kitty tried to sit up. 'He'd ruin me,' she whispered, her face twisting, and with a hiss of pain she collapsed back onto the pillow.

'Oh my Lord,' cried the older woman, 'it's started already.'

'Is she all right?'

Mrs Ferris bit her lips. 'Go and see if the carriage is here.'

The carriage driver, in his wet oilskins, was persuaded to come in and give Mary a hand down the stairs with her friend.

He clicked his tongue. 'Shame,' he said, 'she left it too late.'

Racked with pain, doubling over, Kitty could hardly put one foot in front of the other. 'Oh God, oh-god-oh-god-oh-god …' she whimpered through colourless lips, while her eyes rolled with terror.

Mary was horrified. 'You can't send her home like this. Can't she stay here, Mrs Ferris,' she begged, 'just till she's over the worst?'

Her employer was having none of it. 'Out!' she shrilled. 'Get her out!' The change in the old woman was shocking. 'My job's finished. She can die on someone else's doorstep.'

Mary gasped. From the fright in her eyes it was clear Kitty had heard. 'It's all right, darlin',' she reassured her, 'I'll see you home.'

The girl shook her head. 'I'll be all right. You stop here.'

'Stop here you will and no mistake, my girl,' said Mrs Ferris. 'If she don't make it and the law gets pulled in you'll drop me right in it.'

'I won't!' she protested. 'Don't you trust me?'

'Oh yes, I trust you, 'cause you ain't going!'

'I have to.' She let go of the sick girl for a moment, and grabbed her shawl and hat from the hall stand as they stumbled past. 'Oh,' she remembered, 'my bag!' It was upstairs, with Pauly's tin whistle and her savings, nearly seven shillings. She would need that.

She dashed upstairs.

The front door was already closed when she started down and Mrs Ferris was barring her way at the bottom of the stairs.

'Let me go!' cried Mary. When her employer climbed up to the third step and stood with her arms outstretched, Mary pushed her out of the way and the older woman went sprawling, banging against the wall.

'Ow, me head!' she shrieked. 'You slut, you scabby little shyster!'

Mary held onto the banister and manoeuvred her way past the swathes of widow's weeds that would have tangled her feet had she not kicked out. Mrs Ferris gave a cry of pain. Without looking back, Mary made for the door. As she fought to open it, the house seemed to contract around her, and then, with an almost muscular spasm, spat her out into the street and banged the door shut behind her.

'Stop! Wait! Driver!' He heard her and reined in the horses, jumping down to bundle her into the carriage, glad to have another pair of hands to help. Groaning and crying, Kitty rocked on her seat and Mary wept, too. 'Did you really think I would leave you alone?'

'Oh, Mary, what have I done?'

'Hush, darlin', I know it's bad. Try and hang on while we get you home. But look, we'd best get your drawers off, in case we have to stop in a hurry.'

There was hardly time to marvel at the velvet seats and the quilted interior. Barely a couple of miles up the Whitechapel Road her friend's cries became bloodcurdling screams. The driver pulled on the reins. Kitty's eyes swivelled towards the window, showing the whites. 'This isn't ...' she gasped through gritted teeth.

'Go on, driver!' shouted Mary. 'Go on! Take her home.'

'But this is the hospital, Miss. They'll know what to do.' He jumped down and opened the door, rain slanting in the streetlamp and reflecting wet on his oilskins.

'Kitty?' Mary asked.

'No,' wept her friend. 'No hospitals. Take me to Hampstead.'

'Hampstead? You sure?'

She was certain.

Mumbling a curse under his breath, the driver climbed back up on his perch.

It took forever to get there. Mile after mile, breathing in shuddering gasps, digging her fingernails into Mary's arm, Kitty fought her body's natural impulses. Sweat and tears mingled on her cheeks and where she'd bitten her lip, there was blood. They swung into a driveway and slowed. Mary heard a soft, 'Whoah!' and the carriage crunched to a standstill on the gravel.

There were steps to negotiate before the coachman could ring the doorbell. 'Oh,' Kitty groaned as a manservant opened the door.

'Quick!' Mary cried as Kitty slid to the floor. 'Help me, someone. Fetch newspapers, cushions, smelling salts. Make her comfortable.' The doorman panicked and he and the driver ran about like slapstick comics, opening doors, calling for help, tugging on bell-pulls.

'What's going on?' A sweaty, bald man strutted into the hall, in shirtsleeves, a fancy waistcoat stretched across his fat belly. He had a glass of brandy in one hand, a cigar in the other and the smell of smoke mingled strangely with the smell of blood. 'Jesus Christ!' he cried as he realised what was happening. 'Not here! Not here! Get her into bed!'

'You can't move her,' Mary protested.

'Get up, woman!'

'I can't.' Kitty's voice was weak. 'I'm sorry.' She leaned back in Mary's arms to straighten her back and heave. Mary was beginning to feel that she would bear the scars of her friend's bone-white grip forever when a terrible sound escaped her throat, inch by painful inch, seeming to echo around the marble hall. At last it ended and the grip on Mary's arm went slack.

'Oh, my God,' said the coach driver as something dark and wet slid out from between Kitty's legs along the floor. He ran to the open front door and vomited over the railings. 'Sorry guv'nor,' he said when he came in, shielding his eyes with his hand, his face greenish in the light. 'I was all for dropping them off at the hospital but she wasn't having none of that.'

'Get this mess cleaned up,' growled the fat man.

'This *mess?*' Mary could hardly get the words out. 'This mess is your ...' She looked again. 'Your son, your baby son.'

'Not mine, by God. No way is it mine!'

Tears rolled down her face; she couldn't stop them. Mrs Ferris had denied that this was their responsibility but it was. It was so! This was a baby and, given a few months more, it might have lived. 'Oh, Jesus, Mary and Joseph, this is terrible, so it is!' She crossed herself. 'Holy Father, forgive us all!' She turned to the fat man, her fists curled, as she spat at him, 'You did this, you wicked old devil, you!'

'Do I know you?' He stared at her drunkenly, weaving about, continuing to suck on his cigar as if there was no blood on the floor, no foetus, no sick woman, no servants standing around gawping in a state of shock.

Mary shrank under his withering gaze.

'Bloody Irish bog-hopper,' he sneered and threw his cigar on the floor. As he trod on it, mashing it into the marble, she understood that this was how he saw himself treating her.

'Nobby,' whispered Kitty through ashen lips. 'Nobby, it's all right, darlin'. The babby's gone.'

'*Nobby!*' cried Mary, her hands flying up. Of course, she knew him now: the fat man who she'd last seen visiting one prossie or another in the neighbourhood. 'Oh, Kitty, no, not this one! Sweet Jesus, no!' She scrambled to her feet. 'You and *him*? He's a monster, so he is – the plague of my life! For isn't he a pimp and a slaver, Kitty? He sells little children.'

Kitty's eyebrows rose clownishly on her chalk-white face. She shook her head.

'No-o.' Her mouth formed the word but no sound came out. Her dress was now saturated and blood began to pool around her. Her eyes closed.

Nobby stepped back from the carnage for fear of dirtying his slippers.

'Will you not get a doctor, for the love of God?' cried Mary.

'At least show willing, ye useless get! Else you'll have two dead bodies on your hands.'

'Who the hell are you to tell me what to do?' He kicked a sodden fold of Kitty's dress and it smeared the marble red. 'Get the hell out of my house, you slapper, you slag!'

His face was ugly, pink and pompous, boiled like an overdone gammon and, before she knew what she'd done, she'd hit him.

'You filth! You maggot!' she screamed. 'That's for Kitty, who just might die because of you!'

His beady eyes popped. He swelled. He spluttered. He raised his fist to retaliate.

'D'you really not know who I am?' she cried, dancing back. 'I'm the black widow spider come to poison your dreams. You think, you just think, where you might have seen me before!'

His servants watched, enjoying the spectacle of Mister Streeter in trouble. *They* knew who she was. They dusted her portraits every day.

He tried to take a breath to fuel his fuddled brain, but he was forced to cough, double over with coughing, wheezing and spluttering, fighting for breath. As his neck swelled over his collar, his eyes were sucked into the fat of his eyelids, his lips turned blue, and he fell to his knees. He slid backwards in the blood and fell forward, cracking his chin hard on the unforgiving floor. As his last breath whistled and phlegm gurgled in his throat, the household turned their heads away.

Mary backed out of the door. 'I'll get a doctor,' she said. 'Look after her.'

Chapter 27

'What does it say?'

John had spent the last five minutes groaning with his head in his hands. Now he sat up, his face blotchy with tears.

'What does *what* say?' Archie turned to the train window, expecting to see words on a hoarding or a factory building, but there was nothing, just sodden fields and villages rushing headlong into the city murk. He would have welcomed some fresh air – he had an appalling headache – but the smoke would have been unbearable. John's pipe was bad enough.

'Quinn's letter from Hegarty, what does it say?'

'I'm not going to read …' He was indignant.

'Horseshit,' said John. 'It might be important.'

A squall of rain lashed the window as Archie retrieved the letter from his pocket, unfolded it a second time and smoothed the stiff paper on his lap. When he read, *'Me own darling,'* he found that his palms were sweating, his heart beating fast. He was afraid, he realised, that he would discover that Mary and Hegarty were lovers. As he read on, his fears diminished. Mary would have none of the tinker. Apparently he had written several times before, care of the workhouse, but having received no reply had decided he would come looking for her. This was the important news she had missed. The hand was crabbed and unsteady, the spelling appalling but, between them, they managed to make out the gist of it.

> 'What hapen to Pauly God rest him was truly a naxidant I sware. Nuttin to do wid me at all and don you go saying it was. As for what happen after well I tort you wood a com wid me. It was why I did the deed after all for want of the muny for the bot of us to start a new life. You shud not a run of to the workus. They teld me the babby dide and just as well out of it wid no daddy to fend for it. But I wood a loved it I sware to God as if it was my own. I wisht you wood have teld me.'

'She had a baby then,' said John, surprised.

'And it died. Poor girl, she's been through it. A penniless young widow, the workhouse, John, and Hegarty on her tail.'

'I wonder whose it was, his or Pauly's?'

'*As if it was my own*, he says. Sounds like it was their child, the Quinns.' He was beginning to see the sequence here. 'Tyrell found some monogrammed cufflinks under her bed in Coppermill Lane, from the robbery: *the deed*. He has an idea that Hegarty gave them to her or left them behind when he went off to London.'

'I wouldn't want to have been in her shoes when she gave him his marching orders, Archie.'

'Knowing him, he'd have smacked her around a bit, for sure, even raped her, or both. Maybe that caused her baby to be stillborn.'

'I know he denies it here.' John indicated the place in the letter. 'But my guess is he had something to do with her husband's death. What do you think?'

'Pauly fell off some scaffolding, she told me.'

'Fell or was pushed?'

'It was rotten wood,' said Archie. 'Neglect on the part of the builder.'

'Mmm,' said John, with a jerk of his chin. 'Maybe ...'

*

The cabby gave them a strange look when they asked him to take them to Mount Street. 'Mount Street?' he repeated, wrinkling his nose as though he could smell something putrid. 'In the Old Nichol?'

'I imagine so.'

'Been there before, 'ave you, sir?'

'Never.'

'Ah.'

He set them down at the end of a tottering, ramshackle street, where ancient, top-heavy buildings cut out most of the daylight. Farmyard sounds dinned in their ears, barking, screeching, grunting, braying. And appalling smells brought tears to their eyes, handkerchiefs to their noses.

'Thirteen'll be up the other end, but I can't get the carriage down there, sir. It's too narrow.'

'Hegarty lives here?' Archie grimaced at the foul-smelling slurry round their feet. What about his smart Italian boots and his fine clothes?

'What about my Clara?' wailed John.

The cab-driver repeated, firmly, 'This here's your Mount Street, sir. There is just the one.'

'Poor baby!' John was appalled. 'There'll be cholera and typhoid ...'

'Watch your step, gents,' the cabby said as Archie paid him. 'Hide anything of value. They'll have it off you, quick as a wink.'

'Will you wait for us?'

'Not on your life,' he said, abandoning his manners. Jerking the reins he was off into the rain, his whip flying, his wheels churning up the mud.

There was no help for it. They had to find Clara. In their hurry to catch the train, they'd left their umbrellas behind and were drenched in no time. There was no shelter to be had in these gaping doorways. Archie lent John his cane to lean on as they skirted piles of animal dung, greasy newspapers, fish bones. Archie stumbled along, occasionally stepping in things indescribable. Old crones watched them from doorways, their hands busy with some sort of knitting or hand-weaving. Despite the rain they must have felt that the air outside was preferable to indoors. Drunks sat propped against the houses, their heads in their hands, mud on their clothes. Scrofulous children ran in and out on bare feet, their faces pinched and marked with bruises. A woman tried to sell them a sheep's trotter from her window. 'Here you are, dear, only thruppence.'

'You're joking!' snorted Archie, wincing and trying not to retch.

'Three a'pence, then, dear. Make a lovely stew.'

To think that this was London, the capital of England, the hub of the Empire, its magnificent buildings and bridges and sewage system the envy of the world! This squalid disgrace, the Old Nichol, was what lay behind the grand facade. They could scarcely speak, but their eyes were busy, watching out for pickpockets and peering through glassless windows where shoe-menders and cabinet makers were at work. From an upstairs window came the sound of a busy loom. They were just as likely to see a donkey or a dog peeping from behind a ragged curtain as a human being.

'Good day,' said Archie, raising his hat to a snaggle-haired woman wheeling a rusty baby carriage. 'Could you tell me, has a man come down here on a horse? He had a small child with him, a little girl.' She looked through him and continued on her way, shaking her head dumbly. He noticed the pram held no child but rather an apple crate, a table-leg and other sticks to make a fire.

'You inspectors, yous two?' There was a dirty hand on Archie's arm, tugging him across to a dark doorway. ''Ere, mister,' a man begged, 'you gotta see this. Me and the missus and her ma and five little kids, all in the one room, mate, one bed, if you want to do something about it.'

Archie assured the poor man that they were not inspectors who could rehouse his family nor were they police, but simply a father and his friend looking for a little girl stolen by a wicked thug.

'I 'opes you find 'er,' said the ragged man, 'and then again I hopes you don't. There's kiddies killed round 'ere for the clothes they stand up in.'

John's eyes filled with tears. 'Oh don't say that. Clara, where are you, sweetheart?'

The street seemed to have ears, windows upstairs and down filled with drawn faces gazing after them, and they heard whispers, repeating snatches of their own conversation, *'Wicked varmint … little girl taken … for her clothes …'* Archie was sure he heard the word *'horse'* but when he looked around the window was blank, the speaker vanished.

He felt a tug at his sleeve: a stunted child with his hand outstretched and a livid bump on his forehead. And then a flash of bare legs as his mate dodged into a passage, with a glint of silver chain dangling from his hand. 'Hey!' he shouted, 'My watch!' He hadn't felt it go. He gave chase, only to confront a burly man with a poker in his fist. The boy was nowhere to be seen.

'Archie!' yelled John. 'Forget it, man.'

Yes, they had to get on. 'Be my guest,' he murmured. He would rather lose his damned watch than his life.

Number thirteen was no better than the rest, an ancient shambles with a costermonger's battered barrow tipped up against the wall. The door was missing – long used up for firewood – Archie imagined, and a dirty blanket covered a rotting window-frame. A dark passage led down between three or four closed doors on the left and stairs on the right, its banisters and some of its treads torn away. They knocked on the first door and a man appeared, wearing a cloth cap.

'What?'

They said they were looking for an Irishman, name of Hegarty.

'Wrong house, mate.' He had almost shut the door in their faces when a woman's voice piped up.

'Could be him over the shed, Bill.' She came to the door, a youngish woman with hollow eyes, missing teeth, bare feet, wearing a dirty apron over a dark dress. 'You ain't the police, are you?' Assured that they weren't, she went on, 'Down the passage to the end and out the back. Watch your step, it's a bit mucky. You want the door opposite. Her downstairs will see to you.'

They followed her directions and arrived in what had once been a backyard. Some greedy landlord had knocked down all the fences between the yards and built adjoining wooden shacks, looking like stables but swarming with humanity. Every inch of spare ground had been utilised. Off to one side was the privy. Under the ill-fitting door there oozed a foul mess leavened with ashes and bricks dropped in as stepping stones. Archie, stomach heaving, pulled his coat collar across his mouth. Dear God, you wouldn't keep an animal like this. Across from this cesspool was a small passage minus doors, front and back, and in there, the poor shadow of a chestnut horse was tossing its head, chewing on the bit still in its mouth. Next was a door marked 13A.

It gave at their first knock and closed behind them on squealing hinges. Inside they found a nest of drying matchboxes and the wood, labels and sandpaper to make more. A ragged woman looked up from a table, lit by a candle. Around her were huddled half-a-dozen children of varying ages, all dipping brushes into a bowl of glue and sticking according to ability. While the mother was dealing with her visitors, Archie saw a glue brush find its way into a small mouth where it was hungrily sucked. Poking out from sacks of finished matchboxes were various bits of broken furniture, an iron bedstead and other heaps of old rags which might have been beds. A vile-smelling crock of glue bubbled away over the fire, a bucket of water beside it.

'Mind where you're walking,' snapped the woman, continuing her work.

'Tommo Hegarty?'

'Up there.' The woman pointed with her chin to a ladder poking up through a hole in the ceiling.

'Just go up, shall we?'

'I wouldn't. Best give him a shout.'

Too late: John was already halfway up when a cudgel swiped through the hole, swishing the air. John just managed to duck and the blow glanced off his shoulder. He dropped the cane, which Archie took up and unsheathed the sword inside.

There was a child's muffled squeal. She was alive.

'Clara! Papa's come to get you, darling!'

'Come any further and I'll do for her, so I will.'

Oh God, what now? Archie, below John, could see nothing but the back of his friend's quaking knees. He heard a faint mewling as though the little girl were gagged.

'Let her go, you bastard!' John was quivering with anger or fear. The ladder shook.

'Don't I know you?'

262

Archie could just see, over John's shoulder, framed in the dark hole, the engorged face of the man he'd last seen trying to sever his hand from his wrist. He wished he'd gone up the ladder first – he could have jabbed the sword in his face.

'John, come down. John!' he hissed, but John refused to look down.

'We've met,' said John, his voice hoarse with unshed tears. 'Untie her, for God's sake, man. She's just a baby.'

'D'ye have Mary Quinn there?'

'For Christ's sake!' said John. 'Clara, sweetheart!'

'We'll take you to her,' Archie spoke up, mentally crossing his fingers. They really should have thought this through; a plan would have been …

'Who's that?'

'The painter,' he called up. 'We've also met.'

'Fetch her here, painter.'

'We can't.' He cast about for a convincing lie. 'The police have her in Walthamstow.'

'The devil ye say!'

'They found out she's Brian Rooney's little sister. They think she can help them find him, and you too. They're probably on their way here now.'

There was a moment's pause while the kidnapper digested this. The only sounds were Clara's snuffling and whimpering and John's heavy breathing. The matchbox makers had all stopped work to watch the entertainment. For a man forced to live by his wits, Tommo was slow. 'Shut yer mouth, brat!' he snarled. There was the thump of a boot against soft flesh and Clara's shriek of pain.

John shouted, 'No!'

'You get out of here now, or I'll split the babby's head.'

Archie felt John's hesitation, saw his friend's foot lower, hover above the next rung down, heard him whine hopelessly, 'Give her to me.'

'Look, look,' Archie put in quickly, 'will you take money?'

'Eh?'

'Money – I have twenty.' Archie's free hand went to his inside pocket.

'Guineas.'

'Pounds. Four fives.'

'Give it here, then.'

'You give us Clara and we'll pass up the money.'

'Like hell you will. You'll pay me first …'

Looking down for the money John saw the blade Archie was holding flat against the ladder and made signs that Archie should give it to him. Archie shook his head. He'd sooner part with twenty pounds than let John loose with a sword. He would have dropped the weapon out of harm's way were it not for the children gazing up. John wrested the hilt from Archie's grasp, throwing him off-balance and nicking his fingers. Letting go of the money, which was instantly snatched up by small fingers, and just managing to catch hold of the ladder with his left hand, he looked up. It was too late. John was up the ladder and flashing steel.

Archie clambered up behind, his heart in his mouth. Oh Christ. Like some swashbuckling hero, John had adopted a fencing pose, demanding, 'Give me my daughter, *now*!'

Archie could have told him that Hegarty didn't play fair, didn't play games at all. With a single up-thrust of his cudgel Hegarty disarmed John just as he'd taken the carving knife off Archie three months back. The thin blade went skittering across the floor and Hegarty trapped it under his foot, bent and picked it up.

'John!' screamed Archie, too late. Tommo ran him through.

John doubled up over his wound and sprawled along the floor, driving the sword in up to the ebony handle.

When Archie looked up from his friend, Hegarty was gone. There was a door at the side of the room, open to the elements, and Hegarty, with Clara over his shoulder like a bundle of washing, was rapidly descending another ladder, into a yard.

'Stop!' yelled Archie. 'Stop, murderer!' He reached the open doorway and saw Hegarty kick the ladder away, mount his horse and gallop away down an alley. It was too high to jump.

Archie slid down the ladder he had come up by, his fingers stinging where the blade had caught them. He found himself being steadied by the matchbox maker. 'Mind out!' she cried, but he was already smashing a path through plywood and glue into the stinking yard.

'Fetch a doctor,' he bellowed. 'A policeman!' Nobody moved. It was twenty minutes before he found either and, by the time he got back to Mount Street, John was dead.

Chapter 28

Mary Quinn got off the bus and walked the rest of the way. Now that she had made up her mind what to do, she was calm.

Kitty would be all right, the doctor had said, though she probably wouldn't be able to have any more babies. Miscarrying like that – it was a crying shame. 'Feed her raw liver and Guinness,' he told the servants. 'Poor lady, she's lost a lot of blood.'

Nobby Streeter was a goner. What a way to go! 'Heart attack,' the doctor said he'd written on the death certificate. 'Who's the next of kin?'

They all looked at each other, silently plotting. Kitty, they said, most likely. Nobby had no children and he'd married the showgirl, they were sure, for hadn't they had that big party to celebrate only last year?

Liars. Mary had said nothing. The ruse might keep Kitty safe in bed until she recovered, then she could sell a few jewels and dresses and Archie's portraits of Mary, for where else would they go? Mary felt she had the right to donate them to her friend's cause. When the lawyers, or whoever's business it was, came to sell the house and contents they'd find Kitty gone, and the servants packed and picking over the chattels.

There were plenty more fat fish in the sea like Nobby Streeter. And, with her luck, Kitty was the girl to land one.

As for Mrs Ferris, she would train up another 'assistant' and carry on the 'practice', as she called it. Mary would miss her room, the smart modern kitchen, the regular meals and regular wages, but she'd be easier in her mind, so she would.

She pushed open the door of the police station and went up to the counter.

'I'm Mary Quinn,' she announced, wearily.

'Mary?'

Mrs Kington was sitting on the bench, looking so washed out, so dull-eyed, Mary knew something terrible had brought her here. Perhaps the tile-maker had finally taken an overdose, in which case the woman was better off, altogether. But what Mrs Kington had to say, fighting tears as she spoke, drove the breath from Mary's body.

'Not Clara!' She shuddered, as fear crawled up her back. She clasped her hands to her breast. 'Not Tommo – dear God, not Tommo.'

'It's you he really wants.'

'Of course he does,' Mary cried, her mind filling again with death and loss, 'poor little Clara …'

'He's desperate.' Mrs Kington still had that cold suspicious look about her.

'He must know, d'ye think? He must know it was me put him in the frame for Wylie's. He wants to stop me speaking up!'

The other woman's eyes widened once, then straightway dulled with the salt of her own fear.

A door opened in the back. It was the sergeant with the moustache, the one she'd met on her first visit to the police station. He stared at her. 'Mary Quinn!' was all he said and her heart shrank. 'Come on, you.' He thumbed the way behind him. 'Beckett, bring your notebook!'

She could feel Mrs Kington's eyes boring into her back, heard her words following like knives. 'It's all your fault, you stupid girl, bringing him down on our heads!'

They told her Dolly was dead, that they believed Tommo Hegarty had murdered her.

Her hands flew to her cheeks. 'That *was* him at the door! Oh Dolly, Dolly … I *saw* him, with his posh boots, sitting across from me! I knew *them*, if nothing else.' She told Sergeant Tyrell that she had seen Hegarty wearing the boots outside Wylie's shop but hadn't put two and two together. She said she had watched from behind the cellar door but had been too afraid to do anything. Still sobbing, she vowed, 'I'll swing for the bastard, so I will.'

Sergeant Tyrell's look scoured her dry. 'If you'd been honest with us from the start,' he said, 'Dolly Brett would still be alive, Archie Price would be in one piece and Clara Kington would be sitting at home playing with her dolls. *If* you'd told us from the beginning that you knew Hegarty, knew the murdering swine.'

'But I …'

'No more lies! We know who you are, Mary Quinn.' His voice cut like a razor. 'You're sister to Brian Rooney, a villain, a wanted man! And you never let on, just scurried around in the shadows like a rat, with never a squeak!' He paused for breath. 'When you saw Hegarty outside Wylie's you knew damn fine who he was, and you might even have guessed what he was about.'

'Oh, no.' She swallowed hard. It was a blow, a punch in the gut, taking her breath away. But they'd got it so wrong. 'I didn't know what to do for the best.' She found a bit of rag up her sleeve and scuffed at her nose, her eyes. She'd never have gone to them at all if Mrs Chinnery hadn't made her. As for telling them she knew Tommo, and how she knew him, they'd have dragged it out of her about Brian and where to find him.

The sergeant continued to scold her while the scowling constable wrote it all down. 'So you did nothing. You went skulking home after work with the fire raging round you, a man's body roasting at the heart of it. Two days you left it, until you were sure he'd got away.' His eyes glittered. 'Wasting Archie Price's time with all that picture-drawing …'

This was the very chair she'd sat in, breathing in the smell of him, a smell she'd later come to recognise as oil paint and turps. His chair was empty now.

Constable Beckett scribbled in his notebook, twirls and twiddles that could have said anything and the sergeant next to him still grinding his axe, his moustache quivering, bubbles of spit catching on the ends. 'Nothing to say? No excuses for letting a madman loose to kill and kidnap and steal and maim some more? I hold you responsible, Mary Quinn!'

She nodded, knowing he was right. She should have killed the rat when she had the chance. Slit his throat while he was sleeping. God knows she had cause enough. No woman should suffer what he'd done to her, let alone one about to give birth. And so what if they'd hanged her for it? Wouldn't she have saved everyone all kinds of misery?

There was a disturbance in the front of the station. A butcher's boy had come with a message, he said, for Mary Quinn. When they took her out to him, Mrs Kington was still there on her bench, scrunched into a silent ball of misery.

'Well, go on then, here she is.' The sergeant was annoyed at the interruption.

'You Mary Quinn?'

'Yes,' she whispered.

'This is for you.' He handed her a little knitted sock.

'It's Clara's!' cried both women at once.

Mrs Kington snatched it and held it to her face, breathing in her little girl's smell. 'Where is she?' she screamed.

The boy seemed pleased at the effect he was having. His rosy cheeks glowed. 'He said Mary Quinn's to meet him on the marshes, by the pumping station, within the hour. He'll leave the kiddie for anybody as wants her.'

'Oh God.'

'In the cold and the rain?' wondered the policeman.

Mary snatched up her shawl.

'Wait! It's a trick!' cried the sergeant. 'Think! How did Hegarty know the girl would be here? It's some scheme they've concocted together.'

'Nothing of the sort, sir,' she said quietly. 'Sure, and isn't our Blessed Lord giving me this one chance to make up for all the bad things I've done?'

'He'll kill you!' said the constable, who seemed a gentler soul than the other.

'No, he will not. I'll be all right.'

I must do this, she thought. Nobody need know how very afraid I am. Nobody need know that Tommo has already killed one baby, and I several more.

'We'll take the mule cart.' Mrs Kington was up on her feet now, bringing her shawl over her head.

The sergeant huffed a sigh and said, 'Beckett, go with them. Hide in the back. We'll put some sacks over you.'

The butcher-boy looked worried. 'The geezer said no police, no one.'

'Right you, out!' said the sergeant, showing the boy the door. 'Now, Quinn,' he said, turning to her, 'you and Mrs Kington take the mule cart as far as the bottom end of Coppermill and you girl, you go on from there – on your own. Give us time to get a couple of armed officers on the river in a boat. He'll be an easy target on that open ground. Just don't get too close to him. We need you alive to give evidence at his trial.'

'No,' she said firmly, her tears forgotten now, 'no guns at all. You might hit the baby. Won't we do it the way he wants? You can arrest him later.'

'But suppose …'

'No.'

Chapter 29

The rain had stopped when the posse of policemen and detectives caught up with Lizzie, sitting in the mule cart beside the deserted pumping station, alternately kissing Clara and examining her for hurt. Apart from rope burns and bruises, she was intact, though her poor little eyes were all puffy, her cheeks streaked with dirt and tears and snot. She howled and sobbed and clung to her mother, and Lizzie sobbed back.

'Get after him,' she exhorted them, hugging the child to her. Poor Clara was wet through and freezing. 'Kill the bastard!'

But there was no sign of Hegarty or Mary Quinn.

'Which way'd they go?' asked Tyrell.

'I didn't see. They were gone by the time I came along. Left my poor baby tied to the railings.' Her voice broke. She had to get Clara into the warm with some food inside her. She opened her shawl and tied the shivering toddler to her. Oh, God, her lips were turning blue. 'It's all right, darling, Mama's got you.' She began turning the mule, murmuring comfort all the while.

'Look here,' said Beckett, pointing at the ground. 'Hoofprints! He had a horse?' he asked Lizzie, who confirmed it with a nod. 'There's more, see, leading to the towpath.'

'Heading for London, looks like,' said Tyrell, and went to speak to the men in the boat, who primed their pistols and started rowing down river. 'Shoot to kill!' he called after them. 'Beckett, you come with me.'

He turned towards the pumping station and walked about, his eyes to the ground, looking for something in the fading light. 'Here it is,' he cried. 'This is where they went.' They were staring at a manhole cover, the moss torn around the edges. Lizzie was about to gee the mule when she heard the scrape of iron on stone and had to look back. 'Down you go, Beckett.' Intrigued, she and Clara watched PC Beckett climb inside and disappear down the manhole.

'Fresh mud on the rungs,' he reported back, his voice sounding hollow and strange.

What was it, a sewer, a water-pipe?

'Two sets of footprints heading off down the passage. Shall I follow them, Sarge?'

Tyrell thought for a moment. 'No, it's getting dark and we don't have a lantern. Get back up here.' Meanwhile he blew his whistle for the people in the boat to turn round and come back, muttering, 'They set the horse free to lead us astray.' Having replaced the manhole cover he said to the constable, 'They'll be making for the railway station, I'm sure. We can get there quicker in the mule cart – if Mrs Kington will kindly give us a lift.'

A detective appeared, leading Hegarty's horse. He'd found it abandoned, he said, cropping the winter grass along the towpath. It was starving. So was Clara. Lizzie just wanted to get her home.

'You'll want to wait for your husband,' Tyrell suggested.

Lizzie supposed she should – Clara kept crying for her Papa. 'Papa fall down,' she kept saying.

'It's warm in the station and I'm sure my wife will find the kiddie something to eat.'

Would food take away the memory of the dreadful afternoon,

wondered Lizzie. Would Clara be scarred for life? If Lizzie loved her and made every waking moment a joy for her could she keep at bay those nightmares of savagery and abuse that John suffered? She was her father's daughter after all.

*

Clara was solemnly munching her way through a doorstep of bread and jam when the door swung open. 'Unca Art!'

'Oh, thank God!' But the door swung closed and where was John? For a split second, before his discovery of Clara safe on her lap, Lizzie saw a look of defeat on Archie's face and her heart missed a beat. Oh God, oh John.

'I'm so sorry,' he muttered grimly.

She said, as evenly as she could for the child's sake, 'How did it happen?' biting her lips against tears.

When he told her about the sword-stick she threw up her hands, 'Archie, you shouldn't have let him …'

He'd wanted to give the kidnapper money, a ransom. He was sure he would have taken it in exchange for the little girl who was clearly trying his patience, but John had snatched the sword from his hand.

'Show me!' Gently she unwound a bloody handkerchief from around Archie's hand. 'Oh John, you fool!' she muttered as she exposed a fresh line of nasty cuts from the palm across two fingers. 'Lord, a little deeper and he'd have had them off, and that would have been Hegarty's work done for him.' She asked for a bowl of boiled water and cleaned the wounds, binding the hand again with a handkerchief of her own. It was warm from her pocket and as she finished she found Archie gazing at her with a look no newly widowed woman should witness. 'There now,' she said, averting her eyes.

'Kiss better, Mama,' demanded Clara, who had followed the operation with interest.

'No need,' said Archie.

'Another time,' said Lizzie, simultaneously.

'Kiss better *now*,' insisted the toddler, and because she'd been so badly mishandled, Lizzie indulged her. She lifted his bandaged palm to her lips and, as she gently kissed it, Clara beamed with satisfaction.

Oh, Archie, thought Lizzie, then hastily collected herself. Oh, John, what was going on in that addled brain of yours? Stupid, romantic pipe-dreams. No doubt he'd seen himself as a knight in shining armour, waggling the sword in the face of a desperate murderer. What was he thinking? Invincible, he was not.

He was dead. He was properly dead, at last. The tears that came were in memory of the young man she'd married, with his bright hopes and charming ways: her darling who had died, to all intents and purposes, three years before. For the stranger who had shared her bed since then, she felt nothing but anger.

Archie took Clara from her, jam and soggy pants notwithstanding and, with coins appearing from her ears and nose and pretending to be after her bread and jam, soon had her smiling, if reluctantly. His encircling arm was a comfort and both mother and daughter nestled into him as questions were answered and answers questioned.

He and John had been chasing their tails through the slums of Bethnal Green, looking for Clara and her kidnapper. When they finally ran the thug to ground, to draw the creature out of his lair, Archie had directed him to this very police station, saying that Mary was being held here, hoping that the police would be able to arrest him. He had come, believing the lie. Now it was Lizzie's turn to describe how it had gone here: the butcher's boy, the sock, the exchange.

'Mary just happened to be here?'

Lizzie sighed. 'She came to give herself up,' she said. 'To confess.'

'To what?' Archie appeared nonplussed.

'Well, I – to being Rooney's sister, I suppose – all that.' Poor Archie, she thought, he'd played right into Hegarty's hands.

She described how Sergeant Tyrell had traced the Irish couple to the subway under the marshes. 'It must be the one *you* found – the rat-run.' He grunted agreement and she continued the story, how rather than follow his quarry underground Tyrell had taken a posse of policemen to ambush the pair when they came out of the underground passage near the railway station.

'She left her bag,' she said, indicating a shadowy object under the bench. He handed Clara back and pulled out the battered old shopping bag, but there were no clues as to where she had been or where she was going, just clothes and a comb and a tin whistle.

'She wouldn't have left these behind, especially the whistle. It was her husband's. She must think she's coming back.'

'I don't think so, Archie. I'm so sorry.'

He made a moue of regret and changed the subject. 'Is Clara all right?' he asked over the child's head. She knew what he meant and nodded assurance. Absently she kissed her daughter's dark curls for comfort as he opened the door. Following his gaze she could see a little clump of home-goers sheltering in a shop doorway opposite from a sudden downpour. Many of the stores were already closed. It must be nearly teatime. She thought she knew how his mind was working. Surely Hegarty would want to avoid public transport at this time of day?

'Why would Hegarty go by train when he had a horse to ride?' he asked, coming back in. 'It would have taken two, easily. You know, I don't think he was heading for the trains at all. He's hiding out in the tunnel, I'll bet.'

'Don't!' intercepted Lizzie. 'Don't even think about it. Look at the state of you.' He was almost grey with grief and exhaustion, his tawny-brown eyes bloodshot. 'Clara's safe. Let the police find Mary.' But she might as well have saved her breath. She knew he cared for Mary, his 'bit of rough' as John had put it so crudely, but he wasn't in love with the Irish girl, he couldn't be. It was Lizzie he loved and they both knew it. John had known it, too, and sooner or later they would acknowledge that they belonged together. No, poor Archie was consumed with guilt. He felt responsible for Mary's troubles, and he wouldn't rest until he had put them right. Once the girl was settled, Lizzie was sure he would come to her.

Tyrell and a troop of half-a-dozen disgruntled men came back, wet and heavy with their sense of failure. Once again, the villain had slipped through their fingers. He may only have been an ill-bred, ignorant tinker, but Mad Tommo Hegarty had kept one step ahead of the police all along. In the ensuing melee of uniforms, the brewing of the healing cuppa, the exchange of information, the writing up of notes, only she saw Archie slip quietly out of the door.

Chapter 30

The pinging bell announced his dive into the tobacconists, the first shop down that was still open.

'All right to use your cellar, Bert?'

'What?'

'Don't play the innocent, mate. This is an emergency!'

'You ain't police?'

'Bert, what is this? You know me.'

'Yeah I do, but you work for them.' He finished closing his shutters, chewing on his thoughts. 'Sorry, Arch, but I gotta be careful.'

'Too late to be careful, Bert. The police already know about the passage. That murder down the road? The seamstress? *She* had a cellar.'

'Oh, right. What, you in a hurry, are you?'

'Bit. Friend of mine's in trouble down there.'

Bert went and locked the door, put up the Closed sign. 'You'll need a light, Arch,' he said. 'Hang on.' He took a lamp down from its niche on the wall and handed it over. 'Here you are, mate,' he said. 'Better take some matches and another candle, just in case. Good luck to you.'

'Thanks.' He took a step towards the door at the back of the shop.

'Nah, this way, pal.' He went behind the counter and lifted a hatch in the floor. 'Down here. Watch out for low beams, there ain't much headroom. Careful as you go.'

*

Ducking through crumbling doorways, twitching away cobwebs, he was sure he was right. Whatever happened, he mustn't panic Hegarty. The Irishman had brought Mary down here to reach the Railway Tavern without being seen. Why, though? Was he under orders? Or was Hegarty doing this off his own bat? He was fond of the girl, so Rooney had said, but she was a saleable commodity to his masters. More valuable than a two-year-old toddler. Hence the swap. Either that or, heaven forbid, they had found out she was a witness to Wylie's murder and intended to blow the whistle on him. So why not simply silence her? Finish it? No – and Archie had to hang onto this hope – Hegarty and his cronies wanted to keep Mary alive. *For whatever reason, they wanted her to live.*

He hurried on, heedless of the muddy puddles, as shadows fled from his lantern and rats' eyes glowed red. Here, under the High Street shops, the passage was a continuous tunnel, one side a brick wall, the other side and ceiling raw clay shored up with pit props. Occasionally, on a sturdy locked door there might be written the name of the premises above: *The Dolls' Hospital, Cox's the Draper's, Marsh Street Congregational Church, Sir George Monoux Boys' School,* or simply *121-123 High Street.* Sometimes, he was able to locate his position by the smells that wafted down. Just above here, the fishmonger conducted his business; this must be the bakers, all yeasty; up there was the coffee house, there the oil shop.

A faint whiff of old smoke and the board announcing '*Daniel Wylie, Second-hand Furniture Store*' gave him pause. Just nine or ten feet above his head, he thought, with a queasy feeling, was the burnt-out shell of a shop, soon to be replaced with a garish music hall, all gilt and red plush. Down here, where he was standing right now, a gang of foul murderers had gathered, not so long ago, waiting to be let up into the shop.

Sighing, he saw his breath forming mist. Come on, Arch, he told himself firmly, don't dilly-dally. You're only halfway there.

On he went, meeting no one, though he heard shuffles and scuffles that might have been watchers in the shadows, might have been the draught flapping a piece of dirty rag. There were no voices or footfalls indicating policemen coming to his aid or even ragamuffins who could be pressed into service. He was on his own in this alien world.

At last the dark air sharpened with a familiar tang and he stood, sniffing like a blind mole. 'Ale.' The whisper bloomed in the dank netherworld.

This was it then: Mowbray's tavern, on the corner of High Street and St James. He played light over the door in the wall but found no number or name, no knocker or bell push, no grille or keyhole, just a small shutter for those inside to slide across and identify callers. There on the wet ground, pooled in the lantern light, were the clear boot prints of a man. A small circle bit into the tread of the heel, showing where a thumb-tack had been driven. In front, and less clear, were the prints of a woman's worn-out shoes. Only the tips of the soles registered. Experimenting, he rocked on the balls of his feet and imagined Mary up on her toes as an arm round her neck forced her in through the door. She hadn't gone willingly.

Oh Mary, what can I *do?*

For long moments he dithered. If he knocked and demanded her safe return he'd be inviting trouble. Probably get his head bashed in for his pains. He had nothing to bargain with. No money in his pockets. His best bet was to get help fast.

But which way? *Which way, for God's sake?* He couldn't think. He'd go back the way he'd come, calling in at the police station when he reached Bert's. He stopped in his tracks. That would take too long. They could have tortured poor Mary by the time the police turned up, or even killed her, finding out what she knew. No, no, he'd continue under the crossroads to Coppermill Lane and hope to find a cellar door open. Up and out onto the street and he'd saunter into the public house as though nothing had happened, as though he was still thinking about that monumental picture Mowbray had wanted him to paint. He could say he was going to buy the canvas and needed to check the measurements. Yes, he was sure he could pull it off. He'd make some excuse to leave the bar. Take a wrong turning to the privy, or something. Somehow he'd find her; somehow he'd get her out of there.

But it would be all up if he ran into Hegarty. Hegarty would blow his cover wide open.

Perhaps the first idea was best. He turned again, in a homeward direction. No – what he'd do *before* going into the pub, he'd knock on doors and find someone to take a message up the road to Tyrell. Get some reinforcements.

Better hurry, he thought, seeing the tunnel yawning before him and breaking into a run.

A few steps past Mowbray's premises he tripped and went sprawling over a fall of stones, loosened by the weight of traffic on the wet road above. Bert's lantern smashed and, in the blinding blackness, he sucked his teeth in pain. As he'd gone down he'd put out his hands flat to save himself and opened up the sword cuts. Lizzie's handkerchief was small protection.

While he was digging in his pocket for a fresh candle and matches, he noticed light straining through a crack in the brickwork. This must be an extension of Mowbray's cellar, presumably, nice and cool for storing wine. It must have been built under the road decades before, when pipes of running water and gas were undreamed of. Soon all the main highways in Walthamstow were to be dug up to lay pipes and sewers. The excavations would destroy much of this underworld.

A thought struck him: perhaps this was where they had put Mary. He knelt up and as he put his eye to the crack, he found the wall to be wet with a steady trickle of water from the street above. This was what had caused the roof-fall and softened the mortar between the bricks. It was dangerous. There were only nine or ten feet of earth and clay between the road and the tunnel roof. Suppose there was subsidence. A brewery dray delivering barrels of beer to the pub could easily sink into it, bringing horses and driver down with it. The wall was no protection. A hefty kick could bring that down. The cellar and its contents would be buried. He put his eye to the crack again. Mary?

Though the place was vaulted with weight-bearing arches as you might expect in a pub cellar, someone was using this damp and windowless place as a bedroom. People were expected to sleep down here! A number of people, by the look of it. There were three – no four – small beds and a baby's cot within his narrow field of vision. This was a dormitory. Servants' quarters, perhaps? A cheap stopover for travellers? The furniture was pretty basic. That carved wooden chandelier he could see further off was very like one he had put in that painting of Ida Sutton. He remembered it particularly as he'd had to invent another branch for one that was missing. Daniel Wylie had quipped that it was a pity Archie couldn't have fashioned the eighth branch as well as he'd drawn it. He blinked. One, two, three … only seven branches … Good Lord, it was the same chandelier! Ignoring his smarting hand, he found his penknife and began scraping away at the damp mortar. Inferior materials had their uses. That picture frame, whose top and corner he could now see, carved with fruit and nuts, was surely one he'd had his eye on. Not the painting, which was a not very good landscape which he'd intended scrapping or painting over. But the frame was made of rich cherry wood, and Wylie had been selling it for four shillings, if he remembered correctly. He'd assumed it had been destroyed in the fire.

He managed to scratch away another inch or two of crumbling mortar, lengthening the bright slit to reveal a windowless room, and yes, many of the furnishings – the mirror, the folding screen, the whatnot, the tallboy – could all have been part of Wylie's stock. Small enough to have been lowered down into Wylie's underground storeroom after the shooting, before the fire. Waste not, want not! If this wasn't proof that Mowbray's minions had burgled the shop after killing the proprietor then what was? Setting fire to the shop was a ruse to hide the burglary as well as the murder.

A door opened beyond the chandelier and a boy of five or six, a skinny little chap in a nightgown at least two sizes too big, came in retching and heaving, too slowly, evidently, for the man behind him. He rudely hoofed him into the room and slammed the door. No way to treat a sick child, thought Archie, as he watched the boy fall onto one of the beds and lie there, staring at the ceiling as if traumatised, his hands clasped tight across his chest. Another child, a slightly older girl, her face pale and sleep-starved, came from outside Archie's vision and knelt beside the boy's bed as if praying. She didn't touch him but her eyes never left the younger child's face. As the door opened again, another man came in. Both children stiffened, the girl recoiling against the bed, the little boy shaking his head in terror and wailing, 'No, no, not me. Not me!'

'You!' barked the man, a well-dressed, familiar figure. Lord, it

283

was Abel Stevens, a one-time drinking companion of Archie's. 'You, boy, come here. Now! I shan't tell you again.' You could hear the schoolmaster in his voice. 'Are you the one I had last time? Get up, sonny, let me see your face.' The boy's lower lip drooped. He was about to cry. 'Ah yes, the pretty one. Jim, if I remember rightly. Are you clean? Good, come with me, boy.'

As Abel walked the boy to the door he fondled the blond curls. What was this, private tuition? As they went through into the next room, Abel's hand slipped to the hem of the boy's nightgown and lifted it, touching the boy's skinny buttocks.

Jesus, thought Archie, springing away. What was this? As he rummaged through his mind for clues and connections, he leaned against the wall for support, knowing exactly what it was. Streeter was running a sex ring, he shouldn't forget that, and this was Mowbray's end of it – child prostitution.

'Dear God!' he muttered and, stepping backwards, fell over his lantern with a clatter.

'Get away from the wall, you!'

He hadn't heard the bolts sliding back or the Railway Tavern's cellar door opening. A man stood there, perhaps ten yards away, holding a lantern up high. He was holding a pistol, levelling it at this shadowy Peeping Tom.

'Come into the light,' he cried. 'Come where I can see you or I'll shoot.'

'You scum, Mowbray!' breathed Archie, blinking the tears from his eyes. His fingers wrapped in Lizzie's handkerchief, balled around his open penknife but he couldn't argue with a gun, or with the ruffians lined up behind it, one smacking a cudgel into his palm.

Rocky with sickness and disgust, Archie ran, abandoning the lantern, bouncing blind off the sides of the tunnel, falling over debris when a shot sounded over his head. Missed! He stumbled on under the crossroads and into Coppermill Lane. As he closed the door to the first cellar, he heard someone else falling over his lantern, the sounds of breaking glass and cursing. One at least, maybe two in pursuit.

His heart was racing as he blundered through four or five more cellars, ducking through rough curtains, using the dim light from the cracks and knotholes in the floorboards above to guide him. He heard pounding feet, rough voices and the first door slamming back on its hinges. When he came to another door, he latched it behind him. He couldn't outrun them. He had to make a stand sooner or later, but one against two? It was poor odds. He looked around, just making out the dim bulk of the brick-built copper. He felt over it for the wooden handle of the lid, which lifted off with a sucking sigh. Protection of sorts. And inside the tub – a copper stick! Used for heaving out boiling wet sheets, the stick was as strong as a policeman's truncheon. He must look like a Greek hoplite going into battle, with his baton and shield, he thought, as he flattened himself against the wall.

A faint glow, outlining the door like beading, soon grew brighter and, as the door burst open, he heard himself growl. He stuck out his foot to trip the lantern bearer, at the same time beating wildly with his stick until the howling stopped and the body slid away. It was difficult to see: the attackers' lantern had been knocked to the ground. A black shape charged him, butted up against his shield and was thrown off. Archie flailed with the copper stick but failed to connect. He felt the sharp edge of the brick tub nudging him in the back. He was trapped. Something whacked the stick from his hand. Fingers clawed at his face, searching for his eyes. Height gave him an advantage and he brought his knee up sharply. The hand gripping his chin went slack and he was able to reach around inside the tub for a weapon – a scrubbing brush, anything. He found a long metal handle, gripped it tight and smashed it over the head of his assailant. There was a grunt, an exhalation, and the body fell at his feet. He felt in his pocket for matches and struck one on the wall of the wash-tub.

'Good grief!'

The flame revealed two men on the floor, one moving, about to crawl out of the door, one not. Hegarty was the one he'd decked with the long-handled enamelled dipper used to bail out the tub. Archie kicked the door onto the escapee's head, knocking him sideways. He rolled the man away from the door with his boot and hit him over the head with the dipper. Pulling the door to, he fastened the latch against further trouble. Damn, there was no bolt. These doors were meant to stay unlocked. *Improvise, improvise,* he urged himself. There wasn't much: a washboard ended up jammed in the gap under the door. Best he could do.

There was movement behind him and he turned in time to catch Hegarty reaching for his cudgel. A kick in the face settled him. Archie kicked the weapon into the shadows for the police to find. Swallowing his distaste, he went through the tinker's greasy pockets and found a roll of banknotes. So – he *had* sold Mary to Streeter. This must be the payment. She was probably on her way to Hampstead at this very moment. Now what? He couldn't just leave these creatures to crawl back home to their masters with the news that their racket had been rumbled. No one involved in this filthy trade could be allowed to escape.

He replaced the money and hung Tommo's coat on the mangle. He removed the tinker's foul-smelling shirt. Working silently, he used his penknife to cut and rip both his victims' shirts into strips to tie them with, knowing that these two were the least in the game. How many others were involved? There were the clients, like Abel of all people. There were the grumpy old domino players, providing a front for Mowbray's activities. There were the procurers, combing the streets and whispering empty promises in poor children's ears, and there were the keepers, ghastly men like Partridge and Mowbray, providing the premises. And right at the top there was Streeter, he was sure of it, the ringleader. Street urchins were rich pickings, there for the taking. If he couldn't exploit them one way, by shipping them abroad, he'd do it another.

Hegarty groaned, opening one eye and then the other, tugging at his bonds, rattling the mangle to which Archie had tied him. Good, he thought, perhaps he'd get some answers before he went for the police.

As he tipped the wretch under the chin with the copper stick, he noticed red weals on his cheek. Someone had raked him with her fingernails. 'Where's Mary?' he barked. 'What have you done with her?'

Hegarty snarled, 'Why'd I tell you, gobshite?'

Archie let the stick do its work. 'Because I'll knock your fucking head off if you don't.'

Hegarty spat blood. 'I've sold her.'

'You bastard! You'd *sell* her into a life of shame? I thought you loved her.'

Even in pain the man's lip had a sly curl. 'I got a good price.'

'Who bought her?' Archie rasped. He was within a sandy whisker of clubbing the man to death. 'Tell me!'

Tommo twisted his head away. Archie wasn't playing games and they both knew it. 'The highest bidder.'

So she was probably already on her way to Hampstead. Archie struggled to his feet. 'I must go to her.'

'Sure and she won't thank you for that, boy,' he taunted. 'For won't she be livin' the life of Riley? She'll be made, and she knows it. She'll have silk sheets and a carriage to ride in. Everything she wants. And what could you give her, eh, *boyo?*' he sneered. 'A crust of bread? A pot to piss in?'

Archie couldn't answer, couldn't see straight, couldn't think for the rage boiling inside him. He swung his stick and knocked the man out cold, and then, his jaw knotting in determination, his three finger ends useless without fully grown nails, he picked and jabbed at Hegarty's bonds, using his teeth as well, until the villain's dirty hands were untied. Filthy hands, bloody hands. He placed them carefully on the lower roller of the mangle. It was made for the job. He turned the screw that brought the rollers together. If Hegarty came round and tried to move he would find his fingers trapped. That was all Archie intended at first.

He started up the cellar steps and looked back at the evil worm. *'Leave it, leave it,'* he told himself, even as he stepped back down. Vengeance was a shameful thing, it would haunt him forever, but wasn't it justice? For John's death twice over, for Clara's dreadful ordeal, for his own beating and for Mary, sold into slavery? For those poor little creatures of corruption up the road? He gripped the winding handle with both hands, brought it up and up, heard the mechanism creak, the heavy rollers begin to turn. Sweat ran down his face. But when he felt the bones of resistance, he could only press his lips together and blink at tears that sprang into his eyes. He couldn't go through with it. A rumble and a crack, and it would have been over with. Hegarty would never have been able to hurt another soul. But Archie stepped away, letting go the wheel. The body sagged as it was released and, trembling at what he had so nearly become, Archie re-tied the thug's bonds.

With his breath shuddering in his chest, he ran up the cellar steps and gave the door an almighty kick. 'Quickly,' he shouted, before he could change his mind again, 'fetch a policeman!'

'Oh no, mate, we don't have no truck with them,' came the muffled reply. The people in the cottage must have had their ears glued to the crack.

'Open the door, for Christ's sake, man – before I kick it in!'

Chapter 31

From way, way off – through the thick darkness it came, borne on the rushing wind – the plaintive sound of a penny whistle. Lilting, soaring, weeping. He was playing for her.

'Will you wait, Pauly? I'm comin', darlin',' she breathed. In her mind she hummed the tune and the words came back to her. '*And in her right hand, a silver dagger ...*' Their duet. '*All men are false, says my mother/ They'll tell you wicked, lovin' lies ...*' Now she was singing, sparkling clear and full-throated, putting in the beautiful grace notes. '*For I've been warned, and I've ...*'

'*I've decided ...*' she whispered aloud but her lips hardly moved. She licked them. They were so dry. Then she remembered. Held her breath.

Were they still here?

She listened hard.

Downstairs, through the floor, the sound of men's voices, raucous laughter, the clink of glasses.

But in here? In this room? Just a faint skittering of mice, a ticking clock. Were there really no vicious brown boots, no harsh voices?

'*Will ye shut your noise, ye bitch! Shut it, or you'll get a taste o' this.*'

And the other man reminding him there were to be no marks

on her face or anywhere that would show. Streeter wouldn't want damaged goods.

She should have kept quiet about that one dropping dead on the floor of his own house. She'd have saved herself a crack on the skull.

Sweet Jesus, but it was so sore. She lifted her hand to the place above her ear and gingerly prodded. Ouch. It was sticky, and all down her face.

Opening her eyes at last, she tried to peer at her fingers for blood. Couldn't see a thing. The room was in darkness. They'd gone and taken the lamp with them. She felt about her. Bare floorboards. Splinters. Dust balls. Husks of spiders. And a smell like sweaty old shoes. Where was she? She only lifted her head an inch off the floor and she bumped it – bed-springs! He'd knocked her out and rolled her under the bed. Out of the way, like so much rubbish, with the cold belly of a chamber-pot pressing against her cheek. She'd have to get out, somehow, before they came back and were at her again.

'Nobby says you can sing, Mrs Quinn. He likes a bird that sings. As do I.'

'Come on, now, Mary, darlin', sing for Mister Mowbray. Sing for your own Tommo. It's why I brought you.'

Sing for Tommo? That'd be the day!

That was how they'd started, and when she'd clamped her mouth shut, the threats had turned into the pinching and twisting of her nipples and other parts. And soon they'd gone beyond any idea of her singing.

Even if she wanted to, her throat was soon squeezed dry with throttling. She'd tried calling for help when that fellow come to the door saying they were needed downstairs. Only a croak came out, and look where it had got her.

Tommo had swung the shillelagh and that was the last she knew of it.

Something was happening now. A rumpus downstairs – shouting and crashing and glass breaking. Saints preserve us, what was going on? As she crossed herself, the door opened, letting in light and a man yelling, 'Anyone here?'

She tried calling out again, but no one heard her from under the bed and the door closed without her.

She thought that if she drew up her knees a bit, dug in her heels, made a real effort, she could wriggle out. Stand up then, if she could, and call out of the window.

She readied herself, but only her thoughts moved.

Oh God. She would stay here, losing blood, getting weaker and weaker, and die.

And God said, or Pauly said, or Brian or the dead babby up in heaven said, 'Pull yourself together, Mary. Move anything at all – arse, elbows, shoulders, fingers. Shuffle and wriggle and push and slide. Forget about the pain. You're not dead yet, darlin'.'

Chapter 32

It didn't take the old man long to find a policeman. There were more than a few about, on foot and on horseback; their lanterns were on the marshes, on the towpath.

The one place they didn't expect to see any action was number eleven Coppermill Lane, but Grandpa did as he was bid, flapping his bony hands to make them hurry.

Satisfied that help was on its way, Archie went back to his post at the cellar door while the old woman put the kettle on. The rest of the ragged little family jumped around like fleas, desperate to feast their eyes on the men trussed up like chickens in their cellar, but wary of Archie and his copper stick and the wild look in his eye. When armed policemen appeared in the doorway, the children dissolved like sugar in tea, up the ladder to the bedroom, behind the wooden settle, nudging each other. 'Blimey, Elbert, see that shooter in his belt!' They would have melted into the woodwork if they could.

After a good deal of whistle-blowing, calling off the hunt, Sergeant Tyrell came in with Constable Beckett in tow.

Archie raised a lighted candle, allowing them precedence down the steps, glad to hand over to them, now. Halfway down his legs gave out and he sank to sitting, suddenly and utterly exhausted.

'Two of the buggers!' cried Beckett. 'Still breathing!' He sounded almost disappointed.

'By crikey!' said Tyrell, when he reached them. 'It's only Hegarty!'

'Where's Mary Quinn, then?' Constable Beckett broke in. 'She run off?'

Archie broke into a cold sweat. Fighting sudden nausea, he blurted out, 'She's been sold to Streeter – on her way to Hampstead, no doubt.' He pulled himself up on the railings but his head swam and he had to sit down again.

*

The elderly couple whose cottage it was made Archie strong sweet tea for shock, on Sergeant Tyrell's instructions, before scurrying next door with their family, bursting with news, happily deferring to the police claim on their kitchen. A costermonger's barrow was requisitioned from one of the houses in the lane and the two prisoners were carted off to jail, properly handcuffed and hobbled.

Gradually the little room filled with a hubbub of law. enforcement officers – day shift and night shift, plain clothes and uniforms, specials and volunteers. At Sergeant Tyrell's nod, they fell quiet. Archie felt a prod in his back and, smearing sweat and tears from his face, gripping the table for strength, he told them about Mowbray's vile establishment. 'Through a crack in the wall … little children being used for sex,' he muttered, 'molested, servicing foul men …'

'What!'

'My God!'

Archie stared at his tea leaves, seeing a bleak future for those poor kids, and for Mary, too. Gone for a life as Streeter's whore, after all she'd been through.

A clattering of hooves outside heralded the arrival of

reinforcements from Waltham Abbey: two men on horseback. Striding windswept into the room, the shorter of the two introduced himself as Inspector Nash and his colleague as Sergeant Young. He had a fair idea of the case but not the latest developments. Tyrell drew him aside, filling him in on events, sotto voce, gesturing at Archie, at the cellar door, at Archie again, towards the pub up the road, and back again to Archie.

Nash came over and patted him on the shoulder. 'Nice work, Mister Price. But you rest easy now. We'll take it from here.' The newcomer made for the cellar. 'Step aside, lads, let the dog see the rabbit!' He rattled down the steps and his sergeant followed with a light.

Twenty minutes later he was back, slower of step and looking grim. 'Bastards,' he hissed. 'Just as you said, Mister Price. Some poor little girl … and that cot, did you see the baby's cot?' An in-breath whistled through his teeth. 'Felt like knocking the wall down on top of the whole damn lot of them, but for the kids. Don't you worry, mate, we'll get 'em.'

He had the men organised in no time. It didn't look as if Mowbray was expecting them, he said, so they would mount their attack on two fronts. 'You, you and you, with me – we'll take them up the back passage, so to speak. Give the buggers a taste of their own medicine, eh? The rest of you – through the front door. You're all armed? Pistols primed? Now remember your training. Shoot to maim, not kill. I want them taken alive, if you can possibly manage it.'

The room emptied fast until there were just Archie and Beckett left sitting at the table. Beckett was supposed to be taking Archie's statement while Tyrell finished making notes.

'Horrible, foul.' The constable seemed almost as stunned as Archie. 'Hard to believe there's *monsters* who would even think of …' He sat, shaking his head dumbly, unable to form the words. 'I mean the innocence of children is supposed to be …' He cleared his throat, rubbed his forehead in pain, but he still couldn't leave it. 'And that pub's been there forever – before the railway. My dad still calls it *The Plough*. It was a country pub back then, served the workers at the coppermill.'

'Last place you'd expect to find a "knocking shop" of any description,' put in Tyrell, looking up.

'And the neighbours the last to snitch, looks like. They must've known about that passage for what, ten, twenty year or more and we had no idea. As for them poor kids …'

'It must have been a proper cellar when Mowbray bought it,' Tyrell reminded him, 'for storing barrels and that. Don't suppose many people know about the change of purpose.'

Beckett sat up, bristling. 'You telling me people round here don't know what's going on under their noses, in their own cellars? They're liars if they say not.'

'They live in fear,' Archie pointed out wearily. 'What can they do? One step out of line and Mowbray will send the boys round to do them over, maim them and their kids, trash their shops. As for telling the police, it's more than their lives are worth.'

'Mowbray? You reckon he's the top man?'

'Who else?' asked Archie. 'Round here anyway. He has the power, the money, the guns – and he has the biggest interest in keeping the passage open. It's not only a thieves' rat-run, he can smuggle children through, and his clients can get in and out without being seen.' He tried to imagine what it must be like for decent people like Bob Cheshire, Bert the tobacconist, Williams the dairyman, for all the other shopkeepers trying to make an honest living, knowing the uses to which their cellars were being put. He drew in a quick breath. 'That's it!' he burst out. 'There's your motive!' But they looked blank. 'Wylie!' he cried, startling them. 'Suppose he objected? Suppose he dug in his heels, threatened to brick up the access? Suppose he said he was going to the police? Maybe the bonfire – putting him up on a pile of chairs – was to make an example of him!'

'An example!' breathed Beckett, horrified. 'If you'd seen the state of him, poor bleeder, burned to a crisp. If that was an example it was way over the top!'

'But it worked, didn't it?' said Tyrell. 'Nobody said a dickey-bird.'

Just then shots rang out from the direction of the Railway Tavern. Tyrell went to the door to look. 'Come on, son, time to go.' Archie struggled to his feet. 'Not you, Arch, you stop where you are. We'll come and get you if you're needed.'

He wouldn't have been much use, he realised, for the next he knew, Beckett was shaking him awake. 'Archie! Come on! We've found her.'

Outside the Tavern he found his way blocked by an ugly huddle of men, handcuffed and roped together, ready to trudge the long mile up the road to the police cells. He recognised Lionel Partridge and some roughneck Tyrell had referred to as 'Bully' Watkins and, oh God, there was Abel Stevens again.

'Archie! Thank God,' said Stevens. 'You'll vouch for me, won't you? Tell them this is all a dreadful mistake.'

Archie winced, knowing he'd seen what he'd seen and the police inspector after him. Good God, though: Abel, of all people. He didn't look depraved. None of them did. Was it in their eyes – a salacious sort of gleam or a bestial dullness? Was there slackness about their mouths? No. In fact only their dishevelled appearance and occasional gashes and abrasions singled them out from curious bystanders.

297

'This way, Mister Price.' There was Beckett with a hand under his elbow, steering him in the right direction.

'No, Abe,' he called back over his shoulder. 'You'll get no help from me.'

Beckett stopped to help a fellow officer disarm a well-dressed and struggling gent, one whose nostrils flared like those on a roundabout horse as he protested his innocence, but it did him no good. Like his clients, Sebastian Mowbray was handcuffed and hobbled and forced to join the shuffling crew making their way up the road. He stared at Archie. *'You?'* In his astonishment he quite forgot to close his mouth. 'In spite of my offer? You must be the worst kind of *fool,*' he snarled. 'Or can you afford to throw good money away?' Gathering up a mouthful of drool he spat in Archie's face. 'You *worm!* You *grass!*' He was hustled on, cursing heavily, flinging the vilest words over his shoulder. Then, 'You'll be sorry …'

Never, thought Archie, breathing hard, wiping his face on his sleeve. I'll never be sorry for putting a stop to devils like you and your kind.

'All right, Arch?' Sergeant Tyrell was holding open the door for a troupe of barefoot children to file through, wide-eyed at the dark night and wrapped in blankets. He scowled. 'No, not really, eh?' he said, as he met Archie's eyes. 'Hold on, I'll be with you in a minute.'

He had a couple of Salvation Army officers with him. One, a captain, was carrying a tiny child – a toddler in the regulation nightshirt, a child no older than Clara. It had clearly only just stopped crying, its face all snotty as it took shuddering recovery breaths. So the cot *had* been occupied! Fiercely gripping his other hand was the golden-haired child Archie had seen Stevens summon – name of Jim. Poor little mite.

'Beckett, go and fetch the doctor, will you? I'll just see this lot on their merry way. Come on, you lot, chop, chop.'

'Nice bowl of soup waiting for you up the road,' cajoled the Captain.

'And a bath,' added his comrade-in-arms.

Archie sighed. He supposed this was the best that could be done for them tonight. Perhaps they would be placed in loving families as time went on, and hopefully the younger ones would forget how they had been abused and come to live normal, useful lives. But what about the older ones?

Bringing up the rear one such, a skinny wretch of seven or eight, tugged on his sleeve. ''Ere, I seen you, en' I? You're the geezer wanted a candle.'

'My God!' Archie was appalled, recognising him. The boy had had freedom of sorts when they'd met in the passage. 'What happened – how did they get you?'

The boy wiped his nose upwards on his palm, stared at the ground and muttered, almost in shame, 'Nah, knocked on the door, din I?'

'What? You …' But there was no point in describing the crass stupidity of the act. The kid had plainly found out the hard way. 'Didn't you know what went on in here?'

'Kind of.'

'You didn't, you couldn't …'

'I was 'ungry, mister,' said the boy. 'They feeds ye down there. Makes you look tasty.'

Tasty? Dear God, is that what they called it? Was he so desperate? Archie released his breath in dismay. Such need was beyond him.

The boy continued to hover for a moment or two before giving Archie a sort of salute and galloping along to catch up with his mates. Hopefully he'd find what he needed with the Sally Army.

In the bar-room, overturned and dismembered furniture wore the scars of battle, bullet holes and splintered wood. Broken bottles and tankards rolled about in a swill of booze, with dominoes, broken clay pipes and sticky playing cards.

'This way,' said Tyrell, heading for a door behind the bar.

At last.

All the doors on the landing were open, except one. With a sense of awful foreboding he followed the policeman inside.

She lay on the bed, her head bandaged crudely with a man's handkerchief.

'Mary! Oh my God, what's he done to you?' He sat beside her, depressing the bedsprings. She hissed with pain.

'Careful.' Tyrell had taken a chair against the wall. 'She's taken a beating,' he said, unnecessarily. 'We missed her first time round. She was under the bed, apparently. Managed to wriggle out.' His notebook was open on his lap, his pencil poised. 'I don't think she's too bad, but Beckett's gone for the doctor, anyway.'

Archie nodded.

The front of her blouse was ripped open and Archie pulled the edges together to make her decent. Oh God, she was in a state. The clear blue of her eyes, the black of her lashes were startling in a face so white.

'Archie!' She managed a smile. 'You look … done in.'

'Never mind about me, look at you! Was it …? Did Hegarty do this?'

Her nod was one of assent and resignation. It was no more than she expected from the man. Damn him. He fought for control. It wasn't anger she wanted now. He rubbed her palm with his thumb and, noticing her fingernails with blood caught under them, turned to Tyrell with an unspoken question.

The policeman waggled his head from side to side, unsure.

'Could be his, could be where she's touched her own head. We'll know soon enough.'

Hegarty's face was scratched. If the blood under her nails matched his, it would certainly help the case against him.

Tyrell busied himself washing a china tooth-mug clean with water from the ewer and filling it. Archie held it to Mary's dry lips and she sipped with difficulty, swallowed painfully and croaked a word, her fingers flying to her throat.

'You don't have to talk, Mary.'

She frowned, ignoring his advice. She was determined. 'He – he –' Her voice ran over gravel. 'He all but strangled me.'

Now he noticed the red marks encircling the beautiful column of her neck. 'Who? Hegarty?'

She drank thirstily, then pushed the tooth-mug away and lay back on the pillow. When she spoke again, her words were clearer. 'Tommo thinks …' She swallowed. 'Thinks he – he made a deal to sell me to – to Nobby Streeter.' She gave a short, bitter laugh. 'But Nobby's dead, so he is.'

'Dead?'

'An accident,' she said, with a fierce nod.

'You were there?'

'I was.' Between sips of water she told them the bones of it, that she'd been staying with her old friend, Kitty. 'She said she met you, Archie, at Streeter's.'

He felt his colour rising and acted surprised, wondering if Kitty had perhaps told her friend how the relationship had progressed to intimacy. There was at least one nude painting of Kitty now out in the world. His smile was fixed as Mary continued, her words rasping over a swollen throat.

She and Kitty had, long ago, dreamt of forming a duet and treading the boards together at the Hackney Empire. So, when they met up, Kitty took Mary to see her manager. 'And …' She held out her hands to express surprise. 'Who should it be but Nobby?'

'He said as much at his party when she came on to sing. But I didn't know she was your friend.'

'Yes, Kitty's my friend. Since we were girls.' She cleared her throat. 'We – we sang to Nobby, so we did, and he said yes, he'd give us a start, and, as he was seeing us out, the, em …' She cleared her throat again. 'The rain came in at the door and wet his marble hallway and he, breathing in the cold air, well, he started coughing – such a fit of it …' She gave a little cough in sympathy. 'And somehow he lost his footing, slipping in the water, and gave his chin such a crack on the floor he upped and died. A heart attack, the doctor said.' After this speech she took the cup from Archie and hid her face in it.

Archie regarded her through narrow eyes. Hmm. She had it off a little too pat, hardly pausing for breath and not looking at him directly at all. But perhaps there was some truth in it, if Nobby really was dead.

'You're sure about this, Mary? There was no struggle? No one put out a foot to trip him up?'

'No, Archie, not at all.'

'See, what I don't understand, Mary,' he said, carefully, 'is if Streeter was willing to buy you from Tommo, why didn't he just snatch you up there and then, when he had you within his grasp as it were?'

She shook her head. 'I don't think he knew me at first, Archie, all neat and trim and clean. He may have had the drink taken. Or mebbes,' she said, hoarsely, 'mebbes, he thought he could get more from me as a singer.'

It was a possibility. In happier times she had a sweet voice.

'Tommo called me a liar …' Her hands fisted on the bed and she touched her bandaged head, Hegarty's signature. 'He throttled me – first, because he didn't believe me, then because he did. Then someone called him out and he hit me over the head to be done with it.'

'Bastard,' growled Archie, 'I thought he was supposed to be fond of you.'

'That's Tommo for ye.' She hunched her shoulders a little, the nearest she could get to a shrug in her weakened state.

'Well, he's under lock and key, right now, him and his pals,' Tyrell broke in. 'They'll all hang if I have anything to do with it. The evidence is piling up. We've got the bugger for Dolly Brett's murder, if nothing else. And your testimony will tie him in with Wylie's, too – though the one pulling the trigger was probably Sebastian Mowbray. We have the gun now – Beckett took it off him. With a bit of luck we can prove it's the same weapon as shot Daniel Wylie.'

'You can do that?' Archie asked.

'Just have to match the markings on the bullets we took from the shop to the screw of his gun barrel, and we have him.'

Mary, too, drew in a long wondering breath. 'So it wasn't Tommo killed Mister Wylie?'

'He was there, though – accomplice to murder.'

'But I … ' She seemed agitated, biting deep into her lip.

'Don't upset yourself, Mary.'

'Where is that blessed doctor?' demanded Tyrell. 'He should be here by now.'

She sniffed, tried to control her tears. 'It's – it's what I came to tell you, Sergeant, at the police station, but you wouldn't … '

'I know. Sorry about that, Mrs Quinn,' said the policeman. 'I was a bit 'ard on you, perhaps. But we was so worried about little

Clara Kington, poor little scrap. Lucky you turned up, as it 'appened. I must say, that was a brave thing you done there, very brave, putting yourself at risk to save a child.'

'Oh,' she said, looking a little distracted. 'Yes, Clara – is she all right?'

Apart from losing her father, thought Archie, but now was not the time to tell Mary that John was dead. He put on a smile. 'She's fine, thanks to you. Chomping her way through a slab of bread and jam last time I saw her. She had a narrow escape. That bastard would have killed her, or sold her, without a moment's hesitation, if you hadn't come forward.'

Mary said, 'He killed Brian, you know, my brother, Brian Rooney. He bragged about it, so he did. Killed him and robbed him of his cash.' So that was *Rooney's* money in Hegarty's pocket, *Rooney's* horse he was riding. Mary's tears were flowing freely, and across the room Tyrell's pencil was scratching for England.

'Mary! I'm so sorry!' Because that was also Archie's fault – in sending Rooney after Hegarty. For her sake, he'd sent him to his death. No doubt she'd been fond of that brother of hers, scoundrel though he was.

When the doctor arrived they left the room to allow him to examine her. After a while he let them back in. To Archie's relief Mary was sitting up in a chair with a spanking white bandage on her head.

'Well,' said Doctor Anthony, 'she has a few bruises and a nasty place on her head. But it will heal. Nothing a few days' rest won't cure.'

'She can go home?'

'She could if she had one to go to, someone to look after her. I suppose …' He turned to Sergeant Tyrell. 'Have you finished at Coppermill Lane? Can she go back there?'

'Thing is, Dolly Brett was only a tenant. She sub-let to Mary.'

'Don't worry,' she said, 'I'll get the bus back to Hampstead.'

'Not in that state you won't, young lady.'

'Can't she stop here for a few days?' Archie asked. 'I'll look after her – I'll sleep next door,' he added, blushing fiercely.

Mary shot him a grateful glance, but the policeman was shaking his head, his face grim. This place was the scene of a heinous crime and off limits to the public. The police had already set up a cordon.

'Perhaps Mrs Reeves has room. I'll go and see,' Archie offered, though the very thought of the long trek to the top of the High Street and back again was exhausting. 'Otherwise – you'd better come back with me, Mary. I'll sleep on the couch.'

But neither recourse was necessary, for there, waiting patiently in the mule-cart outside was Lizzie, with Clara soundly asleep in the back, piled with shawls and blankets.

She'd been at the police station, waiting for news, when the message came for armed policemen to go to the Railway Tavern. Clara was asleep, she said, so she'd stayed put for a while. But no news came and, when she couldn't bear not knowing any longer, she took matters into her own hands and loaded the sleeping child into the cart. Mrs Tyrell had insisted on the blankets and a hot-water bottle or two. Passing gangs of shuffling prisoners on their way to the police cells, and barefoot children filing into the Salvation Army Hall, she had pieced together the turn of events. On reaching the pub she'd gathered from police officers on cordon duty that Archie and Mary were both still alive, so she'd decided to wait and see if she could be of any help.

'*Lizzie, Lizzie, Lizzie,*' breathed Archie, his eyes shining. '*Darling girl …*'

Chapter 33

With the interval almost over, the 'auditorium' was filling up again. They'd had the back door open while people went to refresh their glasses and themselves, to let in the summer air, let out some of the tobacco smoke. Now they closed them. A hand-bell was rung and the stragglers wended their way back to their tables. The saloon bar buzzed with anticipation.

They'd enjoyed the earlier acts: performing dogs, a magician and the comic, Dan Leno, who had them in stitches with his story of a woman whose greed had her eating oysters in the mirror to make them seem more. Archie, drawing the man's picture for the *Journal,* had glowed with pleasure to see Lizzie hooting with laughter.

He watched her now, sipping her port and lemon, chatting to Charlotte on the next table, beautiful and animated, more so than she'd ever been while John was alive. Charlotte wanted to decorate her new shop with Lizzie's tiles. William Mowbray had also seized the opportunity, earlier on, to ask for her catalogue and price for re-tiling his entrance hall in the Art Nouveau style. It was all the rage and everybody wanted Lizzie's designs. Taking on that apprentice and the new maid would help her meet the demand, and Archie would do what he could to lighten her load.

Now here was Percy ringing his hand-bell, mounting his rostrum, brushing off his waistcoat and taking up the gavel, as

Mrs Reeves and the barman went down each side of the auditorium, adjusting the houselights to dim.

'Ladies and gentlemen, welcome back to our evening of variety. I was saying just now to Mrs Reeves, couple o' years' time, the Horse and Groom will be no more!'

Cries of *'Shame!'* rang out and those who hadn't heard the news banged their tables with their fists and tankards and shouted *'No!'* and *'We won't let it happen!'* Lizzie widened her eyes at Archie, for they were two of the privileged few 'in' on the secret.

Percy banged the gavel to quiet the uproar. 'Now then, now then, don't take on, ladies and gentlemen. The good news is that we're opening up down the road. New premises ...'

While Percy briefed them on the new Walthamstow Palace that would soon grace the High Street, amid all the *oohs* and *ahs* and cheers of relief, Lizzie, now wreathed in smiles, rubbed Archie's thigh under the table. For it had been at his suggestion that Percy Reeves had taken over where Mowbray had been obliged to leave off, and gone in with Nellie Wylie to bring the music hall into being. Nellie had her insurance money and Percy and Bertha would have money from the sale of this place and their savings. They had advertised for partners and been overwhelmed with local interest. Even Archie had put up some money, from the sale of the *'Carrington Sisters'* at the Summer Exhibition, now that Cedric was no longer in a position to purchase it himself. The notoriety of their father had added a certain *frisson* to the girls' portrait and more than a few hundred pounds to its price.

Wylie's site had already been cleared and the foundations were going in for a four-storey building with twin turrets. When Archie had put it to the Board that he might paint a mural for the foyer they had pounced on his offer, but wouldn't hear of him doing it for nothing. Which was what he'd rather hoped they'd say.

Percy wanted to get on now. Repeated and hefty banging of the gavel gradually restored the audience to order. 'Thank you, thank you, one and all, on behalf of Mrs Reeves and myself, for your good wishes. But it'll be *you*r music hall, *your* Palace of Varieties, don't forget. We couldn't do it without you. And the artistes, of course. Where would we be without our artistes?'

An impatient heckle, *'Get on with it, Perce!'* came from the darkened back of the room and an irritated shushing in the vicinity.

The gavel banged again.

'For goodness' sake,' said Lizzie under her breath, 'someone take the wretched thing away from him.'

Archie squeezed her hand. They were both on edge.

'And now, ladies and gentlemen, the act you've all been waiting for. Ireland may lay claim to them but they are Kitty and Mary – our very own – *Flowers of Burren!*'

A fiddle started in on a rising slide which shattered into a cascade of merry jigging notes and the curtains parted to show the player, stamping his foot and fiddling like mad. He stepped back as a chap playing a penny whistle joined him, same rhythm, but harmonising with squeals and wails of his own. Then came a bodhran, the Irish drum she'd told them about, played fast and furious to emphasise the beat. All three instrumentalists took another step backwards to make room on the little stage for the girls, who strode in, from either side, clapping their hands in time, wearing long, close-fitting dresses and jackets tailored from a green silky material that Mrs Reeves had found in the market.

They joined hands and greeted their audience with warm smiles. Their hair was piled up and studded with flowers. Apart from their colouring, dark and fair, they could almost have been sisters. When they began to sing, their voices were sweet and true and *'Phil the Fluter's Ball'* had every foot and finger tapping. Next came 'Paddy MacGintee's Goat', followed by – a change of mood – the lovely 'Marble Halls'. It was their signature tune and one many customers had heard Mary sing solo in the bar, 'singing for her supper' as she'd put it the last time he'd heard her there. Archie had wondered then, how many of The Horse and Groom's patrons knew that Mary did most of her singing practice around the pots and pans, kettles and washtubs of Lizzie's little cottage? That the maid-of-all-work, her wages paid by a friendly painter, had played a vital role in getting the tile-making business back on its feet?

Not for much longer, though. With Kitty joining her, now, for the first time singing the descant, and with the proper instruments, the song was twice as poignant, twice as moving, the voices pure magic. The Walthamstow Palace had better hurry up and be built or Percy would never be able to afford them.

Dashing tears from her eyes, and clapping for all she was worth, Lizzie remarked, 'That came from the heart.'

Archie, his own sketch of the band splashed with damp spots, muttered, 'All she's been through and she can still sing.'

'With so much feeling, Archie.'

It was grief – that fiery crucible – that had shaped her, shaped them both. He understood that Kitty had had her fair share of it. But that mad man had killed Dolly Brett, Brian Rooney and – it had come out at the trial – he'd killed Pauly Quinn, too, by laying rotten planks on the scaffold poles for him to step onto. He'd said he was only obeying orders. Josiah Fox, the builder, was a cheapskate who used inferior materials and when Pauly complained on behalf of the men, Fox had had to get rid of him. Mowbray sent his man, Hegarty, to do the job. This time, other former employees bore witness to what had happened, and Fox went down.

Mary's evidence had been crucial in the case against Sebastian Mowbray. From the witness box she'd rounded on Hegarty, accusing him of raping her. 'One way or another he killed my unborn baby. Sure, an' he was sorry about it after, he said, and wanted me to go to America for a new life. That's why he agreed to kill the old Squire in the forest and did for Mister Kington – to get money for the passage. But I wouldn't go to the end of the street with your man and I told him so. Well, he wouldn't take no for an answer and was ever after writing me letters that I couldn't read, knocking at the Workhouse door for me. Following me. He made my life a misery, so he did.'

When she moved in with Dolly she'd begged the matron not to give her away. And she thought the good woman had kept her word. But then she'd heard Hegarty was back in Walthamstow working for Sebastian Mowbray. It was why she had gone to the police – with only a few days' hesitation – to report seeing Hegarty behaving strangely outside Daniel Wylie's place prior to the murder.

With Streeter dead and Mowbray and his cronies in custody, and now that the underground passage was headline news, various other witnesses came forward to corroborate her story and to swear they had seen and heard the gang going through to Wylie's cellar around noon on that fatal day. They had even heard them calling for someone to let them up into the shop. Mowbray's gun proved to be the one that had killed Wylie and various pieces of furniture, found in Mowbray's underground brothel and for which he was unable to produce bills of sale, were identified as having been stolen from Daniel's shop.

There was no question in the minds of the jury that Sebastian Mowbray and his entire gang were corrupt, murdering slavers, with a list of illegal activities as long as your arm. The ringleaders were hanged, others got life in prison and the rest were shipped off to the colonies.

Some long months later, when Tommo Hegarty had been tried and found guilty of multiple murders – Paul Quinn, Squire Timothy Mowbray, John Kington, Daniel Wylie, Dorothy Brett and Brian Rooney, to name but six – he was hanged. Other crimes were taken into consideration, such as rape, threatening behaviour, at least three cases of theft, child abduction, and assisting in the running of a brothel. All in all, the people of Walthamstow thought they were well shot of him. When the fuss had died down, when Archie and Mary were alone in the studio, waiting for Kitty to join them to have her picture drawn for tonight's poster, Mary confessed.

'You know I told a lie, Archie?'

'Oh?' Another one? And which, of all the lies she had told him, was this? He still didn't believe she'd been staying with Kitty when she disappeared that time. But it was her business, nothing to do with him.

'I did *not* see Tommo outside Mister Wylie's shop that time. I hadn't seen him in months.'

'Yes you did, you described him to me. He was wearing a three-piece summer suit, remember? A brown derby hat.' Her mouth firmed into a stubborn line and she shook her head. 'You saw him banging on the window,' he persisted, 'and Daniel Wylie let him in.'

'I made it up.'

Archie was astounded. He'd turned away from his sketch to stare at her and found those blue eyes shining with truth. Mary Quinn really hadn't seen anyone outside the store, no one at all.

'You framed him,' he marvelled.

'I did.' Her lips squeezed tight. She took a deep breath. 'I swore on the Bible in court and I told a lie, Archie, and I'm surely going

311

to hell for it. But I'd do it again, if it meant that bastard would get his deserts. I'm telling you because I drew you into it and you got hurt and you saw things you shouldn't and ...' Her eyes filled up.

'I see.'

What could he say? It had been her lie that had uncovered that whole nasty mess of corruption and goodness knows what. She had started it.

He promised that no one would hear of it from him.

*

'And this next song,' Mary announced, as the applause eventually died down, 'is called *'The Silver Dagger'*. It's one of our favourites.'

Like everyone else, Lizzie sat spellbound from the first words: *'Don't sing love-songs, you'll wake my mother.'* It was a song about a woman whose bad experiences with a handsome, fickle husband led her to sleep with a silver dagger by her side, in order to kill her daughter's lover should he dare show his face. All men are liars, the warning went.

Lord, thought Archie uncomfortably, she was looking straight at him. They both were!

As the song drew to a close, the words, *'For I've been warned and I've decided / To sleep alone all of my life'*, resonated in a ringing silence before tumultuous applause made the lamplight flicker. Next stop, the Hackney Empire.

More from Honno

Short stories; Classics; Autobiography; Fiction
Founded in 1986 to publish the best of women's writing,
Honno publishes a wide range of titles from Welsh women.

A Time for Silence, *Thorne Moore*

Be careful when you look into your family history. You may not like what you find... 1933: Gwen is a loyal wife but her duty to her husband John will have a terrible price for herself and her children. Now: When Sarah finds her grandparents' ruined farm she becomes obsessed with restoring it and turning it back into a home.

Eden's Garden, *Juliet Greenwood*

Sometimes you have to run away, sometimes you have to come home: Two women a century apart struggling with love, family duty, long buried secrets, and their own creative ambitions.

The Mysterious Death of Miss Austen,
Lindsay Ashford

No-one has ever been able to provide a satisfactory explanation for the tragically early death of Jane Austen. A shocking new possibility emerges in this intriguing novel...

GWASG MENYWOD CYMRU
WELSH WOMEN'S PRESS

All Honno titles can be ordered online at
www.honno.co.uk
twitter.com/honno
facebook.com/honnopress

ABOUT HONNO

Honno Welsh Women's Press was set up in 1986 by a group of women who felt strongly that women in Wales needed wider opportunities to see their writing in print and to become involved in the publishing process. Our aim is to develop the writing talents of women in Wales, give them new and exciting opportunities to see their work published and often to give them their first 'break' as a writer.

Honno is registered as a community co-operative. Any profit that Honno makes is invested in the publishing programme. Women from Wales and around the world have expressed their support for Honno. Each supporter has a vote at the Annual General Meeting.

For more information and to buy our publications, please write to Honno at the address below, or visit our website: www.honno.co.uk

Honno, 14 Creative Units, Aberystwyth Arts Centre
Aberystwyth, Ceredigion SY23 3GL

Honno Friends

We are very grateful for the support of the Honno Friends:
Gwyneth Tyson Roberts, Jenny Sabine, Beryl Thomas.

For more information on how you can become a
Honno Friend, see: http://www.honno.co.uk/friends.php